## HELPLESS DEFIANCE

A feeling of dreadful anticipation crept over her scalp as his warm grasp tightened on her chin. Then his other arm banded her waist and she was locked against him, unable to breathe without feeling the press of his chest against her.

"So you will not fight," he said. "I wonder if I can make you do so. I think I would enjoy the pleasure of subduing you, Mademoiselle Genevieve."

Still holding her gaze, with the most agonizing slowness, he lowered his head to take her mouth with his own.

Tears filled her eyes as she recognized her helplessness in the face of the invader. There were no doors to bar, no defenses to throw up. He held her and explored her with a devastating intimacy that the sheltered girl, for all her crusading bravado, her defiant refusal to abide by the conventions, could never have imagined . . .

# ROMANCE FROM FERN MICHAELS

DEAR EMILY                    (0-8217-4952-8, $5.99)

WISH LIST                     (0-8217-5228-6, $6.99)


## AND IN HARDCOVER:

VEGAS RICH                    (1-57566-057-1, $25.00)

# RECKLESS
# SEDUCTION

## Jane Feather

Zebra Books
Kensington Publishing Corp.
http://www.zebrabooks.com

ZEBRA BOOKS are published by

Kensington Publishing Corp.
850 Third Avenue
New York, NY 10022

First Printing: September, 1987
10 9 8 7 6 5 4 3 2

Printed in the United States of America

*Chapter 1*

The April sun was hot, pouring in through the open window of the second floor room, and Dominic Delacroix pushed back his chair with a scrape on the smooth polished oak boards. The sound was swallowed up in the greater noise from the slave exchange on the floor below where, despite the heat, the auction was proceeding as efficiently as ever beneath the swift patter and decisive hammer of Jean Maspero. Dominic went to the window, hoping for a breath of air. If it was like this in April, there would be little quarter offered for August, he reflected, wiping his brow with a crisp linen handkerchief. But then only fools and dreamers expected mercy from a Louisiana summer. All others, once the *saison des visites* reached a close, would flee New Orleans and the threat of yellow fever for the relative cool of their plantations.

For Dominic Delacroix, the sea beckoned, the fresh winds offering surcease from the swamp heat and mosquitoes, and a British Indiaman promising the rich prizes of war. Although, in this year of war, 1814, the British were becoming most protective of their merchant ships. Dominic's lips curved in a sardonic smile that, nevertheless, contained a degree of self-mockery. Somehow, evading the British blockade was proving a more challenging business than

5

merely preying on the ungainly ships of commerce. And the goods his swift fleet of privateers brought to the beleaguered southern states did much to raise a smile on the faces of the aristocratic planters, their overindulged ladies, the affluent business men and their womenfolk for whom the prospect of a diminution in the supply of luxuries could only be viewed with horror.

Chartres Street, below his window, was crowded with the buyers and sellers of human flesh. Maspero's Exchange stood on the corner of Chartres and St. Louis, and the ground floor of the building was open onto both streets, offering maximum views to the prospective purchasers packing the auction room and spilling onto the banquette outside. The bells of the Church of St. Louis struck the hour, and the two figures that he had been expecting turned onto Chartres Street from St. Peter, walking toward Maspero's Exchange. There was a third figure, however, in addition to the ripely luscious Mademoiselle Elise Latour and her cousin, Nicolas St. Denis. Dominic frowned and the turquoise eyes darkened with irritation. St. Denis was well aware of his instructions. In the early stages of this game, he should contrive to be the only chaperone during the "accidental" meetings between Dominic Delacroix and the gorgeous but fortunately somewhat empty-headed and susceptible Elise.

The three figures drew closer, and it became clear from her dress and bearing that the third person was no maidservant. Her gown, with its modest lace inset at the neck, was the demurely correct afternoon gown of a debutante. The brim of her ruched silk bonnet decorously shielded her face from both the depredations of the sun's rays and any vulgar oglings. Dominic debated, in the face of this annoying addition to the party, whether to go downstairs or not, whether to follow the original plan whereby he would find himself so conveniently on the same stretch of banquette as Mademoiselle Latour. An invitation to take goûter at La

6

Gallier in the square would have been most natural and quite unimpeachable in the company of the lady's cousin, Monsieur Delacroix's good friend. But he did not wish for the acquaintanceship of Mademoiselle Elise Latour and Dominic Delacroix to become common knowledge within the Latour family, and presumably the accompanying lady was a friend of the family. But then, if he did not meet with Nicolas St. Denis now, how could he receive the invitation to Madame Latour's soirée this evening? The invitation was central to the plan and could certainly not be issued by anyone but Nicolas, and could only be issued serendipitously since Dominic Delacroix was not an automatic addition to the receiving lists of the majority of hostesses in New Orleans. That sardonic smile curved his lips again. It was not a pleasant smile and did nothing to soften the set of a finely drawn mouth or to relax the taut line of a determined jaw. Hopefully, the invitation would then be pressed most flatteringly by Mademoiselle Elise.

He had just decided that the presence of an onlooker to the proceedings was a nuisance that must be absorbed, when something quite extraordinary occurred. For the last few minutes of his cogitations, he had been aware on the periphery of the general cacophony below of a high-pitched, childish wailing accompanied by a keening sound rising to a pitch of hysteria. Such audible evidences of distress were only to be expected in the business being transacted at street level and sufficiently familiar not to have intruded too dramatically on his thoughts. That did not seem to be the case with the unknown young lady accompanying his quarry. A most unladylike exclamation escaped from her lips, and the next minute she was pushing her way into the Exchange through the astounded crowd, which parted before her impetuous progress like a *gâteau* beneath the knife. She was now out of his sight, and the uproar below increased. Curious, Dominic crossed the room and went out into the inner gallery overlooking the auction room.

7

"I would like to know, Mr. King, who gave you permission to sell Amelie and the baby?" The young woman stood in the middle of the room confronting a tall, thin individual whose ascetic-looking countenance bore an expression of enraged, disbelieving shock. As well it might, the watcher in the gallery reflected, amused interest replacing the irritation in the blue eyes.

"That, if I may say so, Mademoiselle Genevieve, is not your concern," Mr. King spat. "It is the concern of your father's overseer."

"Under Mr. Carter's management, sir, families were *never* parted," the young crusader declared, meeting him eye for eye.

"Mr. Carter is no longer overseer. I am," she was informed. "And I will do as I see fit."

"Not in this instance." Mademoiselle Genevieve swung round, walking to the block where a child of about three stood in a ragged shirt that barely reached his knees, sobbing and stretching his arms out to a distraught woman being held to one side of the room. Genevieve lifted the child and carried him over to the woman. She directed a hard stare at the driver holding the mother's arms. He glanced nervously about the now almost silent room, looking for help, instructions, anything from Maspero, who stood immobile, from Mr. King, who seemed momentarily struck dumb. Then, slowly, the driver released his grip. Genevieve put the child into its mother's arms. "Go straight back to the house, Amelie," she said gently. The woman, clutching her child, looked involuntarily at the overseer, the man who held the true power, and saw, to her unutterable amazement, that for this moment he seemed powerless. She left the Exchange, expecting at any minute to be seized and dragged back, back into the nightmare that was life, after all, but no one stopped her.

"Monsieur Latour will hear of this, mademoiselle, make no mistake." The overseer spoke into the charged silence, his

8

voice low, quivering with the malice of the publicly defeated.

"You do surprise me, Mr. King," she responded, with a smile that dripped contempt. Turning on her heel, Mademoiselle Genevieve walked through the crowd, back to her companions still standing on the banquette.

Dominic Delacroix whistled softly, brown fly-away eyebrows raised in surprise. That had been a most fascinating spectacle—not particularly edifying, certainly, but quite fascinating. He hurried down the steps of the gallery and made his own way across the seething auction room and outside, coming within earshot of Nicolas, Elise, and the formidable Mademoiselle Genevieve.

"Are you run quite mad, Genevieve?" Nicolas demanded. "Just think what your father will say. To go into a public auction room and . . ." He shuddered, rendered speechless at the horrifying ramifications of the event.

"Only think what will be said if anyone gets to hear of it," Elise whimpered. "And I will be implicated because I was here with you . . . Papa . . ." Her voice faded, tears beginning to well in the magnificent deep-blue eyes. They were tears of fright, and no one acquainted with Monsieur Victor Latour would doubt that they were genuine and the fear well founded.

Genevieve shrugged. "I will do what I can to spare you, Elise. It is likely that he will be so enraged with me that he will have little energy left to dwell on your part which was, after all, both involuntary and negligible."

Dominic Delacroix coughed. "Nicolas, well met. I was taking a breath of air at my office window and thought I recognized you turning into the street." He removed his curly brimmed hat and bowed to the ladies. *"Enchanté,* Mademoiselle Latour. I can scarce believe my good fortune in meeting you again so soon."

Elise curtsied, blushing prettily. "Monsieur Delacroix, how delightful," she murmured. The tears had miraculously dried, their residue simply making the blue eyes even more

9

lustrous as she peeped up at him through her eyelashes. It was an entirely satisfactory reaction, Dominic reflected complacently, offering her a most special smile as he brushed her fingertips with his lips. Genevieve blinked and shot her cousin Nicolas a look brimming with questions. Elise had a tendency to flirt, to be sure, but this particular gentleman was not at all like her usual courtly suitors. He was older for a start, and there was a coiled tension about him, a hint of—of what? For the moment Genevieve could not put her finger on the particular quality that was communicating itself to her, sending little chilly ripples up and down her spine.

"I beg your pardon," Nicolas said hastily. "May I present Monsieur Delacroix, Genevieve. Dominic, my cousin, Mademoiselle Latour's stepsister, Mademoiselle Genevieve."

So that's who the firebrand was. The daughter, presumably, of Latour's second wife who, like his first, had died in childbirth. The third wife had so far managed to avoid the perils of the accouchement bed, much to the irascible Latour's disgust, if rumor were true. The old gentleman was still hankering for a son—an event that Nicolas, for one, would regard with some considerable dismay. Dominic, having so far restrained his curiosity in the interests of furthering the original purpose of this meeting, now turned to look at Elise's companion properly for the first time. She was younger than Elise by perhaps three years and, on first glance, quite unable to hold a candle to the elder's rich, luxuriant beauty. On second glance, too, he decided. Where Elise was magnificently endowed with curves and indentations, the little sister rather resembled a flat plain relieved here and there by small hillocks. She was something less than middle height and gave the distinct impression of tiny-boned fragility. However, the performance he had just witnessed was somewhat at odds with this impression of delicacy.

"Mademoiselle Genevieve. Your servant." He bowed

punctiliously and met a direct and frankly inquiring look from a pair of the most unusual eyes he had ever seen. Pure gold—no, he amended; tawny gold—tiger's eyes. Large, too, framed in thick, straight golden eyelashes. A small, straight nose, beautifully formed over an equally straight mouth—a far cry from Elise's full-lipped, rosebud pout, but as he looked, Mademoiselle Genevieve smiled. Helen of Troy would be advised to look to her laurels, Dominic decided, more than a little surprised at himself for such a flight of fancy. After Rosemarie, he had had no time for the art of dalliance, despised susceptibility to the charms of the fair sex unless it were deliberately implied to achieve a purpose, but in this instance he could begin to imagine launching a small fleet if that smile requested it of him.

Well, well, Genevieve thought. So that's who the gentleman is. No gentleman at all. "Monsieur Delacroix," she said, curtsying demurely. "I do not appear to have had my sister's good fortune."

"Your pardon, mademoiselle?" He frowned, somewhat nonplussed at a statement that seemed not to make sense, except that he had formed the unmistakable impression that this very young lady rarely spoke less than sense.

She smiled again, but kept her eyes lowered. "Why, in not having made your acquaintance earlier," said Genevieve.

Was she mocking him? wondered Dominic, discovering to his surprise that the idea piqued his interest rather than his annoyance. His lips twitched, and the smile this time was not sardonic. "You do me too much honor, Mademoiselle Genevieve."

"Oh, surely not, sir," she demurred.

"Genevieve, your manners! I must crave indulgence for my baby sister, Monsieur Delacroix." Elise spoke with a nervous little titter. "She is not really out yet, and I am afraid still considers she has the license to behave with the child's lack of decorum." The words were uttered with a degree of

11

venom. Elise's baby sister had always had the devil's own way of monopolizing attention, and it did not suit the beauty in the least, and particularly not in this instance.

Her interruption served also to remind Dominic that paying undue attention to Mademoiselle Genevieve was not the object of this afternoon's exercise, and he had no desire to antagonize Mademoiselle Latour. He offered the latter a smile of complete understanding that relegated baby sister to her correct place in the scheme of things. Genevieve intercepted the smile, and a flash sparked for a second in the tawny eyes—a flash instantly extinguished.

"I was on my way to La Gallier to take *goûter*," he said, with another low bow. "Would it be most presumptious of me to invite your cousin, Nicolas?"

Nicolas looked at Elise, and there was just the correct moment of hesitation before she said, "Why, Monsieur Delacroix, we were on our way there, ourselves." Her eyelashes fluttered.

"Then, may I have the honor of inviting you to share my table?" he begged. "I am sure Mademoiselle Genevieve would enjoy a *pâtisserie*." He offered a kindly smile, brimming with condescension—a smile that infuriated its recipient but did much to placate Mademoiselle Latour.

"You are too kind, sir. We should be delighted." Elise laid her hand on Dominic's proffered arm clad in blue superfine, Dresden lace frothing at the wide cuff. Her cousin was thus left to offer escort to her stepsister.

"I do not wish to be a killjoy," Genevieve said, "but I fear that I do not have the time to take tea this afternoon. I must return home immediately to ensure that all is well with Amelie and the baby. There is no knowing what Mr. King will do in revenge if I do not forestall him."

An uncomfortable silence fell at this unpalatable reminder of the earlier disgracefully indecorous scene. Elise flushed with annoyance. "Monsieur Delacroix does not wish to concern himself with such matters. Have you not made a sufficient spectacle of yourself for one day?"

"I do not recall asking Monsieur Delacroix to concern himself," her sister said icily. "And I am not about to make a spectacle of myself. I intend simply to return home. Nicolas must decide which of us he chooses to chaperone."

What a troublesome girl she was! The tolerant amusement died from the turquoise eyes as Dominic waited for Nicolas to assert the mastery of the male and the elder. He needed only to tell Mademoiselle Genevieve that her wishes took second place and the girl would surely have no choice but to accede. Except that Nicolas did not say that. "Well . . . well, perhaps we should return home, Elise," he muttered. "There is bound to be trouble, you know."

Dominic felt the strands of his carefully laid plan begin to slide through his fingers. He could not stand here on the banquette like a dumb idiot, yet the politeness that he had to maintain if he were to play the game successfully forbade him to press his invitation. If only Nicolas would gather his wits. "Perhaps I shall be more fortunate on another occasion," he said blandly. "Some occasion when Mademoiselle Genevieve's engagements need not take precedence." He allowed a slight note of polite incredulity to creep into the statement, amazement that the wishes of a schoolroom miss should overrule those of her elders.

"I am desolated to discommode you, sir," snapped Genevieve, "but I am afraid I am concerned with matters of more moment than tea and *pâtisseries.*"

"Quite so." He bowed. "Slave trading, if I understood it correctly. A most unusual activity for a young lady, if I might say so." The bright blue eyes held no warmth as they locked with the tawny ones of Mademoiselle Genevieve; in fact they held an inexplicable warning. Danger, she thought, with an illuminating flash of recognition. Dominic Delacroix is a dangerous man and foolish Elise does not realize it. His

13

voice continued smoothly: "I could not help witnessing your so . . . so courageous, shall we say . . . stand in the Exchange."

Fortunately, at this moment Nicolas recollected himself. "Since we are unable to accept your invitation, Dominic, perhaps we can extend one of our own. This evening, my aunt is receiving. I would be delighted to introduce you if you should happen to be free."

"Yes, indeed," Elise fluttered, trying to mask her eagerness. "My stepmother would be pleased to welcome you."

"And, dare I hope that my presence would not displease others?" The pretty words emerged without effort, but their effect was somewhat blunted by a noise, something between a snort and a giggle, from the inconvenient Mademoiselle Genevieve. "I beg your pardon, mademoiselle." He turned toward her. "Did you say something?"

"No, no, indeed not, monsieur, I do not think I could participate with any skill in this conversation, so would not presume to enter it."

Genevieve Latour clearly recovered rapidly from both setbacks. Dominic decided that he would relish the opportunity for a private confrontation when his responses would not need to be constrained by an audience. However, for the moment he chose to ignore her remark and turned his full attention to Elise. "I should be honored to accept your invitation. Until this evening, Mademoiselle Latour, Nicolas." He touched his hat. "I expect you will be in bed, Mademoiselle Genevieve, but I am sure we will meet again." Turning on his heel, he walked away from them. It had been a small enough victory, but he derived some satisfaction from the indignant tiger's eyes riveted on his back.

"So, you think Hélène will be pleased to welcome such a one as Dominic Delacroix to her drawing room?" Genevieve mused, looking after the tall, broad-shouldered figure

14

moving away with a long, easy stride that seemed to eat up the yards.

"Of course she will," Elise insisted with a degree too much vehemence. "What can you possibly know of such things? You are still only a baby."

"Maybe," her young sister murmured, having no need to rise to the provocation. "But I *do* know that Monsieur Delacroix is not at all respectable, and I do not think that Lorenzo will look with equanimity on his betrothed's extending such a doe-eyed, effusive welcome to one of that reputation. He may tolerate your ordinary flirtations, but not this."

Elise, for all her porcelain beauty and softly rounded figure, had inherited her fair share of the Latour temper, and an exceedingly unpleasant scene threatened. Nicolas stepped in hastily. "You do not know what you are talking about, Genevieve. The Delacroix are one of the oldest Creole families in the Quarter. They are received everywhere."

"But *Dominic* Delacroix is not willingly received," his young cousin persisted with her customary obstinacy and accuracy. "Not by ladies . . . or, at least . . ." Imps of mischief danced in the tawny eyes, she added, "Perhaps by the ladies of Rampart Street, but not by Hélène and her friends."

"That is enough!" Nicolas declared firmly as they turned onto Royal Street. "Dominic Delacroix is a friend of mine and that fact should be enough for you."

"Dear me, Nicolas." The irrepressible Genevieve shook her head in mock reproof. "Numbering privateers amongst your friends! Whatever will Papa say?"

"Your father will have little enough to say to me, once Mr. King regales him with the tale of your little adventure this afternoon," Nicolas retorted.

That statement was undeniably true and succeeded in diverting Genevieve's attention for the moment. "Mr. King must have had some ulterior motive for attempting to sell Amelie and the baby. I must discover what it is if I am to ensure that he cannot do such a thing again. I do not think Papa will take Mr. King's side publicly against mine, however, whatever he might say in private. He would not consider it correct to do so, do you not agree, Elise?"

Elise shrugged, unwilling to offer reassurance. Unlike her sister, she had difficulty switching moods and was inclined to bear grudges. "It is a matter of supreme indifference to me," she declared loftily. "I cannot imagine why you should concern yourself with such affairs. It is most undignified."

"Is it indeed?" Genevieve's eyes snapped. "No more undignified than clandestine meetings, artfully arranged, with a privateer. And you need not deny that that meeting was arranged. It was as plain as day to anyone with half an eye. *I* should like to know why Nicolas is sufficiently intimate with a privateer to risk Hélène's discomfort by inviting such a disreputable figure to her drawing room." With that, Mademoiselle Genevieve flounced up the curving steps to the portico of a graceful, double-fronted house occupying a large proportion of Royal Street. The central door swung open as her hand reached for the knocker. She inclined her head in acknowledgement to the impassive butler and went into the large hall that ran the length of the house and was flanked on either side by a square *salle de compagnie*.

Her cousin and stepsister followed, both rendered silent by the butler's presence, and both, for separate reasons, distinctly uncomfortable at the embarrassing insight of their far-seeing relative. As they knew from painful experience, Genevieve, once she got her teeth into something, rarely let go until she had worried the matter to death.

"Oh, there you all are." Hélène Latour appeared from the parlor on the left of the hall. Her brown eyes were more than usually anxious this afternoon, and she patted her dark hair

16

nervously, frowning at her stepdaughters who were not that much younger than herself but over whom she was supposed to exercise some form of authority. "There is such an uproar in the slave quarters. It is something to do with Amelie, but no one will tell me anything, and if your father comes home to find everything so unsettled . . . Oh, dear . . ." Her voice, never much more than a whisper, faded in defeat.

"You had best prepare yourself for an explosion, Hélène," Genevieve said with a briskness not undiluted by compassion. Her stepmother paled and her hands quivered.

"Oh, dear," she said again, tremulously. "Why? What has happened?"

"Genevieve saw fit to enter Maspero's Exchange in the middle of a public auction and forbid Mr. King to sell Amelie and the baby," Elise announced with a brutal lack of frills. "It will be the scandal of the season. We shall never live it down."

Hélène leaned against one of the Ionic pilasters framing the doorway of the parlor. "How could you, Genevieve?" she faltered. "Victor . . ."

"Will not be best pleased," Genevieve finished for her in rueful understatement. "I am sorry, Hélène, but I could not do otherwise. You know it has never been Latour practice to separate families. I do not know what lay behind it on this occasion, but I intend to find out before Papa returns. I will need all the defense I can muster."

"But I am receiving this evening," Hélène whimpered. "If Victor is enraged, it will affect the entire household, and I shall have the headache, I know I shall."

"Please, Hélène." Genevieve took her arm, turning her back into the *salle de compagnie*. "You must not work yourself up in this way. You know it is bad for you. Why do you not lie down for a little while?"

"Perhaps it would be best," her stepmother agreed. She added in pathetic revelation, "Victor will not disturb me if he believes I am not feeling quite the thing. Elise, would you see to the arrangements for this evening? I was going to do the flowers in the ballroom, but you have such a delicate touch . . ." She offered a pleading little smile to which not even Elise was impervious.

"Of course," Elise reassured. "You must lie down and gather your strength. I will see to everything, and you must not concern yourself about this other matter." A dismissive hand banished the troublesome business of Genevieve's indecorous involvement in the affair of Amelie, the baby, and the overseer into outer darkness. "When Papa comes in, we shall all keep out of his way . . . except Genevieve," she added, shooting her sister a malicious glance. "It is her responsibility, after all, to draw the fire."

"And when have I shirked the responsibility?" Genevieve asked with a hint of a smile. "The blame is mine, and I acknowledge it freely. However, you must excuse me while I attempt to gather a defense."

She left the two women and Nicolas, knowing that the three of them would enjoy a discussion of her heinous behavior even while Hélène fluttered and trembled at the prospect of the forthcoming uproar. Elise and Nicolas were probably hoping that the inevitable scene and turmoil would effectively mask their introduction of Dominic Delacroix into the respectable drawing room of Hélène Latour. But why had the invitation been issued in the first place? If Elise had decided to pursue a flirtation with the privateer, then she was being more than ordinarily foolish. The rigidly correct Don Lorenzo Byaz would not stand for it, and if anything occurred to upset *that* match, Victor Latour's rage would know no bounds. And why, knowing that as he must, was Nicolas colluding—aiding and abetting, in fact? It was most definitely not in his interests to fall foul of his relative who might decide to look elsewhere for an heir.

It was most puzzling. Genevieve shook her head, then

dismissed the puzzle for the moment as the matter of her own self-preservation loomed large. She hurried down the hall and out onto the long porticoed gallery running the width of the house at the back. The gallery, where the family took their meals in warm weather and pursued those leisure activities conducive to idleness, overlooked a large walled courtyard that provided absolute seclusion from the hustle and bustle of the Quarter. Indeed, it was hard to imagine that this fragrant, cobbled square of mellow stone, where a fountain plashed melodiously and banana trees offered wide-leafed shade, was actually situated in the midst of a city.

The kitchen that served the house was a long, low building at the left of the courtyard, and it was there that Genevieve now made her way. When she returned to the main house a half hour later, she was in full possession of the sordid facts of an all-too-common tale. Its recounting would do little to turn aside Victor Latour's wrath, but it would ensure that it fell also on the head of the overseer, and would safeguard Amelie and her child from sale by Mr. King in the future. And for more than that, Genevieve knew from bitter experience, it would be foolish to hope.

"So, what have you discovered in your missionary zeal?" Elise inquired, looking up from her embroidery as Genevieve came up the steps to the gallery. Her tone was as sharp as the question. Quite clearly, Genevieve had not been forgiven for her afternoon's work or for her uncomfortably pointed remarks.

Genevieve did not immediately answer the question. "Where is Nicolas?" She poured tea from the silver pot resting on a low table and sat down in a deep rocking chair, sipping appreciatively at the steaming liquid in the delicate flutted cup.

"In his apartments, I imagine." Elise gestured vaguely toward the *garçonnière* at the rear of the courtyard, then took a chocolate tipped *langue de chat* from the plate, beside the teapot, popping it whole between her lips before helping herself to another one with eager fingers.

"You'll get fat," Genevieve observed with the regrettable want of diplomacy frequently to be found in younger siblings. "But I don't imagine Don Lorenzo will mind. He is developing something of an embonpoint himself. Then, of course, one can't have too much of a good thing, can one?" She smiled with deceptive innocence over her teacup. "Unless, of course, Lorenzo has ceased to be a good thing? Usurped, perhaps, by one Dominic Delacroix?"

The crash of the great front door shivered the glass in the windows of the cabinets opening onto the gallery. The two girls froze, the mischief of one and the indignation of the other subsumed under an immediate watchful tension, the familial pinpricks of irritation vanished under their shared trepidation. Genevieve placed her teacup on the table and gave her sister a rueful grimace. The door to the gallery flew open, and Victor Latour filled the opening, his normally rubicund face crimson hued, eyes blazing, barrel chest swelling with apoplectic fury. Elise shrank back against the cushions of her sofa and watched with reluctant admiration as her stepsister rose to her feet slowly, squaring her shoulders. How was it that Genevieve could face the full blast of that fearsome rage without appearing to flinch? She had always been able to do it—the only person on God's earth, in Elise's opinion, who refused to show fear before Victor Latour. Not that that refusal benefitted her in any way—if anything, it increased his fury, but, somehow, Genevieve always seemed to emerge from the torrents of rage unmarked, her spirit intact.

"You dare to drag the name of Latour across the floor of a public auction room?" Victor Latour bellowed, standing to one side of the wide-flung door, an imperative forefinger pointing back into the house. "You dare to meddle in the business of my overseer!"

20

"There were reasons," Genevieve said, forcing herself to follow the direction of that forefinger, walking through the door, past the rigid figure without flinching, although her flesh crept in expectation of the blow that might or might not be delivered. On this occasion, Victor stayed his hand, but his daughter took little comfort from the restraint. She had a rocky road to travel before his anger would be played out and the matter drawn to an end.

# Chapter 2

"But Dominic, you promised!" Angelique pouted prettily, twining herself around the lean sinewy body beside her. The evening sun sent a golden bar of light across the bed, touching the two naked figures with the day's last finger of warmth.

"That was before this imperative matter arose," Dominic explained, patiently still although it was Angelique's second attempt in the last hour to persuade him to change his mind. He stroked lazily down the long, creamy gold back as she pressed herself against him.

"But why cannot you deal with it some other time? You have not taken me to the theater for months." Even as she spoke, Angelique realized that she had pushed too far. The turquoise eyes beside her glazed beneath a thin sheen of ice as he sat up in one neat movement, swinging himself off the bed.

"That is enough. Have you not learned that I cannot abide whining? I do not come here to be badgered and hagridden, and if I do not satisfy your wants, my dear, you had best look around you for another provider."

Angelique shivered at the cold, expressionless tone, at the words she knew he meant. Dominic Delacroix would have no compunction about drawing their arrangement to a close.

It would be done with grace and a degree of generosity, so long as she had not forfeited any rights to the latter, but he would not think twice about it. There was no shortage of quadroons, as beautiful and delicate as Angelique, who would count Dominic Delacroix as the summit of their ambition.

She sprang from the bed, cajoling words of apology on her lips, as she caressed his length with knowing hands, filled the basin from the ewer of warm water and began to sponge him, performing the service as he stood, seemingly indifferent, his face a mask. She fluttered around him, helping him with his shirt, his pantaloons, kneeling to draw on his stockings and maneuver his feet into his boots. Then he walked over to the mirror above the dresser where he very deliberately arranged his cravat, inserting a diamond-head pin in the folds, before shrugging into the coat of blue superfine that he had been wearing earlier when he had met the Latour sisters and their cousin outside Maspero's Exchange.

Angelique waited anxiously for the smile that would tell her her lapse had been forgiven, for a word, at least, but Dominic's face remained impassive as he shook out the lace ruffles at his wrists. It was impossible to tell whether he was still angry with her, or whether, as so often happened, his mind was elsewhere, had abruptly switched from the sensuous pleasures available to him in this enchanting little house on Rampart Street to the formulation of some plan, to the unraveling of some knotty problem plaguing his life outside these silken walls. Angelique was always excluded from that other life and, indeed, would not have wanted to be included. She had her own friends, a pleasantly idle existence, no shortage of luxuries, clothes, servants; her only obligation, to be willingly available whenever her provider required her, and she must *never* discommode him in any way, or cause him the least annoyance. She had transgressed those last rules with her pestering this afternoon, and knew from painful experience that withdrawal would probably follow and she would not see Dominic for several weeks as he demonstrated how easily he could do without her. During those weeks, she would live on a knife edge of anxiety, wondering if he would ever return, or if she would simply receive the formal notification breaking their contract with a generous payment that would not begin to compensate for the greater losses.

He walked to the bedroom door, and she ran to open it for him, standing on tiptoe to brush her lips across his mouth, pressing her bare breasts against his chest, feeling the lace and lawn of his shirt, cool and smooth against her skin. She did not dare ask when he would return, but her lip trembled slightly, and the brown eyes swam as she stood aside to let him pass. Dominic paused on the landing outside, then, almost absently, touched the tip of her nose with a long forefinger. "Take a friend to the St. Charles with you, Angel. You may use my box as I have no need of it this evening."

Angelique's face lit up. "I will come to the door with you, Dominic."

He shook his head brusquely. "No, I do not have the time to wait for you to fetch a robe." He moved unhurriedly down the stairs—unhurriedly, yet he was out on Rampart Street before Angelique had pushed her arms into the silk peignoir.

The sun was setting as Dominic strode down the street in the direction of the square and his own house on Chartres Street. That visit to Angelique had been unscheduled, but his only half-successful encounter with Elise Latour and her relatives had unsettled him, and he did not care to be unsettled; it clouded the mind which, in Dominic's business, was a dangerous condition. Angelique had done her work well, but he had gained clarity of thought at the expense of time, and if he was to make a seemly appearance at the Latour residence, he would have to hurry with his dressing and dinner. Dominic Delacroix did not like to be hurried any more than he liked to be unsettled, and for much the same reasons.

24

Silas was waiting for him in the cool, lofty chamber opening onto the rear second-floor gallery overlooking the courtyard. "Knee britches, monsieur?" he asked, running a clothes brush lovingly over a silver-gray velvet coat.

"Yes, I think so." That sardonic smile touched Dominic's lips. "One mustn't appear lacking in respect to Madame Latour, for all that she will be hard pressed to extend a gracious welcome to such an uninvited guest."

Silas, who was not party to the details of his master's plans, contented himself with a grunt and began to sharpen the razor on the leather strop. He was a burly man with a sailor's pigtail, hands rough and calloused from years before the mast, but he shaved Dominic with incongruous delicacy and the utmost care. In the same manner, he assisted him into the fine lace and velvet of his evening clothes, brushing and smoothing until satisfied that Dominic's appearance was appropriately immaculate.

"I took the liberty of informing the kitchen that you would dine in the courtyard, monsieur," he informed his master. "'Tis a fine evening, and you'll be glad of the fresh air, I'll be bound." There was a faint note of longing in his voice and Dominic chuckled.

"We'll be back at sea soon enough, Silas. I've just this one matter to tie up, then we'll be off in search of a prize or two."

"And the new anchorage, monsieur?" Silas asked the question casually, as if the answer were a matter of supreme indifference to him. It was the most sensible attitude, he had discovered long ago. Since he could not be sure such questions would receive an answer, it was wise to cultivate indifference.

Dominic shrugged. "That, Silas, is the very matter I have in hand." He strolled out onto the gallery and down the outside staircase to the courtyard where a candlelit table was laid beneath a tall magnolia tree, its waxen blossoms in full, fragrant bloom. The attentive manservant drew back his chair, filled his glass, and served him from the dishes brought

25

from the kitchen at the rear of the courtyard to be placed in readiness upon a side table.

It was a delightful evening with the moon hanging full in the sky and the scents of verbena and yellow jasmine heavy in the air. Dominic ate in a leisurely manner, deliberately controlling his impatience to be off about the evening's business, and equally deliberately refusing to allow himself to think of that business, dwelling instead on the beauty of the evening, the rich bouquet of the excellent burgundy in his glass, and the subtlety of the sauces enhancing the food on his plate. As a result, he was refreshed and relaxed when the bell on his front door peeled and a few minutes later, Nicolas St. Denis was announced.

"Why, Nicolas, what a pleasant surprise," Dominic murmured, waving his guest to a chair. "You will join me in a glass of wine?"

"Thank you." Nicolas took the offered seat and smiled awkwardly. The older man always made him feel gauche, a bumbling schoolboy who needed to mind his manners. "I hope you will forgive the intrusion, but I thought it might be . . . uh . . . be more politic if I were to accompany you to the soirée." He flushed slightly. One really did not like to imply that one's guest might not be welcome under one's family's roof, however undeniably true it was.

Dominic smiled, fully conscious of his companion's confusion. "A good thought, Nicolas," he reassured. "I am most grateful to you. It would be quite embarrassing to be turned away from the door." He smiled kindly, but managed nevertheless to convey that it was, of course, quite ridiculous to imagine Dominic Delacroix in such an embarrassing predicament.

"Mademoiselle Latour is in good health, I trust, and intending to grace the soirée?"

"Most certainly," Nicolas assured him. He would have liked to have added that Elise awaited Dominic's arrival most eagerly, but, somehow, although such a statement

26

would be a mere drop in the ocean of his treachery, he could not forsake the strict rules of his Creole upbringing sufficiently to discuss a lady in that fashion.

"It was unfortunate about this afternoon," Dominic continued smoothly, filling his guest's glass. "It would have been preferable had you contrived to be alone with Mademoiselle Latour when we met."

Nicolas squirmed, recognizing the rebuke beneath the gentle tones, the implacable warning lurking behind the smile. "Yes, I must apologize for that, Dominic, but Genevieve is . . . is . . ."

"A tiresome child," Dominic finished for him, still smiling. "I rather gathered that." He sipped his wine thoughtfully. "Also somewhat forceful. You seemed to have some difficulty gainsaying her." The smile was switched off like a doused candle, and Nicolas felt his cheeks warm.

"I could not have allowed her to return to Royal Street unchaperoned," he protested.

"No, of course not," Dominic concurred easily, "but, was that your only option? Could she not have been obliged to fall in with yours and her sister's plans?"

"Genevieve does not, in general, fall in with other people's plans," Nicolas said with a sigh. "But you need not fear that she will be in the way tonight."

"I am relieved to hear it." Dominic rose from the table. "I think it is time you presented me to your aunt. I am most anxious to renew my acquaintance with Mademoiselle Latour, also, and to exchange a few words with your uncle. Shall we go?" A fly-away eybrow lifted, and Nicolas made haste to get to his feet.

It was but a short distance to the Latour house on Royal Street, and the two men walked through the soft spring evening, both lost in their own thoughts. But while Dominic could guess fairly accurately the tumultuous reflections of his companion, Nicolas could not begin to hazard what thoughts formed behind the smooth brow and untroubled eyes of Monsieur Delacroix.

As they turned onto Royal Street, it became clear that a party was in progress. Carriages passed along the narrow thoroughfare, turning in through the grilled porte cochere of the large mansion to unload their passengers in the courtyard at the end of the wide-paved driveway. The guests made their way across the lamplit courtyard, beneath the lattices and pergolas hung with fragrant blooms and delicate greenery, to be received by their hostess on the rear gallery.

The strains of music from French horn, violin, and pianoforte drifted through the gallery's open doors behind Hélène. The musicians were ensconced at the street end of the long ballroom contrived by throwing open the doors between the *salle de compagnie* and the dining room, and the young people were dancing there, well away from their gossiping elders gathered on the gallery and at the far end of the room.

Elise had been released from her receiving duties at her stepmother's side soon after the arrival of Don Lorenzo Byaz, and was moving across the polished dance floor, partnered by her fiancé, when her cousin and Dominic Delacroix entered the house, like other pedestrians, from the front verandah on Royal Street. Elise saw them over Lorenzo's shoulder and her eyelashes fluttered. Dominic smiled and one eyebrow lifted infinitesimally. Elise promptly lowered her eyes demurely and Dominic's smile broadened.

Elise knew that she outshone every girl in the room with the candle glow catching the russet lights in her hair, piled artlessly in loose curls atop her head, and the richness of her figure in the blue Grecian-style gown that exactly matched her eyes. And Elise knew that there was only one man in the room worthy of her beauty—and that man was not her fiancé. Lorenzo was a magnificent catch, of course; wealthy, aristocratic and, as his wife, she would be mistress of Villafranca, the Byaz plantation outside New Orleans, as

28

well as the magnificent town house that almost rivaled the Latour establishment. Elise wanted all of these things as passionately as Victor Latour wanted the alliance, but she also knew that once Elise Latour became Madame Byaz, she must bid farewell to the possibility of all excitement, to the gentle spice of flirtation, to those moments when the maiden's heart beat faster as she contemplated a handsome countenance and wondered—just wondered.

It was not sensible, of course, but Dominic Delacroix had made no secret of how he was drawn to her on the three occasions that they had met, and there was something infinitely exciting about him; the man everyone needed although they hated having to admit to that need. He made no secret of his disdain for his "customers," or for the rules and regulations of the rigidly correct Creole existence that was as much his background as it was Elise's. But when he looked at her, Elise saw only admiration. When he spoke to her, she heard only compliments in the soft voice. To her knowledge, he had never singled out another Creole lady for his attentions, although there were those willing to risk a little. Why should she not indulge just a tiny bit in an innocent, harmless flirtation? And besides, it would do Lorenzo no harm to be a little less complacent. His eagerness and praise for her grace and beauty had diminished in extravagance since the betrothal had been formalized and, on occasion, he seemed to behave toward her as if they were already married, as if she were already his possession. No, it would do him no harm to realize that even a man like Dominic Delacroix, supposedly impervious to female charms, was not immune to Mademoiselle Latour.

Dominic, Nicolas beside him, made his way through the crowded room toward his hostess. He seemed not to notice the minute lull in the conversations around him, the startled glances, swiftly averted, but Nicolas noticed them and wished as he had so often done in the last weeks, that he had never had dealings with Monsieur Delacroix. He had still not worked out how he was to explain this guest's inclusion in his aunt's soirée to Victor Latour, beyond the rather ingenuous excuse that he knew his new friend from one of the *salle d'escrime* on Exchange Alley, which was, after all, where they had first met. He was a Delacroix, when all was said and done, and if one happened to meet accidentally in the street and was invited to take a glass of wine with him, it would be discourteous, when pleading a prior family engagement, not to invite him to come along. It was very feeble, but would have to do, Nicolas decided disconsolately. Victor thought him an idiot, anyway, so would probably not see anything odd in this further example of stupidity.

"Hélène," Nicolas greeted his young aunt with a brilliant smile. "May I introduce a good friend of mine. I happened to meet him in the street as I was on my way, and made sure you would be glad to welcome him." Laying his hand lightly on Dominic's velvet arm, he announced, "Dominic Delacroix."

Hélène, for all the fragility of her nerves, for all her fear of her husband, had been brought up in the strict school of a Creole lady, and would have cut out her tongue rather than reveal in public an iota of discourteous surprise. With barely a flicker, she welcomed Nicolas's companion, smiling warmly as she pressed a glass of iced champagne upon him and quietly introduced him to the group beside them. Everyone responded with the same immaculate courtesy, and Dominic was hard pressed to keep a straight face as he imagined the seething speculation, not unmixed with indignation, that would replace the well-bred smiles once he was no longer in the room. However, he bowed, sipped his champagne, chatted amiably until he espied a lady in a purple turban consuming, with a degree of determination, dragées from a chased silver bowl.

"You will excuse me," he murmured. "I must pay my respects to my aunt." This gentle reminder that the privateer was a Delacroix, and as such should be as much accepted in the drawing rooms of society as any other member of his family, did much for Hélène's peace of mind and, in fact, created a degree of confusion amongst those others who had simply been waiting for his departure to cry their outrage. One could not refuse to know a Delacroix.

"*Tante* Louise, how delightful." Dominic bowed before the elderly dowager.

"What the devil are you doing here, you rascal?" The dowager, with no need for politeness, raised her lorgnette and examined her nephew closely.

Dominic's eyes twinkled as he raised her hand to his lips. "I am acquainted with Nicolas St. Denis, *tante*. He was kind enough to invite me."

"Nonsense!" Louise dismissed the statement with all the contempt it deserved. "What dealings do you have with Latour?"

"At the moment, none but those I have with most people in this room," he replied easily.

"At the moment, eh?" The old lady regarded him shrewdly. "You've some mischief in mind for the future, then?"

"How could you think such a thing?" Dominic chided gently. "I never plan mischief, madame, only necessity."

"Ah." The old lady nodded her head in comprehension. "You need something from Latour, then." She cackled with laughter. "I wish you luck, nephew. He's as hard a man as you. You will be well partnered." She took another dragée from the depleted bowl and waved a hand in dismissal. Dominic accepted his congé with a further bow, and turned his attention back to the room.

Victor Latour was on the gallery, looking ill at ease as he attempted to make small talk with a group of ladies. The man was not cut out for drawing-room affairs. He was much more at home in the clubs with his cronies, or riding around his vast sugarcane plantation, or managing the affairs of his shipyard on Lake Borgne. He looked more than ordinarily choleric, Dominic thought, examining the bucolic figure dispassionately. Something must have happened to exacerbate that notoriously short fuse. But, of course—the tiresome Mademoiselle Genevieve with her penchant for slave trading. Dominic examined the occupants of the *grande salle* again. There was no sign of that diminutive figure with the tiger's eyes, and small though she was, Dominic was convinced her presence could not possibly go unnoticed by anyone who had once met her.

Mademoiselle Latour, however, was very much in evidence, and much in beauty. Of course, if he could come to an easy understanding with Victor Latour, it would not be necessary to pursue matters with Mademoiselle Elise, but then, the former was highly unlikely, and Dominic believed in hedging his bets. He moved toward the dancers and was gratified to see Elise instantly say something to her partner, something that brought them both out of the dance. Don Lorenzo left her, crossing the hall to the supper room set up in the parlor opposite, and Dominic appeared beside the lady.

"Good evening, Mademoiselle Latour. This is a delightful party, is it not?"

"I am so glad you were able to join us, monsieur." Elise turned the full beam of those magnificent blue eyes upon him.

"The pleasure is all mine," he said softly. "But a crowded ballroom leaves much to be desired, I fear, as a setting for a tête-à-tête."

Elise's eyes narrowed as she contemplated her response to this bold invitation. No man she had known hitherto would have dared venture such an outrageous suggestion. Lorenzo, if he heard of it, would probably demand satisfaction with swords in St. Anthony's Garden. The thought struck her as immensely amusing, but she was obliged to swallow her giggle as Lorenzo himself appeared with the glass of orange-flower water that she had begged him to procure.

"Thank you, Lorenzo." Smiling prettily, she took the

proffered refreshment. "Are you acquainted with Monsieur Delacroix?"

"I have not had the pleasure," her fiancé said in a tone of voice that suggested pleasure was not forthcoming at this moment, either. The aquiline Castilian features were set in severe lines of disapproval.

Dominic took a pinch of snuff from a gilded onyx box and regarded the young Spaniard, mild amusement in the turquoise eyes. "I have seen you fence, Don Lorenzo, at Arnaud's. You were a worthy opponent, as I recall, for the *maître d'armes*. Perhaps we may have a match one day."

Why was it that the seemingly polite suggestion carried the indefinable tinge of a challenge? Elise blinked and felt a surge of excitement. Could Monsieur Delacroix possibly be hinting to her that he would match his swordplay with her fiancé for *her?* It was an outrageous idea, of course, but as she glanced up at him, the corners of that chiseled mouth lifted in a smile that was as conspiratorial as it was full of promise. So overcome was she by this exhilarating reflection that Elise did not notice that the smile was absent from his eyes, which bore a hooded expression almost of boredom.

Vain little fool, Dominic thought dispassionately—just like all the others of her breed. She was going to make matters very easy for him, and that stiff-necked Castilian was only going to help things along unless he lightened up a little. "Would you permit me to solicit your fiancée for the next dance?" He bowed to Lorenzo who could do nothing but return the bow stiffly as he gave his permission for the dance.

"I am afraid that your fiancé disapproves of me," Dominic observed with a little laugh, holding the voluptuous figure lightly yet managing to convey an intimacy that shocked Elise even as it delighted her.

"Oh, Lorenzo disapproves of anything that he does not understand," she said airily.

"And he does not understand me?" The fly-away eyebrows

lifted and Elise giggled a little. It was not at all proper to be discussing her fiancé in this manner. "Do *you* understand me, Mademoiselle Latour?"

"I am not sufficiently acquainted with you, monsieur," Elise managed in stifled tones.

"A situation I hope to remedy," Dominic said smoothly, wishing perversely that the girl would make it a little more difficult for him. He had never enjoyed challengeless games.

"You should not say such things, Monsieur Delacroix," Elise now reproached him. "I am betrothed."

"Yes, so you are," he agreed. "But that does not mean that we cannot become acquainted, does it?"

"No . . . no, I suppose it does not." Elise felt a wave of heat creeping up her neck. This was the most dreadfully dangerous conversation, yet it was utterly irresistible.

"Perhaps you would like to take a turn about the garden," her partner said. "It is a most beautiful evening. We could become acquainted under the moonlight."

"I do not think Lorenzo would permit it," Elise said at last. "Even with a chaperone, it would be considered . . . well, peculiar."

Dominic was silent for a moment, then he said gently, "I had not thought to seek Don Lorenzo's permission, and I am not, myself, accustomed to chaperones."

"I think perhaps we should talk of something else," Elise murmured.

"Of course," he agreed, and began to talk of the opera.

Elise hardly attended to his remarks; her mind was in such a whirl. What possible harm could there be? A little walk, a little conversation about more than these social pleasantries, a kiss—No, not that. Not even Lorenzo had kissed her, except for the most decorous salute on her brow or cheek. Genevieve was always saying that she considered Lorenzo distinctly poor-spirited in this matter, for all that he was only behaving according to strict convention. Genevieve also said that she could not imagine getting married without having experienced some flash of passion. But then, Genevieve was always saying such shocking things, always talking about matters that she was far too young to know anything about. But the idea of her sister having a flirtation with Dominic Delacroix on the eve of her marriage would surely stun even the seemingly unshockable Genevieve. It would give Elise an advantage that she had never before had, a pinnacle from which she could condescend in a most satisfying manner. And no one else need know. Genevieve would never betray her.

"I sometimes walk a little in the side garden before retiring," she said breathlessly. "I find it helps me to sleep after the excitements of a party."

Dominic, who had decided he had sown sufficient seeds for one night and was preparing to abandon the beauty before launching a renewed attack on the next occasion, hid his surprise. His hand pressed for an instant against her waist, imparting a patch of warmth that increased Elise's breathlessness; other than that, he simply inclined his head in acknowledgement. Then the music ceased and he returned her to Lorenzo with punctilious thanks to them both.

Elise, as she watched him make his way to the gallery and the elders of the company, wondered if he had understood her to mean what she thought she had meant, although, in all truth, her statement had seemed to spring to her lips without volition. Just the thought of saying such a shameless thing brought hot color to her cheeks and a mist of sweat to her palms. Perhaps he thought it was simply a piece of small talk, an inoffensive, unimportant statement. Nonsense, of course he would not think such a thing. He would know that she was quite shameless, and was probably utterly disgusted that she should have responded to a meaningless flirtatious remark with such a disgraceful implied invitation. She could almost see the way Genevieve's eyebrows would lift incredulously if she heard of it.

"It is too hot in here, Lorenzo," she said, suddenly pettish.

"Escort me out to the courtyard, if you please."

Lorenzo was all attention. It was quite right and proper for delicate ladies to be overcome by heat when they had been dancing so indefatigably.

"What the deuce is Delacroix doing here?" Victor Latour hissed at his nephew. He gazed at the elegant figure engaged in seemingly animated conversation with Madame Fourchet. The devil was amazingly personable. No one would think, to look at him, that he was a rogue—the blackest sheep ever known to the Delacroix, or to any other Orleanian family, for that matter. Except that the service he provided by running the British blockade with his privateers was one they could none of them do without.

"He is a friend of mine, uncle," Nicolas began his prepared speech. "I met him at a *salle d'escrime,* and we had several passages. He is a superb swordsman."

"Of course he is," Victor snapped. "You would hardly expect anything else. The man's no sword*player!* The instrument's a weapon for him, not a toy, and he's not welcome in my house."

"I beg your pardon, sir." Nicolas struggled to collect his thoughts, which always scattered when he was under attack from Latour. "I felt it would be discourteous in the extreme to refuse to extend the invitation this evening. I met him in the street, you understand, and our dealings in the past have always been pleasant, and he invited me to take a glass of wine with him this evening, which, of course, I could not because Hélène was receiving and—"

"Oh, do stop wittering, man," Victor interrupted impatiently. "Delacroix would not have expected to be invited here. He's hardly some naive unsophisticate." The accusatory glare that accompanied this statement left Nicolas in no doubt as to who was deserving of such a description. "However you spend your time when you are about town is of no importance, as well you know. You may enjoy what company you please, but you need to exercise some discrimination in whom you introduce to my wife and your cousins. Genevieve has no sense of decorum as it is, without your setting her such an appalling example."

Latour's color deepened as he remembered his daughter's scandalous conduct and the shamelessly matter-of-fact manner in which she had told him that his overseer had been taking his revenge on Amelie because the slave had dared to refuse him her body, and her husband had actually attempted to defend her. Victor, unlike the majority of his fellow planters, disapproved mightily of relations between his free employees and his slaves. It made for confusion and dissension, and Mr. King, as a result of Genevieve's disclosures, was in need of another job, and Victor in need of another overseer. It was a problem that he did not care for, and one that he would not have had to contend with, if his daughter had kept her nose out of matters that did not concern her.

"Monsieur Latour." Victor was torn out of this unpleasant reverie by something no more pleasant. Dominic Delacroix was paying his respects to his host, and the host was obliged to respond in kind. Nicolas, with a sigh of relief, took a discreet departure. Dominic did not need his help further. Surely, he had done all that was required of him.

## Chapter 3

The cabinet was lit only by a shaft of moonlight from the window midway up the outside wall. The darkness did not bother Genevieve who, in the five hours of her imprisonment, had come to know intimately every nook and cranny, every obstacle in the small room that served as a storeroom for kitchen supplies. It was one of two cabinets situated at the corners of the rear gallery, and its fellow opposite was used as an office by Victor Latour. Sounds of the party continued to drift under the door, and Genevieve sat glumly on a pickle barrel, alternately nibbling on a dry biscuit and dipping her finger into a jar of strawberry preserve. It was a distinctly inadequate supper when compared with the delicacies laid out for the guests; however, she supposed she should be grateful for small mercies since her only significant complaint at the present was boredom.

Licking her fingers, she got up and dragged the barrel over beneath the window. The view of the side garden below was hardly thrilling, but it made a change, and the night air was pleasantly soft on her face as she propped her chin on the sill. The crunch of gravel below brought her up on tiptoe, peering over the edge of the window. The figure standing in the shadows was unmistakable. So, he had decided to act upon the invitation, Genevieve mused. But why? What could

Dominic Delacroix possibly find to amuse him in the decorous entertainment offered by Hélène Latour? Was it Elise who had taken his fancy? Surely not. Elise was beautiful, certainly, accomplished enough for the correct marriage that was her destiny, innocent and simple in the manner considered *de rigueur* for a Creole maiden. But those were not qualities likely to appeal to such a one as Monsieur Delacroix, if rumor were true, and there was little reason to doubt it.

Another figure appeared on the lawn, coming from the front of the house, and the watcher at the window recognized her cousin. Genevieve considered eavesdropping to be a perfectly legitimate activity, and particularly when it was the only diversion offered to her, so she strained her ears into the night gloom, concentrating with every fiber of her being as the two men came together in the shadow of the wall beneath her window.

"Has it gone well, Dominic?" Nicolas asked, a note of anxiety in his voice, almost pleading, Genevieve thought. "Did you talk with Latour?"

"Not beyond the courtesies," Dominic replied. "But then I did not expect more on this occasion." A flare sparked in the dark, then the glow of a cigar tip as Dominic drew deeply and with a small sigh of pleasure, the aromatic smoke curling in the air. "But the ground has been prepared, and he cannot deny me now when I call upon him at his office. Not when I have been welcomed as a guest in his house."

"And Elise?" Nicolas sounded distinctly hesitant. "If all goes well with her father you will not need—"

"How unsubtle you are, Nicolas," Dominic mocked gently. "Your cousin, I do assure you, would be most disappointed if I did not pursue our . . . our acquaintance. Indeed, I expect her to join me at any minute, so perhaps you would like to make yourself scarce, since I do not think she wishes for a chaperone any more than I."

"You promised me she would not be hurt," Nicolas said,

with a catch of desperation in his voice. "I would not have agreed—"

"I do not recall that you were in a position to do otherwise," the older man interrupted coldly. Genevieve's scalp prickled. She understood nothing of what was being said, but so far she had heard nothing to dispel her earlier conviction that Dominic Delacroix was a very dangerous man.

"But if she is discovered here, alone in the garden with you, it will create the most dreadful scandal."

"The suggestion was Mademoiselle Latour's, Nicolas, I do assure you. I would not have had the temerity to make it myself, this early on in our acquaintanceship."

Idiot Elise! Genevieve bit her lip in annoyance, wishing she could make some sense of this conversation.

"Don Lorenzo . . ." Nicolas began miserably.

"Is a blind, complacent fool," the other broke in bluntly. "Your cousin, my dear fellow, is ripe for the picking, and the sooner that arrogant Castilian sweeps her off her feet and beds her, with or without the vows, the more likely he is to find her still virtuous."

Genevieve nodded in sage agreement. She had been of the same opinion herself for weeks. Elise swung between panic and dismay at the prospect of the passionless years of marital duty, for all that in her heart of hearts she could conceive of no alternative life and would be devastated at the thought it might be denied her. But Genevieve knew and understood how she hankered for the romantic adventure, the fantasy to be indulged just once before she became the rich, respectable, aristocratic matron. However, if Elise thought she could have that adventure with Dominic Delacroix, she was going to burn more than her fingers in the fire; Genevieve was convinced of it. But she still did not know why Dominic seemed inclined to encourage the maiden's foolishness, or what part Nicolas was playing in all this.

"You promised that her reputation would not suffer,"

Nicolas was insisting now, his voice low and urgent.

"That is up to the lady." Dominic laughed, and Genevieve felt that prickle again. It was not a reassuring laugh. "I do not need to ruin her reputation to achieve my object. If, however, she should insist upon . . ." He laughed again, and the tip of his cigar glowed bright. "Run along now, my dear Nicolas. You have discharged your debt, and I absolve you from all further responsibility."

Debt? Sweet heaven, what was going on? Genevieve watched as Nicolas turned and made his way slowly back to the house. Well, whatever it was, it clearly had to be stopped. Foolish Elise might be, spiteful, too, on occasion, but they were sisters, and if one was getting into waters too deep and too hot, then it was up to the other to fish her out. Genevieve did not stop to consider whether her rescue attempt would be gratefully received by her sister, although it did occur to her that Monsieur Delacroix would probably not be best pleased at her interference, but then his feelings in the matter were supremely unimportant.

While she was pondering, her eye caught a pale glimmer against the trees. Elise, her hair and gown covered with a gauzy shawl, came slipping across the lawn. Dominic ground out his cigar on the gravel at his feet and took a step toward her. "I hardly dared hope I understood you correctly," he said softly, his voice vibrant with a husky warmth.

Genevieve scowled. No wonder Elise was fluttering and simpering. Who wouldn't be when on the receiving end of that voice? Tightening her grip on the windowsill, she hitched herself up, scrabbling for purchase on the plastered wall with her toes as she scrambled onto the ledge. The window was a good eight feet above ground level outside, and Genevieve swung her legs over the sill, twisted awkwardly until her back was to the garden, then lowered herself over, hanging onto the ledge with her fingertips, preparing to drop.

"What in the world!" Dominic swung round at the rustle behind him and stared at the pendent figure. In two strides, he had reached her and clasped her waist strongly. "Let go. I have you safe."

"I can manage myself," Genevieve protested with a mutter, suddenly overwhelmingly conscious of his physical nearness. Her body was held hard against his, and when she released her tight grip on the ledge, she felt herself sink into his hold, helplessly dependent. She kicked her legs in the air, a reflex action that brought an infuriating chuckle from her captor/rescuer. He set her on her feet and she straightened her skirts, brushing the dirt from her hands, the busy movements giving her time to regain her composure.

"An unorthodox method of egress," Dominic observed, regarding her with exasperation not untinged with amusement. It somehow seemed entirely inevitable that this meddlesome creature should have dropped out of the sky into the middle of his carefully laid plan of campaign, once again to wreak havoc.

"Maybe so, monsieur, but it was the only one available to me," she informed him, attempting to retie the ribbon that confined her hair. "The door being locked—from the outside, you understand."

"Ah." He nodded his comprehension. "This afternoon's business as Maspero's Exchange, I presume?" He couldn't help smiling. Her efforts to tidy her hair were singularly unsuccessful. It was the most extraordinary color, ash blond streaked with deep-gold bands, the whole luxuriant mass cascading over her shoulders, catching the moonlight. Tawny eyes and silver-gold hair made the most unusual combination, as unusual as the person herself, he decided. Not at all like the rest of her breed—as different in her way as Rosemarie. But then Rosemarie had not come from the Creole breeding ground. He frowned. What the devil was he doing thinking like that?

"Yes, exactly so," she agreed matter-of-factly. "However,

I achieved my object, so do not really mind the consequences. I was becoming a little bored, though, so I thought I would come down and join you." She smiled benignly. "You have no objection, I trust, Elise?"

Elise stared at her. "Papa locked you in the cabinet?"

Genevieve nodded cheerfully. "Where did you think I was?"

"In your chamber, naturally."

"Oh, well that probably would have satisfied him, except that I told him Mr. King had attempted to rape Amelie and she had resisted, which was why he was selling her. After that, only the cabinet would do."

Elise gasped in unfeigned shock at this appalling speech and Dominic murmured, "Remarkably forebearing of him, I would have said."

For a second, those tiger's eyes flashed, then Genevieve shrugged. "You are entitled to your opinion, monsieur. But do not let me disturb your tête-à-tête with my sister. I will just stroll around the garden and stretch my legs for a few minutes." There was no possibility of misunderstanding her. However shocked they might appear to be at her earlier behavior, she had just reminded them that they stood condemned in an infinitely more compromising position.

"I do not know what you can mean," Elise protested. "There was no question of a tête-à-tête. How could you think such a thing? I just came out for a breath of air. It is so hot in the house. I did not know Monsieur Delacroix was of the same mind."

"No, of course you did not," Genevieve concurred calmly. "Has Don Lorenzo departed already? I cannot imagine him permitting you to take the night air without his accompanying you. And I'm sure, even then, he'd insist on a chaperone."

There was a moment when Dominic thought that he would be required physically to separate the warring sisters. Elise's hand trembled on the verge of lashing out at the other's blandly smiling face, then, recollecting their audience, she bit her lip, turned on her heel and went back toward the house.

Dominic took a cigar from his inside pocket, lit it, and inhaled thoughtfully. He glanced up at the window of the cabinet and then back at Genevieve. How long had she been listening? Was her unconventional arrival prompted by pure mischief, simply by that tiresome tendency that he had already witnessed to interfere in the affairs of others, or did it have a more serious intent?

"You do not consider yourself to be in danger of opprobrium by *our* unchaperoned meeting?" he inquired.

"Oh, I am in so much trouble already, a little more will make no difference," she replied airily. "Besides, *I* am not betrothed, and might still be excused the impropriety on the grounds of a childish lack of awareness. And I do not think, Monsieur Delacroix, that anyone would imagine you might be interested in a clandestine meeting with the baby of the family."

Baby of the family, she may be, Dominic thought grimly, but when it came to awareness, she could beat her elders to flinders. Just how much had she heard? Had she been listening when he was talking to Nicolas? Well, he was wasting his time here, now, thanks to this self-styled baby, and nothing would be gained by fruitless speculation. There was always tomorrow. "You are quite right," he agreed smoothly. "And it is time I bade my hosts farewell. So I will give you good night, Mademoiselle Genevieve."

He had turned away when she spoke, her voice suddenly hesitant. "Monsieur Delacroix?"

"Yes?" He turned back to her. She gave him a slightly rueful smile.

"I do not think I can climb back through the window unaided. It is a little far off the ground."

He examined the window and the wall, then bent his gaze on Genevieve with a mocking deliberation. "For one so small, it is a little high, I agree. Perhaps you should return by more conventional means."

Genevieve swallowed the bitter pill of his justifiable vengeance. "I cannot do so undetected, monsieur."

"No," he agreed silkily. "I do not imagine you can. But did I not hear you to say that you were in so much trouble already, a little more would make no difference?"

"That may be so, but there seems little point in courting it." She clasped her hands behind her back and met his gaze.

"I quite agree with you. But that seems to be a lesson you are only just learning." He smiled. "You should have thought of it before you decided to drop from the skies in such a dramatic fashion." The gloves now well and truly shed, Dominic bowed, bade her a second good night, and strode off into the dark.

Genevieve sat down on a carved stone bench and reviewed the situation. It was not encouraging. She may have saved Elise from the consequences of her foolishness for this time, but that did not mean that her sister would not persist in her indiscretion. One thing was clear: Dominic Delacroix would not be easily prevented from accomplishing whatever goal he had in mind. As for her, she was stranded outside the window of her prison, her only option to wait until the household had retired when she could perhaps creep back undetected, always supposing, of course, that the key to the door would still be in the lock so that at least she could get back into the cabinet. But she was no magician, and could hardly relock the door from the outside while she was on the inside. It rather looked as if she were heading for an abrupt exile on the Lake Borgne plantation where Victor would assume that she could get up to no further tricks. And, once banished, she would be able to do nothing to save Elise from whatever *she* was up to. Perhaps she could find Nicolas. He would help her without question, but then he'd quite legitimately want to know what she was doing outside and what had prompted her escape. And since he appeared to be in cahoots with the privateer, she could hardly tell him she had overheard their conversation.

Genevieve had just decided that she would have to rely upon her own wits when her nostrils caught the aromatic scent of tobacco that had departed with Dominic. He reappeared from around the corner of the house and strolled casually across to her.

"Still here?" he murmured. "I was sure you would have solved your problem by now."

"It is insoluble," she stated. "But clearly you enjoy turning the knife in the wound, Monsieur Delacroix. It is hardly chivalrous to refuse to help me, then to make mock of my predicament."

"No, it is not," he agreed casually. "But then, you see, mademoiselle, I am not known for my chivalry."

"For some reason, monsieur, I do not find that statement at all a revelation," she retorted, getting to her feet. "Please don't let me keep you." Her lips moved in the semblance of a polite smile.

"Do you really think you could?" he inquired with a degree of interest.

Genevieve bit her lip, unable to think of a dignified reply since neither "yes" nor "no" struck her as suitable.

Her infuriating companion nodded his satisfaction. "It is always wise not to attempt to answer the unanswerable." Then, with sudden decision, he tossed away his cigar and brushed his hands together. "It's well past your bedtime. Up with you, now."

Genevieve's jaw dropped, but he took her by the shoulders and spun her round before he bent, grasped her tightly around the knees and lifted her straight up to the window. Her fingers curled around the ledge, then she was hoisted higher. Her feet found his shoulders, and the next minute she was sitting on the windowsill, blinking down at him. It had all happened so fast, her body had been twisted, lifted, turned as if she were a doll that could be manipulated at will. But she was where she wanted to be, and objecting to the methods that had been employed to get her there was hardly appropriate, so she said, "Thank you, Monsieur Delacroix. To what do I owe the change of heart?"

"I cannot imagine," he drawled, dusting off his velvet-covered shoulders. "I expect I had too much champagne. I am sure I shall regret the chivalrous impulse."

Genevieve could not help smiling since, if she had anything to do with it, she rather suspected that he would indeed regret it. "Well, I am most grateful to you since you have saved me from certain banishment to the country," she informed him.

Dominic groaned. "I knew I should not have yielded. I have the unmistakable impression that this city would be a deal more peaceful if you were not in it, Genevieve Latour. If you wish to show your gratitude for my kindness, you will contrive to keep out of my way in the future."

"I do not think I can promise to do that," she said quietly. "Not if you intend to make trouble for my sister."

His indrawn breath rasped sharply in the still air. "You have overlarge ears, Genevieve, and rather less sense than I credited you with, if you think to challenge me."

"Is that a threat, Monsieur Delacroix?" She had not meant to say anything about what she had overheard. Why had the words just tumbled out like that? Now, she had opened a veritable Pandora's box, and for what purpose? He would be much harder to circumvent, if he was on his guard against her.

Dominic stepped up to the wall, reached up and grasped her ankles that she had neglectfully left dangling. His fingers circled them easily, and the pressure he applied verged on the uncomfortable. For one moment, Genevieve thought he meant to pull her down off her perch. But instead, he asked a prosaic question in a voice that contained not a shred of emotion. "How old are you, Genevieve? Sixteen, seventeen?"

"Neither," she replied, making her voice respond in the

47

same neutral tone that he had used. "I turned eighteen last month."

"Mmm. You look younger."

"It is because I am small," she offered, forgetting for a moment the sinister fashion in which this discussion had started.

His eyebrows lifted and the turquoise eyes gleamed in the moonlight. "That must be the reason." That hint of mockery was there again. "Well, mademoiselle, I can give you twelve years, years that I have spent a long way from the schoolroom, in pursuits that, if you had a shred of maidenly modesty, which I doubt, would shock you. I do not need to issue threats, my child. I will simply repeat: You have less sense than I credited you for, if you think to challenge me." With that, he released her ankles and walked off, whistling a cheerful, insouciant little tune.

For some reason, the carelessly merry sound made Genevieve shiver with a tingle of apprehension. He had not attempted to deny her accusation, which, in itself, was most disconcerting, and she had been warned, as bluntly as it was possible to be, to keep out of his business. But it was not a warning she either could or should heed. She had always had a tendency toward the crusader, and once she had taken up a cause, she found it impossible to give it up. Dominic Delacroix was up to no good, and Elise, for some obscure reason, was designated victim. But not if Genevieve had anything to do with it.

On this rousing thought, she swung her legs over the sill and dropped back into her prison. Her ankles still retained the warmth of his grip, she noted distractedly. In fact, for some reason, the entire surface of her skin tingled as if she had been touched all over by hands other than her own. She had certainly been "handled" this evening in the most unfamiliar—no, she amended ruefully, *familiar* fashion. If Elise had been touched like that— But then she wouldn't have been. It was unthinkable that anyone would treat Elise in that cavalier, unconcerned fashion, as if she were no more than the child Dominic had called Genevieve. But then Elise would not have been clambering in and out of windows like a tomboy. She would never have put herself in the position of having to, Genevieve thought disconsolately, looking around the cabinet as a wash of weariness broke over her.

The only sounds from the house now were those of the servants clearing up after the party; everyone else was away to the comforts of feather mattresses and lawn sheets. And where was she supposed to sleep? There was barely sufficient free floor space to curl up on, even supposing the wooden boards were inviting. Victor Latour was a bad man to cross. But then his younger daughter had known that since she'd first become aware of the real world. She sank down in a corner, her back propped in the angle of the walls. Elise had obviously forgotten that fact if she was thinking of jeopardizing her marriage with Don Lorenzo Byaz.

It was dawn before the sound of the key turning in the lock brought Genevieve out of the wretched half doze that was all her uncomfortable position would permit in the way of sleep. Hélène Latour stood in the doorway, holding her robe across her breasts, her hair disheveled. "He said I might," she whispered. "I could not sleep properly, knowing you were in here."

Genevieve stood up, wincing as her crampled muscles protested momentarily. "Poor Hélène." She put her arms around the other woman, knowing full well the night Hélène would have submitted to, in order to achieve this concession for her stepdaughter. It was not the sort of knowledge considered appropriate for a *jeune fille de la maison,* but Hélène was so close in age to her husband's daughters, so much in need of friendship and support when she had emerged, six months before, petrified with shock, from the two-week honeymoon spent closeted with her new husband in the big nuptial bedchamber, that she had been unable to hold back from the sympathetic warmth offered to her.

Now, she smiled wanly, and leaned for a minute against Genevieve, drawing from the girl's strength, a strength seemingly undiminished by the hours of acute, lonely, physical discomfort. "My thanks, Hélène," Genevieve said. "He will be going to his office soon, then you will be able to sleep."

Hélène nodded. "And you, also. But I do wish you would try not to anger him, Genevieve."

"I do not do it on purpose." Genevieve smiled, although she knew the smile was not going to reassure Hélène. "Sometimes, it cannot be helped if I am to do the right thing."

"I wish you did not always feel that you have to do the right thing." Hélène sighed. "Oh, dear, that does not sound like something one should say, does it?"

Genevieve chuckled. "You should be ashamed of yourself, *Maman.*" In spite of the chuckle, though, she found herself thinking that life would be a lot less hazardous at times, if she were to ignore her managing conscience. She had already this evening drawn herself an opponent as formidable as Victor Latour—more so, she thought, with that little shiver. She put the thought aside and returned Hélène's embrace with equal warmth—a warmth not untinged by resignation to their shared fate and to their different methods of dealing with that fate.

Genevieve climbed wearily up the stairs to her large, sunny bedchamber opening, like all the others, onto the second-floor balcony at the back of the house. The temptation to fall onto the bed fully clothed was hard to resist, but she was still wearing the afternoon gown of delicately flowered chintz that she had been wearing when they had met Dominic Delacroix outside Maspero's Exchange all those days ago— Days? Well, it certainly felt like it, although common sense told her that it had only been about sixteen hours ago. It seemed a lifetime. Yawning, she kicked off her kid slippers and stepped out of the gown that was now much the worse for wear after the events of the evening, leaving it crumpled on the floor; similarly the single petticoat and her shift. Tabitha would deal with them with her usual soundless efficiency. She sat on the bed to roll down her silk stockings, contemplated the need to wash her face, brush her hair, was still contemplating it as she crawled naked beneath the coverlet, inhaling the lavender freshness of the embroidered pillowcase as she sank into oblivion.

# Chapter 4

The sounds of the levée market below, drifted in through the open window: the calls of the vendors hawking their wares; the excited babble of shoppers haggling in all the tongues of the civilized world as seamen jostled amongst the stalls; the squawk of a parrot; the shriek of a monkey; the incessant gibbering of small-game birds. With the sounds came the smells of decaying produce and river mud, of spices and garlic, furs, and fresh, green, rainwashed vegetables, ripe cheeses, and fresh-caught, glistening fish. But the two men facing each other across the broad mahogany desk in Victor Latour's private office were oblivious of the vibrant scene outside. It was one, after all, that had provided the backdrop for their lives in the city since either had memory.

A vein throbbed in Victor's temple as he struggled for sufficient control to articulate his outrage. The younger man opposite, with the fly-away eyebrows and the carved mouth and jaw, watched his struggles impassively and waited with a polite smile as his host gobbled and the perspiration stood out on his brow.

"You have the temerity to imagine that I would agree to such a proposition?" Victor managed at last. "That *I*, Victor Latour, should go into partnership with a privateer . . .

a rogue . . ."

"You are not so nice in your notions, Monsieur Latour, when it is a matter of trading with a privateer," Dominic interrupted gently, the calm reminder doing nothing for Latour's temper. "You and all your so delicate friends take what I offer most eagerly. It is convenient, is it not, to forget how they were acquired? But if you will permit me to say so, your hands are dirtied, nevertheless, by handling the silks, the velvets, all those little items that are indispensable to a comfortable life; those items that were wrested by main force from some merchantman—stolen, if you will." Dominic laughed, a low laugh of pure pleasure that rang incongruously in the fury-charged atmosphere of the sunny room.

Victor's ears began to buzz, and he knew he must take hold of himself before his pounding heart burst. "Insolent cur," he gasped. "You dare talk to me in that fashion. I will have satisfaction!"

Dominic shook his head and rose to his feet in a leisurely fashion. "I regret, Monsieur Latour, that I could not, in good conscience, meet you. You are a great deal older than I, and I do not think your health would stand up to the strain."

Victor's color changed dramatically, and the thickset frame began to shake. "You mistake me, Delacroix," he hissed. "I would not meet you as a gentleman. I would take a horsewhip to you, rather."

It was Dominic's turn to pale now. The turquoise eyes glittered and his body became very still. "I am very much afraid, Latour, that you will regret that insult." He bowed, clicking his booted heels together, swung round, and left the shipbuilder's office. His horse stood outside the frame building, tethered to the hitching post. The scruffy urchin who unfastened the reins, handing them to Dominic, cringed involuntarily at the sight of those polished eyes, the twist of the mouth, the power coiled in the broad shoulders. Cuffs came the lad's way as often as coins, and he scooted backward as soon as he'd handed over the reins.

"What the devil's the matter with you, boy?" Dominic demanded, as the frightened movement penetrated his ice-locked reverie. Reaching into his pocket, he drew out a coin, leaning down from his horse to hold it out toward the urchin. The boy took a tentative step forward, grabbed his payment, and jumped back against the wall.

"Something's angered monsieur," he muttered.

The darkness lifted on Dominic's face. "Yes, indeed it has, but it is not your responsibility, child, and I'm not inclined to vent my anger on an innocent."

He rode off along the levée, skirting the hubbub of the market, down to the different turmoil of the quay where tall ships swung at anchor, ropes creaked, rigging slapped in the river breeze coming up from the Gulf. *La Danseuse,* true to her name, seemed to skip at her mooring. Delicate, white and gleaming, the frigate was Dominic's pride and joy, and the sight of her was balm to his inflamed spirit. But it was also a painful reminder of his abortive meeting with Victor Latour. He *must* have Latour's cooperation, and he would get it now in the one way left open to him: He would force it. Dominic smiled slightly as he dismounted, tossing the reins to another eager urchin. He would force it, and by the forcing would have his revenge for the insult. He would strike at Latour at the base of his identity—his pride.

He strode up the gangway and onto the well-scrubbed deck. Two sailors, engaged in revarnishing the coaming, made movements as if to rise, but at the wave of his hand, resumed their work. The master of this ship was not one to expect ceremonial reverence, but he demanded implicit obedience, and there wasn't a soul who sailed under him who would deny him that. If common sense failed to convince them of the wisdom, fear was a powerful inducement.

"Morning, monsieur." The bosun appeared from the quarterdeck, wiping his oily hands on a filthy scrap of rag tucked into his belt. "She's ready to sail for the new anchorage, whenever you give the word."

Dominic nodded and mounted the ladder to the quarter-deck from where he could survey his little kingdom. *Danseuse,* on the surface, looked in perfect condition, but her master could see in his mind's eye the patched gash on the waterline. He needed that secluded anchorage and the easy access to the shipyard and its facilities in order to make his repairs, not just to *Danseuse* but to the other ships of his fleet, most of them in need of overhaul before the next foray into the Gulf and the oceans beyond. Such repairs could not be made here, by the quayside. Too much was going on, and too many secrets would be revealed. He needed privacy to conceal his weaknesses. Spies abounded around the quays, Spanish and British sailors with sharp eyes and long tongues. If it hadn't been for the sharp eyes and long tongue of Lucien Gros, he would not have been in this position now, forced out of the safe anchorage on Lake Salvador.

But Lucien had paid the price and was now feeding the sharks, and Dominic would get little achieved by dwelling on his past errors. His plan to repair the damage caused by those errors was formulated, half put into practice, and now required only the finishing touches. How long would it take before the Latour peach dropped into his hand? Dominic frowned. A week, maybe, if he speeded up his approach, sacrificed the grace of subtlety in the interests of expediency. Not something he cared to do, but needs must when the devil drives. He shrugged.

"I'm going below, bosun."

"*Oui,* monsieur." The sailor stepped aside. "Anything I can get you?"

"Coffee," Dominic said. "And brioche. I have not yet breakfasted."

In the master cabin, where the comfort of wood paneling and jewel-toned rugs belied the purpose of a stripped-for-action frigate, Dominic sat at the Chippendale desk, with its tooled leather top, reached for pressed paper and his quill, tapped the pen against his teeth for a thoughtful moment, then began to write. The note was calculated to flatter, to intrigue and, if those were not sufficient, it made the sort of offer no discerning young lady with an eye to her wardrobe could refuse. No discerning, but susceptible young lady, Dominic amended with a disdainful smile.

The note required a nosegay as accompaniment and a messenger. A knock at the door heralded a young cabin boy in his first season, bearing the breakfast tray and regarding his captain with the wide eyes of one looking upon legend. He heard his instructions, received coin to purchase the flowers, and scampered off with the letter in the direction of the Latour house on Royal Street.

Elise was sitting with her sister and Hélène on the patio, sipping café au lait and toying with a plate of rice cakes that the butler had just bought during his daily shopping excursion to the market. She looked in eager surprise at the folded paper and the little bouquet of violets, presented to her on a silver tray. "The writing is not Lorenzo's," she said, holding the paper up to the light.

"Open it," Genevieve demanded with some impatience. "You cannot guess at its author just by peering at it."

"But that is part of the fun," Elise protested. "You are so unromantic, Genevieve. I suppose when you start receiving billets-doux you will criticize the vocabulary and the structure and the handwriting instead of responding to the message."

"Certainly, I shall, if the messages are anything like as sloppy as the ones you have received in the past," her younger sister retorted.

"I cannot help feeling, Elise, that you should not be receiving billets-doux from anyone but Lorenzo," Hélène said in her soft voice. It was but a feeble attempt to exercise the authority of the stepmother, and like all such attempts, failed signally. Elise simply patted her hand absently, before turning her attention to the nosegay.

"Are they not pretty?" She buried her nose in the fragrance, and Genevieve shook her head in exasperation. At this rate, it would be the middle of next week before Elise decided to discover the identity of this admirer. But, at last, the older girl broke the seal and unfolded the sheet of paper, giving a little gasp as she read the bold black signature at the bottom of the equally bold missive.

"Well, tell us!" Genevieve clapped her hands impatiently.

Elise went a little pink. Neither sister had referred to the garden meeting last evening, and Elise knew that Genevieve would never bring it up in front of Hélène, or anyone else not in the secret. Nevertheless, it was with a degree of embarrassment that she murmured, "Monsieur Delacroix."

Genevieve raised her eyebrows. The gentleman clearly didn't waste any time in the pursuit of his purpose. Of course, she still didn't know exactly what that purpose was, Genevieve reminded herself. And she was unlikely to find out by antagonizing Elise.

"Oh, dear," Hélène fluttered. "That is most improper, Elise. I do not think you should acknowledge either the note or the nosegay."

"No, of course you are right, dear Hélène," Elise said soothingly. "I shall ignore it. It is most presumptuous of him." If Hélène was deceived, Genevieve most definitely was not. She could feel the suppressed excitement emanating from her sister, noted the slight tremble of her fingers as she refolded the note and then, instead of discarding it as a presumptuous message from an impertinent gentleman, she thrust it into her workbag on the table.

Genevieve said nothing, however, but resolved to keep a close watch on her sister, and when Elise came downstairs after their siesta, dressed in an afternoon gown of pale flowing muslin, a chip hat perched saucily on the russet curls, Genevieve appeared from the *salle de compagnie*.

"You are going out?" she inquired casually. "It is as hot as Hades."

"You are so vulgar," Elise admonished, drawing on lace-edged mittens. "I am going shopping."

"Oh, then I will come with you." Genevieve moved to the stairs. "I will just fetch my bonnet. It will take but a minute."

"You do not care for shopping," Elise snapped. "And you have just said it is too hot to go out. Why would you want to accompany me?"

"Oh." Genevieve contrived to look hurt as she paused, one foot on the bottom step. "You do not wish for my company?"

Elise offered a placatory smile. "Of course I do, but it is possible that I might . . ." She hesitated, biting her lip in some confusion. "Well, I know it is not quite proper, but it is possible that I might just happen to meet Lorenzo in the Church of St. Louis, if I should stop in for a few minutes' quiet devotion."

Genevieve clicked her tongue against her teeth in mock reproof. "Shame on you, Elise. You are a sly one. I would never have suspected it." A lot slyer than she would *ever* have suspected, Genevieve thought to herself. Elise had always struck her as singularly guileless, but the self-conscious, pleased little giggle that she now gave was quite masterly and would have convinced anyone but Genevieve. "Well, in that case, I would only be de trop and, since I do not wish to spend the afternoon at my prayers in that gloomy mausoleum while you whisper with your betrothed, I will stay here and twiddle my thumbs." With a cheerful wave, she ran up the stairs, leaving a relieved Elise to slip out of the house accompanied only by Tabitha, who had cared for both sisters since they were babies and would no more think to question their actions than she would to disclose

58

those actions.

In her chamber, Genevieve found a straw hat with a wide brim and a veil. If she was going to walk the streets unchaperoned, she had best not advertise the fact. It was far too hot for a pelisse, but a silk shawl with a tasseled fringe provided an adequate wrap that disguised her recognizably diminutive figure. She ran lightly down the stairs from the gallery outside her room, crossed the patio and slipped through the side gate into the driveway. The house still slumbered in the afternoon warmth, and the only activity seemed to come from the kitchen where dinner preparations were under way. Even the stables were quiet, Zaccarius snoring in the shade, a straw hat tipped over his eyes. The master was at his office on the levée, Nicolas, too; Hélène was still resting, and the groom was unlikely to have to bestir himself for one of the *jeunes filles de la maison*.

Out on the street, Genevieve looked up and down, wondering which direction Elise would have taken. Toward the center of town, surely, rather than down to the market and the levée. Her guess was proved correct when she reached the high walls of the Ursuline convent on the next corner and saw Elise and Tabitha moving down the street of the Ursuline toward Chartres Street. Genevieve followed, keeping within the shadows of the buildings, in the shade beneath the elaborate iron work of the lace balconies. Was Elise going to Maspero's Exchange again? Monsieur Delacroix clearly spent time there himself, indeed had talked of having an office in the building. But Elise and Tabitha hurried past the Exchange, quiet this afternoon, its street doors closed. Then Elise stopped outside a shop—an innocent looking mercer's shop.

Genevieve knew the shop. It was where all the Creole ladies bought the fine materials that made up their wardrobes. It was also well known, but never mentioned, that the shop was supplied by Dominic Delacroix and his privateers. She waited until Elise had disappeared inside, then sauntered toward the shop herself. The door stood open onto the banquette, and when she peered inside, there was no sign of Elise. Tabitha, however, sat on a stool in the corner of the store, with hands folded patiently in her gingham lap.

Genevieve stepped into the cool dimness. Tabitha seemed the only occupant. The maid looked up, her eyes opening in startlement at the sight of Genevieve. "Where is Elise, Tabitha?" Genevieve spoke softly, wondering why she felt it necessary to do so.

Tabitha nodded toward a door at the rear of the store. The door was ajar and seemed to lead directly outside to the inevitable courtyard. "Some special bolts of silk out there," she said with a placid smile. "Miss Elise went to look them over."

"Well, I do not think she should keep such good things to herself, do you?" Genevieve said briskly, and walked with determination to the door. Here, she paused, listening in the moment when she was still hidden from any occupants of the courtyard. She heard Elise's laugh—that light, flirtatious laugh that had made her the belle of the *bals de royauté* in her last season and had so endeared her to Don Lorenzo Byaz. The laugh was answered by a low voice, with that vibrant warmth that Genevieve remembered hearing last evening when Dominic Delacroix had greeted Elise in the garden.

Taking a deep breath, she raised her veil and pushed open the courtyard door. "Tabitha says you are having a preview of some special silks, Elise." She spoke lightly but clearly, smiling as she crossed the courtyard to where the two stood looking at her, Elise with astonished chagrin, Dominic with suddenly narrowed eyes. "Will you not share the treat? Good afternoon, Monsieur Delacroix. Is this your store, by any chance? You are, in some way, a merchant, are you not?"

Dominic massaged the palm of one hand with the thumb

of the other and regarded her steadily, and in silence. The implication that he was a mere shopkeeper was a minor irritation compared with the much greater one of her presence. Something was going to have to be done about Mademoiselle Genevieve.

"What are you doing here?" Elise found her voice at last.

"Well, I decided that perhaps I would join you in church, after all," she said with a blithe smile. "I have a host of sins for which to do penance."

"A meddlesome nature and impertinent tongue being only two of them," Dominic murmured, pointedly turning back to the long table that was piled with bolts of material of every type and color. "Mademoiselle Latour, may I suggest the cream satin? It will look very well with your hair . . ."

"What a consummate courtier you are, monsieur," Genevieve broke in. "So experienced in the matter of female dress, as experienced as any merchant-tailor, I dare swear."

The silence in the courtyard became suddenly menacing; even the birds fell quiet, the breeze stilled. Genevieve felt that prickle of apprehension, a prickle that became the full-blown shudder of panic. She had mentally castigated Elise for not realizing that Dominic Delacroix was a dangerous man, and now *she* was guilty of the much greater foolishness—that of not heeding her own advice. That provocation had been a piece of pure self-indulgence. She should have stayed still and quiet in a corner of the courtyard, providing Elise with the impeccable chaperonage that was her only purpose. Or had she another purpose? One she had not acknowledged and did not want to admit, even to herself. Had she for some inexplicable reason wanted to draw the privateer's attention away from Elise and full onto herself? Well, she had certainly succeeded in doing that.

Dominic stood looking at her, his body as still as it had been in Victor Latour's office that morning, and Genevieve felt his anger as a palpable force that sent a quiver up her

61

spine and dried her mouth. Somehow, she managed not to drop her eyes under the cold, hard stare, but it took every ounce of willpower. Then he spoke, his voice soft, yet it seemed to shriek in the silence. "Mademoiselle Latour, I will send someone to assist you with the materials. You will do me great honor if you do not stint in your choice, since anything you decide upon this afternoon will be my gift. But if you will excuse me for a moment, I have some merchandise within doors that I would show your sister." His hand closed over Genevieve's wrist. She pulled back, casting Elise a glance almost of desperation. But there was no help forthcoming in that quarter. Elise's white face revealed her own alarm, and the bewilderment of one who did not know why she was alarmed.

"Come," he said, drawing Genevieve beside him. "You will be most interested in what I have to show you." Raising his voice, he called, "Marcus! Will you come and help the lady." A burly man, a heavy gold ring in his ear, looking as if he had been transplanted from his natural habitat, the deck of a ship, appeared instantly from the house, and Dominic marched toward a building at the rear of the small courtyard. Genevieve lengthened her stride to keep up, for some reason determined that it should not look to anyone that she was being forced to participate in this errand, although the fingers circling her wrist made it clear that she had no option.

"I do not care for shopping," she gasped breathlessly, as he pushed open a door into the gloomy interior of a storeroom. "You can have nothing in here that would interest me." Then, unable to help herself, she declared, "Besides, I do not have the necessary currency, unlike my sister."

"And just what is the necessary currency?" he asked, kicking the door shut behind him, closing out the sunshine and the reassuring murmur of voices. "Pray tell me, mademoiselle. I am fascinated. I should also like to know what you think your sister is buying—apart from the mercer's wares."

Thus confronted, Genevieve found herself at a loss. He was standing very close to her in the gloom enlivened only by a mote-encrusted bar of sunshine coming through a window set high in the wall, and his voice was clipped and derisive. She could not be in a worse position than she was now; the privateer could not be any more threatening than he was now. With sudden decision, she metaphorically stripped off the gloves. "Whatever that reason may be, therein lies the currency. My sister is buying an adventure that she thinks is innocent enough and will be of limited duration; and she is buying nourishment for her vanity." The tawny eyes challenged him to deny it.

Dominic nodded slowly. "You have some courage, for all that you are a foolhardy, interfering, insolent little madam in need of a strong hand."

Genevieve gasped indignantly, and his laugh ridiculed her indignation as if it were of no more account than that of a thwarted child's.

"Perhaps you do have the correct currency," he said suddenly, catching her chin between finger and thumb. "Shall we see whether you do, my dear Genevieve?" She looked up into the bright blue gaze that contained an indefinable something—indefinable, yet it brought her nerve endings throbbing to the surface of her skin. There was no warmth in that gaze, only curiosity and the absolute knowledge of his power. A feeling of dreadful anticipation crept over her scalp as his warm grasp tightened on her chin. Then his other hand banded her waist and she was locked against him, unable to breathe without feeling the press of his chest against her breasts. She fought the urge to struggle, knowing that it would be simply demeaning, would only increase his power. The turquoise eyes mocked, and she felt he could see inside her skull, knew exactly what she was thinking and would bring down her barriers if he chose.

As if in confirmation, he said, "So you will not fight. I wonder if I can make you do so. I think I would enjoy the pleasure of subduing you, Mademoiselle Geneviève, so much your father's daughter." Still holding her gaze, with the most agonizing slowness, he lowered his head to take her mouth with his own. A tremor ran through her body, and she leaped against him as if she had been struck by lightning. The involuntary reaction caused him to increase the pressure of his mouth, brutal almost in its searing thoroughness that forced her lips apart for the deep invasion of his thrusting tongue. Tears filled her eyes as she recognized her helplessness in the face of the invader. There were no doors to bar, no defenses to throw up. He held her and explored her with a devastating intimacy that the sheltered girl, for all her crusading bravado, her defiant refusal to abide by the conventions, could never have imagined.

Then something else seemed to happen to intrude on her distress. A slow-spreading warmth surprised her, filled her, causing the rigidity to leave her body, her mouth to relax. Her tight-shut eyes flickered open and met the equally sudden surprise in the turquoise ones above. The arm around her waist loosened, ceased to be a bond, became a firm, warm presence. His hand flattened against the curve of her hip, drawing her closer as the fingers left her chin to stroke her eyelids closed again, then traced the delicate lines of her face. The kiss moved to the corner of her mouth, playful and amazingly sweet.

When Dominic at last raised his head, he continued to hold her for a minute, looking down at her swollen lips, heavy eyes, the flushed vulnerability of her expression. For a moment there was warmth in his gaze, then his eyes became shuttered and he released her. "I seem to have underestimated my powers of persuasion," he drawled. "Subjugation was hardly necessary, was it? It seems you are well endowed with the correct currency, Mademoiselle Genevieve."

Her face paled, the tawny eyes deepened with humiliation as the insulting words embedded the shards of mortification in her soul. With a little choking sound, Genevieve turned away, searching for some words of her own. But the only ones that came were questions. "Why? What do you want with us?"

"Why should you imagine I want anything of you?" He shrugged carelessly and lit one of his little cigars, narrowing his eyes against the smoke as he watched her.

"It is something to do with my father," she hazarded, hearing those strange words again: that he would enjoy subduing her, so much her father's daughter. "You would revenge yourself on my father through his daughter?"

He just laughed. "You flatter yourself, my dear. Should I wish for revenge against your father, I would use stronger weapons than his daughter's frailty."

In essence, that was the truth, Dominic reflected. He had intended to use Elise's foolishness, to play on her vanity, in order to achieve Latour's compliance, and after this morning's exchange, he would have derived extra pleasure from the other's capitulation. But he had not intended to harm the girl. It would be quite superfluous to do so. She would have learned a significant lesson, certainly, but he would have returned her, intact, to her father and, if Victor played his cards right, the fiancé would have been none the wiser. But then, the frailty of her maidenhood was a matter of supreme indifference to him. He now preferred his women experienced in the ways of pleasure, knowing and skilled. Initiating the uninitiated seemed a tedious task, and taking by force what was so readily and pleasurably available elsewhere seemed utterly pointless. But his plan had been constructed around the elder Latour girl—a weak vessel to be easily manipulated, just like her cousin, Nicolas. He had not bargained for this particular scion of the Latour family whose predilection for popping up when least wanted had ceased to be merely annoying, and had become a habit that *must* be quashed. In fact, Dominic decided, it was his civic duty, as well as imperative to his own interests, to break her of it. There had been a moment there when he seemed to have forgotten that, when the body in his hands had softened, become pliant, eager.

He swung on his heel and flung open the door onto the courtyard. "I have finished with you for the moment, Mademoiselle Genevieve. You may rejoin your sister. If you did not enjoy the last few minutes, I suggest you bear in mind that if you intrude upon my consciousness again, what will follow will make what has just past seem like Mardi Gras."

Somehow, Genevieve managed to walk past him with her head high, although the hot tide of humiliation continued to break over her in relentless waves. The entire episode had taken no more than five minutes, yet she found herself surprised to see that Elise still stood beside the long table where the servant was cutting a length of the cream satin as if nothing untoward had occurred. Elise looked at her sister, and Genevieve read considerable annoyance in the magnificent blue eyes. It was not hard to guess the reason for that annoyance. Genevieve had just had a tête-à-tête with Dominic Delacroix, something Elise had been endeavoring to arrange for days. In Elise's opinion, it was yet another example of the younger girl's ability to monopolize events, and for the moment she forgot that she would rather have dropped into a snake pit than have taken her sister's place with the icily furious Dominic Delacroix. Then she noticed Genevieve's pallor, the strain in her eyes, the tension in her shoulders, and Elise shot an alarmed look at the man walking behind her.

His face was impassive, eyes unreadable as he reached her. "Forgive me, Mademoiselle Latour, but I have pressing business to attend to. Please feel free to give Marcus whatever instructions you wish as regards the materials." Taking her hand, he raised it to his lips. Elise tried to read some special attention in the gesture, but no amount of self-deception could invest it with anything more than courtesy and, while his lips curved in a smile of sorts, she could derive nothing personal from it. The only satisfaction lay in the fact that he left the courtyard without so much as a glance at Genevieve, who might just as well not have been there.

"Let us go home, Elise," Genevieve said in a low voice indicative of her sudden weariness. "You cannot have any further business here."

"No, thanks to your interference," Elise hissed. "Why must you be always meddling? I think it is just that you are envious. You cannot bear me to receive attention that you do not." She turned away to give Marcus the address to which the materials should be sent.

The accusation was so far from the truth that Genevieve could have laughed. Had Elise received the attention just bestowed upon her sister, she would be in screaming hysterics. She heard the instructions to Marcus in disbelief. Surely, after the events of this afternoon, Elise was not going to compromise herself further by accepting the privateer's gift? But then Elise knew nothing except that Dominic Delacroix was courting her, and she probably drew no distinction in the game of gallantry between the gift of a nosegay of violets and materials worth perhaps thirty piasters. Looking at the beautiful, vacuous face, the large, bovine eyes, Genevieve discarded all thoughts of confiding her conviction that Dominic Delacroix was simply using Elise for his own, as yet unrevealed, purpose. She had intended to tell her of the conversation between Nicolas and the privateer that she had overheard last night, but now decided against it. Elise would not believe it, and would probably put it down again to jealousy on Genevieve's part. The one thing Genevieve knew she could not do would be to reveal what had happened during those dreadful minutes in the storeroom. Such mortification one kept to oneself.

It was time to confront Nicolas. Without the truth, she was fumbling in the dark, and one thing she had learned this afternoon, if she was to enter the lists against Dominic Delacroix: She would need the brightest illumination, or be utterly lost.

# Chapter 5

Nicolas paced the apartments in the *garconnière* that he had occupied since he had reached puberty. He did not think that he had ever suffered such mortification in those years as he had late this afternoon. Dominic Delacroix, with a blistering tongue, had stripped him of every last vestige of adult dignity, worse even than Victor Latour's contempt. At least, with the latter, one knew that it was applied indiscriminately. But why should *he,* Nicolas St. Denis, be held responsible for his young cousin's damnable meddling? It was not his fault that she had overheard their conversation last night, although Dominic seemed to think he should have known that she was in the cabinet. And it was not his fault that she had insisted on accompanying them to Maspero's Exchange, either. What excuse could he have found for confining to himself and Elise a supposedly innocent walk about town? Genevieve would have guessed at once that there was a hidden agenda, and once something caught her attention, she worried it to death. Which was exactly what was happening now, and he had to stop it; find some way of allaying her suspicions, or keeping her out of the way. His instructions on this score had been crystal clear, and it would take a braver man than Nicolas to defy the orders of Dominic Delacroix. No threats had accompanied the edict, but those turquoise eyes had contained an expression that sent chills down his spine. He could still see it now.

A sharp rap at the paneled door interrupted this miserable reverie. *"Entrez,"* he called, not sorry for the diversion. He was sorry, however, when his visitor marched into the room, closing the door decisively behind her.

"We have to talk, Nicolas," Genevieve said in uncompromising accents. "What is between you and Dominic Delacroix? This debt that you must discharge?"

Nicolas was so taken aback that he made no attempt to deny the charge. What was the point, anyway? He knew what she had overheard. "It is my business," he said with as much force as he could muster. "A private matter. I am entitled to some privacy, am I not?"

"That rather depends," Genevieve stated, perching on the arm of an overstuffed chair and swinging a sandaled foot nonchalantly. "But I think, in this instance, if your business involves others, and they are quite unwitting participants in the affair, then you are not entitled to your privacy. Why is Elise being pursued by the privateer? Why did he wish for an introduction to this house?"

Nicolas pressed his fingers to his temples, feeling like a hunted animal under this remorseless catechism. "No one is going to come to any harm," he said weakly. "Dominic wishes to do business with your father, that is all. But he needed to meet him before he could broach the subject, and it seemed more politic that he should do so initially at a social gathering."

Genevieve stared incredulously. "Dominic Delacroix doing business with Papa! You have windmills in your head, Nicolas, if you think Papa would agree to such a proposal."

Nicolas, who now knew the details of Latour's reaction to the proposition, held his tongue. But his infuriating cousin continued to look at him expectantly, and he realized that she was waiting for an answer to her first question. "Elise will not come to harm," he repeated. "I can say no more than that, but you must trust me."

"Trust you!" she ejaculated scornfully. "I would not trust you any further than I could throw you, Nicolas, after this business. If you will not tell me the truth, then I shall lay the whole before Papa."

Nicolas went the color of chalk. "You would not."

"If you force me to, I will," she said definitely. "I am no tattle tale, as well you know, but something stinks to high heaven around here!" She let the inelegant statement lie between them, watching as her cousin resumed his restless pacing. At last, Nicolas seemed to come to a decision.

"Why should your father not do business with Dominic? Why, when he buys his merchandise without batting an eyelid, should he consider it beneath him to provide a service for which he would be well paid?" There was a note of venomous anger in the question, and Genevieve began to perceive why Nicolas had lent himself to whatever nefarious business was afoot. He loathed his guardian, who, after all, had never given him reason to do otherwise. "He is not usually so nice when it comes to money, is he?"

"No," she agreed neutrally. "But what Creole would enter into an open partnership with such a notorious rogue? It would hardly be gentlemanly, now would it? What does the privateer want of him?"

"A secluded anchorage on Lake Borgne, near the shipyard where his vessels can avail themselves of the facilities. The place Dominic has decided upon is situated on your father's plantation."

Genevieve pursed her lips in amazement. "He would implicate Papa, then, in his piracy. Surely you can see that, Nicolas. Papa would be a business partner, aiding and abetting in a business that only this war legitimizes. He would never agree."

"He must," Nicolas said flatly.

"Why must he?" She looked at him, holding her breath as she waited for his answer.

71

"Because, my dear little cousin, Dominic Delacroix wants it, and he will be satisfied with nothing less." Nicolas gave a short laugh. "It is not possible to deny Delacroix."

"You do not find it so, at all events," she said sharply, trying to ignore the little voice that told her Nicolas spoke only the truth. "He holds something over you."

"Yes." Nicolas sighed. "But, believe me, Genevieve, I would not have agreed to play a part in this if I did not know that no harm would be done except that your father would be forced to swallow his pride, for once."

She heard Dominic's voice of the previous evening: I do not recall you were in a position to do otherwise. Deciding, out of charity, not to challenge her cousin's assertion, she asked, "What lever does he have, Nicolas?"

"I lost heavily at play," he told her, relief showing in his eyes as he finally unburdened himself. "I do not know how it happened, but my IOUs totaled more than twenty thousand piasters." Genevieve gasped. "I was at my wits' end, Genevieve."

"I can imagine," she said drily. "Were you drunk?"

"Probably." Nicolas ruffled his hair in bewilderment. "There was this woman . . . Oh, I do not know, exactly. I lost my head, could not manage to keep her satisfied however much I spent. She took me to the gaming rooms . . . I . . . Oh, well, never mind. It is not a story for your ears."

Genevieve could not help her peal of laughter. "You are worried about the propriety of talking to me of whores, in the middle of this squalid little mess?"

"It is not amusing," Nicolas said stiffly. "Anyway, one day, when I did not know where to turn, Dominic came up to me in the *salle d'escrime*. He had bought up all my IOUs, and he wanted only a favor in order to destroy them." He looked at Genevieve pathetically. "It was such a simple thing to do, Genevieve, just to arrange an introduction to Elise, and an invitation to the house so that he could meet my uncle

72

socially. How could I refuse? Why should I have refused?"

"Did you know why he wanted this?"

"I did not ask, at first," he admitted with obvious reluctance. "I was so overjoyed at this stroke of fortune that I did not question my luck."

"But then you did find out?" she prompted.

Nicolas sighed again. "Yes. And I still saw no reason why I should not go through with it. No one was to be hurt."

"You keep saying that," Genevieve mused. "Why do I have the impression that you are trying to convince yourself? I can see your point about Papa. It will do him no real harm to do business with the privateer. In fact, I could enjoy as much as you the prospect of his defeat, but what does the privateer want with Elise?"

"To . . . to persuade Latour should he prove reluctant," Nicolas told her. "He promised me she would—"

"Come to no harm," Genevieve interrupted. "Yes, I heard you the first several times. How is Elise to persuade Papa? Her powers are no greater than anyone else's."

Nicolas was silent for long moments, wondering if he could fob Genevieve off with some half truth that would satisfy her sufficiently to ensure her withdrawal from the arena. Thus would Dominic also be satisfied, and Nicolas could breathe easy once again. But creative imagination was not Nicolas's long suit, and he knew that the longer he tossed ideas around under his cousin's unnerving gaze, the less chance he had of convincing her that what he finally came up with was the truth.

"Perhaps I can help," Genevieve said suddenly. "Elise, for reasons that escape me, appears to find that arrogant bastard appealing. I am sorry if I have shocked you," she said sardonically, seeing his face. "But there are no other words to describe him." She could feel her cheeks warm at the memory of this afternoon's encounter and found herself wondering how it was possible to feel such detestation for someone. Detestation, pure and simple? Was that what she felt? No. Not pure and simple. The recognition brought her up short, and for a minute she was silent. Then she forced her mind back to the subject at hand. "I do not believe that he is encouraging her just for amusement value. So . . ." Abruptly, her eyes widened. "What a fool I've been! I've been trying to prevent her from compromising herself, and that is exactly what he wants, isn't it? Elise Latour, with a slur on her reputation, would be no wife for Don Lorenzo Byaz. I had seen that, but somehow had not taken it as seriously as I should have. You and I know that it is only foolishness on Elise's part, but it could easily be made to appear much more than that. How is Don Lorenzo to discover his fiancée's indiscretions? But then Papa will be told first, so that he may save the match by agreeing to work with Monsieur Delacroix. Is that not so?"

Nicolas nodded eagerly. "It is not so very bad, is it? Elise's foolishness is largely responsible, after all, and her father will put a stop to it quickly enough. No one will suffer except Victor, who will have to swallow his pride."

Genevieve shook her head slowly. "It is not bad enough, Nicolas. An occasional unchaperoned meeting, an inappropriate gift—the idle foolishness of a silly girl. The gossips could get hold of it, perhaps, and Lorenzo would be annoyed, but her true innocence would not be in question, and Papa is not fool enough to give in unless he recognizes the sword of Damocles." Under the clear-eyed gaze, Nicolas winced. "So," she said. "How is Elise to be compromised sufficiently for Papa to recognize the sword of Damocles?"

What could he lose further by telling her? Nicolas thought with weary resignation. He was between the devil and the deep blue sea. Genevieve, when her mind was made up, was as impossible to resist, as impossible to circumvent as Dominic Delacroix. They were two of a kind, the privateer and Nicolas's little cousin. That realization punctured his weariness and he blinked, as if to dispel the extraordinary concept—the extraordinary truth, rather. A flicker of amusement showed in his eyes, to be instantly, prudently doused. Let Genevieve match her wits against Dominic. Why not? Whoever won, Nicolas's position could be no worse, so he might as well enjoy the contest.

"I think that Dominic intends to invite her to an assignation that . . . that will perhaps be of a longer duration than she had expected," he explained in roundabout fashion, having no fear that Genevieve would fail to understand him.

"Overnight?" Outrage flared in the tawny eyes. "And you said he would not harm her!"

"Nothing will happen to her," Nicolas protested. "She will spend the night quite innocently. Dominic is no ravisher, Genevieve."

"You say that so vehemently, as if it were appalling that such a thought might have entered my head," Genevieve retorted. "Anyone capable of concocting such a diabolical scheme simply to achieve some minor goal is capable of anything." And after this afternoon— But that uncompleted thought she kept to herself.

"It is not a minor goal," Nicolas protested. "The perfect anchorage has to be utterly secret, with access to the main waterways, and close to facilities for keeping the vessels in good repair. Can you imagine how few places there are that will fulfill all those requirements?"

"Well, what has he been doing up until now?"

"His last hiding place was betrayed to the British," Nicolas said. "There was an ambush, a battle, some of his ships were hit. His fleet at the moment is anchored in the river, but he does not wish to make repairs in public, and obviously he cannot have all his movements take place under the eyes of the entire population of New Orleans. Until he can find another refuge, his activities must be in abeyance." A nervous smile touched Nicolas's lips. "He is not a patient man, Genevieve, and cannot abide idleness. He has fixed upon the site on your father's plantation and will be satisfied with nothing less."

"I do not care one way or the other whether he hides his ships on the plantation," Genevieve declared, getting to her feet with the determined energy that always alarmed her cousin. "And I do not care if Papa is forced to accede to the privateer's wishes. He will be well served. But I will *not* stand aside while Elise is tossed between them like a piece of driftwood. And I still do not understand how you could have lent yourself to such a scheme. Has it occurred to you what Papa will do to Elise, if, because of her foolish vanity, he suffers such a resounding defeat? He will tear her limb from limb."

"No, he won't," Nicolas said, thankful that on this issue he was sure of his ground. "You are forgetting Lorenzo. Your father could not allow a breath of suspicion to reach him, and he could not possibly revenge himself upon Elise without Lorenzo wanting to know why and what for. No, Victor will simply encourage Lorenzo to hasten the date for the marriage. And that," he added dourly, "would be no bad thing for anyone. Elise is not safe to be let loose."

Genevieve was silent, absorbing this. Nicolas was probably right about Victor's reactions, she decided. But Elise, if subjected to a night of captivity, whether she was physically unharmed or not, was likely to lose her mind with fright. "We have to stop it, Nicolas."

Nicolas heard the "we" with sinking heart. It was one thing to stand aside while Genevieve joined battle with the privateer; quite another to be obliged to participate, particularly in opposition to Delacroix who had already told him in no uncertain terms to remove his meddlesome cousin from the scene in whatever manner necessary. "How do you propose going about such a thing?" he asked, evading the issue of partnership for the moment.

Genevieve frowned, nibbling her bottom lip. "We cannot tell her, can we?" Nicolas's headshake was automatic; the question had been really rhetorical. "Could we contrive to remove her from town? Back to the plantation? Or maybe she could go on a visit to someone."

"That would take time, and I do not think you have that luxury," Nicolas said bluntly. "Dominic is in somewhat of a hurry, and he already has Elise where he wants her."

Genevieve grimaced and failed to notice that Nicolas seemed to have excluded himself from responsibility for the planning. "Yes, and after this afternoon, she is piqued because the assignation did not go as she would have wished, so she will be more than ready to accept another invitation." Her companion made no comment and, after a short silence, Genevieve seemed to come to a decision. "There is only one thing to be done. We must intercept the invitation. Then you must keep Elise out of the way, and I will take her place."

Nicolas stared at her. "*You!* Have you the slightest idea what you would be walking into?"

Genevieve felt a little cold knot in the pit of her stomach. She could guess without too much difficulty. A thwarted Dominic Delacroix was a fearsome prospect. But what options did they have? She gave Nicolas a seemingly careless shrug. "I do not think he will murder me and throw my body into the Mississippi, do you?"

"I would not be so confident of that," Nicolas said soberly. "His opponents get short shrift, and he is not known for his scruples. I cannot allow you to do it."

"I would remind you, cousin, that you are not in a position to allow or disallow anything," Genevieve snapped. "If you remember, this entire tangle is your doing. Anyway, why should Monsieur Delacroix worry about the substitution? I am quite happy to assist him in his plan to achieve Papa's compliance. He will simply have a willing accomplice rather than a petrified victim. And I have a reputation that needs to

77

be preserved, also, do I not? Papa will not care to see my name dragged through the mud."

"Yes, of course, but you are not betrothed to Don Lorenzo Byaz. You know how much that match means to your father, how much he wants the alliance of the two families. He will do anything to ensure that it goes through, and he will not argue for one minute with Dominic's terms."

"But he might argue if it were me," Genevieve agreed with a tiny smile. "Yes, you are probably right. He will try everything to wriggle out of it. But Monsieur Delacroix does not know that and, besides, I am considerably more resourceful than my sister. I may well contrive to achieve my own salvation."

Nicolas looked doubtful, but decided to keep his doubts to himself. It seemed as if, so long as his crusading cousin only required his passive cooperation, he had chosen his side. Dominic could not really lay the blame for the substitution at his door and, if he achieved his goal by using the alternative tool offered to him, would probably not object in the slightest. If his plan failed through some deviousness of Genevieve's, then that would lie between the privateer and the girl. Of course, Nicolas thought, he probably should feel the need to protect his cousin, but if he hadn't felt the need too strongly with the so much more vulnerable Elise, why should he feel it with Genevieve, who was making all the decisions anyway. Nicolas St. Denis sometimes did not like himself very much, but he was under no illusions about his character and had learned to live with himself quite some time ago.

"I will engage to keep Elise out of the way if you wish to take her place," he said. "But do not expect any help from me if your plan rebounds against you. I will have enough to do defending *myself* against Dominic if he discovers my part in the substitution. I am supposed to keep you out of the way, not actively encourage your further interference."

78

The tiger's eyes filled with contempt. "You have my promise, cousin. I will not put you in further jeopardy."

Nicolas flushed a dull crimson, but could find no words of defense. "How will we know when Elise receives the invitation?" he mumbled instead.

Genevieve frowned, contemplating the problem in silence for a minute or two, then her face cleared, and the frown was replaced with a sunny smile. "Amelie," she pronounced. "She will do it for me."

"Do what?" Nicolas asked, still in the dark.

"Intercept messages that come for Elise. I will ask her to bring them to me before giving them to Elise. I will recognize Monsieur Delacroix's handwriting since I saw it clearly on his last letter. All others, Amelie can return to my sister who will be none the wiser."

Nicolas nodded slowly. It would work if Amelie's cooperation could be guaranteed, and after the incident at Maspero's Exchange, she would do anything for Genevieve without question.


It was two days later, when Amelie knocked softly on Genevieve's door in the heat of the afternoon. A messenger, a grimy lad from the docks, had just brought a letter for Mademoiselle Latour. One look at the bold black script, and Genevieve knew that she had what she had been waiting for. She thanked Amelie and dismissed her with a reassuring smile, then began to walk around the sun-barred chamber, tapping the missive in the palm of her hand. Opening letters addressed to others was definitely worse than eavesdropping, she decided ruefully. And if this message was quite innocent, how was she to explain to Elise why the seal was broken?

Well, she had made her decision a long time since, and this was no time to be overly scrupulous. The end must justify the means. With that comforting reflection, decisively, she broke the seal and unfolded the paper. The flowery words somehow struck her as not being in keeping with the hard strokes of the pen, and she had the unmistakable impression that Monsieur Delacroix was not, in general, one for pretty compliments and elegant turns of phrase.

The message, however, was perfectly simple. After an oblique reference to their inconveniently interrupted meeting in the courtyard of the mercer's store, Monsieur Delacroix begged the favor of a few words in private with Mademoiselle Latour. There was a hint that he was a prey to all sorts of tormenting emotions, deeper than any he had previously experienced, and only the sight and sound of Mademoiselle Latour would grant him a measure of respite. Genevieve's lip curled. He had struck exactly the right note. Elise would see the statements as her due; she had heard them often enough from lovesick swains not to doubt their authenticity in this instance. Only Elise was too blind to realize that Dominic Delacroix was no young Creole gentleman with idle hands and empty head, playing the game of dalliance. At the end of the message came the concrete suggestion. Could Mademoiselle Latour see her way to taking a short stroll alone in the side garden that evening? Her humble suitor would wait beside the side gate, near the street. He would wait all evening if necessary, in the desperate hope that she would honor him with a brief sight of her.

Clever, Genevieve thought, refolding the note. Elise would see only a slightly wicked adventure. She would not be leaving her father's grounds, and all that was suggested was a few words, maybe a little handholding, while the sweet music of a lover's torment filled her unattainable ears. But how was she then to be persuaded out of the garden, away from the safety of home, and into a situation where she could be held until Victor Latour capitulated?

Genevieve would find that out this evening. Apprehension

fingered her spine, crept over her scalp. But it was mixed with another feeling, with what she could only identify as excitement. The life of a Creole maiden on the marriage mart most definitely lacked excitement, and Genevieve Latour, sublimely indifferent to the consequences, had pursued that enlivening addition to her life since childhood.

# Chapter 6

"You do not object, then, Victor, if I escort Elise and Genevieve to the *bal de royauté* this evening?" Hélène asked timidly, passing the platter of *grillades* to her husband.

Victor looked around the family dinner table where sat his two daughters in ball gowns, Nicolas in knee britches, all three of them studiously examining their plates, as if afraid to meet his eye and thus, by some ill chance, give him the opportunity to deny the chaperonage that the girls, at least, would need.

"I suppose I have no choice in the matter," he grumbled, with disregard for the realities of life in the Latour household. "If you prefer your duties as stepmother to those of wife."

"Papa, that is not just," Genevieve protested, and a ripple, like breeze in a cornfield, ran round the table.

Victor regarded his younger daughter with a baleful eye. "You, mademoiselle, may stay at home and study your collect," he pronounced. "It may remind you of your duty to your elders."

"Yes, Papa," Genevieve murmured, dropping her eyes submissively, hiding the gleam of satisfaction. She had been racking her brains for an excuse for not accompanying the others this evening. Fatigue, or the headache, would cause an unwelcome stir, since she never suffered from either. Anything more serious would be given the lie by her too healthy complexion and the brightness of her eyes. And it was quite inconceivable that she should simply choose to stay at home with a book, voluntarily eschewing the gaiety. Nothing could have been better than her father's interdiction, and since he would certainly not spend the evening at home if his wife was out, Genevieve was assured of an empty house—no watchful eyes when she slipped out into the side garden.

Something was pressing on her foot. Nicolas, she realized, unable to resist letting her know that he appreciated her strategem. She took a sip of wine, allowing her gaze to skim over him, then returned to the pompano in lemon butter sauce.

"It is such a pity you must stay at home," Hélène lamented, adjusting her lace mantilla as she and Elise stood on the verandah, half an hour later, preparing to descend to the waiting carriage. "It was not necessary to defend me, you know?" She smiled and lowered her voice. "I just do not hear him when he says things like that. He knows it is not true."

Genevieve chuckled. "Your methods are more subtle than mine, Hélène. But I cannot help protesting his injustices, and I do not really regret it."

"How can you not?" Elise gazed at her sister in amazement, the enormous blue eyes shining under the overhead lantern. "*Everyone* will be at the Gerard's this evening. And they always have the best musicians."

Genevieve just shrugged. Not quite everyone would be there. If Elise was expecting a privateer's attention, she would be sadly disappointed. She stood on the verandah, waving them away, then turned back to the hall, just as Nicolas came down the curving staircase, drawing on his gloves, very much the elegant gallant on his way to charm the young ladies of the Creole aristocracy.

"I would say 'take care,'" he whispered. "But I do not

think it is advice you will heed."

"It is a little late for that," she replied drily. "Challenging the privateer is hardly a careful prospect." An exciting and irresistible one, though. But that thought was hers alone, not to be divulged. "If I am not here in the morning, do what you can for Hélène and Elise when the storm breaks, as it surely will."

"What can I do?" he asked with a helpless shrug.

"At least you can tell them the truth, so that when Papa rages they will be armed with foreknowledge," she returned briskly. "Her narrow escape might encourage Elise to show some enthusiasm for an early marriage. I do not think Papa will quarrel with that, either." Her lips twitched and Nicolas shook his head in astonishment. How could she treat such a subject with so much insouciance? Even if Dominic Delacroix accepted the substitution willingly, Victor Latour's revenge on this daughter who had no fiancé's sharp eyes as protection would be terrifying.

Genevieve ran upstairs to her chamber, leaving the door ajar so that she could hear the general commotion that would herald her father's departure for his club. It came within the hour; his bellowed demand for his hat and cane, the scurrying feet of his attendants, the slam of the great front door, then the almost palpable breath of relief as the house settled into silence. It would be an evening of relaxation for the household. There would be music in the slave quarters, and the main house would be deserted since they all knew that Mademoiselle Genevieve would make no arbitrary demands. Already, she could hear the sounds of laughter, voices raised in song, the high-pitched tones of children playing in the courtyard that, for this evening, they could make their own domain.

She would have to leave by the front of the house, with all that activity in the rear, Genevieve decided. She had changed out of her ball gown into a simple dress of apple green cambric with a scalloped neckline and little cap sleeves.

Now, she slipped a dark, heavy cloak around her shoulders, tucking the silver-bright hair beneath the hood. It was a great shame that her stature in no way resembled her sister's. But in the darkness, huddled in the cloak, if she played the shy, speechless coquette, maybe she could pass muster long enough for Dominic to commit himself to the abduction. Then, she would be in a position to talk business with the privateer. That now familiar little prickle ran down her spine again—part apprehension, part anticipation.

The garden was full of shadows, the empty house in semidarkness, candles extinguished in all but the main hall, only *veilleuses* providing a soft welcoming glow in the bedchambers that awaited the return of their occupants. Genevieve closed the great front door behind her, careful to make no more than the slightest click. She stole down the wide verandah steps to the street, hugged the stone wall that confined the side garden, raised the latch on the wrought-iron gate, and slipped inside.

Genevieve had not known what to expect when she made the rendezvous, had thought she was prepared for anything, but when the heavy blanket descended over her head, enclosing her in hot, stifling darkness, and her body was bundled up, her arms pinned to her sides, she fought against the darkness and the restraints with all the fury of a petrified animal. Her teeth sank into the iron arm holding her. Her legs kicked free of the blanket and made contact—a contact that brought a violent expletive from somewhere above her. A hand clamped over her mouth and nose, holding the blanket against her face, cutting off the air supply, and her lungs stretched agonizingly, panic rising in her chest, black spots dancing in the red mist behind her eyes. She stopped her struggles, and instantly the pressure was lifted and fresh, cold air rushed into her lungs. She lay still in the arms holding her, certain that a renewal of resistance would result in the cessation of that wonderful life-giving supply.

She knew that her captor was not Dominic Delacroix.

Apart from the fact that her body would have recognized his in this close proximity, if it had been the privateer, he would have guessed instantly that the light frame in his arms could not have belonged to the generously endowed Elise. She was being carried swiftly, but almost silently, the sound of feet on the banquette barely audible. Then she felt herself hitched up higher against his chest as her carrier climbed upward. Her position changed again, as, with a small grunt, he sat down, still holding her in the confining blackness of the blanket. A door closed, and they lurched forward with the steady clop of hooves. An experimental twist of her body brought that suffocating hand across her mouth and nose again, and Genevieve lay still immediately.

Not a word had been said. The only human sound she had heard had been that oath when she had kicked and bitten her captor. It was eerie and frightening, even though she knew what was happening to her and why. Elise, if subjected to such an experience, would have fainted dead away, and Genevieve felt her anger rise again, full and strong, surpassing her fear. How could he have planned this brutal treatment of a complete innocent? And how could Nicolas mutter comfortingly about how no one would be hurt? Genevieve hurt at this moment and had absolutely no confidence that the experience would improve.

The carriage jolted to a stop. The door opened. Hands wrapped her more tightly, like Cleopatra in her carpet, Genevieve thought with an unlooked for flash of wry humor. Then she felt herself being lifted again, carried down the steps, then up some more and, by the sudden change of atmosphere, she sensed that they were inside a house.

"Any trouble?" It was Dominic Delacroix's voice, and Genevieve stiffened involuntarily.

"A bit," a rough voice returned. "You didn't warn me she was a fighter. Got teeth and claws like an alley cat."

The privateer laughed, and Genevieve boiled with rage in her constraints. "My apologies, Silas. It's the last thing I would have expected of her. Now, had it been her sister . . ." That laugh came again. "Put her in the chamber above-stairs."

They ascended what seemed like a fairly long flight. Then there was the sound of a door opening, and Genevieve suddenly found herself, still wrapped in the blanket, rolled upon the floor. There was a decisive click as the door closed again. Then the sound of a key being turned, and she was at last free to fight clear of her wrappings.

Blinking bemusedly in the light of wax tapers set in a branched candelabra, Genevieve sat up, picking bits of fluff from her mouth with an annoyed grimace. Shaking off the blanket, she stood up, taking stock of herself. She felt bruised and a bit shaken, but apart from that, quite well. Her hair was an impossible mess, her gown creased and twisted, but they were insignificant ills that could be put to right to some extent. She was in a bedchamber, a very elaborate bedchamber of ruched silks and overstuffed pillows. On the dressing table were to be found combs, brushes, hand-mirrors. Genevieve made good use of them and regarded her surroundings with a little frown. It was impossible to imagine Dominic Delacroix, of the quiet elegance and discreet but definite power, inhabiting this vulgarly opulent, mirror-hung room. The bed was hung with crimson satin, the canopy lined in pale blue, the festoons of lace. The long windows were similarly draped. The furniture was ornately carved, the mirrors and picture frames gilded, decorated with cherubs and bunches of fruit. It was most definitely not the bedchamber of a lady, as Genevieve understood the term.

Crossing over to one window, she pulled aside the looped curtain with its fringed tassel and peered out into the dark street. It looked much like any other in the Quarter. The houses opposite had the usual intricate lace balconies and shuttered windows, but there was nothing within her visibility to identify it exactly, and the street was empty, perhaps not surprisingly, given the hour, which an ornate ormolu clock on the armoire told her was ten o'clock. It was too late for people to begin the evening's visiting, and too early for their return.

She turned back to the room, just as the sound of booted feet on the stairs outside reached her. Instinctively, she seized her cloak and tossed it round her shoulders again, drawing the hood over her head, moving into a corner of the room, her back to the door. For some reason, Genevieve felt the greatest need to keep her identity a secret for as long as possible.

The key turned smoothly in the lock, and the door swung open. The hairs on the back of her neck lifted, and her heartbeat drummed in her ears. Sweat made her palms clammy, as her body, of its own accord, registered the presence of Dominic Delacroix. There was a chink of glass, the soft tinkle of pouring liquid, then he spoke. "I must apologize, Mademoiselle Latour, if you found your handling a little rough. It was certainly not my intention to cause you discomfort. But you should not have attempted to fight Silas. You will take a glass of brandy, and I hope you will feel quite restored."

His voice so cool! Blaming *her* for that brutal assault! Fear forgotten, Genevieve swung round to face the room. The hood of her cloak fell back, revealing the shining mass of her silver-gold hair, and the tawny eyes blazed in a face paled by anger. "It is a pity, Monsieur Delacroix, that you did not advise against resistance in your so charming invitation." Her voice shook and then she fell silent under that metallic, azure gaze, feeling his stillness as a palpable force in the deathly quiet. In that moment, Genevieve knew her danger to be acute. How could she have taken so lightly that which she had recognized from the first moment of laying eyes upon the privateer? This was no ordinary man, with ordinary responses. He was dangerous, totally unscrupulous, and he would exact a fearsome penalty for opposition or interference.

Very slowly, Dominic raised the glass in his hand to his lips, threw back his head, and tossed the amber contents down his throat with a twitch of his wrist. Then he replaced the glass carefully on the silver-embossed tray resting on a carved side table. "So," he said, "little sister has decided to offer herself as sacrificial lamb. Is that it?" When Genevieve remained mute, her vocal chords seemingly glued together, he walked over to her.

He moved with lithe ease, a powerful, athletic man carrying an air of indefinable menace with every springing step, and Genevieve shrank back involuntarily. "You will be more comfortable without your cloak." He unlooped the fastening at her neck, his fingers brushing her skin, scorching like burning tapers. The manteau left her shoulders, was tossed onto a chair, and she was held immobile in the grip of that turquoise, glinting gaze. "I wonder, my dear little Genevieve, if you truly realized what that sacrifice would entail," he mused. "For some reason, I had not thought you the stuff of which martyrs are made. Crusaders, missionaries, certainly, those for whom action is their lives' informer, but not for you the passive yielding of martyrdom."

"You do not quite understand." Genevieve found her voice at last and prepared herself to explain that she was here, not with the intent to forestall his plan, but to offer herself as a substitute, in partnership rather than as victim.

"No," he interrupted gently, hooking a finger into the thin gold chain that made a gleaming line around her neck, accentuating the fragility of that slender column and the translucence of her skin. "*You* do not understand. Did I not make myself sufficiently clear to you that afternoon in the storeroom? I had thought to be absolutely lucid as to the consequences of any further interference on your part."

Genevieve swallowed, feeling his bent fingers resting against her throat lift with the involuntary movement. But she managed to speak with a bold defiance, although the tinge of fear shaded her voice. "You were quite lucid, monsieur, but threats do not move me."

His eyes darkened, and his gaze drifted over her face, her neck, the line of her shoulders to her bosom that rose and fell under her swift breath, skimmed down her body, touching her waist, the curve of her hip. "I can only assume, then, that you found the promise irresistibly enticing." His voice was dulcet in its insolent meaning, and his look had stripped her naked.

His free hand slipped over her shoulders, lifted the cascade of hair at her back, slid beneath to palm her scalp and, as she waited, mesmerized by her knowledge of what was about to happen, he brought his mouth to hers. That same lightning bolt tremor ran through her, the slow spreading warmth and, with a hot flush of bewildered shame, she felt herself lean into him, her lips parting beneath his almost before he demanded entrance. Dominic still held her, hooked by the chain at her neck, but his grip shifted, his spread fingers sliding up her throat, kneading the soft skin beneath her jaw. In the deepest recesses of her mind lurked the foreknowledge of the overpowering humiliation that would follow this eager surrender, yet it seemed to make no difference. She seemed to have no control over her responses. It was as if some other person inhabited her body, and the sensation was only pleasurable. Was this what she had come here for, this that she had known since the afternoon in the storeroom would follow a further intrusion into the privateer's life? Her breasts pressed against the deep expanse of his linen-clad chest, her nipples burning against the fine lawn of her underdress as her tongue, tentative and inexperienced, attempted to join with the dance of his.

Then, without freeing her mouth, Dominic moved to clasp her beneath the arms and the knees, and she was lifted, her own arms finding their way around his neck. The bed ropes creaked as he laid her down, and then, finally, he raised his head. But even as she shrank from the expectation of his mockery, the look in his eyes contained only speculation tinged with an amusement that was not unkind.

"You are a treasury of surprises, it would seem. What would you have of me, Genevieve of the tiger's eyes?" he asked softly, reaching to lift away a bright swath of silver hair where it fell across her breast. A long finger trailed over the soft mound, where the upper curve was revealed, lifted above the scalloped neckline of her gown as she lay, arms flung above her head. "You did not come here simply to save your sister from perdition. There was more to this rescue mission than your unfortunate tendency to busy yourself in the affairs of others."

Having only just realized those truths herself, Genevieve was unable to answer him, but the tawny gold eyes were heavy, languorous in the way of a woman experienced in loving, of one who could anticipate the pleasure waiting in the wings. Yet he would have staked his life on her innocence. "Is it a teacher you would have?" he probed, allowing his finger to slip inside the neckline, reaching down to the small, erect crown of her breast. "Is the Creole maiden desirous of learning something of the glory that can lie between man and woman? Is that why you are here, so recklessly defiant of the consequences of interference?"

As if it belonged to someone else, her head moved in almost imperceptible affirmation. Her body shifted on the bed beneath the caress of his finger, and her eyes became deep pools of wanting—wanting something that, so far, she had felt only as a tantalizing hint.

Dominic found himself strangely moved by this curious girl-woman. There was something hauntingly familiar about her eager fearlessness, her warm softness. But she was not at all like Rosemarie in face or form or experience. What was it? He had intended to frighten and humiliate her, to teach her once and for all that her weapons were of the puniest, and her attempt to join battle with his vastly superior strength merely laughable. He had intended to send her home, weeping with mortification, but in all essentials unchanged by the experience. Now, he was not so sure. His anger had left him some minutes before, to be replaced by interest and the unmistakable stirrings of desire. And she was hardly a child. Those eyes, gazing up at him, were most definitely not the eyes of a child. If this was what she wanted, what could he lose by gratifying her? True, instructing the inexperienced was not a pasttime that in general afforded him much satisfaction, but unless he was much mistaken, this golden-eyed sprite would prove a most ardent pupil.

"Then learn you shall. It will be my pleasure." Smiling, he slipped the neck of her gown off one creamy shoulder. The white shoulder strap of her underdress followed, baring the pearly, rose-tipped mound of her breast. His lips trailed over the soft roundness, and he heard her gasp as his tongue flicked the hard crest. For one last time, he raised his eyes, examined her face, saw only what he had seen before. But now the eagerness, the excitement was transparently revealed with her parted lips, the wonder in her eyes. Would she regret this? It was the faint murmur of a conscience that rarely troubled the privateer. "Genevieve, if you would have me stop, speak now, or forever hold your peace." For answer, her hand touched his cheek in a fleeting caress, and Dominic gave a little sigh of resignation to the inevitable.

He kissed the hollow of her throat, felt the pulse beat fast and erratic against his lips. Slipping a hand beneath her, he raised her against him, his fingers feeling for the hooks of her gown. They flew apart with the ease of temptation, and he let her fall to the bed again, hitching himself on one elbow to lean over her as he drew the gown down to her waist before, with tantalizing slowness, doing the same with the thin underdress. His hand, beneath her again, lifted as he drew the wadded material over her hips, and Genevieve felt the cool satin of the coverlet against her bared flesh. For one instant, panic flared. What was happening to her? How was it happening? Why had she allowed—no, invited this? Then the sensation of his palm on her naked abdomen, pressing as it stroked, drove all questioning from her mind. Her head turned from side to side on the bed, the gesture expressing her incoherent bewilderment as her blood poured in swift tumult through her veins. Although she had not yet experienced it, the shape of bodily joy grew in atavastic memory, suffusing her, filling her with liquid warmth.

His hand flattened between her closed thighs, moved in intimate exploration, and the tears of confused pleasure stood out in her eyes, to be instantly hidden as she dropped her eyelids. Dominic took her lips again, as the tender but inexorable trespass brought her to a peak of vibrant desire, the skin of her belly rippling, the muscles beneath growing rigid. Then, with almost demonic knowingness, he raised his hand, leaving her for long seconds, her senses ravished by an arousal that screamed for completion, her soul branded by the recognition of her wanting.

She raised her lashes in a long sweep, her tormented gaze fixing him as he watched her. His eyes were blue flames in a face where the muscles, like those of his arms and shoulders, were ridged with the strain of restraint. She knew then that no degrading mockery would follow this. His own defenses were breached, and his wanting was as open and acknowledged as her own.

She trembled, a slow burn of an age-old triumph creeping over her as he stripped off his pantaloons, shrugged out of his shirt, then drew her beneath him, parting her thighs, her moist, tender flesh to guide his surging, searing entry within. There was the moment of resistance, when she felt the stretched fullness, and he checked, touched the corner of her mouth with his tongue, whispered a tender word of reassurance. Then there was a sharp, rending pain. Her cry was silenced against his mouth, and the hurt receded. Gently, he kissed her eyelids, the tip of her nose, the sensitive corners of her mouth. His hand caressed her breast, stroking

93

the nipple that grew pliant beneath his touch as the tension left her. He eased deeper then, stroking the body beneath him to a wondrous peak of pleasure that astounded her.

Setting a rhythm, smooth and even, Dominic watched her constantly, listening to her body with his own, and when both eyes and body told him she was ready, he increased his pace, driving deeper until she gripped the corded muscles of his upper arms and yielded up her self to be tossed in the maelstrom of glorious sensation. Then, and only then, did he yield the dikes of his own control, sure that the maiden-no-longer beneath him had made a true start along the paths of loving.

Genevieve lay motionless, listening to the quiet tick of the clock, basking in the warmth of his skin pressed close to hers, in the dreamy lethargy, a relaxation more wondrous than any she had ever experienced spilling in her veins, anointing her muscles. So *that* was what so petrified and revolted Hélène? *That* was what the matrons whispered about in the parlor, what Elise feared, even as she wondered and talked nobly about wifely duty. *That* wondrous happening a duty! Her soft, joyous laugh filled the warm, rose-glowing room, startling Dominic out of his own reverie.

"What has amused you, tiger eyes?" Propping himself on one elbow, he leaned over, exploring her face quizzically.

"I appear to be ruined," she said with a little smile.

"On the contrary," he drawled, lifting a lock of silver-gold hair and twisting it around his finger. "You are much improved, to my mind. Virginity is a tedious burden for a passionate woman to bear."

"And am I a passionate woman?" she asked, the question managing to sound like a perfectly ordinary query.

Dominic laughed. "Oh, yes, Genevieve. You are, indeed." With sudden energy, he swung himself from the bed and strode to the door, flinging it wide. "Silas, bring wine and a supper tray, for two."

Genevieve looked at his glorious, unconcerned nakedness

94

as he strode over to the side table and poured brandy into a glass. Men were really most beautiful, she decided; the male form certainly had as much to recommend it to the artist as the female. Although, that would probably depend on the model, of course, in both cases. The one coming over to the bed must surely be unsurpassed with that narrow waist, the slim hips, and long, muscular legs lightly masked with fair curling hair.

Dominic read the message in that wide-eyed, uninhibited appraisal, and a smile touched his eyes, curved his mouth.

"Passionate, you may be, sprite, but I suggest you slip between the sheets before Silas comes in. It would not bother him in the slightest, but unless *you* are something less or more than I believe you to be, it should concern you."

It was impossible not to understand. Less of an innocent, more of a whore. Genevieve got off the bed, pulling the covers back and putting herself between them. She was hardly in a position to protest the truth. She had arrived in this room the virginal *jeune fille,* and had proceeded to behave like the most shameless wanton. She did not think that Dominic's statement had been intended to hurt or humiliate her; it had been a plain statement of fact. It rather seemed as if she had to rethink her conception of herself. Curiously, the idea, far from being either shocking or alarming, was merely exciting.

Silas entered after a sharp knock, bearing a tray of cold meat, cheese, and pastries, a carafe of wine and two glasses. This he placed on the table and, while he could not have failed to notice either Genevieve, propped up against the pillows, or the disorderly heap of her clothes on the floor, his eyes remained strictly in front of him. As he walked to the door, however, he said, "A word with you, monsieur."

Dominic, in the act of stepping into his pantaloons, frowned. "Well, speak up." He fastened the waistband and trod over to the table, pouring wine into one glass and refilling his own with brandy.

"Angelique . . ." Silas coughed. "She was desirous of knowing when the room would be free."

"You may tell her that I do not know," Dominic snapped. "She would be well advised to pass the night elsewhere."

"Very well, monsieur." Silas bowed, his face expressionless, and left the room.

"Who is Angelique?" Genevieve asked, reaching to take the glass of ruby wine that Dominic held out to her.

His face closed as if a shutter had been dropped. "No concern of yours. Drink your wine."

"But is this her house?" Genevieve persisted in blatant disregard of the warning. "I did not think, somehow, that this could be your bedchamber."

Dominic sighed and attempted to temper the sharp snub that rose to his lips. "To the extent that this house belongs to me, this is my bedchamber. But, as it happens, I do not live here."

"No, Angelique does." Genevieve sipped her wine and looked around the room again. "She is perhaps a quadroon *placée?*"

Dominic sighed again. "Exactly so. I do not wish to continue with this catechism. Angelique has nothing to do with you, nor you with her. Is it quite clear?"

Genevieve shrugged. The matter was hardly worth quarreling over, and it was hardly surprising that Dominic Delacroix should have a quadroon mistress; not nearly as surprising as that Genevieve Latour should be sitting up in the bed of the quadroon *placée,* the only difference between them was that one earned her keep by giving what the other had rendered with a free and eager spirit.

"When will you send Papa the ultimatum?" she asked, changing the line of questioning to one every bit as interesting, helping herself to a cheese tartlet from the plate he had placed on the coverlet beside her.

"When will I *what?*" The question stung like a lash, and Genevieve realized with sinking heart that she had just betrayed Nicolas. She had not intended to reveal that she knew all the details of Dominic's plan, but wanted merely to imply that she had guessed in general terms and was willing to help him, so that he would not need to use her sister. But the events of the evening had eroded her caution. The privateer was still a most dangerous man, for all that he had just given her such a tender, joyous gift.

"I can see that it is incumbent upon me to teach Nicolas the advisability of keeping a still tongue in his head—at least where my affairs are concerned," Dominic said, softly, menacingly thoughtful.

"Please . . ." Genevieve stammered. "You must not blame Nicolas. I forced him to tell me."

Those fly-away eyebrows lifted incredulously. "Resourceful, I know you to be; tiresomely willful and determined, I know you to be, but do not expect me to believe, my dear Genevieve, that you have the means to force a grown man to reveal what he knows he must not reveal. Unless, perhaps, you have access to thumbscrew and rack?"

"No, of course I do not, but Nicolas knew that by telling me, he would not make difficulties for you. You see . . ." She was having trouble explaining under an unflinching, ice-coated stare. If only he would move, just a twitch of a muscle, the flicker of an eyelash. The utter stillness was more intimidating than anything she could ever have imagined. When the silence continued, she drew breath and resumed. "I came here tonight intending to offer myself as Elise's substitute in your plan to . . ." Blackmail was the word, of course, but somehow she didn't think she could use it. "To compel Papa in the matter of the anchorage."

"I see. And what led you to assume that you would do as well, mademoiselle?" he asked coldly. "It is a matter of currency, as you so correctly deduced the other day. I do not believe that you have the correct coin."

A flush of anger stained her cheekbones. "After what has just occurred between us, I do not see how you can say that.

97

You may tell Papa in all truth that I am a spoiled virgin—a fact you could broadcast to all and sundry simply by returning me to Royal Street, with a degree of ceremony, in broad daylight. The story will be on every tongue within the hour."

"I see." Dominic came to the foot of the bed. He braced his arms on the wooden bar that was used to smooth the surface of the feather mattress when the bed was made and surveyed her. "Very well worked out. I congratulate you." There was open mockery in his voice. "And do you believe the sacrifice of your unblemished reputation will be sufficient inducement for your father?"

"I am as much his daughter as Elise," Genevieve retorted.

"Indubitably," he agreed smoothly. "But you have no highly desirable suitor panting at your heels. *You* would certainly suffer from the loss of your reputation, since no eligible alliance could ever then be made for you, but, tell me; why should that concern your father beyond a fleeting moment of lost pride—a loss that he might well count as more easily borne than that involved in agreeing to partnership with a privateer."

It was undeniably true. Genevieve dropped her eyes to the coverlet, tracing the embroidered pattern with a fingernail. "No, you are right. He would not be overly concerned. I daresay he would send me to the Ursulines to become a nun, and consider me well disposed of."

A rich laugh suddenly, startlingly, rang through the room, and she looked up, amazed. The turquoise eyes now shone with enjoyment. "That would be a most disastrous fate, for you *and* the Ursulines," he chuckled. "Definitely to be avoided at all costs. A nun!" For a moment, his laughter got the better of him, and his shoulders shook as he looked at her, propped up against the pillows, that ash-blond river pouring over her shoulders, the tawny gold eyes sparkling with indignation. "No . . . no." He shook his head. "We must definitely avoid that!"

"Oh, would you stop laughing!" Genevieve demanded crossly. "I do not like to be laughed at."

"You should not present me with such a magnificently absurd image," he offered in meager apology, turning back to the supper tray and the brandy bottle. "We must find a way to return you home with no one being any the wiser."

"But what will you do about the anchorage?" Genevieve persisted. "You cannot still intend to use Elise."

"And why not?" he asked gently. "I can assure you that now I know the true nature of the opposition, and I shall be able to circumvent it without difficulty on a future occasion."

Genevieve had no doubt of that. She would not be allowed the opportunity to prevent Elise from falling into the trap another time. "I have only to tell her the truth," she said stoutly. "Nicolas may be a coward, but I think, in this instance, he would corroborate my story."

The turquoise eyes darkened ominously. "Why should she believe you? It is a somewhat fantastic story, is it not? And I do not think your sister is well endowed with sense, common or otherwise." The open contempt in his voice made her wince, yet she could not deny it. The silence lengthened, then Dominic shrugged. "As it happens, I have decided to abandon that plan, so you may put your mind at rest as regards your precious sister."

"Why do you not simply take what you want?" Genevieve asked thoughtfully. "The lake frontage of the plantation is considerable and exposed, but there is a deep bayou, hidding from the lake and never visited, to my knowledge, because of the swampland surrounding it. There is no reason why anyone should ever know that you were there. There would only be danger of discovery during the summer months, anyway, when the family is in residence and Papa takes an active interest in the land. But I could warn you of any possible danger . . ." Her voice trailed off as she felt the glittering blue gaze boring into her.

"This bayou—how would I find it?" He walked over to a *secretaire* in the corner, sat down and pulled pen and paper toward him.

"I could show you," Genevieve said tentatively to his back, wondering what he was doing. "It is only accessible by water, but if you were to take your ship, and I were to accompany you—"

"And how would you explain an absence of several days?" Dominic interrupted, writing busily.

"Do not laugh again, but I am in the habit of spending time in the convent, studying Latin and higher mathematics with the mother superior." She paused as the figure at the writing table swung round, subjecting her to a close scrutiny, eyebrows lifted. Then he nodded and returned to his penmanship. "It would not be questioned if I said I would be spending a day or so in retreat," Genevieve finished.

Dominic did not immediately respond, but instead read through what he had just written and dusted the ink briskly with the sandcaster before rising and going to the door. Opening it, he called again for Silas. When the man appeared, almost before the echo of his name had died down, he stood in the doorway, waiting as his master folded the sheet before handing it to him. "Take this to the Latour house. Deliver it yourself into the hands of Nicolas St. Denis. No one else will do, you understand?"

"Yes, monsieur." Silas bobbed his head. "Will there be anything else tonight, monsieur?"

"No." Dominic shook his head. "You will wake me at dawn." The sailor-servant left the room, and Dominic came over to the bed. There was intent in his blue eyes, a clear intent that set Genevieve's nerve endings tingling. "If you have supped sufficiently, I think it is time to advance your education beyond the pages of the primer." A long-fingered hand took the sheet at her neck and drew it down slowly, revealing her body inch by inch. Genevieve felt her heartbeat quicken. Her eyes seemed riveted on the intricately worked

100

gold signet ring he wore, gleaming against her pale skin as his fingers stroked with feather lightness across her belly.

"What did you write to Nicolas? Do . . . do you agree to my plan?" The words fluttered between her lips in a futile attempt to regain her hold on reality as she obeyed the pressure of a hand on her shoulder, pushing her to lie flat.

"You must learn never to mix business with pleasure, my Genevieve," her mentor said softly, bending to flick her navel with his tongue. "Just as you must learn a little patience. I will tell you what I wish you to know, and only when I am ready to do so."

Genevieve would have protested this arrogance had she been able, had she considered it important enough to do so. Maybe another Genevieve, in another world would have done so, but the second lesson of the day was requiring an active response, a powerful demand that she not simply lie and receive, but that she give, that she learn how to give back the pleasure that was given to her. It was an all-absorbing exercise, she found, one involving the discovery of shapes and contours, the most wonderful hardnesses and softnesses beneath her exploring fingers, the discovery of what delighted the body that was her playground, and ultimately the discovery of the power of the pleasure-giver.

The Genevieve Latour who eventually fell asleep, locked in the arms of the privateer, in the bedchamber of a quadroon *placée* on Rampart Street, had progressed a long way down the paths of loving, and bore only superficial resemblance to the *jeune fille* who had set out full of crusading zeal a few short hours before.

## Chapter 7

The rich aroma of coffee assailed Genevieve's nostrils, bringing her out of sleep and into startled awareness of unfamiliar surroundings. The room was in darkness, relieved only by the soft light of a *veilleuse* on the mantel.

"Good morning, Genevieve." The greeting came from beside her and was delivered in the most matter-of-fact tone, a tone that belied the overpowering sensation of strangeness as her skin registered the direct contact of the sheets and the warmth of another body as naked as her own.

"Is it morning?" she asked, curiously reluctant to look at her companion. "It is so dark."

"It is very early morning," she was informed. "Might I draw your attention to the tray at your elbow? If you would pour the coffee, then we might both be able to face the new day with a degree of awareness."

Genevieve sat up slowly, drawing the sheet over her breasts with a nervous twitch, and peered blearily at the table beside the bed. A linen-covered tray stood there, steam rising from the twin spouts of a silver coffeepot and milk jug. A basket of hot, flaky rolls gave off the most enticing scent of fresh baking, and she sniffed hungrily.

Dominic hitched himself up against the headboard, regarding her with a smile in his eyes as she carefully poured hot milk into a wide, shallow cup, then topped it up with dark, strong coffee. Her tongue peeped between her lips as she concentrated on the very ordinary activity, except that pouring a man's café au lait, when ensconced in bed beside him, could hardly have been an ordinary activity for her. "Thank you." He took the cup with a polite smile.

Genevieve poured her own coffee, offering him the basket of rolls with punctilious courtesy and, when he refused with equal formality, helped herself. The business of eating and drinking made conversation unnecessary which, Genevieve reflected, was very fortunate since she had not the faintest idea what to say. What topics were suitable for such a moment? Did one ask if one's companion had slept well? Did one make polite inquiries about his planned day? Offer information about one's own?

Dominic's lips twitched—her thoughts were transparently easy to devine. She was a most appealing figure to wake up beside, he reflected. The morning after was always a harsh test, but Genevieve's skin was dewy and fresh. Her tousled, shining hair enchantingly tumbled over her bare shoulders, falling over the creamy swell of her breasts, revealed by the disarranged sheet. The tawny eyes were bright and clear, and when he reached a long finger to brush a crumb from her lips, she looked at him and laughed with a most seductive absence of affectation, although with more than a hint of shyness.

"There is no need to be shy," he said gently, tracing the curve of her mouth. "You are not regretful, are you?"

She shook her head vigorously, the ash-blond hair swirling in silver emphasis. "How could I regret that . . . that . . ." She sighed, finding herself quite inarticulate. "I do not know how to describe how I feel, but I am like a well that has been filled with pleasure."

"And will continue to be so filled," he promised. "Once you have learned to give and receive in that manner, no one can take it from you." He kissed her lightly, then handed her his empty cup. "Pour me some more. I must get dressed. Nicolas will be here to take you home shortly."

Genevieve felt a sudden stab of desolation. He had spoken as if the continued supply of pleasure had nothing to do with him; as if his role of instructor, now completed, made her ready to be launched upon the world. But pride forbade questioning on that score. "Why is Nicolas to come?" she asked instead, busying herself with the coffee and milk.

"He will escort you home as if you have both been taking a pre-breakfast walk," Dominic told her. "Even if your absence last night has been discovered, the consequences will be confined simply to your own household."

"No one will have discovered it," she said. "Tabitha does not come to my chamber until I ring, and no one else will be up before nine o'clock at the earliest, not after last night's *bal de royauté*."

He nodded, buttoning his shirt. "That is what I had hoped. There is hot water in the jug if you wish to wash."

Genevieve, accepting the cue, pushed aside the covers and swung her legs to the floor. Still sitting on the edge of the bed, however, she stared at the floor for a minute, frowning deeply.

"What is it?" Dominic fastened the waistband of his pantaloons and came over to her, lifting her chin with a long forefinger. "Something is troubling you, sprite."

Emboldened by his tone and the use of the nickname he had used during their lovemaking, Genevieve said hesitantly, "I would like to ask a question."

"Then ask it," he said. "You are not, in general, backward in coming forward." His tone was teasing and she smiled hesitantly.

"Last night, when . . ." She was being ridiculous; it was a simple enough question. It was just embarrassing that her knowledge was so limited that she was obliged to ask it. Genevieve took a deep breath. "When, at the very last, you withdrew in that way, that was to ensure that I did

104

not conceive?"

"Yes," he replied briskly. "I have no interest in raising up a tribe of bastards."

"Neither do I, as it happens," Genevieve retorted, nettled by his tone.

"I did not imagine that you did. Get dressed now. Nicolas will be here soon."

"There is no need to be so dismissive," Genevieve snapped. "It is not my fault that I am not as well informed about such matters as I am sure your quadroon mistress is."

Dominic, to her increased irritation, burst out laughing. "Since you have not, hitherto, had the need to be so informed, that is hardly surprising." Still chuckling, he went to the door. "Stay in this room until I come for you."

Genevieve yielded to the childish yet vaguely satisfying urge to put her tongue out at the closed door, then turned her back on it and went over to the basin and jug on the washstand. She felt the eyes on her back as she drew the washcloth slowly down her body, one breast cradled in her palm. Her movements stilled as her scalp seemed to contract with unease. Of course no one was watching her. She had not heard the door open. Breaking free of the hypnotic shackles of fear, she spun round.

A woman stood in the doorway, the doorknob in her hand. Large brown eyes subjected Genevieve to a clear and objective appraisal, as if she were being inspected on the auction block, Genevieve thought with a sick thud. She had seen such things often enough, but never before had she truly been able to imagine what it felt like to be examined with such brutal candor. The woman was very beautiful with a fair creamy skin, as fair as Genevieve's own, and lustrous dark hair that hung in loose ringlets to her shoulders. She wore a wrapper of midnight blue, adorned with lace ruffles, a wide sash outlining a slender waist and accentuating the curves of bosom and hip.

"What do you want?" Genevieve whispered, wishing she

had something with which to cover herself, but her clothes were on a chair at the other side of the room, and only a small towel hanging beside the washstand offered itself. Somehow, she felt that an ineffectual attempt to shield her nakedness would be more undignified that simply standing still, so she stood still.

The woman did not answer her, but then she didn't need to, Genevieve thought with a flash of illumination. She could only be Angelique, and it was quite clear what she wanted: She wanted to weigh up the opposition. The banging of a door knocker sounded from downstairs and the woman jumped, a look of fear standing out in the brown eyes, then she had gone, as soundlessly as she had come, the door closing inaudibly behind her.

Shaken, Genevieve dressed rapidly. There had been nothing friendly about that examination; quite the reverse. Naked hostility had shone in the huge liquid eyes, and a degree of contempt as she judged Genevieve's physical charms. Of course, the usurper *was* a mite lacking in stature and curve, Genevieve was obliged to own, as she brushed her hair with borrowed brush. And it was hardly surprising that Angelique would resent her presence, in *her* bedchamber, *her* bed, with *her* protector. In fact, what had possessed Dominic to do such a thing? But then, of course, he had not intended sharing that bed with his proposed victim. Presumably Angelique's cooperation had been gained for a different scenario from the one that had been played out.

Genevieve went over to the window, drawing back the curtains to look out on the street she had seen the previous night. It was now full daylight, although only seven o'clock, and there was still nothing to identify the street, but Genevieve was in little doubt that it was Rampart Street— where else did a Creole gentleman keep his quadroon mistress?

"Nicolas is here." Dominic spoke from the doorway.

"What did you tell him?" Genevieve found that it mattered

what he had said to her cousin.

"Nothing." Smiling, he came over to her. "It is for you to say what you wish. I merely gave him instructions to ensure that you were returned home without a blemish on your honor." Picking up her cloak, he draped it over her shoulders, drawing the hood up, carefully tucking her hair away. Then his hands cupped her face. "I think you should make your preparations for a retreat with the Ursulines."

"When?" She could not deny the swift beating of her heart at the thought that last night was not to be the beginning and the end. And in this moment of turmoil, she forgot to mention Angelique's unsettling visitation.

"As soon as you can arrange it." Dominic brushed her lips lightly with his own. "Come here tomorrow afternoon. I will be waiting for you."

"But I do not know where 'here' is," she reminded him. "And I do not know how I could contrive to leave the house in the middle of the day without being noticed."

Dominic's eyebrows lifted. "Mademoiselle Genevieve, do not play coquettish games. I do not find them amusing. If you wish to come here tomorrow afternoon, you will contrive. You forget, perhaps, that I have been made annoyingly aware of your resourcefulness and your willfulness. If you set your mind to something, you will achieve it." He laughed, but there was no mockery in the sound. "It is a quality I share, sprite. We are two of a kind, so do not attempt to deceive one who knows you as well as you know yourself."

That familiar little prickle ran down her spine at these words. Perhaps he did know her as well as she knew herself. Perhaps they were two of a kind. If they were not, how could what had happened have happened, and what in the name of goodness did she think she was doing? "I will be here," she said quietly. "It is Rampart Street, is it not?"

"Just so. You will recognize the house if you look carefully when you leave now. Let us go downstairs." Cupping her elbow, he eased her toward the door.

There was to be no passionate farewell, then? No soft words of remembrance? No gently romantic acknowledgement of the pleasure exchanged? The privateer had a day's work ahead, clearly, and was anxious to be about his business and to be done with this business. Genevieve shrugged. Far be it for her to intrude! She marched down the stairs that she had not seen on her coming into this house. That blanket-wrapped abduction seemed to have happened in another lifetime to another person.

Nicolas stood in the square hallway, his face drawn, eyes heavily ringed; whether with anxiety, conscience, or simply lack of sleep, Genevieve could not tell. But it was abundantly clear, from the look he shot the privateer, that he was not about to do anything to annoy that gentleman—like, for instance, demanding satisfaction for the dastardly kidnapping of his cousin.

"Good morning, Nicolas," she greeted cheerfully. "Did you enjoy the ball? I hope it came up to Elise's expectations. Monsieur Delacroix." She turned as she reached the hall, holding out her hand to the privateer who stood on the stair behind her. "My thanks for your hospitality."

Laughter danced in the turquoise eyes. He raised her hand to his lips. "The pleasure was all mine, mademoiselle. I hope it will be repeated in the near future."

Inclining her head in faint acknowledgement, she sketched a curtsy before turning back to her cousin. "If you are ready, Nicolas?"

"Yes, yes, of course." Nicolas sprang to open the front door, but was forestalled by Silas, who stood impassively as they went past him out onto Rampart Street. Genevieve automatically drew her hood closer around her face. *No* respectable lady could ever find a reason for traversing this street. But then, of course, she hardly qualified as respectable, did she? A giggle escaped her and she hastily turned it into a cough, glancing behind her at the house, fixing it in her memory. Her gaze drifted up to the second floor, to the window she had looked from earlier, and encountered the intent scrutiny of a pair of brown eyes. A shiver ran down her spine, but as she looked, a figure appeared behind Angelique, hands curled on her shoulders. It was Dominic, turning his mistress away from the window—back to bed?

What if he was? Genevieve demanded angrily of herself. It was none of her business. What lay between a man and his quadroon *placée* was out of the frame of reference of any Creole lady, be she wife, sister, aunt, mother, or even mistress.

"I do not understand what has happened." Nicolas was speaking, his voice low but urgent. "Why is Dominic not using you to compel my uncle's cooperation?"

"He quite rightly guessed that Papa would probably not find my reputation enough of an inducement," she replied. "But he has agreed to leave Elise alone."

"To give up his plan?" Nicolas stopped on the banquette, looking at her incredulously. "I have never known him to give up something on which he has set his heart. What did you say to persuade him?"

"I told him I would help him," Genevieve said dismissively. "As we discussed, you and I."

"But how?"

"That is no business of yours, Nicolas." She looked at him contemptuously. "It is better that you not know. You are released from your obligation. Is that not enough for you?"

Nicolas flushed in angry discomfiture. "I suppose you imagine I have not been lying awake, worried out of my mind about you?"

"You had no cause for concern," she said shortly. "Did you not get a message delivered by Silas?"

"Yes, I did. And it did little to put my mind at rest. It was simply an order that I present myself to that house by seven o'clock this morning. I had no idea what had happened."

"The matter is at an end," Genevieve told him. "If you manage to avoid getting into impossible debt in the future, then maybe you will avoid dragging your relatives into the mire with you." It was harsh, and she knew it, but she found it hard to forgive Nicolas for what might have happened to Elise. Although, even while she thought this, an inconvenient little voice nagged at her conscience, telling her that if it hadn't been for Nicolas and his cowardly stupidity, she would never have experienced last night, or be facing the prospect of an exciting, undrawn future quite outside the experience of a maiden on the marriage mart.

"Who is she?" Angelique demanded as Dominic drew her away from the window. "You did not say you would sleep with her."

"It was not my intention," he said. "And she is nothing to do with you, do you understand?"

"But you bring her here, to my house," Angelique protested, although she knew she shouldn't.

"It is *my* house," she was reminded. "And I do what I please in it. She will be coming here again, and when she does, you will pay a visit to a friend." Dominic ran a hand over his chin and frowned. He needed a shave and a bath. In other circumstances, he would have had both here, but Angelique was looking aggrieved and disconsolate, and he was in no mood to deal with a scene. "Tell Silas we are leaving," he instructed briefly, going to the armoire for his coat.

"Will you not stay for breakfast?" Angelique, recollecting herself, smiled and stood on tiptoe to kiss his mouth. "I will shave you myself, and prepare oysters in the way you like them, and we can eat them in bed."

Dominic glanced at the tumbled bed, the pillows that bore the imprint of Genevieve's head. For some reason, a rerun with Angelique as partner had little appeal. He shook his head. "No, not this morning, Angel. I have work to do on my ship."

"Will you come to me this evening?" She was twining herself around him, and he could smell the strong sickly sweet fragrance of her favorite lily of the valley perfume. Genevieve, he recalled, had smelled of soap and lavender water, unsophisticated, certainly, but pleasantly refreshing.

"Maybe," he replied shortly, taking her arms from around his neck. "It depends. Tomorrow afternoon, however, I do not wish you to be here. *Tu comprends?*"

Angelique lowered her head, hiding the flash of fury in the brown eyes. She did indeed understand. "As you wish, Dominic," she murmured, and he was too distracted to hear more than the submission he expected in her voice.

He left with Silas five minutes later, and Angelique spent the next half hour wreaking havoc in the kitchen with the china, her slaves cowering against the walls as this seemingly limitless fury expended itself. They all knew that the master had spent the night in Angelique's bed with another woman, and it did nothing for Angelique's consequence in their eyes.

Once the storm had passed, however, Angelique went up to her bedchamber. The brown eyes were coldly determined, and the little maid who scurried around laying out her clothes, brushing her hair, passing the paint and powder, kept well out of the way of the too quick hands and the serrated tongue. Whoever was responsible for upsetting her mistress so dreadfully was clearly going to suffer, the child decided, with a little shiver. Angelique was well known for the fearsomeness and duration of her grudges.

Dressed to her satisfaction, Angelique put on the turban that law required all quadroons to wear as identification, and left the house, the maid accompanying her. They walked down to the river, skirting the levée market and turning into a narrow street of dilapidated houses, whose sagging floors and peeling paintwork bore witness to the depredations caused by the flooding Mississippi, the fearsome attacks of hurricanes, the constant, ineradicable dampness of humidity and river mist.

It was the home of gaming hells, brothels, coffeehouses, and wineshops, frequented by the riverboat men, the sailors, and all those with money to burn and a taste for the unsavory. Angelique walked briskly, ignoring the ribald calls from open doorways, stepping over the occasional drunkard stretched upon the banquette. The rise of the levée was on their left, topped with scrub grass and mock orange trees. Clotheslines flapped in the breeze above the odorous piles of rubbish, adding to the general air of desolation and neglect. At a small dark doorway, Angelique told her companion to wait.

The child cowered against the wall, looking nervously up and down the street. There were few people around, but those there were were not of the type to inspire confidence. She peered in through the doorway, into a dim room with sawdust on the floor, and a most pervasive odor that she could not begin to identify. It was heady, a mixture of alcohol, of incense, of strange herbal potions. Angelique was at the rear of the room, deep in conversation with an old woman wrapped in brightly colored scraps of material, her hair bound in tight pigtails standing out like corkscrews over her head. She was bent over a small round table, its top formed of stretched hide, rattling something in the palm of her hand. With a flick of her wrist, she tossed whatever it was onto the leather surface, and the two women looked closely. The child, slipping into the room, saw white bones forming a random pattern on the table. There was a whispered consultation, then the old woman creaked over to a shelf on which reposed jars, sackcloth pouches, and carved boxes. Muttering, she ran her hand along the contents of the shelf before finding what she sought. She brought the pouch over

112

to Angelique. A flash of silver shone for an instant in the dust-laden dimness before her fingers curled over the coin Angelique held out. The child swiftly returned to the street and was waiting, to all intents and purposes, in quiet obedience, when her mistress emerged.

Dominic, sublimely unaware of the havoc he had caused, went back to the unsullied peace of his house on Chartres Street, where he bathed, shaved, consumed a leisurely breakfast and contemplated the pleasurable prospect of stealing an anchorage from Victor Latour, under his very eyes, and with the connivance of his own daughter. The privateer preferred a subtle vengeance and found utterly delicious the idea that Latour should be unaware of the theft of his land; that his cooperation in Dominic's plans should be unwitting. And the daughter? A passionate sprite with silver-gold hair and tawny eyes. Dominic smiled to himself. She would come to no harm at his hands, but when they had exhausted the possibilities that each had to offer the other, it would be a most knowledgeable and skillful woman he gifted to whichever young Creole blood was lucky enough to attract Genevieve's fancy, and was considered an eligible suitor by Victor.

Rising from the breakfast table in the courtyard, he went through the house to the front hall where Silas was waiting to hand him his curly brimmed beaver and cane. "You are going to *Danseuse,* monsieur?" There was no mistaking the wistful note in his voice.

"No." Dominic drew on his gloves. "To the office at the Exchange. I have some charts there that I want to examine."

The sailor's eyes gleamed. "Plans for the next voyage, monsieur?"

Dominic smiled. "Maybe, Silas, maybe," he said airily, and walked out onto Chartres Street. At the banquette, he turned and looked back at Silas, standing in the doorway. "If you've a mind for a stroll, pay a visit to *Danseuse* and tell the

113

bosun to have a half crew assembled for a short sail—two days, maybe three—in inland waters."

Silas beamed. "Yes, monsieur. With pleasure, monsieur. Right away, monsieur."

Chuckling, Dominic sauntered unhurriedly in the direction of Maspero's Exchange. Preparations were being made for an auction later in the day, and the auctioneer greeted his tenant with the offer of a julep and the suggestion that he might like to look over the day's stock. If any pleased him, Maspero would be happy to hold his bid.

"The julep I'll accept gladly, Jean." Dominic followed the auctioneer into his inner office. "But I'm not buying at the moment."

Maspero looked at his guest shrewdly as he handed him a frosted silver goblet. "Plans afoot, eh?"

"Possibly." Dominic returned as vague an answer as he had to a similar question from Silas. The auctioneer was no more fooled than the sailor, but politely changed the subject. One did not press a man about his affairs, after all. And the privateer was notoriously closed mouthed, as befitted a man in such a business. Only thus could one be sure of reasonable safety.

Alone in his second-floor office, Dominic laid navigation charts of Lake Borgne upon the table. He had spent many hours pouring over them as he had planned the original anchorage on Latour's property. But that site fronted the lake and Genevieve had talked of a bayou, surrounded by swamp, inland from the lake. He was taking a risk, of course, that she knew what was involved in a secluded harbor for a fleet of frigates and clippers—deep water was a must. But what did a Creole maiden know about a ship's draught? Perhaps he'd been a fool to accept her suggestion so easily. In the cold light of day, he knew why he had done so, of course. Having met, in the shape of Mademoiselle Genevieve, an insurmountable obstacle to the achievement of his

114

goal, he had readily latched onto the offer of an alternative.

The sound of footsteps and whispered voices clearly in altercation beyond his door brought a frown to his brow. He straightened from the charts on the table and went to the door. Maspero knew that the privateer received no uninvited visitors in his office, and it sounded remarkably as if someone was demanding entrance. He flung open the door. A slight figure in a bright calico gown, a turban wrapped around her head, somewhat down-at-heel boots upon her feet, was engaged in vociferous, if low-voiced argument with the auctioneer.

"What the *hell* are you doing here?" Dominic demanded of Genevieve Latour, seizing her wrist and hauling her into the room before the astonished gaze of the auctioneer.

"I wished to see if my disguise would pass," she said cheerfully, looking around the room with fascinated eyes. "It seems that it did. Monsieur Maspero was not about to permit a quadroon to sully his upstairs regions." An acrid note lurked in her voice.

"How did you know to find me here?" he asked, ignoring both the note and the statement.

She shrugged. "I did not. But I knew it was possible, and if you were not it would not have mattered. I would have proved my point anyway." Wandering to the table, she bent over the charts. "Are you looking for the anchorage?"

"As it happens," he agreed, somewhat bemused by this visitation, although recognizing that he should not have been. Experience should have taught him that Genevieve did not make a habit of turning up in orthodox fashion and only when expected. "Have you no maid with you?"

"How could I have?" She laughed. "I cannot pay clandestine visits in this guise to a house on Rampart Street in the company of my maid. This was just a trial run, if you like. It was amazingly easily accomplished."

"I had little doubt that you would find it so," he said drily.

"Where on earth did you acquire those dreadful clothes?"

"Amelie procured them for me," she informed him with a serene smile. "Perhaps you do not remember her, but—"

"I remember only too well," Dominic interrupted. "Take the turban off, at least while you are in this room. And since you are here, you may help me. Where is the anchorage you have in mind?" Coming to stand beside her, he bent over the chart, then slowly stood upright again. That fresh, distinctive scent of young, delicate skin and silky hair was utterly distracting. "On second thought, it can wait a minute," he murmured, tilting her chin. "Did I kiss you this morning?"

"Not properly," she said, a slight quaver in her voice. She seemed to be swallowed up in that turquoise gaze, her own eyes riveted on his mouth, her lips tingling in expectation of that remembered sensation—the firm softness of his against hers.

His mouth curved. "I did not think I could have done. I would have remembered if I had. I think I should remedy the omission, don't you?"

Genevieve could only nod, the long golden sweep of her eyelashes fanning on her cheekbones as her arms slipped around his neck, and she came up on tiptoe, bringing her face eagerly to his.

Dominic tasted deeply of her sweetness, feeling the soft yielding of her body as she reached against him. His hands ran down her back to cup her buttocks, drawing her against the rising shaft of his desire. She responded with all the passion she had evinced during the night, her mouth opening as she pressed her body against him, moving sensuously, sinuously, bringing his arousal to a throbbing peak. His breathing ragged, at last he drew back. "Ah, but you could drive a man to his ruin, sprite," he said thickly. "And will do so one day, unless I am much mistaken."

But not you, Genevieve thought, trying to still her fast beating heart that pushed the hot swift blood through her veins while her pulse fluttered like a wounded bird in the palm of a hand. Dominic Delacroix could never be brought to ruin at the hands of a woman, however passionate she might be. She smiled in what she hoped was a light, flirtatious manner and tossed her hair over her shoulder. "Such flattery, monsieur. I declare I do not know where to look."

A frown darkened the blue eyes. "Don't play the coquette, Genevieve. It does not suit you. Your responses are true, and they are what make you special. You have no need to play games. You are not Elise."

The reproof was delivered in the tones of schoolmaster to erring pupil, and Genevieve bit her lip in awkward discomfiture. What made it particularly galling was that she knew he was right. Elise's affectations sounded simply ridiculous on her stepsister's tongue. In fact, Genevieve privately thought that they sounded ridiculous even coming from Elise, and she could not imagine what had possessed her to try to emulate her. It seemed a good point at which to change the subject. "Did you not want me to show you the anchorage?"

"Yes." To her relief, Dominic accepted the changed tack as ending the topic and returned to his scrutiny of the map. "This is the site I had originally chosen." Pointing with the sharp tip of a pair of compasses, he indicated the spot. "Show me yours."

Genevieve stabbed with her finger at a faint blue spot some miles inland from the lake and, judging by the surrounding area, it was well and truly isolated from the inhabited parts of the plantation. Dominic frowned. "How deep is it?"

She shrugged. "I do not know exactly, not having sounded it, but it will take a frigate's draught. And the channel, too. I know it looks narrow and, indeed it is, but it will suffice, and is deep enough."

117

"Now, how do you know that?" He looked at her with interest. She had used nautical terms with an ease that bespoke familiarity.

"One of the slaves who used to work in the shipyard way back in my grandfather's time, told me. He's retired now and likes to potter around the lake and the bayous. As a child, I used to love going to the yard when I could escape from the house, and old Sam sometimes took me out in his boat." She smiled a little guiltily. "He still does, actually, but Hélène is so frightened of what will happen if Papa finds out that I very rarely go now. It is most irksome that putting up one's hair and wearing long skirts should mean such tedious restrictions on one's activities."

Dominic chuckled. "I have seen no indications that you accept those restrictions, Mademoiselle Genevieve. Or, indeed, *any* restrictions. Have this channel and bayou ever been sailed by a vessel with a frigate's draught?"

"Sam said that many years ago, when the Americans were trying to secure free navigation of the Mississippi from the Spanish, a few privateers sailed into Lake Borgne. The Spaniards pursued them, but they disappeared in the night. According to Sam, they hid in the bayou until the Spaniards had given up, then returned the way they had come."

Dominic nodded thoughtfully. It seemed a plausible enough story and, if true, certainly indicated that the hiding place was secure.

"When shall we go and investigate it?" Genevieve asked, looking up from the map. "I have already told Hélène that I wish to spend some time with the Ursulines." She laughed a little self-consciously. "Hélène tried very hard not to show how pleased she was, but her life is much more peaceful when I am not around."

"Mmmm. I can certainly see her point," Dominic concurred, absently but with absolute truth. Genevieve grimaced. It didn't sound as if he were teasing her. "The sooner the better," he went on with brisk decision. "I will take only *Daneuse* on this exploration and, if it will do, arrange for the rest of the fleet to remove there immediately. When you come to Rampart Street tomorrow afternoon, I will have made the necessary arrangements and will tell you how you should proceed."

Genevieve wondered if she dared ask the question that had been nagging at her since leaving the house that morning. Then decided that she had little enough to lose. "Dominic, is there nowhere else that we can meet?"

"Why?" He shot her a puzzled look as he folded up the chart.

Genevieve sighed and said awkwardly, "Well . . . well it is Angelique's house."

"Goddammit! It is *not* Angelique's house," he exploded with restrained irritation. "It is *my* house. Why do you women persist in maintaining that it is not?"

So Angelique had also objected, and clearly to no avail. Genevieve wondered whether to tell him of that strange, unnerving visitation in the bedchamber, then decided against it. He would undoubtedly be angry with the girl, and it seemed hardly fair to add that to her problems. However, she was not ready to give up yet. "But I am uncomfortable there," she said. "You must have another house, one where *you* live."

Dominic's face closed, and the azure gaze contained slivers of ice. "I do not allow *anyone* in my house," he said with cold finality, making Genevieve feel as if her suggestion had been a social solecism of incredible magnitude. "If you are not prepared to come to Rampart Street, then that is your choice. There is no compulsion."

Genevieve said nothing, but busied herself replacing the turban over the bright mass of hair. The desire to tell him that she would not come to Rampart Street warred violently with the knowledge that he would make no attempt to

119

change her mind, would shrug the whole affair off as if it was and had been of no importance. She could bring herself to say neither that she would capitulate nor that she would not. Instead, she found herself walking to the door. Dominic moved to open it for her and then, as she passed, caught the back of her neck between finger and thumb.

"Angelique will not be there, sprite. I am not *that* insensitive."

"She was there last night," she couldn't help saying, as she stood still under the warm pressure of his fingers.

"True enough, but then, if you remember, *you* were responsible for a change of plan that made her presence undesirable, and it was really too late to do anything about it."

It was logical, reasonable even according to some lights, yet she could not like it. But what choice did she have, and he had, at least, given her a face-saving opportunity to capitulate.

"Very well," she agreed in a low voice that conveyed her lack of enthusiasm. The fingers pinched her neck.

"Don't come if you mean to sulk," he warned softly.

Nettled, her head went back against his hold. "As it happens, Monsieur Privateer, I do *not* sulk! I accept the consequences of my actions."

"Good," he stated with calm approval. "I am glad to hear it." He could feel her fury through the skin beneath his fingers and with a sudden movement pulled her back into the room, slamming the door again. "Obviously, you need further convincing."

Genevieve struggled against this kiss, but he held her tight, asserting the mastery of his greater strength, the dominion of shared desire, until she submitted to both. Only then did he release her, declaring with a degree of savage satisfaction, "I do not think you are going to be a restful lover, mademoiselle, but I accept the consequences of my actions also. Now, be off with you before I lose all willpower to deal with the day's business." He sent her through the door with an encouraging smack and no opportunity to say anything further of protest or agreement.

Somehow, she attained the banquette, breathless, yet through her turmoil, certain of the inevitability of her immediate future, although the ramifications of that future remained a mystery.

# Chapter 8

"I cannot imagine why you would want to spend three days locked up in a convent with those dusty nuns," Elise said to Genevieve irreverently, looking up from her pattern book. "Do you not think this will be perfect for that cream satin, Hélène?"

Hélène examined intently the pattern that her step-daughter had chosen for the privateer's gift—not that Hélène was aware that the material had been a gift. "I am not sure about the flounce," she said thoughtfully. "Genevieve, my dear, have you talked to your father about your retreat?"

"Not yet," Genevieve said, wondering as always how the two women could find pattern books so inordinately fascinating. "I thought perhaps you might have mentioned it."

"Oh, dear." Hélène looked immediately guilty, as if she had been sadly remiss. "I did not think to do so. I am sorry, *chère.*"

"No matter." Genevieve shrugged. "He will not object, at all events. I will ask him when he comes home at noon."

"He does not approve of your studies," Elise said unhelpfully. "You had best make sure he believes your reasons are purely pious."

Her younger sister chuckled and declared in a fair

imitation of Victor Latour, "An educated woman is the very devil!"

"Oh, Genevieve, hush. You must have more respect," Hélène chided gently, even though laughter sparked in her eyes. "If we made the flounce deeper, Elise, I think it will look very pretty."

Genevieve got up restlessly and went to the window. Rain poured down in an almost impenetrable wall, flooding the deep ditch running down the center of the street, sending the odorous debris of horse manure, offal, and garbage rushing in the torrent to the canals below the town, and from there into the river. After the recent heatwave, the rain was necessary and welcomed by most inhabitants of the town. But not by Genevieve, who could not imagine how she was to make the rendezvous in Rampart Street this afternoon. It would be hard to leave the house unnoticed, with or without her disguise, since everyone was inside, all the doors and gates closed against the storm. And even if she could contrive her escape, she would arrive in Rampart Street like a rat drowned in a sewer. Dominic would know why she had failed, of course, but that didn't help, somehow. She felt bereft, forlorn, and as frustratedly disappointed as a child denied a birthday party.

"I do not think Papa and Nicolas will return for lunch in this," she said, pacing the room, idly straightening an ornament, flicking through the pages of a journal, and turning the music on the pianoforte.

"Have you nothing to do?" Elise exclaimed. "You are making me so nervous. Why can you not behave like a grown woman, instead of a cabinned child?"

"Probably because I feel like a cabinned child," Genevieve retorted. "I have not been outside for almost twenty-four hours and I am ready to scream."

"Oh, pray do not squabble," Hélène begged. "It is very irksome for Genevieve, Elise, to be kept idle in this way. She needs exercise."

"Like a pony," Elise declared. "It is not ladylike to need exercise."

That made Genevieve laugh in spite of herself. "How right you are, sister dear. I am not at all ladylike, never have been and never will be." She left the *salle de compagnie* and went upstairs. Her calico gown was stuffed at the back of the armoire and she pulled it out, shaking out the creases. It was so hideous that a little rainwater would probably only be an improvement. She glanced out at the rear gallery sheeted with rain. The courtyard was almost invisible below. No one was around, and if a maid was seen hurrying through the downpour, it would be assumed she was on some errand dictated by an unfriendly master. No one would imagine that anyone was voluntarily abroad on an afternoon like this. She would go, and to the devil with the rain!

The loud boom of the gong announcing luncheon brought her back to reality. If the gong was sounded, it meant the master of the house had decided to return. When the ladies ate alone, there was little ceremony. Genevieve tidied her hair and tried out a variety of expressions, looking for the one most expressive of daughterly docility. It was hard to achieve the correct result, she found. Her eyes were too sparkly, her spirit too infused with wicked excitement now that she had definitely made her plans for the afternoon. The idea of Victor Latour's younger daughter preparing to spend an afternoon in the arms of the notorious Dominic Delacroix, while planning to rob her father of a piece of his property—admittedly a piece that was of no use to him, but, nevertheless, it belonged to him—was too delicious for sobriety. Perhaps, she had better forego the terrapin stew, which was a pity since it was one of her favorite dishes, and remain in her chamber during luncheon. Her presence would not be required, as it would be at dinner.

A knock at the door was followed almost immediately by Hélène. "Did you not hear the gong? Your father is here."

"Yes, I thought so. I am not very hungry, Hélène. I think I

will stay up here."

"But there is terrapin stew," Hélène protested. "And you intended to ask your father about your retreat."

Genevieve gave in rapidly. The last thing she wished to do was to draw attention to herself. "Yes, I had forgotten the terrapin stew." She grinned cheerfully. "Even without an appetite, I cannot deprive myself of the treat. Let us go downstairs before Papa starts to bellow." Linking arms with her stepmother, she accompanied her down the wide staircase to the dining room where Victor and Nicolas already sat, and the heavy silver tureen steamed aromatically.

Angelique knew that disobedience was dangerous where Dominic was concerned, but after a careful weighing up of the consequences against the possible advantages, she decided that, in this instance, it was a risk worth taking. The rain would provide her with some excuse. Where could she go for the afternoon in weather like this? And she could always say in feigned innocence that she had assumed the rain would have prevented Dominic and his friend from meeting, and so did not think it necessary to leave the house. If she could get him to accept that, so that he would not be angry, then the rest of her plan should be easy to accomplish.

She dressed with great care in an afternoon gown of blue silk with a low neckline that left little of her magnificent bosom to the imagination. Dominic never made any secret of his appreciation of that endowment and, in general, preferred that it be inadequately covered. Her hair was curled in a mass of ringlets framing her face, a band of silver filigree—a gift of Dominic's—around her brow. Judicious touches of powder and rouge completed the picture, and, with a little nod of satisfaction, Angelique went downstairs to the parlor where she arranged a tray of little cakes and a bottle of Dominic's favorite Spanish wine. He would not refuse refreshment when he arrived, not on a day like this, and Angelique knew that he insisted upon an orderly presentation of hospitality.

With an excess of caution, she went to the window on tiptoe, although there was no one to hear, and looked out onto the rain-drenched street, peering from behind the gauzy curtain. There was no one in sight. Drawing a little pouch from the pocket of her gown, Angelique tiptoed over to the tray, glanced nervously toward the hall doorway, then shook some of the contents into one of the wine glasses. She filled the glass with wine and stirred with her little finger, then anxiously held the liquid up to the light from the window. The powder seemed to have dissolved completely. She sniffed, but, as the mambo had promised, there was no odor except the rich bouquet of the wine. Her hand shook a little as she slipped the pouch back into her pocket. It *had* to work. The mambo had assured her that it never failed.

The doorbell peeled imperatively and Angelique jumped, although she had been expecting it. Her heart pounded and she struggled to compose herself, knowing she would need all her wiles in the next few minutes.

She hurried into the hall just as the little maid opened the door. Dominic, shaking the water from a many-caped overcoat, stepped into the house followed by Silas, clad in sailor's oilskins and bearing an umbrella. They were drenched just by taking the few short steps from the closed carriage that stood at the banquette to the front door. "Damnable weather!" Dominic exclaimed, shrugging out of his coat. Then his eye fell on Angelique, who stood smiling in the parlor doorway. "What the devil are you doing here?" he demanded, his eyes darkening ominously. "I told you I wanted the house to myself this afternoon."

"Oh, pray do not be cross, Dominic," Angelique wheedled, taking his coat and handing it to the maid. "Come into the parlor. You must be wretchedly cold and wet. I have wine for you."

"Just answer the question, please." Brushing off the hand that she laid on his arm, he stalked into the parlor.

"Oh, dear," Angelique murmured tremulously. "Please do not be cross, Dominic. But I thought, since it was raining so hard, that you probably would not come. And, besides, I did not know where to go. I promise I will not be in the way. I will stay here in the parlor, or even in the kitchen if you would prefer." She handed him the glass of wine, still chattering nervously. "This is your house, Dominic, and I would not dream of interfering with the business you have with the . . . the lady."

Dominic frowned at her over the lip of the glass as he took a sip. It did seem a little unreasonable to turn her out of house and home on such a wretched day, and she was always very sensible about his business. He took another, larger sip. Then his frown deepened. "What's the matter with this wine?" He picked up the bottle and examined the label. "It should be all right. This shipment of Rioja was a good one."

"Is it bad?" Angelique asked anxiously. "Perhaps you just imagined it. Take another sip."

Dominic did so, then held the glass up to the light. "It looks clear enough. But there's something the matter with it. Don't open any more bottles until I have had a chance to sample one or two." He put his glass back on the tray. There was about a third left, but he was clearly not going to finish it.

Next time, she would find some stronger-flavored liquid, Angelique decided. At least, his annoyance at her presence in the house had become dissipated in the discussion, and he had taken a fair amount of the potion. She went up to him, slipping her hand inside his coat, running her fingers over his chest, feeling the warmth of his skin beneath the fine lawn of his shirt.

"Can I fetch you something else before your guest arrives?" Her bosom lifted as she moved against him, and Dominic glanced down, seeing her face, pretty beneath the rouge and powder, the glossy lips open over pearly white teeth, the swell of her breasts uplifted by her gown so that the nipples were barely concealed. She would have darkened her nipples with rouge, he knew, in the mistaken impression that nature's gifts required artifice for adornment. Of course, he had never bothered to tell her that it made no difference to him, one way or the other.

Without answering her, he moved away to look out of the window, thus missing the angry flash in the girl's eyes, the sudden set of her mouth caused by this careless dismissal of her charms. Genevieve, he thought, would surely not attempt to come out in this monsoon. He had been racking his brains for a way to help her, had contemplated patrolling the streets in the carriage in the hope of catching sight of that calico-clad figure. But, even supposing she did decide to brave the torrent, she could have taken any number of routes from Royal Street to Rampart, and it seemed a pointless exercise. If he missed her, and then was not here when she arrived, it would add insult to injury. And, dammit! He found that he wanted to see her very badly this afternoon. It was most unusual for him to feel either such a pressing desire to spend time with a woman, or such irritated disappointment at the prospect of being denied her presence.

"Silas?"

"Monsieur?" Silas appeared instantly.

"Take the umbrella and see if you can see her. She'll be wearing maid's costume and a turban." It was little enough succor to offer, but all he could think of. Silas, without a flicker of protest, donned his oilskins again, and went out stoically to patrol the street.

"She will be very wet," Angelique said in tones of concern. "I will prepare a brandy toddy for her. It will help to avert a chill."

She was rewarded by an instant, warm smile. "That is a

128

kind thought, Angel. Do so by all means."

With a little smile of satisfaction, Angelique went out to the kitchen. Not for one minute had Dominic questioned her easy helpfulness, her apparent lack of concern that he was intending to spend the afternoon making love to some scrawny, underdeveloped whore. But then why should he question it? she thought bitterly. He believed absolutely that his established mistress had no right to object to anything he chose to do. He looked after her in exchange for what she had to offer. It was a simple contract—one of the oldest in civilization—and if the woman wanted it to continue, then she must do nothing to upset her protector. Unless she could capture him, body *and* soul. Then would she have the power to alter the balance of power.

Genevieve splashed through a deep puddle, rather resembling a river, and cursed as her broken-down boots filled with water. She had been crazy to attempt this, but one more minute in the house listening to Elise and Hélène discussing flounces and ruffs, and the relative merit of *cord du roi* over merino and she would have smashed something—probably one of the precious French figurines that her own mother had brought as part of her dowry and that would form part of Genevieve's own, she reflected glumly. Her outbursts, like her father's, always had the worst possible consequences, however unintentional; unlike Elise, who contrived to weep and storm without causing the least damage, and always arousing maximum sympathy.

Besides, over lunch, she had obtained her father's approval for a visit to the Ursulines, and she found that she could not contain her need to tell Dominic. It was always possible, if she failed to make contact with him, that he would go off to Lake Borgne without her. He knew where the bayou was and did not really need her to navigate for him. He was presumably far too expert a sailor to need any assistance in the matter at all.

In spite of her heavy cloak, the front of the calico gown was soaked, the darkened material plastered to her legs, where the wind and rain had blown the cloak aside. The turban clung to her scalp, water dripping in a steady, chilling stream down her back. Genevieve did not think she had ever been so wet outside of the bathtub, and she could not remember ever having been more uncomfortable. As she turned onto Rampart Street from Ursulines Street, the thought of her own bedroom, of a steaming bath and Tabitha clucking around her with hot tea and thick towels, rose with almost irresistible force. She was too cold and wet and miserable to face strangers. And Dominic Delacroix, except in one essential, was almost a complete stranger. Why should she imagine that he would be sympathetic to her plight? He would probably laugh and say that he had never expected her to come out in such a storm, so the fault was all her own. He certainly would not be either able or willing to give her what she needed—what only Tabitha could give her.

With a wretched sniff, she stopped in the middle of the river that was the banquette. She would go home. At least her need for exercise and fresh air had been satisfied. But as she turned back, a voice hailed her. "Mademoiselle!" She spun round to see a figure hurrying through the puddles toward her. He wore oilskins and carried a huge umbrella. "Mademoiselle, come with me, please."

It was the man called Silas, her abductor. The man who had no scruples about the methods he used to quench resistance. But then he simply obeyed orders. It was Dominic who lacked the scruples, she remembered. Silas came up with her, holding the umbrella over her. "This way, mademoiselle." He took her arm, turning her up the street. Genevieve shrugged and complied. The succor of the umbrella was offered a little late in the day, she reflected, but it would be churlish to refuse it.

They reached the house, its front door flush with the banquette, and Silas hammered on the knocker. It was flung open instantly by a dry, elegant Dominic, not a hair out of place, not a ruffle disturbed, who said exactly what Genevieve had been afraid he would, and what was the last thing he had meant to say. "You silly child! Whatever possessed you to come out in this? You look like a drowned kitten!" There was exasperation, not amusement, in his voice, and it was too much for Genevieve.

"I needed the exercise," she snapped, turning back to the banquette. "And I find I have not yet had sufficient."

"Come back here!" Dominic grabbed her arm and yanked her into the hall where she stood dripping and indignant. "You're going nowhere but upstairs where you will get out of those wet clothes and into a hot bath." Hustling her toward the stairs, he gave brisk orders to Silas to bring up hot water and a brandy toddy immediately.

Genevieve, in perverse protest at what she wanted more than anything in the world, pushed back against the hand in the small of her back, twisting her head round crossly. She encountered the fixed stare of a pair of large brown eyes. Angelique stood in the parlor doorway, watching and listening with puzzled hostility. Dominic did not sound at all loverlike as he pushed the damp creature up the stairs, which did not seem at all surprising to Angelique, considering the condition of the creature—disheveled, bedraggled, dressed in those dreadful clothes. Perhaps Dominic was not really interested in bedding with her. Probably he just wanted something from her, and this was his way of getting it. The creature was struggling quite foolishly. Surely she knew that one did not resist Dominic Delacroix.

"Will you do as you are told, Genevieve," Dominic said. "I do not want to have to carry you, since I shall get wet myself.

But if you do not get out of those wet clothes, you will catch pneumonia."

"If you would just permit me to return home, I would be able to change my clothes," she retorted. "I did not come here to be bullied like a child in the nursery."

Dominic chuckled suddenly. "No, I am well aware of what you did come here for, and we shall get around to that all in good time." He gave her another imperative shove.

Genevieve, to her mortification, felt herself blushing. She stumbled up the stairs, deciding that further protest would only add to her embarrassment. And she could still feel those brown eyes on her. "You said Angelique would not be here," she accused, sure of her ground on this one, as Dominic pushed her into the bedchamber.

"No, I am sorry," he apologized carelessly. "But she had nowhere to go in this rain. She is not troubled by you, and will certainly not trouble you, so I suggest you stop thinking about her." Unfastening the loop of her cloak, he lifted the heavy waterlogged weight off her shoulders. "Get out of those clothes now. I will give them to Silas when he comes up with your bath, and he will dry them in the kitchen."

"And what, pray, am I supposed to wear?" she demanded in a hopefully sarcastic tone, pulling off the turban and shaking free her rain-darkened hair. "I do not intend wearing anything of Angelique's, at all events."

"No," he agreed with infuriating calm. "Her clothes would not suit you at all." Spinning her round like a top, he unfastened the hooks of her gown, pushing the material off her shoulders. "Step out of this now."

"Well, what am I to wear?" Genevieve stepped away from the wet heap of gaudy material clinging to her ankles.

"I can't see what need there is for you to wear anything," he replied cheerfully, lifting the hem of her shift and drawing it up her body, over her head. With a little smile, he reached out to touch one breast, cradling the cold roundness in the palm of his hand, caressing the nipple until it contracted in a hard, tight bud. Genevieve's breath caught in her throat, and his smile broadened as his other hand began to pay the same attention to her other breast. The sensation deep in her belly was so acute it was almost painful, and her hands came up of their own accord to close over his wrists, circling the sinewy strength. Her tongue ran over her lower lip, and Dominic watched the tiny movement, so expressive of her growing desire, and matching passion blazed in the turquoise eyes. Then there came a loud knock at the door.

"One minute, Silas," Dominic called with a rueful smile. He freed her breasts from that tormenting captivity with obvious reluctance. "Take these off, now." Finger and thumb pulled at the drawstring waist of her frilled pantalettes, and they fell to her ankles with a sighing rustle. Striding to the armoire, he pulled out a garment of richly brocaded silk. "This should provide adequate cover." He dropped the robe over her shoulders. Genevieve was about to reiterate her protest that she would *not* wear something of Angelique's, when he bade Silas enter, and she was obliged to turn her back on the door, hastily thrusting her arms in the sleeves. As she did so, it became clear that the garment could not have belonged to Angelique. The sleeves flapped emptily almost to her knees, and she could have wrapped the sides three times around her body. Walking was quite impossible as her legs and feet had disappeared totally in the folds of material that flopped to the floor, settling around her in a colorful silken sea. So, she just stood still, her back to the room, while whatever preparations were being made went on behind her.

"Take these and dry them, Silas." Dominic picked up her discarded clothing, including her pantalettes, and handed them to the imperturbable sailor. The door closed, and a reflective silence seemed to take the place of the busy, bustling sounds. "Are you, like Lot's wife, turned into a

133

pillar of salt?" The privateer's voice teased, a bubble of amusement in its vibrant depths. "You have not moved for at least ten minutes."

Awkwardly, Genevieve turned round in the swathes of material swaddling her. "Walking does not appear to be an option I have, at the moment. This must belong to a giant."

"It belongs to me," she was informed with a laugh. "But, compared with you, sprite, almost anyone would be a giant. Take it off now and get in the bath." Shrugging out of his coat, he tossed it over a chair and unfastened the mother of pearl buttons at the wrists of his shirt. With careful deliberation, he rolled up his sleeves.

Genevieve swallowed, her eyes riveted on the bronzed forearms where silky fair hair curled over rippling muscles. She had never known anyone but laborers who had suntanned bodies, but the privateer's arms, torso, and face were deeply bronzed with a color so layered that it would take months of confinement away from the sun for it to disappear. He could only have one reason for rolling up his sleeves, she thought distractedly, fumbling with the tasseled girdle of the monstrous robe. It was one thing to be ministered to by Tabitha who would bathe her and dry her and wash her hair in the comfortingly familiar ways she had employed since Genevieve was a baby. But men did not do such things. Did they?

Dominic bent to run his hand through the water in the porcelain hip bath. "Hurry," he directed softly. "It will get cold."

Why did she feel so shy? The other night she had not been. She had offered herself shamelessly, yielding to the powerful demands of her body without thought or inhibition. What was different now? Was it that it was the middle of the afternoon? It was such a ludicrously prosaic thought that an embarrassing giggle threatened. Pure nervousness, she recognized distantly, as, unable to stall further, she pushed the robe off her shoulders and stood naked.

Dominic looked her up and down, his eyes hooded, that little smile playing over his lips. "In with you," he said, pointing to the tub.

She walked across the floor, feeling the texture of the rug, warm and slightly prickly against her bare soles. The wood of the floorboards, where the rug stopped, was cool and smooth in contrast. All her senses seemed abnormally acute: her ears catching the drumming of the rain against the window; the whisper of the bathwater as Dominic drew his spread fingers across its surface; the slight shuffling sound of his buckskin-clad knees as he dropped to the wooden floor beside the tub; her eyes catching the play of light as the wax tapers, lit against the storm dark, were reflected in the swing mirror on the dresser; her nostrils catching the mingled scents of candle wax; a lingering perfume that was not her own; a dustiness from the little track of spilled face powder on the dresser; the clean tang of soap that Dominic was rubbing between his hands; and the wet smell of her hair as it clung in tendrils against her face.

Genevieve reached the tub, stood for a minute, her toes curling against the floor, her calves brushing against Dominic's thigh as he knelt, waiting for her. Slowly, silently, he clasped the ankle nearest him, stroked the sharp pointy bone, ran his hand up her leg, molding her calf, tickling in the soft, sensitive spot behind her knee, stroking up her thigh, then higher to caress her bottom with a light, feathery touch. Genevieve trembled and wondered if she would ever manage to make the move that would take her into the waiting water. The tantalizing exploration of his fingers was sapping her will, leaving her formless, mindless. In an instant, she would sink to her knees beside him.

Then he took his hand away, leaving her skin cold and bereft. "Get in the bath, sprite," he instructed, his voice husky, yet quite determined.

135

She stepped over the rim of the tub, then sat down slowly, sinking into the water's warm benediction.

"Now," Dominic promised softly. "I am going to give you a bath, unlike any you have ever received. Put your head back." Reaching with one hand for a copper jug from which a spiral of steam curled, he lifted the wet mass of her hair with his other hand and poured the hot water in a slow, deliciously comforting stream over her head and shoulders. "You have the most incredible hair," he murmured, his voice a caress as smooth as the hands that now massaged soap into her scalp. "I have never seen such an extraordinary color, and the texture is like satin."

Little shivers of pleasure tiptoed up and down her spine, as she listened to his words and felt the sensuous touch of his hands. Her eyes were shut tight as she yielded her body to the delights of sensation—the warm river of water rinsing the soap from her hair, the vigorous rubbing that made her scalp tingle as he dried the shining mass with a thick towel before wrapping the towel lightly around her head and turning his attention to the rest of her.

Not an inch of her skin escaped the attention of his soaping hands, yet she was not being washed so much as deliberately, skillfully, knowingly aroused. Dominic seemed to be intent on discovering the most sensitive areas of her body, and Genevieve discovered, with considerable surprise, that those areas were not always where she most expected. Her ears, for instance, were obviously not designed simply for hearing. They were devastatingly sensitive to the flicking touch of his tongue, sending paroxysms of a pleasure so intense it verged on pain coursing through her entire body. The same was proved true of her feet. Small and narrow though they were, every millimeter seemed sensitively attached to some other part of her body, so that as he stroked over the soles, ran a soapy finger between her toes, massaged each toe with a firm, pulling movement, some other portion of her body came alive with delight. At the very end, he parted her thighs, spreading her legs wide over the sides of the tub, and her opened body leaped beneath his fingers, the exquisite pleasure simply the logical, inevitable extension of what had gone on before, completing the circle of arousal and fulfillment that had been applied to every inch of her.

When he laid her upon the bed, her skin glowing from a vigorous toweling, Genevieve thought that she had exhausted the possibilities of pleasure; only to discover, as she watched him undress, his movements swift and economical, and watched him come to her, powerful and most amazingly beautiful, his passion rising hard with promise from the base of his flat belly, that both mind and body demanded that the limits be extended.

Dominic stood beside the bed, looking down at her. "I wonder," he said softly, "if you are ready yet to accept without fear *my* need, an ungentle and demanding need for your body."

Genevieve reached out a hand to enclose the pulsing shaft that would enter and fill her. She knew what he meant, knew that previously he had thought only of her, gentling her into pleasure, checking himself lest he scare or hurt her tender inexperience with an unwary movement. Now, he wanted to take what she was learning to give. "I am not afraid," she whispered, kneeling on the bed to take him in her mouth, as he had taught her, concentrating with every stretched nerve in feeling his desire and pleasure through the movements of her lips and tongue and fingers. She felt his hands on her bent head, fingers twisting convulsively in the still damp hair on her neck, heard his breath, fast and uneven, as she moved her hands round to grasp his buttocks, her fingers digging into the hard, driving muscle as his mounting passion spread to enclose and involve her in the tight spiral that he broke abruptly, taking her by surprise as he pushed her urgently onto her back on the bed.

137

She looked up into a stranger's eyes, deep, dark blue oceans of self-enclosed passion. "This time, you must come with me as you are able, sprite," he declared, his voice a low throb as he knelt over her, spreading her thighs wide to receive the thrust of his turgid flesh. Genevieve heard herself whimper as her body closed around him, and her belly tightened, her hips arcing as he pressed deeper, reaching her very core, it seemed. With each thrust, he drove harder, further, beyond the boundaries of her self so that his presence within her became a part of her very self. His head was thrown back, his eyes closed, his hands on her shoulders, so that she bore the weight of his upper body. But she found herself able to bear the weight without difficulty, just as she found that she was able to take responsibility for her own pleasure, matching him thrust for thrust, her fingers biting deep into the flesh of his buttocks as she expressed her urgency the instant before the explosion racked her body, and her cry rang through the room, joined by Dominic's a split second later.

It was an eternity later before the weight of him crushing her breasts, the soft press of his lips against her neck, brought Genevieve back to recognition of her own identity in the world. Her arms were flung wide on either side of her body as they had fallen in the aftermath of that explosion. Her legs were still spread wide around him, her skin damply melded with his. She brought her hand to his back, running a slow caress down the lean, muscular length, and Dominic raised his head and kissed her mouth—a kiss of affirmation, but affirmation of what, Genevieve was unsure.

Slowly, he rolled onto the bed beside her and lay for a moment, his hand resting warmly, possessively on her hip. Then, with a mysterious little laugh, he sat up and swung himself off the bed.

"What is amusing?" she asked, suddenly diffident, now that he had moved away from her.

"Oh, I was not laughing with amusement," he said, "but

138

with satisfaction. It is always most satisfying to be proved right."

"Right about me?" She struggled onto one elbow, brushing her hair out of her eyes.

"Yes, about you." He smiled, bending to kiss her again.

"What about me?" she persisted when he seemed disinclined to elaborate.

Dominic shook his head. "That's for me to know and for you to find out, sprite."

"Well, I do not think I have anything further to learn about this loving," she said, frowning.

Dominic laughed. "Now there you are quite mistaken, my dear Genevieve. You have but scratched the surface, as you shall find out when we sail to Lake Borgne." Casually, he stepped into the bath that still stood before the empty fireplace.

Genevieve sat up. "When will that be? I have Papa's permission for my visit to the Ursulines."

"The day after tomorrow." He splashed the now cold water over his face and neck, and reached for the soap. "Silas will meet you outside the convent walls at three o'clock and bring you to *Danseuse*. We will sail with the afternoon tide."

"What should I bring?"

"Bring?" Dominic looked at her in some puzzlement. "Why should you bring anything? Besides, there is little enough storage room on board."

"But I must bring a portmanteau," Genevieve explained, getting off the bed. "I cannot leave the house for a three-day visit without appearing to take clothes and other necessities. Think how peculiar it would look."

Dominic muttered a soft but not very fierce oath. "Well, if you must bring a portmanteau, I suppose there is little point leaving it empty. Pack whatever you feel you will need, then. *Danseuse* has never had a woman aboard, and I have never sailed with one—neither have the crew," he added. "I hope to God they don't object too vociferously."

"Why should they?" she demanded with a tinge of indignation, taking a sip of the neglected brandy toddy that stood on the side table.

"Sailors are very superstitious. They may consider it back luck," he informed her. "Come and wash my back. It is your turn to return the favor."

## Chapter 9

"You may leave me here, Jonas. I will ring the bell myself."
Genevieve stopped outside the heavy wooden gate set into
the stone wall of the convent and smiled at her companion
who set the portmanteau down on the banquette and looked
at her doubtfully.

"I should see you inside, mademoiselle."

"It is not necessary, really." Genevieve laid a hand on the
bell rope hanging beside the window grill at the top of the
door. "I wish to compose myself before the nuns admit me."

Jonas scratched his grizzled head. Mademoiselle Genevieve could come to no harm outside the convent, and if she
wished to prepare herself alone for entrance into the
hallowed house, then that was her right, and quite
understandable. All the same, he was unsure how Monsieur
Latour would view the matter, and that was the important
consideration.

Genevieve had hoped that one of the young slaves would
have been given the task of accompanying her this
afternoon. With almost anyone but Jonas, who had been in
the Latour household since she could remember, a simple
instruction to leave her would have been obeyed without
question. "You will be late getting back," she said
persuasively. "And I know madame has some commissions

141

for you to execute at the market. I promise you I will ring the bell when you reach the end of the street."

After further cogitation, Jonas nodded. Genevieve was a great favorite of his, and her request was far from unreasonable. Bidding her farewell, he turned up the street, plodding to the corner. There he stopped and looked back. Genevieve, seeing no help for it, pulled the bell rope vigorously, the peal reaching the elderly man, who, with a wave of satisfaction, disappeared around the corner.

Genevieve grabbed up the portmanteau and ran for the opposite corner of the street, before anyone could have time to come and open the gate. Finding an empty street, the nun would assume either a childish prank or a mistake. A closed carriage was waiting on the corner, and the door flew open as she hurried past.

"Where are you off to in such a hurry?" Silas asked, stepping out onto the banquette. "I've been waiting for you."

"I didn't see you," Genevieve said breathlessly, relinquishing the portmanteau. "I had to get away from the convent before anyone opened the door."

Silas merely grunted. The mechanics of this operation from the girl's point of view were of little interest. He was interested only in fulfilling his orders, for all that they did not meet with his approval. He gestured toward the open door of the carriage, and Genevieve scrambled inside, anxious to get off the street and well hidden as soon as possible. Silas and the portmanteau followed, the door slammed, and the carriage lurched forward.

Genevieve peered out of the little window to see which route they would take to the quay. But instead of going down to the levée, they proceeded along Chartres Street, where the carriage drew up outside Maspero's Exchange. "What are we doing here?"

Silas did not immediately reply. He opened the door and sprang down, making another of his mute gestures that she should follow him onto the banquette and into the

Exchange. They went upstairs to the office where Genevieve had found Dominic a few days before. It was empty on this occasion, however.

"Monsieur wants you to change into those clothes," Silas said shortly, indicating a pile of clothes on the table. "I'll be waiting outside for you."

On examination, the neatly folded pile revealed a pair of cloth britches, a lawn shirt, stockings, a knitted cap, and a pair of black shoes with pinchbeck buckles. Genevieve's jaw dropped. She had never in her life worn a pair of britches, although she had on occasion envied the freedom that such attire must accord. Slipping out of the simple gown of sprigged muslin, old, faded and most definitely out of fashion, she pulled on the britches, finding to her amazement that they were a near perfect fit. Although perhaps it was not that amazing, she reflected, pushing her arms into the shirt sleeves. Dominic's vast experience both of dress and the female form must have equipped him to make all sorts of judgments.

There was no mirror in the room, unfortunately, so that she could not examine her appearance when she had finally twisted her hair into a knot beneath the cap and slipped her feet into the shoes. The latter were a trifle large, but a sheet of tissue paper had been beside them, and she used this to pad the toes, assuming quite correctly that this was its intended purpose.

She could not help her slight flush of embarrassment as she opened the door and met Silas's objective scrutiny. It would have been so much better if she could have formed her own impression of what he was seeing. But he seemed satisfied because he gave her a terse nod and gestured toward the stairs. They returned to the carriage where she put her discarded dress, petticoat, and camisole, stockings and shoes, into the portmanteau, which had hitherto contained very little—just hairbrush and comb, ribbons for her hair, and clean undergarments.

"Why am I to dress in this fashion?" she asked to the silent Silas.

He shrugged. "Monsieur's orders."

"Oh." Since Silas clearly judged that to be an all-encompassing answer, Genevieve joined him in silence, and the carriage rattled over the cobbles of the quay.

This time, she jumped out ahead of her companion, looking around eagerly at the ships lining the quayside. Dominic had said his vessel was called *La Danseuse,* and eagerly she examined the names printed upon the swinging bows. Her initial awkwardness in the unfamiliar costume had quite dissipated, to be replaced with a wonderful sense of ease, caused as much by the effectiveness of the disguise as by the fluid comfort of the clothing. No one would see Genevieve Latour in this boyish figure on the quay.

"Over yonder." Silas touched her elbow, and she turned to follow him as, bearing her portmanteau on his shoulder, he loped toward a gangplank between the quay and a dainty, white-hulled frigate.

Genevieve looked for Dominic as she reached the crisp, gleaming deck. She had expected bustle and noise, the confusion of departure, but there was quiet and a deep, tranquil sense of order. Men stood, positioned about the deck, in attitudes of alert readiness. She could see no sign of the ship's master, and Silas was standing at the companion way, beckoning her imperatively. She followed him down the narrow ladder, along a passage and into a square, paneled cabin that came as a complete surprise. Genevieve had not known what to expect of Dominic Delacroix's vessel, but she had thought of piracy, of cutlasses and pistols, of bottles, both empty and full, of desperados with earrings and belts bristling with knives, of narrow, cramped, dirty quarters used only for snatching a few brief moments of sleep between bouts of combat and adventuring. What she found was a room, like any other except for the windows that were round, not square or rectangular. Sun poured through these windows in the ship's stern, deepening the rich polished patina of table and chairs, the luster of the jewel-toned carpet, sparking in the crystal cuts of decanter and glasses, shining off the heavy silver candlesticks. A large bed, in no way resembling a bunk, stood beneath these windows.

Silas deposited her portmanteau on the floor. "Monsieur wishes you to go to the quarterdeck as soon as you have unpacked your belongings." Without another word, he left the cabin, closing the door behind him.

Genevieve felt a surge of excitement too powerful to allow her to unpack her portmanteau. She had never sailed on a vessel of this size, although she had scrambled over the hulls laid up in her father's shipyard, listening attentively to the nautical talk so that the terms and general geography of the ship were familiar to her. But now, a fugitive from convention and all that she knew, she was setting sail on a privateer, right under the eyes of Orleanian society, on a voyage that would bring a significant defeat for her unwitting father and an exceptional amount of shamelessly illicit pleasure for herself. Her eyes lingered for a minute on the big bed. Dominic had said he had never sailed with a woman on board. Perhaps that meant that he had never before shared that bed with a woman. For some reason, Genevieve derived considerable satisfaction from that thought.

She skipped out of the cabin, back along the passage, up the companionway and out onto the sun-soaked deck. The ladder to the high quarterdeck was to be found where expected, and Genevieve climbed nimbly. As she did so, she heard the rattle of the cable in the hawser, the grinding of the capstan, and the sound of stamping feet. Turning at the head of the ladder, Genevieve watched the steady treading of the men upon the deck as they propelled the bars of the capstan. Someone struck up a low, rhythmic chant, quickly picked up by the rest, and Genevieve felt her heart lift with a wondrous sense of freedom, as if she were a bird tossed into the air, feeling her wings for the first time in pursuit of her own flight path.

Suddenly, she heard an order called out from behind her in a voice crisp and decisive. Dominic stood behind the helmsman, hands clasped at his back, his face tense and alert as he looked aloft at the great white sails catching the wind, at the curving banks of the Mississippi, at the busy river traffic, his eyes missing nothing of the scene, his mind calculating from his vision. This was not the Dominic of the ballroom and the bedroom, the impeccably dressed Creole gentleman of the cynical tongue and quizzically raised eyebrow. This was the sailor, the pirate, the adventurer at work in shirtsleeves and britches, the strong bronzed column of his throat rising from the open neck of his shirt, the rich nut-brown thatch of hair ruffled carelessly by the breeze, and Genevieve felt suddenly as if she were an intruder, one who might get in the way of the efficient accomplishment of that work. Instead of going to him, announcing her presence, she went over to the rail, standing at a distance from the master and the helmsman, content to watch as the sailors in the waist of the ship below hurried about their accustomed tasks. Dominic's voice continued to give the course, and the frigate passed down the river, threading her way through the other craft, leaving the water front behind.

The river widened as the city disappeared around a bend, and the wind, with a salt tang, freshened, bringing the knowledge of the open seas of the Gulf ahead. Genevieve pulled off the knitted cap, stuffing it in the pocket of her britches, reveling in the pull of the wind in her hair, whipping the silver-gold streaks across her face.

"Do you like it?"

With a laugh, Genevieve swung round from the rail, looking up at Dominic. She had not noticed him leave the helmsman to come and stand beside her. Now he smiled down at her, the turquoise eyes merry with his own enjoyment, as she nodded enthusiastically in answer to his question.

"Good." Cupping his hands around the flame to shield it from the wind, he lit one of his little cigars, inhaling with a sigh of satisfaction, resting his hands on the rail beside hers. "If you wish to change back into your own clothes, you may do so. I did not want anyone on the quay to see a woman coming aboard, but we are quite safe from prying eyes now."

Genevieve shook her head. "I like wearing these. It felt a little strange at first, but now it's wonderfully liberating." She performed a few steps of a hornpipe for him in illustration, and he chuckled, catching in one hand the tumbled, wind-tangled mass of hair at the nape of her neck.

"You need to keep this out of your eyes." Holding her hair with one hand, he pulled the knotted kerchief from around his neck and twisted it deftly around the thick, shining strands, tying it in a neat bow. "There, that's better." He ran his eyes over the slight frame and then frowned. "You should be wearing a camisole under that shirt, Genevieve."

Flushing, she looked down at her front, seeing the unmistakable swell of her breasts against the thin material, the dark peak of her nipples standing out. "I did not realize," she muttered. "It felt so wonderful to be free of all those layers and buttons and laces."

"Well, if you intend to keep to this costume, you must wear something beneath it," he told her without equivocation. "Apart from the fact that I do not care to have displayed what is for my eyes alone, it is not good for morale to dangle the unattainable before my crew."

"I did not realize," she repeated, unsure whether it would be better to be accused of naive ingenuousness, or of deliberate wantonness.

"Fortunately for you," Dominic said with a dry little smile, making it clear that the former accusation was definitely preferable, "I understood that. Go below and do something about it."

When she returned on deck some ten minutes later, she

147

found Dominic on the poop deck, engaged in conversation with Silas and the bosun. All around her, the business of sailing the ship continued, the man laughing, joking and singing as they handled ropes and blocks, climbed aloft in the rigging to trim sails, spliced rope. Genevieve found a sheltered corner of the deck, leeward of the wheel, where the afternoon sun shone warmly. There she sat cross-legged, tipping her face to the sun and the breeze, closing her eyes, allowing her body simply to absorb sounds, smells, and sensations. The deck beneath her, hard yet warm, shifted with the motion of the hull. The rail at her back imprinted itself on her skin through the shirt. She was aware of the scents of the swamp, salt, tar, and oil, the creak of the rigging, the tremendous flap of the mainsail as the helmsman put the wheel hard over. The banks of the river were cut with channels and bayous carving their way inland; fishermen in canoes and small rowboats pulled in the crawfish and crab, the oysters and baby alligators that constituted the river's rich harvest, and Genevieve listened to their shouts, the rapid patois of the bayou. For this moment, she was at one with her surroundings, as elemental as the river, the wood, the mud, the breeze, or the sun's glow, and she was at peace.

Dominic watched her, even as he listened to the bosun's report of a weakening of the patch over the gash at *Danseuse*'s waterline. His eyes were curiously softened, his lips curved unconsciously. Silas, who had already decided that the presence of the little mademoiselle boded ill for all sorts of reasons that he could not put his finger on, was even more alarmed at his master's expression. Monsieur had only once, to Silas's knowledge, succumbed to the wiles of the fair sex. He took his pleasure, certainly, but had neither the time nor the inclination for lingering too long or too intensely with any one female. And he had never, in the years Silas had known him—the years of privateering—yielded to whim or impulse in his dealings with women; *never* involved them in business! Yet here was this diminutive creature, firmly ensconced on board, and monsieur's face bore an expression the old sailor had never seen before.

"If this anchorage will serve our purpose, bosun, we'll be able to haul her up and take a good look," Dominic said, almost absently. "Until then, keep the pumps going." Leaving the two sailors, he strolled across the deck to the entranced Genevieve.

"Who is she?" the bosun demanded of Silas, staring, a deep frown between the beetle brows.

Silas shrugged. "Daughter of Latour. Monsieur needs her in this business of the anchorage, it seems."

"Since when has monsieur needed the help of a woman? Let alone a slip of a girl?" the bosun declared, spitting over the rail.

Silas shrugged again. "His business, I reckon." That indisputable truth served to end the exchange, and the two went about their business.

Genevieve opened her eyes when a shadow fell across her, blocking out the sun's warmth and light. "I was not asleep," she murmured, stretching luxuriously. "Bewitched, I think."

"As you appeared." He dropped to the deck beside her.

"Does my costume now satisfy your notions of decency, monsieur?" she asked, an impish gleam in the tawny eyes.

"Do not make light of a serious matter," he chided, closing his own eyes with a little sigh of pleasure.

Genevieve, after an instant's consideration, decided that the admonition was not to be taken seriously. "Will we sail up one of these little rivers into Lake Borgne?"

"No, we are going to sail down to the delta, then come up through Breton Sound," Dominic informed her.

"But is that not a very long way around?" Genevieve sat up curiously. Any one of the little tributaries of the Mississippi would take them directly into Lake Borgne within a few hours, but to sail down to the Mississippi Delta and then back up the coast through the sound would take much longer.

"Are you so anxious to curtail the voyage?" Dominic asked lazily. "I have not been at sea for so long that I am reluctant to stay only in inland waterways."

"I do not think that is your only reason." Genevieve regarded him through narrowed eyes. "The privateer does not waste precious time simply to satisfy a wanderlust."

Dominic gave a low laugh. "What a perspicacious child you are! No, indeed he does not. I do not wish anyone with eyes to see to realize that Lake Borgne is my destination. We are seen sailing into the Gulf and from there our destination is anyone's guess. We can beat up the coast, and no one will be any the wiser."

"Wind's backing to the east, monsieur," the helmsman sang out, and Dominic pulled himself to his feet.

"Very well, we'll wear ship," he said, strolling over to the wheel.

Genevieve stood up, watching as the men ran to their appointed stations, bringing the frigate round close hauled on the starboard tack. It was a fascinating operation, and she found herself wishing she could take some part in this business of sailing. The huge sails filled, and *La Danseuse* heeled slightly on the rippling waters of the wide river, her decks aslant so that Genevieve grabbed the rail automatically. There was another bellowed order, and men ran for the rigging, swinging themselves into the shrouds as they climbed, agile as monkeys, to loose the topsail.

Dominic had not said she was confined to the quarterdeck and, indeed, Genevieve could not think of a good reason why she should remain where she was when all the activity was below on the main decks. Down there, among the crew, she might, with careful observation and her ears open, learn something of the sailor's craft. She climbed back down the ladder, taking up a position against the lower deck rail, gazing up at the men at work in the rigging. It could not be that difficult to climb up there. They all made it seem remarkably easy, at any event. She'd watched men in the shipyard repairing struts and shrouds, perched way above the deck, clinging one-handedly, laughing and singing, as relaxed as if they were in an armchair before the fire.

A lad, not much older than twelve, swung himself onto a small platform at the top of the mizzen mast. It seemed dizzyingly high, but the rigging provided a solid enough ladder. He must have the most magnificent view, Genevieve mused, right out across the land and ahead to the delta and the Gulf. The decision to join him seemed to make itself, and she had kicked off her shoes and jumped for the mizzen shrouds almost without realizing it. Once there, it became very clear that the business was not as easy as it looked. Her feet and fingers seemed to reject the unfamiliar steps as she curled both around the rigging, but Genevieve was not one to give up once she had set her mind to something. Controlling the sick little flutters in the pit of her belly, she climbed steadily, looking down through her feet only once. That once was quite enough. After that, she kept her eyes up, trained on her goal, which did not seem to come much closer as her suddenly frail and unorthodox stepladder swung unkindly in the wind.

Silas saw her first. His jaw dropped as he gazed at the unmistakable, tiny figure swarming up the rigging, the sun shining off the silver hair. "Monsieur?" He touched the arm of his master whose attention was given to the helmsman. Dominic turned, then his gaze followed Silas's pointing finger.

"Sweet Jesus!" His face paled beneath the suntan. "What the devil will she decide to do next?" He ran to the quarterdeck rail and bellowed up at her. "Genevieve! Come down this instant!"

Genevieve heard the shout but set her teeth grimly. Having got this far, she was not about to deprive herself of success. Besides, the mizzen top was now a lot closer than the deck beneath, and she did not know how much longer her aching fingers would hold purchase on the prickly, cutting ropes of the shrouds.

At the master's shout, the crew, to a man, turned to stare upward. The sight of the ship's unusual passenger clambering to the mizzen top was surprising enough, but it was not that that caused their amazed whispers. It was the fact that the figure continued to climb, disregarding monsieur's order, even when that order was repeated at increased volume. Did she not know the penalty for insubordination?

"Doesn't seem to hear you, monsieur," Silas remarked laconically.

"Oh, she hears me all right," Dominic said through clenched teeth. "And by God, she'll not suffer from selective deafness a second time! Bring her down!" His knuckles whitened as he clenched the rail; his heart pounded as her foot slipped, and the rigging swayed violently under her convulsive grabbing at the shrouds. One false move, and she would plummet a hundred feet to her death on the deck beneath. It was always possible, of course, that she might consider such a fate preferable to the one he had in store for her when he got his hands on her. Fury fed fear, fear fed fury as he watched Silas's rapid progress up the rigging, and Genevieve at last reached the mizzen top and the safety of the platform. From the security of that vantage point, she peered down at the circle of upturned faces far below and to Dominic's white-hot rage, waved cheerfully.

"Didn't you hear monsieur tell you to go back down?" her fellow occupant of the mizzen top asked with a fearful curiosity.

Genevieve, who was seriously doubting her ability to descend in the manner of her ascent, mumbled something vaguely, and looked around. The view was every bit as stupendous as she had imagined, but whether it was worth the fearful effort of the climb, she was not at all sure; any more than she was sure how she was going to get down again.

The lad peered over. "Here comes Silas," he observed. "Wonder why. He doesn't come up here much."

Silas reached the platform and regarded Genevieve appraisingly. The girl was scared, he decided, which might make their descent somewhat troublesome.

"Monsieur wants you on deck, mademoiselle," he said briskly.

"I'll come in a few minutes," she said, offering a shaky little smile. "I've only just got here so I might as well enjoy the view."

Silas was not fooled by the brave words. "Monsieur wants you *now*. If I don't get you down, he'll come for you himself. You don't want that to happen." This last was said with all the confidence of one who knew what he was talking about, and Genevieve felt a prickle of apprehension that had nothing to do with her fear of the climb. "Follow me," Silas went on. "I'll guide your feet. Just put them where I direct and don't look down."

He moved back down the rigging, leaving enough space for Genevieve. She lowered herself gingerly over the platform, and then froze, clinging in panic to the flimsy rope. "I can't, Silas."

The agonized whisper reached him, and he swore under his breath. Reaching up, he grasped her ankle, his hand warm, firm and comforting. "Yes, you can. I'm going to hold your ankle all the way."

Dominic chewed his lip, guessing at what was causing the delay even though he could hear nothing of what was said. Silas could only be holding her in that manner for one reason. Genevieve wouldn't be the first to need gentling from that unstable height. Many a young lad on his first voyage had been petrified with panic and vertigo up there, and Silas was using established practice. He probably should have gone for her himself, Dominic thought in angry, frustrated helplessness as he paced the quarterdeck, not taking his eyes off the scene being played out way above him. At last, however, when he was about to spring for the shrouds, Genevieve moved backward, slowly but definitely. Silas climbed down further, holding her ankle so that she came with him. Dominic heaved a sigh of relief and went down to the main deck to wait for them.

Genevieve kept her eyes fixed on the pattern of the rigging in her hands, concentrating only on the feel of the rope and the warm security of the fingers circling her ankle, obeying those fingers blindly as she placed her feet where they directed. Time seemed to stop and there was only this steady, rhythmic progress among the creaking rope and stiff, shivering canvas, a progress that would eventually bring her to solid deck beneath her feet so long as she did not allow her mind to wander.

"Just a few more yards," she heard Silas say in calm reassurance, then she felt hands around her waist, and she was swung through the air to land solidly on the deck.

Her knees began to shake uncontrollably, and she grabbed the rail as the aftermath of panic slowly receded and she was able to take in her surroundings again. There was total silence, eerie in its absolute quality, and Dominic was standing in that dreadful, motionless way. Then he spoke, his voice quiet and even. "Did you hear me tell you to come down?"

Genevieve swallowed and thought rapidly. Would denial save her skin? Somehow, she thought it would probably do the opposite. There was no way she could not have heard that deep, carrying instruction. "I was almost at the top," she said, lifting her chin. "I wanted to finish what I had started."

"I see." Dominic inclined his head in a pleasant gesture of comprehension. "Then you will not object to repeating the journey, will you?" He smiled with his lips only, and gestured toward the rigging.

The color drained from her face. "Dominic, no . . . I do not wish to . . . I ca . . . cannot."

"I think you will find that you can," he said, still in the same pleasant, even tone. "You and I will go up together and look at the view. I'm sure you did not spend sufficient time in

154

the mizzen top to see all that there is to see. We should be able to see the Gulf."

Her mouth seemed to fill with sawdust, and her palms misted, clammy and cold. Wordlessly, she shook her head, no longer aware of the interested stares of their audience, conscious only of that glinting azure gaze, the coiled tension in the powerful frame standing so close to her that she could almost feel the heat of his skin. And again, she was overpoweringly conscious of impending danger. "Please . . ." she managed, her voice a mere thread. "I cannot."

"I will give you a choice," he said. "Either you climb the rigging again, or I will put you ashore—here." He looked over her shoulder at the banks of the river and, as if hypnotized by the sense of menace, her head turned to follow his eyes, to look into the swampy, forbidding distance, stretching, green, unwelcoming and seemingly uninhabited by any living thing that moved upright, on two feet. "There is no place on *La Danseuse* for those who do not know how to obey orders, or who cannot be taught to do so."

Genevieve knew with absolute, cold certainty that he meant it. He would do exactly as he said, without compunction or scruple, and no one would make a move to help her. This was Monsieur Delacroix's private kingdom where he ruled supreme, and she had always known what she risked by venturing into that dominion. She glanced up at the mizzen top and unconsciously stiffened her shoulders. What she had done once, she could do again. She turned and swung herself up onto the mizzen shrouds.

Silas nodded thoughtfully. Monsieur had not gone soft, after all, for all that he'd had that strange look in his eye earlier. He was treating the girl like any novice cabin boy. The rule was always the same. Send 'em up again immediately, before they had time to dwell on the first fright, otherwise they'd never be able to go aloft another time, which, in most cases, would be the end of a promising maritime career. Not that the mademoiselle had a promising maritime career ahead of her, he remembered with a sudden, puzzled frown. But then, she'd disobeyed orders, of course. It was an appropriate enough penalty that monsieur had chosen. Anyone else would have found themselves lashed at the gratings.

"I'm right behind you." Dominic's voice, as calm as ever, reached Genevieve, and the rigging shook as he leaped for the shrouds. "Go at your own pace. You are not going to fall."

Just why, when he was forcing her to do this dreadful thing, did he sound so reassuring? Genevieve gritted her teeth, forcing her raw fingers to claw around the rope as her aching legs climbed upward. For two pins, she would kick backward and catch that expressionless, domineering bastard unawares and topple him from his precious rigging to fall among the grinning circle of sailors on the deck beneath. Busily contemplating such a satisfying revenge, Genevieve barely noticed the distance and reached the mizzen top in an amazingly short time.

Dominic swung himself onto the platform behind her. Its previous occupant had descended in the wake of Silas and Genevieve, and they were alone up among the sails and clouds and wheeling seabirds. Genevieve sank down on the planking, catching her breath, examining her reddened palms with a pained grimace.

"Let me see." Dominic turned her hands up. "I'll put some salve on them when we go down."

"Such consideration," she snapped. "Why should you care? By the time I get down again, there'll be no skin left. *If* I get down again," she added glumly.

Her companion made no response, but merely took a cigar from his shirt pocket, struck a flint and lit the tobacco, narrowing his eyes against the smoke as he walked to the edge of the platform and examined the horizon. He was no longer angry, but neither was he prepared to enter an acrimonious discussion on the punishment he had imposed. It had been both deserved and necessary if she were to understand the realities of life aboard his ship. It had also not done her any harm to push herself beyond the threshold of fear. It was a lesson she might be glad of one day. So he smoked in silence and gazed out at the horizon, and Genevieve fumed in silence, dreading the descent, yet knowing that this time she would manage it without panic; knowing, too, that it would only be in the most extraordinary circumstance that she would again defy the privateer publicly on his own ground.

They made the descent, Dominic first. But he did not guide her feet as Silas had done, although Genevieve knew somehow that had she needed it, he would have done so without hesitation. When they reached the deck, he ordered brusquely, "Go below and take off those britches. Stay there until I come to you."

He walked off without a second glance, back to the quarterdeck, and a thoroughly exhausted Genevieve went meekly down to the cabin, wondering whether anything could be salvaged of this adventure.

It was an hour later when Dominic, deciding that she had had long enough to contemplate the lessons of the afternoon, went below to join her. He found her, still fully dressed, fast asleep on the bed, her sore hands curled open on the pillow near her head. With that tiny, enigmatic smile that had so disturbed Silas, he went over to the table and poured wine, taking a sip as he turned back to the bed. "Genevieve?"

The straight lashes swept up and she stretched, blinking bemusedly as if uncertain where she was. Then her eyes shot wide open and she sat up. "I fell asleep."

"That was certainly the impression I had formed," he responded gravely. "I thought I told you to take off those britches. It is quite clear that you can get up to far too much trouble wearing them."

"But I like wearing them," Genevieve said, then bit her lip

as his eyes darkened ominously. "I would have taken them off, only I fell asleep."

Dominic put his glass down and came over to the bed. A flat palm on her shoulder pushed her onto her back. "I am very much afraid, Mademoiselle Genevieve, that you are a great deal too accustomed to having your own way. The fact that you simply wish to do something is *not* sufficient reason for doing it. Particularly in those cases where *I* do not wish you to do it." His fingers moved deftly on the buckle of her belt, unfastened it, then undid the buttons at her waist.

"But why should what you wish be more important than what I wish?" Genevieve demanded, incensed at the very clear injustice of his statement. She pushed impatiently at his busy hands.

"Because I am older and stronger than you, and you are on my ship," he told her, brushing away her hands as if they were irritating mosquitoes.

"I might find the last reason to be worth considering," said Genevieve, with an assumption of dignity hard to maintain as her nether garments were tugged over her hips. "But the first two are purely incidental."

"Oh, are they, indeed?" The turquoise eyes narrowed speculatively. "Perhaps I should demonstrate how convincing greater age and strength can be." A final pull, and her britches were yanked off her feet.

"Oh, what are you doing?" Genevieve tugged at her shirt in a vain attempt to cover her nakedness, feeling suddenly too vulnerable to be having this discussion.

"Merely doing what you had refused to do for yourself," he said calmly, putting one knee on the bed beside her, taking her wrists in one hand and pushing the shirt up to her waist with the other.

Genevieve squirmed uncomfortably as his eyes raked her body, bared from the waist down. "If you wish to prove that you are stronger than I, you do not need to," she said, through a suddenly constricted throat.

158

"No?" he said, a pensive light in the blue eyes. "Perhaps I do not want to prove my greater bodily strength, but the emotional and physical sway one body can hold over another. There are chains that bind more securely than any that man can manufacture, Genevieve."

Genevieve tensed, feeling a hard knot of resistance in her belly. She did not like lying here, held in bond by his gleaming, speculative eyes and the hand at her wrists. It felt like a game that she did not want to play. But when she turned her head in denial on the pillow, away from the steady, azure gaze, he bent his head and his lips brushed the tender sensitive skin on her neck, just below her ear. A little shiver ran over her, and her bared flesh seemed to come alive. She closed her eyes tight and concentrated her will on resistance and denial. Dominic smiled, but she did not see the smile, hearing only his voice, light and amused.

"Such a stubborn sprite! But I shall prove my point, never fear." His lips took hers, and she tasted salt and wine and sun as his mouth, firm and warm, pressed against her own with an unexpected tenderness, becoming a gentle invasion that brought her defenses crashing down. Her head lay still on the pillow, and she forgot to resist. His hand, warm on her abdomen, stroked, a finger playing in her navel as the kiss deepened and the invasion became infused with determination. As Genevieve felt that purpose, could almost taste it, was inhaling it with every breath, she marshaled her defenses again, contracting the muscles in her belly, pressing her thighs tightly together, setting her lips.

Dominic laughed softly against her mouth, and his fingers moved to unbutton the shirt. Genevieve curled her legs and pushed against him with her knees. "I do not want this," she gasped, twisting onto her side with her knees drawn up, wishing she could bring her captive arms around to hold herself fast against the invader. Yet, in the deepest recesses of her soul, she knew that she did want this, that her protests were purely form, were the last-ditch attempt to deny her

159

knowledge of the chains he had described—a knowledge that Dominic had given her and so knew that she possessed.

Her wrists were released, and the bed frame shifted as he removed his knee and stood up. "In these matters, nothing will happen that you do not wish," he said evenly. "I have no need to take what is not freely given, and the pretense is not a game that amuses me."

Genevieve swallowed in disbelief at this abrupt volte-face. One minute, he had been laughing and tender, the next, fervent in a demand for a response that matched his own, and then, this—dismissive, cool, putting the pupil in her place as if she had not construed her Latin verse correctly. Tears of mortification pricked behind her eyes, and she shivered, devastatingly conscious of her half-naked body and the sense that she was quite alone, alone with a harsh and unpredictable stranger and no familiar supports. Without a word, she did the only thing that came to mind, pulling back the coverlet on the bed and crawling beneath its warm concealment.

Dominic drank deeply of his wine, allowing his regret for that unthinkingly sharp speech to rise unhindered by excuse. Genevieve was not Angelique. She was quite unlike any of the women, except one, who had hitherto graced his bed, and he had neither the right nor the justification to forget that. He bore considerable responsibility for her, something he had always avoided in the past—since Rosemarie, at least, he amended, accepting the familiar pang that accompanied the thought. But by yielding to the whim—no, to the most powerful desire—to teach this indomitable, reckless, ingenuous sprite what there was to learn about the glories of loving, he had implicitly shouldered the responsibility that she should not suffer from it. She had not knowingly been playing some game of the teasing coquette, and now he could feel the bewildered hurt radiating from the curled and completely silent mound beneath the cover. He had also intended to do something about her scraped hands,

160

Dominic remembered with another stab of guilt. But that would have to wait until he had healed the greater wound. Stripping off his clothes, he pulled aside the cover and slipped in beside her, drawing her body against him as his lips nuzzled her neck, and he whispered gentle reassurance until the tightly coiled frame relaxed, and she rolled onto her back, the tawny eyes, candid in their puzzled desire, gazing into his.

"Mea culpa, sweet sprite," he whispered, kissing the tip of her nose. "I was expecting you to run before you can walk. I will try not to do it again."

Genevieve was not sure she quite understood what he meant, but she could not fail to understand what his body was telling her. The adventure was going to be salvaged and, at some point, when she could sit quiet and ponder, she would try to understand what had happened and ensure that it did not happen again.

## *Chapter 10*

Angelique was in despair. Dominic was leaving her again without having availed himself of what she knew so well how to offer, of what, until the last few weeks, had never before been rejected. As always, he had drained to the last drop, the thick, strong, sweet coffee that she knew he liked, and the dose of the love philter with it, but his farewell kiss was perfunctory, the turquoise eyes bland. He seemed not to notice her perfume, the care she had taken with rouge and powder, the gauzy wrapper that barely concealed the naked, oiled and powdered body beneath. All the arts and wiles she had learned seemed powerless to break through her protector's polite indifference, and if he was now indifferent to her, how long would it be before their arrangement would be terminated? A man did not keep a mistress who had ceased to please him.

Her eyes swam with tears and she put her arms around his neck, pressing herself to him. If he would just put his hands on her, feel the soft, warm curves beneath her robe, then surely he would not be able to resist, and they would go upstairs to that bedchamber that he only entered these days when that scrawny, scruffy little slut in her calico gown and turban came to the house.

But he simply laid his hands on her shoulders and put her

162

from him. "Not now, Angel. I am in a hurry."

"You are always in a hurry," she whispered plaintively. "I do not know why you come here to see me if you do not have time for—"

"I do come, do I not?" he interrupted, that dreaded note of impatience in his voice. "You may start to worry when I do not."

Angelique trembled and stepped back, not daring to say another word in case she heard in return the final words of rejection. So long as he did not say them, so long as he continued to come here for whatever reason, she was safe and could keep trying to rekindle his interest. If the mambo's philter had not worked, then she would try the bocor. Maybe the good magic of the priestess was less effective than the bad magic of the sorceror. Maybe she should transfer her attentions to the cause of Dominic's waning interest. If she could disable the creature in some way, then surely he would come back to her.

Dominic stepped through the front door she held for him, then paused, turning back to her. "Angel, I will not object if you choose to . . . to expand your business a little. I would not impose complete abstinence on you. It would hardly be just." Without waiting to see the effect of these kindly words, he stepped onto the banquette.

Angelique gasped, pressing the back of her hand to her lips. She would have rather he had abused her, imprisoned her, insisted that she keep herself chaste for him whether he wanted her or not, anything but tell her that he was no longer interested in her exclusive attentions. The next step was inevitable and would not be long delayed.

Dominic strode off down the street, completely oblivious of the terror his words had caused, or of the vicious flames of loathing they had fanned. As far as he was concerned, he treated Angelique with scrupulous fairness and consideration. It did not occur to him that she might object to anything he did or said while he continued to honor his side

163

of the bargain, maintaining her in the standard to which she had become accustomed. He was quite happy to continue doing that for the time being, or until Angelique found herself another protector, which she would do soon enough, as young and lovely as she was. He stepped around a group of children dancing on the banquette and went into the cool dimness of a wine shop. The proprietor nodded and placed, without comment, an absinthe on the marble-topped counter. Dominic tossed the fiery spirit down his throat in one neat movement, then made his way into a back room where three men sat around a table waiting for him. They rose instantly as he came in.

"Gentlemen." Dominic greeted them with a brief inclination of his head and sat down, gesturing to them to follow suit. "You will take the fleet to the new anchorage on tomorrow's tide. You will have your crews sober and in good order by then." It was statement not question and received with grunts of assent. "Have the ships hauled up, cleaned, the repairs made, canvas and shrouds ready for sea within the month."

"Where do we go, then, monsieur?" a gray-bearded, grizzle-haired captain ventured, filling a shot glass with absinthe.

Dominic smiled and lit a cigar, keeping his audience in suspense for the time it took. "It seems that some people need our assistance," he said carefully. "And you all know how anxious we are to be of service." A rumble of laughter went around the table. "Apparently, these people are not happy being subservient to the Spanish. There are those in New Orleans who would help them gain independence, but someone must take the guns and powder." His smile broadened. "I have been requested to place my fleet at the disposal of these ... uh ... liberators. In exchange for a substantial consideration, of course."

"Honduras?" The sharp question came from a swarthy man, his right cheek grotesquely puckered with scar tissue.

Thick blue smoke curled from the pipe he cradled in the palm of a gnarled hand.

"Shrewd guess, Jake," Dominic said. "After we have made our delivery, we shall see what spoils of war are sailing the seas. We can't come back empty-handed, now, can we? I'd hate to disappoint all our customers."

Someone chuckled. "An Indiaman? We'll be running the British blockade both ways, then."

"Indeed, we will," Dominic agreed in accents of considerable satisfaction, and the turquoise eyes glinted. "Adds a little spice to the venture, wouldn't you agree?"

"Your suitor is become a trifle impatient, Mademoiselle Latour," Victor announced with an attempt at joviality, marching onto the rear gallery where his wife and daughters were sitting, as motionless as possible, gasping in the abnormally fierce heat of this first week in May.

"I do not understand, Papa." Elise dabbed at her upper lip with a lace handkerchief and looked a little fearfully at her father who was so clearly trying to give the impression of bonhomie.

He shook a finger at her. "Do not play the little innocent with me, mademoiselle. It seems you have been tormenting him quite shamelessly, and nothing will serve to satisfy him but an early date for the wedding. We have decided upon four weeks today. You will be married from Trianon and spend your honeymoon there. Your stepmother will arrange the nuptial suite."

"But the *lit à ciel,* Victor," Hélène murmured faintly. "How shall we have the canopy completed in four weeks?" The sunburst of azure satin which lined the canopy and gave the bed its name was barely begun, and Elise could not be put to bed to await her husband on the wedding night unless it was in place.

Victor frowned. "Those details are hardly my province,

madame. You have had ample time since the betrothal. Next, you'll be asking me about initialing and embroidering the girl's linen, or her wedding dress or *robes d'interieur!"*

"Oh, no, Victor, of course I would not," denied poor Hélène.

Genevieve choked on an inconvenient giggle at the absurd thought of her father's involving himself in such matters. It was amusing enough simply to hear the words on his lips. She turned the giggle into a violent coughing spasm, but her father's next words killed all desire to laugh.

"We will remove to Trianon at the end of the week."

That was in three days' time. She could not leave New Orleans so abruptly, without the chance to make plans with Dominic for the summer. She did not even know if she would see him before then. Since their return from Lake Borgne, he would send her a brief message, always given to the discreet Amelie, saying when he would be at the Rampart Street house. It was up to Genevieve whether she made the assignation or not. On the occasions when she could not, nothing was ever said, no questions ever asked. He had told her that she could send him a message to Maspero's if ever she was in dire need. But the implication was clear—that approach was to be used only in an emergency.

Genevieve knew that this secrecy was to protect her. The privateer was not concerned about covering his own tracks, but he was most insistent on Genevieve's using the utmost caution. She was both touched and amused by it. Such scruples seemed rather out of character for the devil-may-care Dominic that she knew, one who found society's conventions and prohibitions contemptible and made no secret of it. There were many times when she was prepared to throw caution to the winds herself, when the stuffy rituals of the house on Royal Street, when the role of *jeune fille bien élevée,* being prepared for the altar, stifled her to the point where she felt almost physically breathless, and she wanted to scream from the rooftops that she was not what she seemed. She was the wanton mistress of the most notorious privateer in New Orleans and loved every minute of it. But on the one occasion when she had been unwise enough to express this frustration to Dominic, he had scolded her as if she were a self-willed, naive five-year-old and sent her home, unloved and unfulfilled.

Now, she spoke rapidly. "Papa, would it not be best if we were to postpone our departure until the end of next week? Three days will not be sufficient time for Hélène to see to those wedding preparations, which can only be managed in the city. There will still be three weeks to arrange the reception at the plantation."

"It would be easier, Victor," Hélène said tentatively. "We must see the dressmaker and the—"

"Oh, very well," he interrupted brusquely. "The end of next week, then. What's the matter with you, mademoiselle? Cat got your tongue?" he demanded suddenly of Elise who had not said a word.

She was very pale, twisting her handkerchief in her lap. "I am just a little surprised," she said in a low voice. "Lorenzo did not say anything to me about wishing to hurry the date. I had thought it was to be a Christmas wedding."

Victor regarded her with a degree of exasperation. Women were all the same. Marriage and child-rearing was their destiny. They were bred to it from the cradle; they talked of nothing else. Yet when the time came, they behaved as if they were about to be sacrificed at some devil's altar. This match he had arranged for his elder daughter was one anyone would be proud of, and she had never shown any reluctance before. Now, she was looking as if it was the last thing she wanted. Shaking his head in complete incomprehension, he stomped off the gallery and went back to his office.

As soon as he had gone, Elise began to weep. Hélène rushed to comfort her, and Genevieve sat and thought. She knew what was petrifying Elise. It was the thought of those two weeks locked up with her new husband, seeing no one except the maid, who would bring their food and water for washing and deal with the various receptacles they would inevitably need; being subjected to whatever it was that husbands subjected their wives to, which eventually led to the horrors of the accouchement bed. Hélène had hinted enough after her own honeymoon, although she had never been absolutely explicit about all the details, since such knowledge must only be garnered by the bride on her wedding night.

Genevieve wondered if she dared help Elise with a little preparation. But how could she do that without revealing her secret? And she could *never* allow Elise to know that secret. Her sister would not believe it, anyway. She would be unable to believe such a shocking story of anyone she knew, let alone her stepsister. It would probably send her into convulsions! And, more than anything, she would be decimated by the idea that it was Dominic Delacroix who had initiated Genevieve. The abrupt withdrawal of his attentions had sent the beauty into a chagrined sulk that had lasted for weeks.

That thought brought her full circle. She had managed to win a week's reprieve, but how could she be sure of seeing Dominic in that week? He rarely, if ever, communicated his plans, although she knew that he was making preparations for the removal of the fleet to Lake Borgne. The anchorage had entirely met with his approval and, after that first disastrous afternoon, the expedition had been pure joy for Genevieve. He had taken her fishing in a little boat, and they had lit a fire on the banks of the bayou and cooked the catfish, eating it with their fingers. The arrogant, dangerous, elegant, powerful Dominic Delacroix had disappeared, replaced by a laughing, carefree, disheveled pirate who knew how to fish and cook under the stars, who licked greasy fingers, his and hers, and made love on a blanket in the silver wash of the moon.

"Why are you smiling?" Elise demanded with sudden petulance, sniffling pathetically. "You look like a cat that has just had the cream. I suppose it's the thought that you'll be rid of me in four weeks."

"Oh, don't be absurd." Somehow, Elise always managed to destroy Genevieve's finer feelings. "If I'm at all pleased at the thought of your marriage, it is for you. Do not pretend that you will not enjoy the consequence of being Madame Byaz, mistress of Villafranca. Once the honeymoon is over, and you go to your own house, you will have all your visits of congratulation, and you will receive on Thursdays and give a grand soirée. You will love it, Elise."

Elise did begin to look a little more cheerful, and Hélène, taking her cue from Genevieve, began to expatiate on the joys of being one's own mistress, on how wonderful it was when one was not simply a daughter but was invested with the importance and independence of wifehood.

"And Lorenzo is not exactly repulsive," Genevieve put in practically. "In fact, you always said you liked him better than any of your other courtiers."

"Oh, you are such a baby!" Elise said. "That is not the point, but you do not understand such things yet, does she, Hélène?"

Hélène looked a little uncertain. She was never entirely sure how much her younger stepdaughter did understand about the workings of the world. But she suspected it was rather more than anyone, and Elise in particular, thought.

Genevieve laughed. "You do not need to answer that, *chère* Hélène. I am going upstairs. It is too hot to sit outside."

Once in her own chamber, she paced restlessly, chewing her lip. She would have to leave Dominic a message at Maspero's, but to do that, she must creep out of the house unseen, in her quadroon's disguise—this afternoon, during the siesta that, in this heat, the entire household would take. Even Victor and Nicolas would retreat to their chambers after lunch before going back to the office on the levée in the cooler late afternoon.

At one-thirty, Genevieve was walking briskly, despite the heat, in the shade of the lace balconies, toward Chartres Street. She was not sure what impulse caused her to change direction and walk instead to Rampart Street, except that there was just the faintest possibility that she might see Dominic, or perhaps Silas. She did not think she would have the courage to knock on the door of Dominic's house if she was not sure he was there. The thought of confronting the cold loathing in Angelique's brown eyes when Dominic was not in the house was too intimidating. It was not as if she could blame the quadroon since she was certain she would feel the same way if some other woman supplanted her in her own house and in her own bed. But Dominic would not permit even the beginning of a discussion on the subject.

Genevieve was only mildly curious as to how much time Dominic spent with his mistress. She assumed that it must be sufficient to repay the cost of the house and Angelique's keep, but it was not really a matter that concerned her. A Creole gentleman of Dominic's sophistication and a quadroon *placée* were inevitable and inextricable partners.

As she turned onto Rampart Street where front doors stood open and the balconies were alive with desultorily chattering women, their gowns butterfly bright and varied, little maids waving huge fans to stir the hothouse air around them, Angelique come out of her house, unattended, and crossed onto Dumaine Street. There was an air of purpose in her step, yet she somehow managed to convey a furtiveness as she glanced over her shoulder, looked to right and left, then increased her speed. If Angelique was on the street, it was reasonable to assume that Dominic was not in the house. Genevieve found her feet following the direction Angelique's had taken. Like Angelique, she kept in the shadow of the house walls, and she adapted her pace to that of the woman in front. Why was she following her? The

170

question reared its head vaguely and inconsequentially. She *was* following her. What did it matter why? There was little else to occupy her on this indolent afternoon, and besides, she could never resist the possibility of expanding her horizons.

The pursuit took her into an area of the Quarter where no respectable woman would be seen. Flies buzzed over stinking piles of rubbish steaming in the heat. Women hung in open doorways, their gowns disheveled, exhibiting their charms to the passersby. Sailors rollicked drunkenly along the banquette, succumbing occasionally to the blatant displays of grimy female flesh so that there would be a mumbled exchange, the flash of a coin, and client and whore would disappear up the rickety outside stairs to the chambers above.

Genevieve attempted to ignore the ribald calls, the lewd suggestions that accompanied her progress. Hands grabbed at her, touched salaciously, but no serious attempt was made to detain her. However, her heart was beating uncomfortably fast, and she could feel the sweat dampening her gown between her breasts and under her arms. It was the sweat of fear as much as that caused by rapid walking in the heat, but to retrace her steps was as alarming a prospect as to continue. And it was always possible that Angelique's destination would take them out of these brothel-lined streets faster than retreat.

Her foot caught on an uneven brick in the banquette and she stumbled, grabbing convulsively at the nearest stable object, which turned out to be a bare, brawny forearm heavily tatooed. Words of apology fell from her lips as she attempted to move on, but her savior had other ideas, it seemed. His hand slid familiarly around her waist, and she smelled the rankness of stale liquor on his breath as he brought his mouth to hers. She put her hand against his face and pushed with all her might, at the same time bringing her knee up with a vicious chop. With the bellow of an enraged bull, her captor released her, and she was off and running without a backward glance, although the yells pursued her, and for a heart-stopping moment she heard the pounding of feet. But both died away eventually and she slowed her pace, realizing that Angelique was no longer in front of her. She realized why a few seconds later. Coming abreast of a doorway where hung a brightly beaded curtain, she heard a whispered exchange. Then a man pushed past her from the street, through the curtain, and she saw within the deep-green gown and scarlet shawl of her quarry.

Genevieve stepped back from the curtained doorway, standing against the wall as she wondered what to do now. She had no idea where she was, or how to get back into familiar territory. And whatever Angelique was doing inside the house was not something she was going to find out, even if she wanted to. In fact, Genevieve found that her curiosity had faded, and she was deeply regretting the thoughtless whim that had led her to this place.

"If you're coming to service, you'd better hurry. The houngan is ready." The harsh whisper was thrown at her as a man, dressed in white, stuck his head through the curtain and looked up and down the street. Genevieve blinked like an idiot, and her feet seemed rooted to the banquette. The houngan? She had heard the word before, but the reference would not come to her. The man disappeared into the house and the bead curtain rattled.

Voodoo! The houngan was a voodoo priest, Jonas had told her. Angelique had come to attend a voodoo service, to which Genevieve had just been invited. Genevieve found herself inside the dim interior beyond the bead curtain in much the same way as she had found herself on *La Danseuse*'s rigging on her way to the mizzen top—no conscious decision made in either case. So long as she kept out of Angelique's way, there would be no danger. The light was dim, and her disguise was perfectly convincing, blending in beautifully with the clothing of the others crowding the room.

A pole, carved to resemble a snake, stood in the center, a cloth-covered altar beneath. Genevieve hung back against the wall, and when a gourd, decorated with snake vertebrae, was passed to her, took a tentative sip of the aromatic contents. It was a powerful, fiery spirit of some herbal mixture, and her eyes streamed as the liquid burned its way down her gullet. No one else seemed to have difficulties with it, and the gourd was emptied and refilled many times as it was passed around the room. A chicken was tethered by one leg to the central pole, and Genevieve watched with a sort of repelled fascination as the bird was washed and dried with great care and tenderness. Then one of the white-robed acolytes poured something from another gourd down its throat, while another held its beak open.

The houngan, for such she assumed him to be judging by his elaborate robes and mask, lit a candle with slow, ceremonious movements, then began to dribble something on the earthen floor. It looked like flour, or ashes, maybe, and the design it made, while clearly, deliberately constructed, was quite incomprehensible to Genevieve. The white-clad assistants began to move around the room, gesticulating with stiff, ritualized movements. Then they began to recite in a flat chant. One of them stopped before Angelique, who had positioned herself at the front of the circle, and Genevieve shrank further into the shadows, straining to decipher the words of the chant, or was it a prayer? She heard the name "Delacroix," and shivered suddenly. The prayer was for Angelique. It asked for the return of her protector's love and for the defeat of the nameless one who had stolen that love from its rightful owner.

A wash of nausea caught Genevieve unawares and the room spun. She leaned against the wall, not daring to move

173

lest she draw attention to herself. Angelique's eyes were closed as the prayer was repeated, her face pallid with the force of her concentration, and her malevolence was almost palpable. Then the assistants moved to someone else in the circle and began another chant, directed toward the special needs of this participant.

She had to get out. The heat in the room was almost insupportable. The rank stench of sweat and tallow wax, the sickly sweet odor of herbs, the bitter burning of the spirit in her belly combined to increase the dizziness and nausea of her fear. But there were too many bodies between her and the curtained doorway. Then a strange sound began, eerie, menacing yet stirring. It was the hollow beat of a drum. Then another joined in, and the rhythm picked up. A space cleared in front of her, and she saw the drummers clearly across the circle, beating with their hands on goatskins, stretched taut across hollow logs. Someone moved into the circle and began to dance, quickly followed by another. Then it seemed that the whole room was in motion, swirling and chanting as the drumbeat quickened and the gourd was passed from hand to hand. Genevieve found herself caught up in the dance, whirling in the smoke-hazed dimness, the mounting frenzy around her as contagious as the plague. Then someone gave a great shout and the crowd fell back as an enormous man leaped into the middle of the circle, his pupils dilated, his eyes wide and staring.

"The loa," the chant went up. "The loa is riding him." Looks of envy and admiration were directed at the wildly gyrating figure, and Genevieve remembered what Jonas had told her. The loa were the gods of the voodoo religion, and at the high point of the service, one of them would deign to enter the body of a participant, to ride him like a horse, and the possessed would speak with the god's voice and act in the manner of the god, and be forever blessed by the possession.

The loa possessing this man must be a particularly

amorous one, Genevieve reflected, nausea and dizziness for the moment forgotten in her utter fascination and the knowledge that no one would ever notice her now. The possessed man was acting like a woman in the throes of the most erotic passion, and the spectators began to join him, imitating his lewd gestures, their bodies falling into the same positions. The drums beat faster, and the hysteria spiraled under the rhythmic, monotonous pounding so that even Genevieve felt herself sliding into the trance of complete absorption. But the instant before she was lost, the possessed one suddenly seized the tethered chicken. A knife flashed, and a hot jet of blood spouted forth from the bird's severed neck, splattering those around. A great cry of exaltation went up, and a gourd caught the flow. The huge man tossed the contents down his throat before falling to the floor to lie, twitching and unconscious.

Heedless of danger, then, Genevieve butted her way through the mass of bodies, but they were quite unaware of her, or of anything outside the supreme exaltation of the moment, and she reached the street in safety. But she didn't stop there. With no sense of direction, she ran, her only object to put as great a distance as possible between herself and the house that served as a temple. She was running along the levée, and a flicker of common sense told her to turn up one of the narrow, fetid alleyways leading back into the town, away from the river.

She thought her heart would burst through her rib cage, so fierce and loud was its pounding. Her legs screamed for relief, and her breath came in painful gasps, rasping in her chest as she emerged onto the blessed familiarity of Chartres Street. But somehow she could not stop running. Her legs seemed to have a life of their own, and she saw nothing but the banquette in front of her racing feet. Innocent pedestrians leaped out of her path if they were lucky enough to realize that she was not going to stop or divert her steps

175

to avoid them. One or two yelled after the turbanned, disheveled quadroon, but nothing halted her frenzied progress until she ran headlong into Dominic Delacroix outside Maspero's.

Dominic had seen her coming down the street, immediately recognizing the gown and turban on that diminutive figure. But he had not the slightest idea why she would be running like a panicked steer, nor why she would be out and about the town in her disguise. But clearly something had to be done before she drew any more unwelcome attention to herself. Deliberately, he stepped into her path and then hung onto her as she struggled to free herself, to continue her flight. Since she seemed incapable of responding to questions, he scooped her off the banquette without further ado, and carted her, still kicking and sobbing inarticulately, away from fascinated ears and eyes, into the Exchange and up to his office. Jean Maspero shrugged expressively as the door slammed under a vigorous kick. The privateer's business was his own, and it would be a very foolish man who would presume to question him, or to put his nose into that business without invitation.

"Calm down, now, Genevieve." Dominic set her on her feet, but maintained a tight grip on her shoulders. "What has happened to cause this panic? Do you realize how much attention you have drawn to yourself? Supposing you had run into someone on the street who knows you?"

Genevieve fought for breath as her chest heaved agonizingly, and her legs began to shake uncontrollably now that the need for motion was gone. Dominic pushed her into a chair and filled a glass with brandy from the decanter on the lowboy. "Drink this slowly." Her hand was trembling so violently that she could hardly get the glass to her lips and, with a muttered oath, he held it for her and would not take it away until she had drunk half the contents.

176

At last, she seemed able to breathe easily, and the quivering ceased with the realization that she was now quite safe, but she still seemed to hear the menacing pounding of the drums, the frenzied chanting. The bright, shocking fountain of blood seemed burned on her retina. "It was so appalling, Dominic," she whispered. "I have never been so frightened."

"No, I should think not," he said very calmly. "You were terrified. Tell me what of."

"Angelique . . ." Somehow the words wouldn't come.

"What has Angelique to do with anything?" Dominic demanded, his eyes taking on that icy glint. "I have told you many times that she is no concern of yours."

Genevieve waved a hand in vague negation as she struggled to find the words to tell him of what she had heard and seen. Angelique *was* her concern, since the quadroon wished her harm, and if Dominic thought that his official mistress was untroubled by his interest in Genevieve then he had to understand that he was quite wrong. "I . . . I followed her," she stammered. "When . . . when she left the house and—"

"You did *what?*" he thundered.

"Please . . . you don't understand," she said hastily. "I do not know why I did it at first, and I know I should not have done, but you must listen to what happened."

Dominic perched himself on the corner of the table at some distance from her chair and regarded her steadily. "This had better be convincing, Genevieve."

There was infinite menace in the soft tones, and she swallowed anxiously. "Voodoo," she said without preamble. "She went to a voodoo service in some dreadful part of town, brothels and drunken sailors and . . ." She shuddered. Dominic said nothing, but he was quite motionless, his mouth set in a grim line and the eyes cold, sharp and piercing as blue icicles.

177

"I went into the temple behind her." Genevieve took a deep breath. "It was quite safe, at least, I thought it was because of the way I am dressed, and only Angelique could have known that I did not belong there, and if I kept in the background, out of her sight—"

"You intruded on a voodoo ceremony?" he asked on a note of total incredulity. "Not even you would dare interfere in something as private as that."

Genevieve hung her head. In her panic, she had not thought of the unprincipled aspect of her actions, that she had been poking and prying into the most secret rites and rituals of another culture. "I did not think. I just went in."

"'Just going in' is a habit you have. It is one I intend to break you of. Now, tell me the rest. I presume I have not yet heard the salient point."

"No." She took another deep, shaky breath. "There were prayers, chants and things, and they seemed to be for people in the audience. There was one for Angelique. It was about you and me."

"Go on," he prompted, still unmoving.

"They were praying that you would go back to Angelique and that something bad would happen to me. I could not understand all the details, but the point was clear enough." She bit her quivering lip. "You cannot imagine how frightening it was to hear such malevolence directed at oneself. Then everyone went wild with the drums, and dancing and the drink . . . some dreadful, fiery spirit—"

"You drank it!" Dominic shook his head in disbelief.

"I was curious," she admitted lamely. "And then I could not seem to get out. It became very confusing with the noise and the dancing. And then they killed the chicken. There was blood everywhere, and I ran. I don't really remember very much after that." Another uncontrollable shudder ran through the slight frame.

"You impulsive, meddlesome little fool!" Dominic pronounced savagely. "You need a damn good hiding, Genevieve."

The recipient of this exasperated, uncompromising statement was too dispirited and emotionally exhausted for protest or defense, even if a convincing form of the latter had come to mind. Her gaze remained riveted on the whorls of a knot of wood in the oak floor at her feet, and a heavy silence settled over the room.

Then Dominic sighed and crossed the room with long, impatient strides. "Just look at you! You look as if you've been put through a mangle." Taking her chin, he tilted her face up to meet his scrutiny. "One of these days, you are going to get really hurt if you do not learn to stop and think before you follow your self-destructive, over-inquisitive nose into whatever trouble happens to crop up." Genevieve said nothing, but two large tears rolled down the sides of the feature under discussion. "Here." Dominic released her chin and pulled a large lawn handkerchief from his britches pocket, handing it to her. "Just as a matter of interest, what were you doing on Rampart Street in those clothes in the first place?"

"I had to get a message to you." Genevieve blew her nose vigorously and dried her eyes. "I thought maybe I might see you, or Silas. If not, I would have come here and left a message with Monsieur Maspero. But I knew you would not really like me to do that except as a last resort." She held out his handkerchief, and he took the scrunched, soggy ball with a pained frown, shoving it back into his pocket.

"So, what is the problem?"

"Elise is to be married in four weeks."

"High time," he said. "That hardly strikes me as a problem; quite the opposite. The sooner she's tucked up in the Castilian's bed, the less likely she is to invite dangerous attentions."

A watery smile enlivened Genevieve's somber countenance. "Yes, that is true. But the difficulty is that she is to be married from Trianon, and we are to remove to the plantation at the end of next week. It was to be in three days' time, but I managed to persuade Papa to delay it. Only, I did not know if I would see you before then, in the ordinary way. If you understand me."

"In the ordinary way, eh?" he mused, a gleam of humor now in the turquoise eyes. "Is it so very ordinary? I had not thought it so, myself. But then, perhaps I do not have as much experience of such matters as you."

A tinge of pink crept into her cheeks. "It is not kind to tease me, monsieur; not when I am already at such a horrible disadvantage."

"If you are at a disadvantage, sprite, it must be for the first time in our acquaintance," he stated drily.

That was far from the truth, Genevieve reflected, and Dominic had to be well aware of it, but the remark was clearly intended to restore to her a modicum of dignity, so she made no attempt to disagree with him. "At all events, I only wanted to let you know that we would be moving to the plantation sooner than I had thought."

He nodded. "I shall be taking *Danseuse* to the anchorage with the rest of the fleet for repairs and refitting before we make our next voyage. You shall act as spy in the enemy camp for me. Keep me informed of your father's movements, of any possibility that someone might develop an inconvenient interest in the swamp."

"When are you sailing again?"

"Soon," said he, uninformatively.

"Where to?"

"That is no concern of yours," he replied dismissively, then changed the subject. "You are not to be frightened of Angelique. Voodoo magic cannot harm you, and I will deal with her myself."

Genevieve shuddered. "Hatred is a very powerful force. I know I should not believe in the magic, but *they* do. And if

180

you believe strongly enough in something, you can make anything happen."

"Now, you are talking nonsense," he said firmly. "And to prove it to you, I want you to come to the house tomorrow night."

Genevieve paled. "I don't think I can, Dominic."

"Yes, you can. Angelique will not be there, but you will see how silly it is to be afraid."

"You said she would not be there before," Genevieve reminded him. "But she was."

Dominic looked rueful. "Yes, I know. It did not strike me as important enough to worry about, and it does not now. But I give you my word that she will not be there tomorrow."

"Will you tell her what I saw and heard?" she asked hesitantly.

Dominic shook his head. "No, I will do you the favor of keeping that piece of interference between ourselves. It would hardly endear you further to Angelique, and on that score I am afraid she would have my support."

"I do not think I wish to talk about it anymore," Genevieve declared, getting up. "You have made your point quite clearly several times."

"Very well, we will say no more about it. But if you ever do anything like that again, Genevieve, and I get to hear about it, you had better put a great deal of distance between you and me."

"You made your point," she repeated wearily, pressing her fingers to her now aching temples. "I must go home. Everyone will have woken after siesta, and I must try to slip in undetected."

Dominic frowned. She looked so pale and wan, so drained of her usual energy and bubbling enthusiasm. "Stay here. I will fetch my carriage and convey you home myself. At least you will be spared the walk, and if I create a diversion at the front door, you will be able to slip in through the side."

She smiled gratefully. He had never offered to help her in

181

her deception before, and she knew that was because he believed that she was doing only what she wished to do, and therefore must arrange matters for herself and shoulder her own risks. It was the premise on which he based his own life after all and not one with which Genevieve would ordinarily argue. But the light kiss he dropped on her brow before leaving the office was most comforting, just as was her certainty that the harshness of his initial reaction to her tale had stemmed from concern rather than simple anger.

# *Chapter 11*

Angelique read Dominic's brief note with hopelessness and fury. She was to arrange to spend tonight elsewhere, leaving the house before nine-thirty. Tomorrow, he would do himself the honor of calling upon her at noon, since he felt it was time for a further discussion of their present arrangements. The black-inked words danced before her eyes. Further discussion could only mean one thing: termination of their agreement. And he was intending to spend the night here with that scrawny creature before delivering the blow to Angelique.

What did she have that Angelique lacked? The girl paced the parlor, little white teeth tearing at her fingernails with nervous violence. If only she could contrive to use the powder from the bocor. It was to be sprinkled in front of the intended victim who must walk upon it, disturbing the prearranged design. This would bring *l'envoi d'un mort* to plague the creature who would surely die within the month. But how was she to sprinkle the powder if she was not to be in the house when the creature came? She could scatter it by the bed, but then Dominic might walk upon it also, and it would defeat the purpose if harm were to befall him. Perhaps she could defy the edict, pretend that she had not received the message so she would still be here when they arrived. But

Silas had delivered the paper himself. Dominic would never believe that she had failed to receive it.

How long would she need to be alone with the creature? Just a minute or two. If Dominic could somehow be delayed for half an hour, the girl would come first, as sometimes happened. She would go straight upstairs, walk through the bocor's powder that Angelique would sprinkle just outside the bedroom doorway. Then Angelique could sweep it up, and no one would be any the wiser. She could leave the house before Dominic arrived, and tomorrow she would be sweet and understanding and agree to everything he said, and wait for the girl to be put out of the way by the sorcerer's magic. Dominic would come back to her, then.

It was a pleasing plan, but how to delay Dominic? She could send him a message, imploring him to meet her at nine-thirty at the Absinthe House. If she sounded desperate enough, hinting vaguely at some dreadful trouble, he would not fail her. He would wait for perhaps half an hour, and then, when she did not make the appointment, he would come to Rampart Street. Angelique, in obedience to his orders would not be here, of course, and she would find an excuse to satisfy him about the broken appointment the next day.

With decision came exultation, and she sat down to compose her missive, smudging the ink with a little water from the flower vase to give the appearance of tearstains. She would not send it until early evening, so Dominic would not have the opportunity to seek her out before nine-thirty. Of course, if he was not dining at home, then he would not receive the message. But she could not make provision for every eventuality. She must trust to luck.

And luck was with Angelique. Dominic received the message, brought by the little maidservant, as he was dressing for dinner. The tumbled words seemed to shriek distress from the smudged paper, and there was no question of his not making the rendezvous. Genevieve would be quite comfortable in the house until he arrived, and since Angelique would be with him, she would not be bothering Genevieve. After dinner, he strolled to the Absinthe House on Bourbon Street. It was a favorite haunt for ladies of shadowy respectability and their protectors, and much frequented by young Creole bloods. Many an evening ended with the challenge that would lead to a dawn meeting in St. Anthony's Garden, and the clash of steel upon steel.

On Rampart Street, Angelique tried to control her impatience, her eyes on the ormolu clock, one of the elaborate *garnitures de cheminée* gifted by Dominic in one of his more indulgent moods. It was fifteen minutes before ten o'clock, and the creature still had not arrived. The powder was sprinkled in the doorway of the bedchamber, but it must be removed before Dominic arrived. How long would he wait for her at the Absinthe House? Was he on foot or on horseback? If the latter, he would reach Rampart Street in ten minutes at the most. Oh, where *was* the creature?

Genevieve hurried up St. Philip Street. It had been impossible to get away from the *salle de compagnie* this evening. Victor had decided to spend the evening at home and had demanded his younger daughter's opposition at the chess board. She was the only person he would play with, outside of his club cronies and, when he demanded a game, could not be denied. Hélène and Elise had been chattering ceaselessly about wedding matters, and Nicolas had sat moodily in an armchair before the empty grate, staring into his brandy goblet. When he had suggested that he would go out and visit some friends, his uncle had told him that they were spending a family evening together and, for once, he could spend time at home. Since Victor, himself, rarely indulged in the pleasures of his own hearth, Nicolas could hardly be blamed for sulking at this hypocritical edict, but his gloom had done little to lighten the heaviness of this family occasion. Genevieve, knowing that he would insist on the usual best-of-three games, had contrived to lose the first two. She was as good a player as her father, and the deception had not been easy. But several inadequately suppressed sighs, fingers pressed to her temples, the occasional weak smile, all led him to demand what the matter was. A faint, brave denial was followed by a mistake that only a tyro would make. He was glad to bring the game to a close, telling her that she needed an early night. All this gadding about during the *saison des visites* was clearly taking its toll, and the sooner they removed to the country the better.

Genevieve had made her obedient way to her chamber, and soon after, had heard the front door close on Victor, off to his club, and then on an exuberant, released Nicolas. Hélène and Elise continued with their chat, and Genevieve made her escape down the gallery stairs and through the side gate.

The clock on the church of St. Louis was striking the hour as she rapped on the brass knocker of the Rampart Street house. The door was opened instantly by the little maidservant she had seen sometimes on her other visits. In general, she saw only Silas and Dominic, although the presence of others in the house was made manifest in the sounds of voices, footsteps, and doors opening and closing.

The child bobbed a curtsy as Genevieve went into the hall. "Monsieur is not here yet, mademoiselle."

"Oh." Genevieve looked around anxiously. Her skin was creeping as if centipedes were on the march up her spine. She did not want to be here at all, and most definitely not without Dominic. It didn't matter that there was no sign of Angelique; that malevolence, the intensity of her loathing was still real in Genevieve's mind and seemed to be embedded in the fabric of the house. She half turned back to the door that the maid had closed, intending to wait outside the house until Dominic came. But that was so silly. She could not allow her life to be ruled by superstition. Genevieve stalked up the stairs, her feet scuffing a line of white powder on the floor before the bedroom door, and went into the familiar, overly opulent chamber, lit only by the glow of the *veilleuse*.

She wandered over to the window, looking into the street for the comforting sight of Dominic, or even for Silas. She had absolute confidence in the monosyllabic Silas. If he was around, no possible harm would befall her. But the street remained empty. The bed was welcoming, though, and she pulled off the turban, shaking out her hair as it fell in a clean, fragrant cloud to her shoulders. The calico gown was tossed onto a chair, and she was about to remove her shift when a whispering sound from beyond the door set her scalp crawling. Her imagination, already brought to fever pitch by the gruesome events of the previous afternoon, now went berserk. She saw rats and slithery vipers mounting an evil guard at the door, conjured up by the venom of the mistress of the house. She saw robed and masked figures, knives in hand, the blood spurting from slashed throats while the drums beat and ashes made strange, circuitous patterns on the floor. A strange noise, half moan, half cry, escaped her lips as she flung wide the door in an unthinking need to confront whatever horror lay beyond.

"What are you doing?" She stared down at the kneeling figure of Angelique, a brush and pan in her hand. The enormous brown eyes gazed up at her, filled with that all-powerful hatred.

"You walked through it," Angelique said in tones of quiet satisfaction. "The pattern was disturbed."

"Through what?" The question seemed to stick in her throat as the slow certainty spread in her veins that she did not want to hear the answer.

"The bocor's powder," said Angelique, rising slowly to her feet, a triumphant glitter in her eyes. *"L'envoie d'un mort* will come to you."

"Messenger from the dead?" Chills rippled across her skin, loosened her gut, and she took a step backward into the room.

Genevieve's palpable fear emboldened Angelique. The quadroon followed her into the chamber. "He will bring you death," she whispered, "and you will join him in the shadows."

"No . . . no . . . You do not know what you are talking about." Genevieve shook her head, one hand pressing against her breast bone. "There is no such thing. I do not believe in your magic." But her voice shook even as she made her denial.

"You *must* believe," Angelique said in the same low voice where intensity throbbed. "You will see, thieving slut, when the messenger brings you the knowledge that you cannot escape."

"You dare call me that!" Anger for a moment superseded her terror, and Genevieve slapped the lovely face that gloated down at her.

Angelique bellowed with fury and struck back, one hand twining in the ash-blond cascade pouring down her enemy's back. And then they were both lost in a whirlwind of fury that transcended all sense of place, of decency, and of purpose. Genevieve knew only that she must not be defeated, because to be so would put her at the mercy of an evil that she could only just begin to grasp. Angelique could think only of bringing the creature to her knees, of driving her from the house. She forgot about Dominic as their hands grabbed, clawed and pulled until the tight, violent circle of hatred was shattered, and she found herself flung against the wall, her opponent torn from her grasp.

Dominic held Genevieve by the waist, her back to him so she could not see his face. But Angelique could, and what she saw brought a whimper of terror from her. "She hurt me," she moaned, her terror making the moan absolutely convincing. "Attacked . . ."

"Lying bitch!" Genevieve, still beyond reason, and completely oblivious of Dominic's hold, leaped for the cowering, hateful figure.

Dominic's arm tightened around her waist, an iron band that felt as if it would cut her in two. "You make one more move toward her, say one more word, and so help me, you will rue it to your dying day!"

It was too much for Genevieve; that he should talk to her in that way, in front of that woman who had threatened to kill her! And he had broken his word. Twisting in his arm, she turned on him with updrawn hand, her outrage and horror blazing in the tawny eyes. Dominic caught her wrist in a numbing grip the instant before her nails made contact with his cheek. Jerking her arm backward, he bent it up behind her back, bringing her body up hard against his. Her breasts beneath the thin shift were flattened against his chest, and as she writhed in his hold, the muscles in her trapped arm and shoulder screeched in agonized protest.

"Do not force me to do something we shall both regret, Genevieve." The words, intense and urgent, were murmured against the rosewater fragrance of her tumbled hair, and slowly, through the mists of unreason, came the realization that it had been more of a request than a threat. She could feel the stillness in the hard, male body pressed against her own, the stillness of control, and gradually she absorbed that stillness herself, and her body became quiescent, her breathing quiet. Then, and only then, did his grip slacken. He put her from him, giving her a little push in the direction of the bed. "Sit down and don't move."

Angelique had watched the way Dominic had subdued the creature, and her eyes were wide with amazed gratification, her tongue running over her lips. Dominic had come to Angelique's defense; he had told the creature to leave her alone. For one wonderful moment, Angelique had thought he was going to beat the usurper who had dared to attack her. Maybe he would if Angelique made much of her injuries. She whimpered again, rubbing her arms gingerly, touching her breasts with a careful, delicate finger, as if they were hurt. Then she saw his eyes—a cold azure fury—and she knew she was lost.

"Out!" Taking her arm, he pushed her through the door. "Don't let me ever lay eyes on you again. Silas!"

"Monsieur?" Silas appeared from the shadows immediately. He had clearly not missed a minute of the scene just played out.

"Get rid of her." Dominic almost hurled the petrified, weeping Angelique into the sailor's arms. "I want her out of this house in the next five minutes. She can collect any possessions tomorrow afternoon, under your supervision."

"Yes, monsieur," said Silas stolidly, propelling his wailing, protesting charge down the stairs in front of him.

Dominic turned back to the room where Genevieve still sat upon the bed. The door closed firmly behind him, and he came to stand, towering over her. "I have never in my life witnessed such a disgusting, disgraceful spectacle! And, believe me, I have seen some sights. How *dared* you behave like some alley cat, entering a physical battle with that whore! You are a Creole, a Latour, for godsake!"

Genevieve's jaw dropped. Whatever she had been expecting it was not this—the conventional outrage of a Creole gentleman at a piece of scandalous behavior by a supposed lady of his own class.

"What did you expect me to do?" she said. "Why should I differentiate between myself and your mistress? We both do the same things with the same man in the same bed in the same house. At your wish, I might add. You do not appear to differentiate between us."

"Do not be absurd," Dominic said, momentarily at a loss for a good retort.

"*You* are being absurd," Genevieve maintained sturdily. "For the privateer who takes such a pride in his own lack of scruple, his own defiance of all convention, you are being more than a little hypocritical, it seems to me, with this nicety of feeling."

"What I do, and what you do, Mademoiselle Genevieve, are two quite different matters," Dominic stated, hanging onto his temper by a thread.

"Then why did you insist that I come to this house?" she challenged him. "It is the house of a kept whore. Why should I behave any differently?"

Dominic Delacroix was, for once, silenced. He had not thought beyond the fact that the house was the most convenient rendezvous. He had certainly not thought that Angelique could possibly object to what he chose to do on his own property, so long as she did not suffer materially. And it had not occurred to him that his chosen rendezvous would inform Genevieve's perception of herself and what took place between them. He knew, for all her definitely questionable behavior, she was still a Creole lady, daughter of an old, aristocratic family, one who would soon be provided with a husband and the children who would inevitably bless the union.

Genevieve did not hesitate to press her advantage. "You broke your word," she accused quietly.

Dominic sighed. "Not intentionally, Genevieve. It seems that Angelique planned to ensure that she was alone in the house with you—"

"Yes, so that she could use her voodoo magic that will bring the messenger from the dead to me." Genevieve interrupted, shuddering as she remembered the terror that had preceded her attack on the quadroon.

Dominic frowned. "Voodoo magic cannot harm you, Genevieve."

"That is easy for you to say," she fired. "You did not walk through the sorcerer's powder and disturb the pattern."

"What are you talking about?" Impatiently, he walked over to the table where glasses and wine stood on a silver tray. "You need a little fortification, I think."

Genevieve took the glass of champagne and sipped before telling him exactly what had transpired between herself and

Angelique until he had made his own dramatic entrance. "You cannot blame me for what I did," she finished, the tawny eyes challenging him.

"I most certainly can," he responded, glad to revert to one area in which he was quite confident that he was right. "*You* do not behave like a street whore under any circumstances. And I do not wish to hear any further nonsense about my treating you in the way I treated Angelique, simply because we have been using this house. You are a Creole damsel whose lost maidenhood will be a secret between the two of us. At some point soon, you will marry and take your place in this society, and this youthful indiscretion will provide you with a hopefully rich memory for the future."

Genevieve shook her head. "No, you are quite wrong."

"You are making me angry again," he said softly. "I have restrained myself with considerable effort, so far. But I cannot promise to continue doing so. I am right because that is the way it must be."

"You do not understand!" Genevieve sprang from the bed. "If this makes you angry, then I am sorry for it, but I cannot help it. Do you think that I have not changed since we met, since . . ." Her hand waved expressively around the room. "Since all this happened? How could I still be the Creole maid preparing for marriage? I was never really suited for the part, anyway, and now it is quite impossible."

Dominic closed his eyes momentarily, marshaling his forces. "You will see that I am right," he said eventually. "This little interlude in your life will soon be over, and you will return to your old life, more mature, certainly, more experienced, much improved, in fact. But you *will* return."

Genevieve had gone even paler than the evening's experiences had left her. "Why will it soon be over?" She tried to sound merely curious, to keep the quaver of anxiety from her voice.

"Because I shall be at sea again, soon. I told you yesterday," he said evenly. "And when . . . if . . . I come back, there will be a lot of water under the bridge, sprite. You will be betrothed, or surrounded by suitors at the very least . . ."

"Take me with you," she asked abruptly. "What you describe would be a living death for me. Let me sail with you. I will not be in the way or expect anything from you. I understand that you do not wish for ties; neither do I. But now that I have had the excitement and the experience of living outside the rules in this way, I cannot be satisfied without it. Why should it be denied me?" She clasped her hands together, her eyes shining as she made this impassioned plea.

She was quite impossible, he thought with a degree of resignation. Genevieve Latour was one of those people who refused to deviate from the path she had set for herself. If she wanted something, she went out and got it, and did not rest until she had done so. He recognized the quality, since he possessed it himself in generous quantity. He also admired it, since, in this world, there were many worthwhile things that could not be done without an indomitable will. However, on this occasion, Mademoiselle Genevieve wanted the impossible, and *his* will must prove dominant.

"You are a spoiled child, Genevieve, who has never learned to take 'no' for an answer. You persist in believing that simply wanting something is sufficient reason for receiving it. I will most certainly not take you with me. I have never heard such a ridiculous idea."

"It is not ridiculous. It might be so for an ordinary woman, but I am not—"

"No," he interrupted drily. "You are not at all ordinary, I grant you that. But you are naive and ingenuous, and you do not know what you are suggesting. Even if I were mad enough to countenance it, my men would be up in arms, and justifiably so. We are not going for a decorous little sail in the Gulf, my dear Genevieve."

"I did not imagine you were," she said, still refusing to give up. "I know about piracy and the British blockade. I know there will be danger. But I don't see why, if I am not concerned, you, and particularly your crew, should be."

She did not know about gunrunning to supply a revolution, Dominic thought grimly. He sighed and brought the discussion to an abrupt, definitive end. "Put your clothes on. It's time you went home."

"I do not usually go home until dawn," she said, sitting on the bed again with a firm thump, wriggling her bare toes and tossing back her hair. "And I think I am owed some compensation for what I have endured this evening. Particularly when you promised that everything would be all right."

He looked at her closely. He could read only a certain calculated mischief in her expression, a sensual darkening of those tiger's eyes. It was as if she had decided to drop the controversial discussion as if it had never been started. Somehow, such willing compliance made him distinctly uneasy, but it was what he had demanded, after all. It would hardly be logical to question it. And besides, the invitation she was extending, as she fell back upon the bed, moving her body with lascivious languor, was utterly irresistible.

*Chapter 12*

Dominic was right to feel uneasy about Genevieve's seemingly ready compliance in the matter of his next voyage. However, she gave him no reason to persist in his uneasiness over the next few weeks, and he allowed himself to relax. The Latour household removed to Trianon, the plantation on Lake Borgne, and the privateer and his fleet set themselves up in the secluded anchorage in the swamp. The air rang with the sound of hammers and saws, was redolent with the smells of varnish and paint as the ships were scraped, repaired and refitted.

Genevieve was a frequent visitor, paddling a canoe through the twisted mangroves, keeping a wary eye out for alligators, and plucking tree crabs from her skirts when they jumped from the overhanging branches as the canoe glided beneath. It was not a journey she enjoyed particularly, but, as she had said prosaically to the privateer, when there was only the one means at one's disposal to achieve one's end, then one had better get on with it. Dominic had simply smiled in agreement, and smoked his cigar, looking out over the smooth waters of the bayou. It was a smile he had often in her company, Genevieve had noticed, and it was rather a nice smile, one that she did not remember seeing often in the early days of their relationship.

Silas remarked on it, too, and he was not the only member of the crew to do so. But the girl seemed to know how to keep herself to herself, and never intruded on the ship's business, although they had all become accustomed to the presence of the figure in a print gown, generally barefoot, the silvery-gold hair tied back with a ribbon. She behaved impeccably—there were no more incidents of the rigging-climbing variety—and monsieur's mood was so equable, barely disturbed by the inevitable irritations and delays of refitting, that her presence was generally considered to be all to the good.

It was a hot Saturday morning at the end of July. Genevieve was lying on her back on the deck, basking in the sun, her belly full of crayfish prepared by the ship's cook, her mouth still savoring the delicate fishy spiciness. As she waited for Dominic to suggest that they go below for a little privacy, she overheard the bosun and *La Danseuse*'s master discussing the all-important matter of acquiring a full complement of hands for the coming voyage.

"I'll go to the quay, monsieur," the bosun was saying. "Plenty of experienced men there, I reckon, who'd be more than glad to sign on with the promise of prize money."

"Try Latour's shipyard, also," Dominic said with a devilish gleam in his eye. "I fancy the idea of stealing his men as well as his land."

The bosun's appreciative laugh rumbled in the still air. "I'll try there tomorrow, monsieur. Bound to have some luck with what we can offer 'em."

Genevieve kept as still as she could, although her blood raced in her veins and her muscles twitched with excitement. She had been racking her brains for a way to achieve her object, had thought of stowing away on one of the other privateers of the fleet, which might have given her a better chance than an attempt to hide on Dominic's vessel. She would declare herself to the captain when they were well and truly on their way, and insist that he have her conveyed to

*Danseuse.* But she could see any number of potential hazards in that arrangement, like the ships all taking a different course from each other, so that she might find herself half an ocean away from Dominic and *Danseuse.* But surely she could produce a disguise that would fool the bosun. He would never see the monsieur's lady companion in a grubby boy in britches, eager to sail with the privateer— not if he wasn't looking for such a thing. And Dominic would have no interest in examining his new crew, not unless one of them was unfortunate enough to draw the master's attention with some error. She had realized that he considered such matters to be the bosun's responsibility. She had also in the last weeks picked up enough technical information about sailing to answer questions knowledgeably. So long as she could keep her hair out of sight and stayed in the background as much as was feasible, it ought to be possible to keep her identity a secret for the few days it would take until they were too far into the Gulf to turn back.

Something nudged her hip. "Wake up, lazy bones. We are going to swim." Dominic's voice, light and amused, drifted down to her, causing her to start guiltily as his foot pressed again into her hip. "You must have been having some very wicked thoughts," he said consideringly. "Judging by your expression."

"Very wicked," she agreed, gathering her wits about her and sitting up on the warm deck. "But they did not include swimming."

"Later," he promised, with the deep smile that made the corners of his eyes crinkle and infused her limbs with a liquid weakness. "Into the dinghy with you, now."

Genevieve clambered over the side of *Danseuse,* springing nimbly into the captain's boat. Dominic followed, took the oars and pulled away, across the bayou and into a narrow, deserted creek. "When will you leave?" Genevieve asked carelessly, trailing a hand through the water, making an ineffectual grab at the bright silver flash of a mullet leaping high out of the water, twisting in the air before falling back beneath the surface again.

Dominic looked at her sharply. He had been waiting for the opportune moment to prepare her for his impending departure, but had been uncertain how she would receive the news. In fact, reluctant though he was to admit it, he was not looking forward to leaving her, and this made the disclosure even more difficult to make. "Tuesday," he said, deciding that simplicity was the best policy.

Tuesday! How on earth was she to find an unimpeachable excuse for her absence by then? At least, Victor was not at Trianon, and Elise was safely ensconced in Villafranca with her new husband, so she would only have to convince Hélène with the deception. "How long do you expect to be gone?" Again, her voice was casual, her eyes closed against the sun, her body lying back in the thwart, apparently relaxed.

"I cannot say," he replied truthfully. "Two months, three, perhaps. It depends on many factors beyond my control."

It would have to be the Ursulines again, Genevieve decided. But this time, she would go on a long retreat to the convent school near the plantation, where she had received most of her education. It would cause no remark, now that Elise was married; Nicolas was in New Orleans with Latour; and Hélène occupied with the social round of the country in the summer. Genevieve's scholastic inclinations were implicitly tolerated if not actively encouraged, and she could say she was going for an indefinite stay to escape the dullness of the summer furnace. It was well known that Mother Thérèse would always welcome her whenever she wished to go, and for as long as she wished to stay.

"At least on the high seas, you will escape this heat," she murmured with carefully calculated wistfulness. "I shall melt and die of boredom."

There was not a trace of hostility in her voice; even the envy carried a note of acceptance. Dominic shipped his oars

198

in the rowlocks and let the boat drift as he reached down and pulled her up against his knees. "I shall miss you, sprite," he said with complete honesty.

Kneeling up on the bottom of the boat, her elbows folded across his lap, she smiled up at him. "Let us not talk of sad things. We have a few days, yet."

It was amazing how mature she had become, Dominic reflected, bending to taste the sweetness of her mouth with a nectar-sipping tongue, feeling the softness of her breasts against his knees, reveling in the promise of her body under the sun. Somewhere, there was a very lucky Creole gentleman waiting in the wings, as yet unaware of exactly how lucky he was going to be.

"Monsieur?"

The bosun turned at the hissed summons. A grimy lad in a pair of britches far too large for him, held up at the waist by a thick belt, and a jerkin that nearly drowned him, was dancing nervously in the shadows of a low building in Monsieur Latour's shipyard. "What is it, lad?" he demanded, obeying the summons of an imperatively beckoning finger.

"Can I sign on, monsieur?" the lad whispered, looking anxiously around. "I've been round ships all my life."

"What are you frightened of, boy?" The bosun looked around, but could see nothing in the busy shipyard scene to justify the lad's very clear nervousness.

"Pa," the boy said. "He'll have my hide if he hears me. Won't let me go, but I got to, monsieur." A pair of golden eyes glowed in the boy's dirty face as he begged with a powerful passion. "I want to go to sea . . . always have, but Pa says I gotta stay here and earn my keep. Please, monsieur, let me sign on."

The bosun thought. He knew well what it was like when the sea bug bit; all the best sailors had it, and they'd all gone to sea no older than this lad, fleeing family and the heaviness of the land for the freedom of wind and waves. If the lad was truly bitten, then he'd provide years of loyal, experienced service once he was trained. Slowly, he nodded. "Be on the wharf with the others, Tuesday night, then," he said. "You'll be picked up by cutter and taken to *Danseuse*. Bring your kit."

"Aye, monsieur." The lady's eyes shone radiantly. "You'll not regret it, monsieur."

"It's to be hoped *you* don't," the bosun said with a short nod. "There's no room on a Delacroix vessel for the faint-hearted or the insubordinate. But if you keep a clear head, do as you're told, and move fast, you'll be all right." He strode off, whistling, leaving Genevieve to melt into the shadows and scamper back through the trees to change out of her borrowed clothes behind a bush. She then sauntered innocently back to the house.

Hélène was sitting in a hammock on the gracious, pillared porch, a glass of lemonade in her hand, a book opened on her taffeta lap. Her eyes, however, were not on the print, but were fixed on the middle distance. She was missing Elise. Fond though she was of Genevieve, the girl was no substitute for her elder sister who shared Hélène's interest in matters of domestic and social moment. Genevieve barely noticed what she wore, absented herself whenever possible from the social round, and had no interest in gossip. If Genevieve were not at Trianon, requiring the presence of her stepmother as chaperone and guardian, Hélène could pay an extended visit to Elise at Villafranca. Victor would not object since his business was keeping him in New Orleans at the moment.

"Good afternoon, Hélène." The light voice of the subject of her thoughts shocked Hélène out of her reverie. Genevieve called to her from across the lush expanse of lawn that was watered night and morning by an army of little boys and girls with watering cans.

"You should not walk in this heat, *chère,*" Hélène

200

admonished weakly. "You will perspire."

Genevieve laughed and ran up the porch steps. "It is too late to prevent that, I fear. After a mere three steps, one resembles a wet rag." She mopped her brow with a lacy handkerchief and sank into a low rocking chair, reaching for the lemonade pitcher. "I would like to visit the convent school for a few weeks, Hélène. Would you mind very much if I left you alone?"

The suggestion fitted so perfectly into Hélène's earlier musings that she started guiltily. It was as if Genevieve had been a party to the thoughts that wished her away from Trianon. "Why, no, *chère,* if that is what you want," she said. "But we must ask your papa for his permission."

Genevieve pulled a distinctly disrespectful face. "I would like to leave on Tuesday morning. Even if I send a message to New Orleans today, I cannot be sure of receiving his response by then."

"But you cannot leave without it," Hélène said with calm certainty.

"I will send the message immediately." Genevieve rose with an energy that made her stepmother feel hot just by contemplating it. "If he has not responded by Tuesday, I shall go anyway. If I am to come back, then you can send for me." She smiled with bland reassurance and went into the relative cool of the high-ceilinged house. The chances of her father's refusing his permission were so remote that she felt quite confident in making that statement to Hélène. And, besides, if her deception were discovered, it would not really matter in the scheme of things. If she could not return to Latour life after her voyage with the privateer, so much the better. Whatever Dominic might say, she knew with absolute certainty that, since she had met him, she had moved an infinity away from the type of woman who could have contemplated the conventional life planned for her. Before, she had been reluctant but resigned, never having been offered an alternative but a nunnery. But things were very different now.

Whatever Dominic might say. Her briskly confident step faltered as she reached the *secretaire*. She had not thought properly of what he would say when he discovered the identity of one of his new crew. That omission, of course, was entirely typical. She sat down, drew a sheet of paper toward her and picked up a pen. Dominic had said she needed to learn to stop and think before following her nose into trouble. Well, she had stopped and was thinking now. It did not seem to affect her decision in the least. The worst he could do was to put her ashore in some inhospitable land, as he had threatened to do before. She would just have to trust to her powers of persuasion. Tapping her pen against her teeth, she felt for the right words with which to address her father, then, satisfied with the composition, wrote rapidly for a few minutes.

The message was given into the hands of a servant, with instructions to make all speed to Monsieur Latour in the city, and to wait for an answer, if he was permitted to do so. Just as he was about to leave, however, Hélène appeared with her own missive. "I thought to visit Elise, if you are to be away," she said to Genevieve. "I do not think your father will object, do you?"

"I cannot imagine why he should," Genevieve responded. "But that is not to say that he will not." Her eyes twinkled mischievously as Hélène tried to look reproving. "It would be best to give the impression that you considered the visit to be purely duty rather than pleasure," she advised solemnly.

"Yes, I have done so," said Hélène, quite failing to see why her matter-of-fact agreement should send her stepdaughter into gales of laughter.

"Poor Hélène." Genevieve squeezed the other woman's arm. "It must be very difficult to be properly dutiful. I think you manage quite admirably."

On the Monday evening, Genevieve paddled her canoe to the bayou. There was an air of expectancy about the men that evening. Even Dominic's usual deep composure contained another element, a tautness as if he was preparing himself, as if the time for holiday idleness was past and the serious business of the world called. Genevieve felt herself considered to be a part of that holiday idleness, felt the absence of his full attention even when they rowed to the little beach on the creek, where he lit a fire and roasted a chicken on a spit. They drank rich, full Spanish wine, and he made a strawberry patch of her body as she lay on the rug beneath the full moon, planting the round red berries where no berries should grow. He plucked the succulent fruit from her with his lips, licking the juice from her skin until she moaned, writhing beneath the questing tongue and the sharp nibbling caress of his teeth.

And at dawn, she left him, knowing that he was ready for her to leave, that he had turned his mind to the exciting realities of work. His farewell kiss was sweet and passionate, and it contained a lingering regret at their parting, but it was a regret that Genevieve knew would be subsumed under the needs and demands of the ship's master, once she was out of sight. Indeed, as she turned to look over her shoulder at him, seeing him standing at the rail of *Danseuse,* the breeze ruffling the nut-brown hair, the turquoise eyes already focused, it seemed, on some distant shore, she felt a sharp pang of misgiving. Perhaps she had no right to intrude on the privateer's private world of danger and camaraderie, to trespass in the personal kingdom where entry had been forbidden her. But it was too late, now, for doubts. She had made up her mind to brave the dangers of Dominic Delacroix's anger, and nothing could be worse than remaining behind in the sweltering monotony of Trianon.

The following evening, Genevieve was one of a number of men and boys waiting on the wharf at her father's shipyard. They were all quiet, staring across the lake for the launch that would take them to the ship. Their kit lay at their feet in bundles and chests. Genevieve had only a cloth-wrapped bundle containing clean linen and a comb. Beneath the knitted cap that was pulled low over her face, her hair was short and neatly cut. Amelie, with great reluctance, had shorn the luxuriant mass, placing a bowl over Genevieve's head and cutting evenly around it. The resulting haircut was hardly a thing of beauty, but it was tidy and ensured that there was no danger of premature discovery from that most distinctive feature, at least. She wore the same overly large garments that she had worn when she met with the bosun, again acquired through the good offices of Amelie. The generous cut ensured that the body beneath remained shapeless and hidden. A few smears of mud and dust on her nose and forehead completed a disguise which, while it might not satisfy someone who was looking for her, would certainly pass muster in a situation where her presence was the last thing anyone would expect.

A low, excited rumble greeted the sight of the launch coming across the lake toward them, the voice of the coxswain calling the strokes carrying in the still evening air. Genevieve scrambled aboard with the others, taking up as little space as she could on the bottom of the cutter as she practiced the art of becoming utterly inconspicuous, the art on which the success of this venture depended.

*Danseuse* loomed white and graceful in the darkness, swinging gently at anchor on the far side of the lake. Genevieve knew that the fleet had left the bayou that afternoon because Dominic was not willing to risk the location of the safe anchorage with men who were as yet untried and who had not proved their loyalty. The rope ladder hung over the stern, bobbing well above Genevieve's head as she stood up with the others in the violently rocking launch. Dominic had always lifted her onto the bottom rung of that ladder. Now she must make the leap unaided. Unwilling to hang back until the last, when she would be noticeable, she plunged into the middle of the group of waiting seamen. As she leaped, a hand came under her backside, giving her a shove that was clearly intended to be helpful. Instead, the shock of that intimate contact brought a yelp to her lips. Just in time, she swallowed the sound and clambered up the ladder as fast as she could to avoid further assistance, tumbling over the rail to land on the familiar deck of *La Danseuse*. Except that it was no longer familiar. Now that her role on board the frigate was different, the surroundings seemed completely alien. She was seeing them through the eyes of a new recruit, a cabin boy who had never been to sea before, and Genevieve Latour, pampered, respected mistress of the vessel's master, was no more.

Her eyes went automatically to the quarterdeck. Dominic stood there, looking down at the new arrivals, the tip of his cigar glowing in the dark, one hand thrust deep into the pocket of his britches.

"Ship's master," a man muttered beside her. "The best that ever sailed these waters, they say. Should come back with some good prize money, I reckon."

Genevieve nodded, then suddenly dropped her eyes as the privateer's gaze seemed to linger on her, and he leaned over the rail. "You, there," he called. "Come over here." Her heart was in her throat and she looked around wildly, then saw to her relief that it was not she who had been addressed. A man behind her ran up to the quarterdeck, pulling on his forelock. "Yes, monsieur?"

Dominic was not ill satisfied with his cursory examination of the newcomers. There was an air of expectancy, an alertness about them that boded well. There was no room on *Danseuse* for the unwilling, the pressed men who would cower under fire and hold back from the ultimate effort. They would only fail in that way, once, certainly, but the personal consequences of their failure were bad for morale. He knew from the bosun that these newcomers were all old hands, experienced seamen who knew what they were getting into, except for one—a young cabin boy whose enthusiasm had taken the bosun's fancy. Dominic picked

205

him out easily enough. A scrawny, undernourished lad. He smiled to himself. A week would make or break him. The bosun believed in rough justice and the regular application of a rope's end in the early days of training.

Genevieve was to have many strange experiences in the next year, but none as strange or as frightening as those she experienced during the next few days. She lost count of the number of times she swallowed her tears and bitterly regretted the impulse that had hurled her into this dreadful, uncomfortable, uncaring adventure. She need not have worried about being inconspicuous; no one took the least bit of notice of her, except to cuff her when she was in the way, or bellow if the decks, which seemed to be her single responsibility, showed the slightest smudge on their pristine whiteness. She had no berth of her own, but was expected to curl up in a corner of the fetid between decks cabin, while the ribald talk went on around her, as the crew, in various states of undress, took what hours of rest were permitted them. She gradually became inured to the glimpses of male nakedness, although she spent most of the time in the cabin with her eyes tight shut, but visits to the heads were sheer torment. She would creep out in the middle of the night, praying that no one else would be there, since privacy was almost nonexistent. Why had this obvious problem not entered her head when she had planned this ridiculous, lunatic journey? One day, she *would* learn to stop and think before following her nose.

She was constantly aware of Dominic, although convinced that he barely noticed the presence of an insignificant cabin boy. Once, when she had swabbed the deck for the sixth time since the early dawn, cold, gray, scummy water slopping around her ankles, he had walked straight across the still damp, freshly cleaned area, leaving muddy footprints, and she had had to start anew before the bosun saw it. There were no excuses, she knew from bitter experience. The temptation to hurl the bucket of scummy water at the master's immaculate, oblivious, white-shirted back had been almost overpowering. But they were not yet far enough into the Gulf for her to declare herself. And after what she had already gone through, Genevieve was determined that Dominic was not going to be able to put her ashore.

It was on their third day into the Gulf that matters reached a head, and the cabin boy finally had to throw in the towel. It was a hot, lazy afternoon, the wind a mere whisper so that the fleet drifted idly on the blue waters, where schools of dolphins played around them, showing off to the amused sailors who leaned over the rail, laughing and applauding at the antics of the graceful creatures. Genevieve sat in the spot on the deck that she had adopted for her own. It was against the hatch, out of the sun, so not popular with anyone else, and relatively secluded, which also made it unpopular with her gregarious fellow travelers.

"Hey, lad!" A voice boomed into her ear. "Come over here. Time for your initiation, we reckon."

She looked up into a circle of grinning, bronzed faces, and realized with a sinking heart that they were up to no good. Boredom played havoc with idle hands and bred mischief that was clearly intended for the shy, scrawny little cabin boy.

"Fancy a swim, then?" A hand, its back masked in black curling hair, caught her beneath one arm and yanked her upright. "In with the porpoises."

"No." Terrified, she shook her head. They could not be intending to throw her overboard, surely! But someone swung her into the air, and the next minute she found herself suspended over the blue ocean far beneath. She heard her scream and the roar of laughter that greeted it, then, miraculously they had returned her to the deck.

Dominic, watching from the quarterdeck, smiled and shrugged, turning back to the helmsman. The bosun was there if the horseplay got out of hand, and there wasn't a man on this ship, including its master, who hadn't endured his own initiation.

"If you don't want to swim for us, lad, then you'll have to dance," someone announced. A cutlass shivered into the deck at her feet, and she jumped back with another scream. There was another burst of laughter. "Let's have his clothes off," someone suggested. "He can't dance properly in those. They're too big for him, anyway."

Genevieve ran, through the grinning circle, taking them momentarily by surprise so that she managed to evade the grabbing hands. Then they were after her, all laughing, all knowing that the pursuit could be as leisurely as they pleased; there was nowhere the lad could run to on this little vessel becalmed in the middle of the Gulf of Mexico. But, to their amazement, the boy hurled himself at the ladder leading to the quarterdeck. The bosun bellowed at him. No member of the crew went up there unless invited, or sent. Swinging his rope's end, he went up after the truant.

Dominic spun round from the wheel at the sounds of commotion, an ominous frown drawing the fly-away eyebrows together, darkening the turquoise eyes so that the bosun began to apologize even as he lunged for the fleeing figure of the cabin boy.

"Dominic, don't let them!" The unmistakable voice of Genevieve Latour spilled from the lips of his cabin boy, and the diminutive figure in its grotesque garments shot behind him, cowering against the rail, seeking the protection of his back.

The bosun stopped dead, his mouth falling open, the rope twitching in his hand. He knew that voice as well as did *Danseuse*'s master. The laughing group of seamen fell silent, crowding round the bottom of the ladder leading to the quarterdeck. As one body, they moved back into the waist of the ship so that they could look up at the drama being played on the deck above.

That eerie, motionless quiet settled on the ship as everyone waited for Monsieur Delacroix to make a move. Then, quite slowly, indolently almost, he reached behind him, his fingers curling in the collar of Genevieve's shirt, and yanked the shrinking figure out in front of him.

"Well, well," said the privateer thoughtfully, regarding his prize with a degree of interest. "It seems that you never learn, do you?" His hand tightened in her shirt collar and jerked upward, forcing Genevieve onto her toes. She swallowed convulsively and began to wish that they had dropped her overboard with the gamboling dolphins. The waiting silence stretched thinly into infinity, and nothing existed but the mingled blues of a glinting azure gaze, of a cloudless sky, and a quiet sea.

"If I had a grain of common sense, I would hand you over to them and turn a blind eye." Dominic spoke at last, the soft voice nevertheless grating in the stillness. "Can you give me one good reason why I should not?" Another jerk on her collar punctuated the question.

Genevieve forced herself to meet his eyes, although her throat had closed so that no words would come forth. But the tawny eyes carried the bold conviction that had brought her to this situation in the first place, and that had enabled her to endure the last few days. It was that that saved her. Had she begged, wept, offered excuse, given way to the fear that she could not hide, the privateer, in his fury, would have left her to fend for herself.

He looked at her for a long moment, then inclined his head. "Very well, you will take your chance with me." He looked past her at the bosun, who still stood, but awkwardly now, quite unsure how he was implicated in this inconceivable muddle, but knowing that in some way, he was responsible. "You will have to manage without a cabin boy, it would seem, bosun. Maybe, in the future, you would examine the credentials of applicants a little more thoroughly." Monsieur's smile was silken, the tone pleasant as he made the request, but the bosun was not deceived. He muttered something inaudible and disappeared down the ladder.

"March!" Dominic snapped suddenly, seizing her belt and pushing Genevieve in front of him, still holding her shirt with his other hand so that her heels barely brushed the deck. She scrambled down the ladder as best she could, enduring the fascinated stares of those hands who did not know who she was, as well as those who did, as she was propelled in this undignified manner across the main deck and down the companionway.

Silas, busily polishing the rich cherry wood of the table in the master's cabin, looked up, startled, as the door crashed open. He had barely noticed the novice cabin boy in the last few days. Now he stared at the tiny figure in monsieur's hands, and recognition dawned gradually. He pursed his lips in a soundless whistle.

"Get out of here, Silas," Dominic ordered curtly.

"Yes, monsieur." The sailor picked up his cloths and polish and left the cabin, closing the door quietly on whatever was about to happen within.

# Chapter 13

In the silence that followed the click of the door, Dominic released his grip on Genevieve and strolled across the cabin to the chart table beneath the porthole. He bent over it for long minutes, making rapid calculations on a piece of paper, seemingly so absorbed in his task that he was oblivious of the still figure, standing where he had left her in the middle of the cabin, in front of his desk.

Genevieve felt excruciatingly awkward and uncomfortable, ignored in this way, yet she seemed to have no choice but to remain where she was. Even walking over to a chair struck her as impossible, although why it should be so, she had no idea. So she just stood and stared at the paneling on the bulwark, as if seeking the answers to the universe in the rich patina.

"So," Dominic said suddenly, straightening up from the chart table. "You have decided to take up piracy, I understand." His tone was blandly conversational as he walked over to the desk and sat down behind it, surveying her with mild curiosity. Genevieve was not deceived, however, and maintained a prudent silence. Dominic linked his hands behind his head, leaning back in his chair, one leg crossed over the other. The sun fingered the rich carpet and the deep patina of the wood. The ordinary sounds of shipboard life filtered under the door, through the open window, but they seemed to have no relevance in this locked circle of menace that contained only the two of them.

"There seems one major snag to this plan of yours," Dominic continued in the same bland, conversational accents. *"La Danseuse* carries no dead weight." He smiled politely, and Genevieve felt the hairs on the nape of her neck lift. She had imagined this scene many times, had expected to be a little scared, defensive, placatory, but she had never imagined the scene where there seemed to be nothing for her to say, nothing for her to do except stand like a rabbit facing the fox, waiting for the horror that she knew was waiting in the wings until Dominic, the orchestrator, chose to usher it on stage.

"So, what can you do to pull your weight?" he inquired, with that same polite smile. "You appear to find the duties of a cabin boy a little hazardous and not entirely to your liking." The fly-away eyebrows lifted. "And I really cannot be interrupted every few minutes because you need rescuing. No, obviously you are not cut out for that role." The turquoise gaze became pensive. "Can you perhaps cook?"

Genevieve shook her head and said stiffly, "I have never tried."

"No, of course you have not," he concurred equably. "Those lily white, Creole hands would not have been expected—"

"They have been scrubbing decks for the last three days," Genevieve interrupted, unable to bear the cool contempt in his voice and eyes. "If you wish me to cook, I will learn."

Dominic shook his head. "I hardly think it would be fair to subject the crew to the experiments of a tyro, just to give you something to do." He glanced around the orderly, sparkling cabin. "I suppose you could keep my possessions in order. Do you sew?"

Genevieve, feeling like a worm on the end of a hook, shook her head in wordless denial.

"No, I suppose you do not," he said. "Such gentle arts would have passed you by. Anyway ..." He shrugged nonchalantly. "Silas would certainly object to being usurped, and he has looked after me so well, for so long, that I am sure I could not become accustomed to a change—particularly one for the worse."

Genevieve thought longingly of the deep-blue sea outside, of the carefree dolphins, and the wheeling, shrieking sea birds diving amongst the spars. She prayed for the metamorphosis that would take her out of this cabin, away from the gem-hard disdain of the privateer, from the knowledge that he was only playing with her; that these apparently sincere questions were part of a devilish game as yet to be revealed. She thought of how it would feel to be out of this cloddish, unskilled, useless body, able to fly and leap freely among the elements where his power to hurt could not touch her.

"Of course, there is one thing that we both know you can do rather well," mused Dominic, closing his eyes with a sigh of apparent relaxation as he rocked back in his chair. "One comfort that you can provide that tends to be lacking on board a ship of war."

Genevieve felt sick, as the horror began to take shape and substance. A clock ticked, loud as the bells of St. Louis in the menacing quiet.

"I assume you would be willing to offer that comfort to those in need?" he said gently. "You would be kept very busy, and would most certainly earn your keep, so you would know that you had discharged your obligations." A kindly smile accompanied this last, and she fought for the words that would not take shape in the turmoil of fury and despair rending her.

With all the leisurely, purposeful menace of a leopard closing on his disabled prey, Dominic rose from behind the desk and came round to her. A hand plucked the knitted cap from her head. His eyebrows almost disappeared into his

213

scalp. "Dear me," he murmured. "Cropping your crowning glory, my dear Genevieve, has not added to your charms in the least." His nose twitched. "Neither does the reek of unwashed humanity and clothes stiff with dirt. You are probably crawling with vermin." To her eternal shame, his fingers moved with practiced skill through the dirt-darkened thatch of ash-blond hair, examining her scalp. "Surprisingly, you are not lousy," he said, brushing his hands together with a grimace of distaste. "But you will scrub yourself from head to toe with lye. I am not prepared to risk contagion for as long as I decide to keep your services to myself."

"Have you any idea how I have been living in the last three days?" Genevieve cried, this final outrage unblocking the damn. "In that filthy cabin with those filthy, lewd men, up to my knees in dirty water—"

"You did not enjoy it, then?" he interrupted. "Surely you did not enter into this deceitful little trespass without realizing that there would be aspects you might not enjoy?" The turquoise eyes filmed with mockery. "Or did you not, as usual, give a thought to the consequences, Mademoiselle Genevieve?"

There was no answer, she found; no answer to the cold scorn in the clipped tones, the knowing glint in his eyes; no answer at all to the absolute knowledge of her powerlessness to alter whatever course Dominic Delacroix had decided upon. And she had no one to blame but herself.

"Take off your clothes." The order shattered the dreadful expectant stillness.

Genevieve swallowed. Her lips moved in a pathetic attempt to form the words of protest, or of question, at least. "Why?" she managed in a croaking whisper.

"Because I tell you to," said the privateer deliberately. "And if you know what is good for you, mademoiselle, while you are aboard my ship, you will learn to respond to my instructions with instant, unthinking obedience."

214

She shook her head involuntarily, the faint stirrings of a spirit that could not be completely squashed infusing her defiance of a statement that she could not accept.

Dominic caught her chin, his fingers hurtful against her jawbone as he forced her face up to meet the unwavering hardness of his gaze. He spoke very softly and almost without expression. "Let me explain something to you. Silas is responsible for looking after those of my possessions that are necessary for my comfort. He keeps them in good order, clean, tidy and always available. And he will treat you in the same way, if I direct him to do so."

"I am not one of your possessions," Genevieve declared. The voiced protest was quavery, but the tiger's eyes, uninhibited by the palpable danger surrounding her, flashed the truth of her outrage.

"You would prefer to be non-exclusive, then, in the granting of your favors?" inquired the privateer silkily. "I have no objections, but, since I do not share my possessions with my crew, you will understand if I choose not to avail myself of what you have to offer."

Genevieve began to shake, black dots dancing in the red mist before her eyes. She had no idea whether he would do the dreadful thing he was threatening, but that he could even think of such a thing was enough to bring the slimy tendrils of terror wreathing clammily around her, immobilizing her as if she were a fly in a spider's web.

"The choice is yours," said the privateer. "Mine or the crew's." Still, she was incapable of speech, and he could feel, through his fingers on her jaw, the tremors racking her. But the cold depths of his anger could not yet be dented by her distress. He could think only of the holds of *La Danseuse* and of the other vessels in the fleet; holds loaded with weapons and gunpowder; of their destination—revolution-torn Honduras; of the incalculable dangers inherent in their mission. And this spoiled, willful, meddlesome girl, seeing, as usual, no reason why she should not gratify her wish, had jumped right into the middle of what promised to be the most hazardous voyage he had yet attempted.

"Well?" he demanded, his fingers tightening on her jaw. "Which is it to be?"

He was going to force her to say it. Genevieve thought of Trianon, of the dull, orderly routine of Victor Latour's household, and for one moment of throbbing intensity, closed her eyes and prayed that when she opened them, that was where she would be. But there was no reprieve. The azure gaze continued to glitter, utterly purposeful; the fingers on her chin bruised their determination that she capitulate, and finally she managed to mouth the necessary word.

A curt nod indicated acceptance, and he released his hold on her chin. "Then, let us return to the point at which this discussion began. Take off your clothes. Or do you wish Silas to do it for you?"

Defeated, Genevieve turned away and began to undo the buttons of her shirt. Dominic strode to the door, flung it wide and bellowed for Silas. The sailor appeared instantly. "Bring hot water and lye soap, immediately."

"Yes, monsieur," Silas said, as stolidly imperturbable as always, in spite of the strangeness of the order and the extraordinary events of the afternoon about which he was now completely informed.

Ignoring the figure fumbling with her clothes in the middle of the cabin, Dominic returned to his absorption at the chart table. When Silas banged at the door a very few minutes later, he bade him enter without raising his head. Genevieve looked around wildly, then jumped for the bed as the door opened. There was no time to seek concealment beneath the covers. All she could do was sit hunched over, her back to the room, a crimson wave of humiliation washing over her. "Take those clothes away. She won't be needing them again," Dominic ordered, his voice abstracted as if the matter were of only minor importance.

"Yes, monsieur." Silas made his customary response, bundled up the pathetic pile of clothing on the carpet and left the cabin.

There was silence. Genevieve continued to sit huddled on the bed, unable to turn back to the room, to look at the author of her wretchedness, and quite unable to make any decision as to her next move. Fortunately, that was decided for her. "The water is there for you to use," he said with heavy sarcasm. "And scrub every inch of yourself, including your hair, with the lye."

Slowly, she got off the bed. A wooden tub stood steaming in the corner of the cabin, well away from the carpet, a cake of harsh-smelling lye soap beside it. She had never used such a thing, although the smell was one that lingered over the slave quarters both on Royal Street and at Trianon.

Dominic watched her sit gingerly in the water and pick up the soap with an involuntary grimace of distaste. "When you touch pitch, it tends to rub off," he said with a mocking smile. "One lesson that maybe you will remember when next you think to mingle with the rougher elements of society." Walking over to a cupboard set into the bulkhead, he turned the key in the lock and pocketed it, then went to the door.

Genevieve summoned up the last shreds of courage and asked hesitantly, "What am I to wear when I have bathed?"

Dominic turned, his hand on the door, and ran his eyes over her in a long, lazy sweep. "You will wear nothing," he pronounced calmly. "Naked, even you are unlikely to attempt to leave this cabin—indeed, it seems the only certain means of restraint I have at my disposal." He paused as she looked at him, dumbfounded. "It will also save time, will it not, when I find I have need of you?" Then he had left, harsh fragments of laughter hanging in the air.

Alone, Genevieve gave way to the pent-up tears, her slight frame wrenched by great sobbing gasps as she scoured herself with the hateful lye. She had always known the danger inherent in crossing the privateer, but she had never conceived of the extent of his power to hurt, or of his willingness to use that power. He had behaved like a stranger, and yet he was not really a stranger even in the manifestation of cruelty. It was still the Dominic Delacroix that she knew, had always known, and it had been blind stupidity that had led her to conjure up the devil in the loving mentor.

Cleansed, her skin reddened by the harsh soap, the smell of disinfectant trapped in her nostrils, she got out of the bath and dried herself. The towel Silas had provided was not big enough to knot around her as a makeshift dress, and examination of the cupboards set into the bulkhead offered nothing to assist her in her predicament. Only the one was locked, and she assumed that behind that door lay Dominic's clothes. The bed linen was the only possibility, but in the end it seemed simpler just to crawl beneath the covers.

The cabin was in darkness when the door opened without ceremony, and Silas entered with a tray piled high with covered dishes from whence emanated the most aromatic steam. These he set upon the table before lighting the oil lamp, filling the cabin with a warm yellow glow. Genevieve closed her eyes against the light and curled up more tightly, as if thus she might be invisible, although the sailor paid the mound in the bed no heed as he set two places at the table, the napery of pristine whiteness, the heavy silver cutlery gleaming in the lamplight, the crystal glasses winking as the intricate cuts caught the light. That task completed to his satisfaction, Silas picked up the tub of water where the soap floated, melting in a pool of scum on the surface, and left the cabin.

Genevieve sat up. Her eyes burned from the storm of weeping that had only just expended itself, and her nose was so stuffed up that she could barely smell the food on the table. But she could not imagine eating. She seemed to have no appetite at all, though she had eaten nothing since early that morning. Meals on the lower deck tended to be substantial but unsubtle, and her delicate Creole palate had had some difficulty adjusting, although the adjustment process had been aided by the ravenous hunger that sea air and hard work produced. Now, however, although the food prepared for the ship's master was clearly of a very different order, she could not contemplate taking even a mouthful. She lay down again, pulling the covers up to her nose.

Dominic came into the cabin, cast a cursory glance at the bed, and went over to the table. He poured wine into the two glasses and sat down, helping himself to the dish of spicy remoulade, breaking a hot roll. "Come and have your dinner," he said. When there was no response from behind him, he repeated the instruction, but in a voice that brought Genevieve out of bed and to her feet almost without realizing it.

"I am not hungry," she said, crossing her arms over her breasts as if she might, in some way, conceal her nakedness.

"Sit down," he said evenly, peeling a large Gulf shrimp and dipping it in the remoulade.

Genevieve did so, but she did no more than that. He could not force her to eat, whatever else he could compel her to do. It seemed, however, that her presence at the table was sufficient. She sipped a little wine and found it comforting. Then she simply sat at the table opposite him until he had completed his meal and had lit a cigar. Taking that as a signal that dinner was now finished, Genevieve got up and went back to bed.

"You are really going to have to improve your skill at entertaining," Dominic observed, swiveling around in his chair to look at her. "I expect a little conversation at the table. Nothing too arduous, if your mental powers are not up to it, but a little small talk, at the very least."

"Go to hell!" Genevieve whispered under the covers. It was his natural habitat, anyway. She found to her amazement that her spirit seemed to be recovering from the crushing blows it had been dealt that afternoon. He would get *nothing* from her except what he compelled. And the pleasure in that would pall soon enough.

Dominic smoked in silence for awhile, then he got up, tossed his cigar out of the porthole and came over to the bed. "Well, if you won't entertain me with your dulcet tones, my dear, we shall have to see what else you can offer." He pulled the cover off her. Instinctively, she curled tighter, like a hedgehog. Although her protective bristles were only in her head, Dominic could almost feel them.

"Turn over," he said quietly, and when she did not immediately comply, he took her by the shoulders and rolled her onto her back. Genevieve covered her eyes with the back of one arm, but, other than that, made no move to avoid his scrutiny; she simply lay as he had placed her. Dominic, in spite of the cold anger that enclosed him in a hard carapace, felt desire stir in his loins. Leaning over her, he touched one softly rounded breast, a feather-light stroke of his finger, moving to flick the rosy nipple, to bring it to life. A shudder ran through the slender body, and he removed his finger as if he had been burned. Her involuntary response had been a shudder of repulsion. Without a word, he replaced the covers and left the cabin.

He spent that night on deck, and Genevieve eventually stopped wondering why he had not taken from her what he had so clearly stated that he would, and fell asleep, able, despite her wretchedness, to luxuriate in the almost forgotten comfort of a feather mattress and clean, fragrant linen.

She woke when Silas entered the cabin bearing a jug of hot water. As before, he behaved as if the mound in the bed did not exist. He left and reappeared within minutes with a tray of coffee, hot milk, and beignets. He was placing these on the table when Dominic came in. "Good morning," said the privateer to the cabin in general. Silas responded cheerfully, but no sound came from the bed. Dominic jerked his head toward the door and Silas nodded, leaving instantly.

"Good morning, Genevieve," Dominic addressed the mound. "Come and have your breakfast."

"I am not hungry," she said clearly. It was as true this morning as it had been the previous evening.

"Nevertheless, I wish you to sit at the table," he said in level tones, mixing café au lait in the two shallow cups.

In dull obedience, she got up and sat at the table. Dominic, instead of sitting opposite her, took his coffee over to the washstand where Silas had left the jug of water, shrugged out of his shirt and sharpened his razor on the leather strop hanging from the bulkhead. Genevieve took a few sips of coffee but ignored the beignets. Dominic finished shaving, washed vigorously, unlocked the cupboard and took out a clean shirt. When he turned back to the table, looking enviably fresh and tidy, his skin glowing after the night under the stars, he found Genevieve intently tracing with her little finger the path of a sunbeam on the table. She seemed to have withdrawn completely into herself. He reached a hand across the dishes and lifted her chin. The tawny eyes seemed sunken and lifeless, the usually mobile features expressionless. She made no attempt to evade his grasp, but just stared into the middle distance over his shoulder.

"Eat," Dominic said.

She shook her head and repeated, "I am not hungry. I would like to go back to bed, please."

He released her chin impatiently. "Very well. But maybe you would care to wash your face and comb what little is left of your hair, first."

"What for?" she asked. "But if you insist . . ." With a tiny shrug, she went over to the washstand. Genevieve found that her nakedness no longer bothered her; nothing seemed to bother her. She was immune from hurt, her self tucked away inside her. When she had washed in a desultory fashion, she climbed back into bed, curled on her side facing the wall, and closed her eyes.

Dominic scratched his head and frowned. During the long reaches of the night, remorse had visited him. It had been a most infrequent and unwelcome visitor in his life, but it was a tenacious one, he had found, as he lay looking up into magnificent star-studded infinity. However many times he reminded himself of the outrageousness of Genevieve's behavior, of the impossible position in which she had placed him, he could no longer feel the conviction that his cruelty—and there was no other word for it—had been justified. In his way, he had behaved as badly as she—in many ways, he was as much the spoiled baby. Thwarted, he had struck out blindly, visiting a vengeance of unthinking severity. But how to undo the consequences of that severity?

Perhaps it would be best to leave her alone to heal herself. He still had to decide what he was to do with her; whether to keep her on board and continue the mission, or whether to turn back and leave her in some safe place ashore, to pick her up from there on his return—if he returned. To add insult to injury, he had no idea how to explain the presence of the daughter of Victor Latour on board *La Danseuse* to the captains under his command and, in all fairness, he could not hide such a significant problem from them. It was a factor that would affect his judgment when it came to making the split-second decisions on which, so often, the safety and success of the fleet depended. Only a self-deceiving fool would pretend otherwise, and Dominic Delacroix was neither.

Leaving the troublesome addition to his crew still nursing her wounds, he went back on deck, summoning Silas with a crooked finger. "Monsieur?"

"Visit the cabin at regular intervals throughout the day and report to me after each visit," Dominic said, sweeping the horizon with his telescope. "Take mademoiselle her lunch and let me know if she eats it." Having disposed, as best he could, of that particular problem, he devoted his attention to the fact that only six sails were visible on the seas, and there were seven of his ships making this voyage.

"Signalman," he called to the sailor in charge of the semaphore flags. "Send to Captain Dubois: Captain Marchand not in sight. Any information?"

The flags dipped and flashed in the bright sun of early morning, and the message was answered. "*Alouette* last seen on port bow, at four bells in the dogwatch, monsieur."

Dominic frowned. Marchand's command had not been seen since early last evening. They sailed without lights during the night watches, so it was not surprising she had not been seen in the dark, but it was now seven in the morning, and it had been daylight for two hours. If *Alouette* had run into part of the British blockade, there was little they could do to help. But if she had been overhauled and captured, then the British fleet would be actively seeking her companions. No intelligent commander would believe in a single gunrunner on an isolated mission, and the British navy tended to have intelligence at its head. Well, there was little he could do but keep a rigorous lookout. He sent someone up to the mizzen top with a telescope and had a similar order signaled to the other vessels. Six top watches should ensure the earliest possible alert, and the frigates, given sufficient warning and a favorable wind, could outrun almost anything on the high seas.

223

## Chapter 14

All that day, Genevieve lay curled in the big bed, oblivious of Silas's comings and goings, of the bowl of turtle soup that appeared at noon, of the sounds of a ship at work. She had discovered that the mind can create its own reality, a universe where the body has no part, a realm safe from the intrusion of inflicted hurts. She was immune to humiliation, to pain, was suspended in her own reality until the shameful memories ceased to plague her. She was unaware, of course, that this blissful retreat was aided by the light-headedness and physical languour brought about by her extended fast. She took only the few sips of water that her body demanded, and left the bed only to use the commode.

Dominic listened to Silas's reports on the catatonic figure beneath the bed covers with a deepening frown. There was still no sign of *Alouette*, but neither had there been any signs of pursuers. All six frigates were now sailing in close formation, messages flashing between them throughout the day as they altered course to draw closer to the coastline of Florida, should flight to safety become necessary. The most hazardous part of the voyage, however, would be the Yucatan Channel that separated the Gulf from the Caribbean. They would be sitting ducks for an ambush if the British played their cards right. But then, they would have to know the privateer's destination. If, of course, *Alouette* and her crew were prisoners, it was highly likely that that destination was now in the British possession.

Dominic paced the quarterdeck, hypothesizing and analyzing, toying with possibilities, trying to explore every possible ramification of the situation. Only thus could he outwit the enemy. He had to think as they would, given a certain set of circumstances. Only he did not know what set of circumstances was the correct one, so plans had to be made to cover all the options. And the thought of Genevieve persistently intruded, throwing him off course. At sunset, he went below, this time prepared to wrestle with the problem of her incompatability with the dinner table.

It was easier said than done, however, and he felt the first stirrings of alarm. The diminutive figure seemed to be fading away before his eyes. It was not so much that she was thinner—a mere two days without food would not show such immediate results—but she seemed to have shrunk, and even when he had got her out of bed, she stood curled over, as if protecting some core. He took a shirt from the neatly folded stack in the bulkhead cupboard and draped it round her shoulders. She made absolutely no attempt to put it on and with a muttered oath, he pushed her arms into the sleeves and buttoned it for her. "This has to stop, Genevieve. It has gone on quite long enough." He tried to hide his impatience, to make his tone firm but kind. "Sit down at the table and eat your soup."

She simply sat and stared at the bowl, but when he held a spoonful to her lips, she turned her head aside. "I am not hungry."

He sighed and bit the bullet. "Genevieve, I am sorry for what I said and did, yesterday. When I am as angry as I was then, I am afraid I have been known to behave in an indefensible way. However, you must bear some responsibility for it; the guilt is not mine alone. But could we please put it behind us, now?"

"It does not matter, anymore," Genevieve said in a dull, flat voice. "I am perfectly all right, just not hungry."

He looked down at her, quelling his exasperation. Then, with sudden decision, he swung her chair away from the table and scooped her into his arms. "It seems, sprite, that I must demonstrate my penitence." Carrying her over to the bed, he laid her down and gently removed the shirt before sitting on the bed beside her.

Genevieve felt the smooth, expert caresses, felt her body begin to come alive, sensation to penetrate the safety of the world she had been inhabiting, and panic shrieked a warning. The world to which these lovely sensations belonged was also the one where the devastation of self occurred, and she knew on some primitive level that she could not risk a repetition of the latter. Her body went rigid beneath his hands as her mind fought for control and won. Then she lay, limp and unresponsive, until Dominic, his lips tight, the turquoise eyes grim, gave up. He strode out of the cabin, the door banging shut in his wake, and Genevieve, without bothering to put on the shirt again, pulled the covers up and resumed the position, which had now became natural.

"Ship to starboard!" the man at the masthead cried suddenly as the master reached the deck.

Dominic grabbed the telescope and peered into the gathering dusk. The lookout sang out that she had altered course and was running down toward them, and then came the shout, "It's *Alouette*, monsieur."

Alone? Dominic wondered, or bearing a fleet of His Majesty's battleships on her tail? The stillness of anticipation settled over him as he waited, ready to make whatever decision was necessary as soon as he could form a relatively accurate picture of the situation.

"She's signaling, monsieur," the signalman said, straining to see through his glass. "Says . . . says, all well."

"Well! And where the hell has she been, in that case?"

Dominic demanded. This signal, accurate to the last word, was transmitted and answered. "Captain Marchand requests permission to come aboard, monsieur."

Dominic frowned. He could hardly entertain *Alouette*'s captain in his cabin, not with Genevieve playing dead. "Tell him I'll join him, and signal to the other captains: Request their presence aboard *Alouette* within the half hour."

A launch was lowered over *Danseuse*'s side, and Silas appeared as if by magic, clearly ready to accompany his captain; only to be told: "I need you to stay here, Silas, and keep an eye on my cabin."

Silas tugged a forelock, but his expression was heavy. "Not cut out to play nursemaid, monsieur," he dared to grumble.

Dominic gave him a sharp look, and then allowed a reluctant smile to touch his eyes. "You will not have to for long. I shall do something about her in the morning, when I have discovered what's been going on with *Alouette*."

It was three bells in the night watch when Dominic returned to *Danseuse,* thoughtful but not displeased. *Alouette* had found herself, in the midnight dark, in the middle of the British blockade. Marchand, as canny and shrewd a captain as any that Dominic had under his command, had turned tail, leading the pursuit a merry dance across the Gulf to the Mexican coast and away from the rest of the privateers. Having lost them, he had returned to his fellows, and Dominic now had a fairly accurate idea of where the British fleet was to be found. They'd be on the alert, now that they knew that at least one ship had evaded the blockade, but whether they would search actively was a question that only time would answer.

In the meantime, something had to be done about Genevieve, who was behaving like the victim of a voodoo death curse. He slept soundly in a hammock, slung among the rigging, until daybreak, when, with set purpose, he summoned the bosun to the quarterdeck. "Have the wash-deck pump rigged," he directed. "Then I want every hand below decks until I give the order to come up. Is that clear?"

"Yes, monsieur." The bosun could not hide his puzzlement though, but he was aware that his standing with the master was more than a trifle rocky since the cabin boy debacle, and he was not about to question the extraordinary order.

"Helmsman?" Dominic turned to the man at the wheel, raising his eyes to the mainsail bellying in the dawn breeze. "Lash the wheel. She'll hold steady on this course for awhile. Then go below with the others." In a very few minutes, Dominic was alone on the deck of an apparent ghost ship. With a nod of satisfaction, he went down the companionway and into his cabin where all was exactly as he had left it the previous evening. He strode over to the bed and looked down at the curled mound. The golden eyelashes fluttered, betraying her awareness.

"Genevieve," he said with clear patience. "Are you going to get up, get dressed and eat your breakfast this morning?"

There was no response, although the eyelashes fluttered again. "Then you leave me no option. Obviously I must do something to stimulate your appetite." He pulled the covers back and picked up the huddled form. She seemed insubstantial, and her limbs remained in the fetal curl even as he held her.

Genevieve had heard his voice, had even understood the words, but she was so buried in her own reverie that nothing seemed to have the power to touch her. A vague question as to what he was going to do with her was dismissed as irrelevant, and she lay motionless as he carried her out of the cabin. Then the realization that she was naked hit her with full force as she felt the sun's warmth on her skin, its light behind her closed eyes. They were on deck and the crew would be everywhere, staring at the bundle in the master's arms. But she could not be hurt anymore, she reminded herself; not if she stayed inside and let her body exist on another, unimportant plane. Those eyes could not hurt her, not if she did not meet them.

Dominic put her down on the deck, and Genevieve curled tightly against the sun-warmed wood, feeling its splintery hardness against her bare flesh, and the sun beamed down upon her. Slowly, she became aware of the quality of the silence, broken only by the creak of the rigging, the flap of a sail, the shrill cry of a seabird. The motion of the hull beneath her body lulled her into the quiet, which she knew with absolute certainty indicated a total lack of humankind. For some reason, only herself and Dominic were up here in the sea air and the sun's warmth. Her eyes opened, scooting along the planking of the deck that stretched before her gaze, as white as it had been when she had mopped and scoured it. Who was responsible for that task now, she wondered distractedly. And then the water hit her.

Dominic, working the pump with one hand, used the other to play the jet of the canvas hose upon the curled figure. The deep waters of the Gulf, while not bitterly cold, were chilly enough on sun-warmed, unprepared flesh, and Genevieve screamed, shocked out of the warm, cottonwool comfort of her daydream to be hurled back into the real world.

Her first reaction was to curl tighter into a ball, minimizing the area of exposed skin, but the water tongued its way into every nook and cranny, stinging her into action so that she staggered onto her feet, stumbling to escape the powerful stream that pursued her mercilessly.

"Damn you! Damn you! Damn you!" she shrieked at the top of her lungs, and Dominic smiled. That sounded *much* healthier.

"Has your appetite returned yet, Genevieve?" he asked, easing off on the pump so that the power of the jet lessened, although he continued to direct it onto her back as she huddled against the deck railing.

"Yes, damn you to hell!" she yelled, and the water ceased

as suddenly as it had begun. She clung, shivering and dripping, to the rail, struggling for breath as the quiet of the deserted deck slowly took over from the chaotic sensations of the last few minutes. Something soft, fluffy, and miraculously dry descended on her shoulders. It was an enormous towel, she realized, and then ceased to realize anything as Dominic began to rub her dry with a vigor that set her skin tingling and left her too breathless to say anything.

"There, that's better," he said at last, lifting the towel from her head. "Come and sit in the sun for a few minutes and you will be properly warmed."

Genevieve raised her head from its resting place on his chest where he had held it as he dried her hair. "I hate you," she said, the fierceness merely emphasized by her quiet tone. "Do you know how much I hate you?"

A smile quirked his lips. "I can make an educated guess," he said, wrapping the damp towel around her. "Come to the quarterdeck now and sit in the sun."

She followed him and her tongue, finally loosened, gave vent to the outrage and the fury that had been bottled up since her involuntary retreat. Dominic listened gravely as he unlashed the helm, gazed up at the sails and made a minute adjustment to the course.

"It might be a good idea if you took the towel off," he interrupted apologetically. "It's a bit damp, you see, and will prevent the sun's getting to your skin."

Genevieve's jaw dropped, but the sense of the suggestion was irrefutable, so she dropped the damp covering and sat down on the deck, throwing her head back with an unconscious, luxuriant sigh. She had forgotten how wonderful the air felt, how wonderful it smelled, fresh and salty and fishy. Then she came back to the present with a jolt. "Where was I?"

"I think you were trying to find some alternative sobriquet to 'bastard,'" he said placidly. "That one has become a little overused in the last few minutes."

"Well, you are," she said.

"I don't think my mother would agree with you," he replied cheerfully, reaching into his top pocket for a cigar. "But I will not attempt to quibble with what you are trying to express. In spite of your somewhat limited vocabulary of curses and vilifications, the message is perfectly clear." He blew smoke into the air in a fragrant blue-tinged ring, and Genevieve, the wind somehow taken from her sails, sat still and found her eyes riveted on his hands: long, elegant fingers curling over the spokes of the wheel, the ripple of muscle in his bare forearms where the soft, fair hair curled.

"Where is the crew?" she asked suddenly as she felt her body begin to follow the thoughts that sprang from her gaze.

Dominic chuckled as he looked at her with shrewd awareness. She had been wearing her nakedness as naturally as if she were clothed, but something had just occurred to make her throbbingly aware of it. "Below," he told her. "They'll stay there until called. However," he said, looking across the stern, "wind's freshening and we'll have to trim the sails in a minute, so perhaps you had better go down to the cabin. I will join you for breakfast shortly."

"Why did you do that to me?" she asked softly as she stood up, knotting the towel sarong-style under her arms.

Dominic knew she was not referring to the bath under the pump. "I have a vicious temper," he said, "and you have the devil's own ability to provoke it. But it was not provoked without cause, Genevieve." He turned from the wheel to hold her gaze with his own. "Your presence on board is going to cause the most damnable complications for everyone. You did what you wanted to do, just as always, as if your decisions and their consequences can exist in a vacuum."

"But I will take responsibility for myself," she said with a puzzled frown. "I do not see why that should cause you difficulties. If anything happens to me on this voyage, that is my responsibility, not yours. You must do what you would have done, had I not been here. That is how you have always behaved, is it not so? Everyone must take their chance and each is responsible for himself."

She really believed it. The golden eyes shone with candor and conviction, and he looked at her helplessly. He could not deny her statement. With anyone else it would have been so. Certainly, if any other woman he could think of had intruded so outrageously and uncompromisingly, he probably would not have felt one iota of responsibility. But this sprite was different, and there was little to be gained by looking for the reasons why that should be so. Deciding to leave that issue, he addressed himself to the one of which he was sure.

"As it happens, the presence of a woman and a stranger on board has far-reaching consequences for everyone. Every man on this ship is aware of the fact that for three days, you shared his quarters, witnessing the intimacies of below-decks life. They are going to find that hard to forgive and impossible to forget. The rest of the fleet . . ." He gestured to the flock of sails spotting the sea around them. "Their captains are going to want to know why they were not informed of the presence of Victor Latour's daughter beforehand, and they are not going to like the idea that she sneaked aboard and managed to remain hidden for three days. They are also going to wonder about their commander, about his ability to make the right decisions for them if he has a woman on board, one of such blatant determination."

Genevieve heard him out in shamefaced silence. Why had she not thought of all those ramifications before she had so blithely pursued her desire? "I will try not to be a nuisance," she said in a small voice when he had finished.

"I would be satisfied if you would promise me that in the future you will stop and think carefully before you leap," he said forcefully. "There is nothing to be done about the present situation, except to make the best of it, but I would like to rest easy at night in the knowledge that you have accepted the need to curb your impulses. Otherwise, God only knows what end is in store for you—not a peaceful one, that's for sure!" Genevieve was silent and he said very quietly, "It is time you grew up, sprite."

Her answer surprised him. "Perhaps it is time we both grew up." The candid tawny eyes met his, and a smile lurked in their golden depths. "I think, Monsieur Delacroix, that we share the same faults. Is the life of a privateer not informed by impulse and love of excitement? By a horror of entrapment in society's coils? Do you not take immense pleasure in shocking the respectable? It could be said that such character traits are not the hallmark of maturity. Is it so very extraordinary that I should feel the same?"

The privateer contemplated this series of questions, a rueful smile playing over the chiseled mouth. "There is one difference between us," he said. "I take no action until I have investigated every possible consequence, and I do not involve the unwilling or unwitting in my adventures."

"I will attempt to learn from you," she promised, an imp of mischief in her eye belying the demure, serious tone. "You have taught me much, and I am quite willing to learn more."

"Go below," he said, turning back to the wheel, but not before she had seen the answering amusement on his face.

In the cabin, Genevieve found Silas engaged in stripping the bed. "You'll not be wanting to get back in here today," he said by way of greeting.

"No," she agreed, picking up from the floor the shirt that Dominic had given her last night. "Do you think you could bring me my clothes, Silas?"

"Not without monsieur's orders," he replied stolidly, gathering up the dirty sheets.

"No, of course not," Genevieve muttered into the air, as he closed the door behind him. "I cannot imagine why I asked." Well, the shirt would have to do. Dropping the towel, she shrugged into the fine lawn and was busy with the buttons when there was a thump at the door. Startled, she heard her

233

voice squeak, "Who is it?"

"Silas," came the reply.

"Come in." When he entered, a tray in his hands, she said, "I am sorry, but I did not realize it was you since you are not in the habit of knocking."

"Depends on circumstances," he replied briefly, placing the tray on the table. "There's bread and warm milk there for you. You've not eaten for over two days, and you'd best start slow." He unscrewed the lid of a silver preserve pot and spooned strawberry jam into the middle of the steaming contents of a silver porringer.

Nursery food, Genevieve thought with a chuckle. It seemed quite incongruous that this burly seaman should be stirring strawberry jam into the nursery posset that he had presumably prepared with his own hands, having decreed like any nursemaid that it was necessary for her well-being.

She sat at the table and began absently to consume the warming, comforting, bland concoction, watching as Silas took fresh linen from a carved oak chest and began to make up the bed, the gnarled, calloused hands moving efficiently, tucking and folding and smoothing. Genevieve, who had never made a bed in her life, could see Dominic's point about not disturbing the status quo when it came to caring for his personal needs.

He came into the cabin at that point, glanced at her almost empty bowl, and accorded her a brief nod of approval before helping himself to coffee.

"Everything all right with *Alouette,* monsieur?" Silas asked casually.

Genevieve's ears pricked. Who or what was *Alouette?* She listened attentively as Dominic explained the situation to the sailor, who responded with a grunt and a nod. It was her first realization, since the voyage began, that danger lurked on those calm blue seas, and it became clear, as the two men talked, that they considered themselves lucky to have so far run up against nothing more threatening than the glimpse of a shark's fin. It also became clear that they both expected trouble in the near future. And Genevieve could not face trouble clad only in the privateer's shirt.

"May Silas return my clothes?" she asked, taking a deep gulp of coffee.

Dominic frowned and shook his head. "No, I'm not having you wearing britches again. When the crew sees you, I want as little as possible to remind them of that time you spent in their quarters." His frown deepened, cutting grooves between the fly-away eyebrows. "It's a pity we can't do anything about your hair."

"That's easily remedied, monsieur," Silas put in. "If mademoiselle would just sit over here." He took a large pair of scissors from a cupboard and flourished them purposefully.

"But it is already so short," Genevieve said nervously, maintaining her seat.

"It's not the length that's the problem, as I see it," Silas said, gesturing toward a chair and shaking out a towel with clear intent.

"You may put yourself quite unreservedly in Silas's hands," Dominic said, amused by her obvious reluctance. "Although, after the barbarism already committed, I cannot imagine why you should worry about further damage."

With a resigned shrug, she took the assigned chair, and Silas draped the towel over her shoulders. The silence in the sunny cabin was broken only by the snip of the scissors and the whisper of coffee as Dominic refilled his cup. He was the picture of relaxation, leaning back in his chair, one leg crossed over the other, watching Silas's handiwork with considerable interest. "Amazing, quite masterly," he said with some awe, when Silas finally replaced the scissors, twitched the towel from Genevieve's shoulders and shook it vigorously, a silver-gold shower of hair floating to the wooden floor.

"Why amazing?" Genevieve put a tentative hand to her head.

"Why don't you look in the mirror and find out?" Dominic advised, returning to his breakfast.

She saw a complete transformation. The pudding basin homogeneity had disappeared to be replaced by a neat, stylish cap, clipped into the nape of her neck, a few feathery tendrils falling in a fringe on her brow. It was short, but it was undoubtedly feminine. Silas was clearly a man of many parts.

"Any suggestions about her clothes, Silas?" Dominic asked. "Obviously what she has on won't do."

"No," Silas agreed laconically, casting an appraising glance at her bare legs and feet. "There's enough material in the shirt," he observed thoughtfully, "but it's not distributed right." Taking her unceremoniously by the shoulders, he turned her around, seizing a handful of the voluminous garment between her shoulder blades. Genevieve stood still and endured the matter-of-fact examination in the spirit in which it was clearly intended.

"Mmm," he pronounced eventually. "Not too much of a problem. You got anything useful in that bundle you brought on board?"

"Clean underthings," she said, without embarrassment. Such an emotion was clearly out of place where Silas was concerned.

"Good. Not sure I could manufacture those for you," he replied. "I'll fetch it." He left the cabin, taking two of Dominic's shirts with him.

"He doesn't approve of me," Genevieve remarked.

Dominic laughed. "No, he does not. But then he does not approve of women in general, and certainly not of the kind who don't seem to know their place in the scheme of things."

"And where is that?" she inquired.

"In bed, or in the kitchen," he informed her succinctly.

"Not, at all events, on board ship."

"Oh." She glanced thoughtfully at the bed, and then back at Dominic. "I suppose it would be a pity to undo all his good work?"

He crooked a finger at her and, smiling, she came over to him, allowing him to draw her between his knees. "I suspect you are incorrigible," he said, lifting the shirt slowly, bending his head to kiss the soft skin as it was revealed, inch by inch. Genevieve shivered as his unshaven jaw rasped across the tenderness of her belly, and his tongue dipped into her navel. Then the prickly fire crept up her body with the shirt. Holding the hem against her shoulders, he turned his attention to her breasts, nibbling their rosy crowns with a sharp insistence that produced the strangest tug in her belly and a liquid fullness in her loins. She looked down at the head, glowing richly burnished against the white skin of her bosom, and her hands went to cup his shoulders, feeling the muscular angularity beneath his shirt. As if in a trance, she moved to explore the feel and shape of his neck, that strong, bronzed column rising from the shirt's open collar. The power of him pulsed against her fingers that moved to trace the whorls and contours of his ears, then slid down, inside his shirt to follow the knobbly path of his spine.

He raised his head and smiled. "You have in mind a little more than dalliance, it would seem."

She nodded her head, reaching her hand even further, until it met the restraint of his belt. Her fingers insinuated themselves inside and reached further to the base of his spine. He inhaled sharply, feeling the insistent, intimate pressure, and, with a sudden movement, he pulled her shirt over her head, obliging her to remove her hand so that her arms could come out of the sleeves. Then, deliberately, not taking his eyes from her face, he unbuttoned his shirt, tugged it free of his belt and shrugged out of it. "Is that enough, or do you wish for more?" he asked, a sensuous, teasing smile curving his mouth.

"More," she said definitely, running her tongue over her lips in that gesture that he had come to look for as indication of the depths of her excitement. Bending, he removed his shoes and stockings, then slowly stood up, unfastened his britches and pushed them, with infinite deliberation, over his hips.

"Mmmm," she murmured with soft satisfaction at the sight of his arousal springing with unmistakable power from the curly nest at the base of his belly. She moved to stand against him, feeling the thrust of that power against her thigh, her nipples pressing against his chest. Her hands moved to palm the lean hips, slipping behind to the hard, muscular buttocks that rippled in response. A light sweat misted her skin as the tension built deep in her belly, and her inner muscles contracted in involuntary preparation as she leaned into him, her grip on his buttocks tightening with the sudden urgency of her passionate need.

"You have a novel way of expressing your hatred, Mademoiselle Geneviève," Dominic teased gently, globing her breasts, tracing tantalizing circles with his thumbs, circumventing the taut, wanting nipples until she thought she would die of the wanting. Her head fell back in a gesture of pure abandonment as her lower body moved with a sinuous urgency against his, seeking the fusion that was for the moment withheld.

"God, but you were made for loving, sprite," he said huskily, his breath rustling against the fast-beating pulse at the base of her throat. "Sometimes I wonder what I have unleashed."

"Then cease wondering," she whispered, "and *know* what you have unleashed."

For a second, he looked down at her. The ivory complexion, lightly kissed by the sun as a result of her days as cabin boy, was flushed delicately; the golden eyes were enormous, deep pools of passion, her lips slightly parted. It was the face of a mature woman who knew her own depths, who knew how to give as well as to receive, who was not afraid to express her desire, nor afraid of another's desire. And he thought, the instant before he kissed her, that only one woman before had had the power to stir him in this way.

She locked her arms around his neck, rising on tiptoe to reach against his length as his hot tongue took possession of the warm sweet cavern of her mouth, and the roughness of his chin rasped deliciously against her cheek. The pressure of his lips made her own tingle, and she inhaled his special fragrance of salt sea and crisp air, and the lingering tang of cigar smoke. When he lifted her against him, without releasing her mouth, she curled her legs around his back and tightened her grip on his neck, knowing without thought what he wanted of her. He took the necessary steps to reach the chart table, bending forward to lay her down so that, in some other world, she could feel the crackling paper against her back. He stood against the table, his hands slipping beneath her buttocks, lifting and cradling, her legs curled around his hips as he entered her, sheathing himself by tormenting degrees in the velvety chamber of her being. She lay, poised on the threshold of wonder, breathless with the knowing expectation of what was to come, her body motionless although the hot blood surged in her veins. He withdrew to the very edge of her body, and the nerve endings at her core tingled and throbbed around the teasing, tantalizing tip of the pleasure-bringer. She heard her voice, as if from a great distance, murmuring the words of joy, then demanding as the waiting became infinity; she thought she could bear the sweet torment no longer. She looked upward into his face, into the softened turquoise eyes that were watching her expressions with intense concentration. Her hips arced upward from the table, insistent, but when he shook his head in unspoken denial of her demand and moved inward only a fraction, she knew that the denial was only to ensure her greater joy. Then he brought one hand from beneath her and touched her at the tender, swollen, nerve-stretched point of fusion, before thrusting deep within. Her body exploded in seemingly limitless pleasure, and the tears of exquisite, indescribable joy squeezed beneath her closed eyelids to lie wet and gleaming on her cheeks. She drew him down to her, holding him tightly against her as he toppled from his own mountain, and they shared the transcendent glory of a loving where both minds and bodies were matched.

# Chapter 15

It was noon when Silas came into the cabin bearing Genevieve's passport to the outside world in the shape of a simply cut, neatly stitched gown, which bore no resemblance, beyond the fine lawn material, to Dominic's shirt. He held it up for her inspection and allowed a small smile of gratification to crack his impassive features at her very obvious pleasure and sincere, complimentary thanks.

"One of monsieur's kerchiefs will serve as a sash, I reckon," he said, going over to the cupboard and flicking through the neat pile of gaily colored scarves. "This will suit." He handed her a large square of turquoise silk. "When you're ready, you're to go to the quarterdeck—and nowhere else," he added sharply, shooting her a look pregnant with warning.

"I would not dream of going anywhere else," Genevieve retorted with as much dignity as she could muster. It was quite true and, if she were to be perfectly honest, just the thought of going on deck and facing the men who had known her during those three dreadful days filled her stomach with butterflies.

Silas merely grunted and left her to get dressed. She had no petticoats with her, since they were incompatible with britches, so she was obliged to make do with only camisole and pantalettes beneath the thin white material. Fortunately, Silas, who had presumably foreseen the lack of respectable undercovering, had left the gown with a degree of fullness, although he had removed a panel from the back and had narrowed and shortened the sleeves. He had used the second shirt to add to the length so that it now grazed her ankles. The turquoise scarf, twisted into a wide strip, made a most satisfactory sash. She experimented with fastening it beneath her breasts in the fashionable Empire style, but decided that the gown was too full to suit that body-skimming design, so she settled for tying it around her waist. She had no suitable footwear. The shoes she had brought with her were not intended for wear with female attire, but it was warm enough to go barefoot. Besides, she enjoyed the feeling of freedom and unrespectability that her stockingless legs and shoeless feet gave her.

It was with a nervously fluttering pulse, however, that she eventually emerged on deck, consciously trying to avoid catching the eye of any of the sailors busy with their appointed tasks. The wind lifted the neat cap of hair and feathered the tendrils of her fringe as she climbed the ladder to the quarterdeck where Dominic was to be found in his usual place behind the helmsman. He was scanning the horizon through his glass and did not immediately notice her as she came to stand beside him. Then, without taking his eye from his glass, he laid one hand on her shoulder in recognition, and she leaned against him with a little sigh of pleasure. It felt so right to be here beside him.

Her nose twitched at the aroma of coffee and hot bread, and she realized guiltily that she was ravenous, even after her breakfast. A young lad whom she recognized as the cook's assistant came up the ladder, deftly bearing a tray on the flat palm of one hand. She turned away in embarrassment, staring out across the flat blue ocean with every appearance of total absorption. Dominic felt her stiffening under his hand and looked down at her averted profile. He nodded his

242

comprehension but said nothing to her, merely gestured to the lad to put the tray on the deck by the forward rail. The lad did so, but his eyes kept sliding to the figure in her white gown, and the speculation was clear. What had been going on in the master's cabin since that extraordinary revelation? Silas wasn't talking, but very few of the men had expected to see the erstwhile cabin boy emerge intact from monsieur's lair.

"Hungry?" Dominic asked, turning her from the rail.

"Famished," she answered, touching her burning cheeks. "I know it is my just deserts, but I am excruciatingly embarrassed."

"You'll get over it," he said carelessly. "If you don't do anything else to attract attention, the fascination will die down."

"I hope so." She dropped cross-legged in front of a tray bearing hot, crusty bread, cheese, lettuce, tomatoes, and olives. There was a pot of coffee and a carafe of red wine. Embarrassment did not appear to have reduced her appetite in the least, she discovered with interest. Perhaps it was simply the result of her fasting. "Where are we sailing to?" It was the first time since their reconciliation that she had had the opportunity to ask the question, and now she waited to see if it would be answered.

Dominic broke off a crust from the loaf, added a wedge of cheese and chewed thoughtfully for a minute as his habitual caution died under the knowledge that it would make no difference now what she knew. "Honduras," he said.

"Why?" Genevieve looked at him curiously. "Is it a good coast for piracy?"

"Not particularly." The privateer chuckled. "Piracy is best conducted, *ma chère,* on the high seas, as far from the coast as possible."

"Then why Honduras?"

Dominic drained his wineglass and stood up. "Come with me." He held his hand down to her and pulled her to her feet.

She followed him down to the main deck, too intrigued now to worry about an audience. At a battened-down hatchway, Dominic beckoned two sailors over, instructing one to fetch a lantern, then he bent and, with the other's assistance, removed the cover. He jumped lightly down into the blackness. "Sit on the edge of the hatch and I'll lift you down." Genevieve did so, feeling his hands strong around her waist, then she was swung through the air to join him in the darkness of the hold. Dominic reached up to receive the lantern and lifted it high, illuminating the cavern, sending shadows flickering against the bulkheads.

Genevieve looked around at crate after crate, nailed down and stacked against the sides. There were wooden barrels, banded with metal strips and, as she peered, her eyes accustoming themselves to the gloom, she made out the distinct elongated roundness of a cannon. She looked up at Dominic, puzzled. His lips were curved in a grim little smile, and the azure gaze was filmed with a mockery that she could have sworn had more than a hint of self-mocking about it.

"I don't understand," she said. "What is in the crates? And why is there a cannon?"

For answer, he walked over to a pile of crates, stooping because of the low headroom and, taking a knife from his belt, pried up the nails in the lid. She stood beside him, holding her breath expectantly as he lifted the lid. Muskets and carbines lay in neat racks, gleaming dully in the lamp's glow, menacing, highly polished, well oiled, primed instruments of death. She shuddered. "All of them?" Her hand waved vaguely around the hold.

"All of them," he affirmed quietly, "contain either weapons or ammunition. The barrels hold gunpowder. There are three heavy cannon."

"You are taking these to Honduras?" He nodded, watching her through narrowed eyes, assessing her reactions, but, also, she knew, waiting to see if she could come up with the reason. She racked her brains, trying to catch onto an elusive memory. Then she remembered. Victor had been talking with two of the town's prominent citizens on the rear gallery at Trianon a few weeks ago and, with her usual inquisitiveness, she had ducked into the cabinet to listen. It had not made a great deal of sense to her at the time: the discussion about a struggle between the people of Honduras and their Spanish masters. There had been talk of the advantages to be gained by the overthrow of the Spanish rule, of the trade and political benefits to be reaped from a grateful liberated population.

"To aid the revolution?" Dominic answered her question with another nod. "You believe it is right, then, for the people?"

At that he laughed. "Right or wrong does not interest me in the slightest, Genevieve. I provide a service for which I and my privateers are well rewarded. That is all that concerns me."

"But that is so self-interested!"

"My dear girl, what do you think motivates those who have bought these weapons and are paying me to transport them? Ideology?" When she was silent, he went on. "No, it is greed, pure and simple. Greed for power, greed for profits. In chaos, both can be found. So, first you create the chaos."

"It is horrible," she whispered. "To create and finance a war for such a purpose."

"I would not dream of defending it," he said casually. "But I am as much an opportunist as your father, and why should I play holier than thou at the expense of my pocket?"

"Papa is involved in this?" But she knew the answer to that without his nod of agreement.

"In some matters, your father is quite willing to do business with a privateer," he said with more than a touch of sarcasm. "At least *I* may be absolved of the charge of hypocrisy."

Genevieve felt an overpowering need to get on deck again and breathe fresh air. Piracy was not the romantic, glamorous, swashbuckling business she had imagined it. It was dirty and dangerous and unscrupulous. But what did that make the privateer? He could not be untouched by the way he chose to earn his living, yet she did not want to think of him in those terms. But, as he said, he was no hypocrite. Perhaps that was why he had shown her his cargo. Such a demonstration was more dramatic than a mere verbal explanation would have been. "Why are you a privateer?" The question came forth without planning.

He shrugged lightly. "I thought you understood that. Did we not agree that it is a life to satisfy one who has no truck with the conventional responsibilities of man's world?"

Somehow, she felt that it was not the whole answer, but for the moment it was the only one she was going to get. They had reached the hatchway again, and he handed the lantern up to the waiting sailor, then lifted Genevieve onto the edge before swinging himself up behind her. Leaving the hands to batten down the hatch again, he strolled back to the quarterdeck, Genevieve following in a sudden dispirited silence. The brightness seemed to have gone out of the day.

"Would you like to sail the ship?" Dominic asked suddenly, the question, as he had hoped, distracting her completely from the revelations of the last half hour.

"May I?" The tawny eyes shone again. "Will it be safe?"

"It will take more than a diminutive sprite to sink *La Danseuse*," he responded with a laugh, leading her over to the wheel. The helmsman, responding to a brief gesture, stepped back, although his surprise seemed to jump out of his skin. "Put your hands on the spokes, like so." Standing behind her, Dominic positioned her hands correctly and held them with warm pressure against the smooth roundness of the spokes, until she had established her balance, legs apart, feet firmly on the deck, shoulders braced. "Keep her steady on her course, now. If you let her come up too much, you will catch the big foresail aback. Do you feel the wind on your right cheek?" He touched her cheekbone, a feather touch that nevertheless sent a quiver down her spine. "Don't let it come any further forward than the bridge of your nose. All right?"

"All right," she agreed, concentrating on her task, her eyes moving from the wheel to the great sail that seemed enormous, as enormous as her responsibility to keep it stretched at just the right fullness, to keep the lively hull of the frigate dancing across the water on her set course. Genevieve did not think she had ever been entrusted with a greater responsibility, and her lower lip disappeared between her teeth. A tiny frown creased the normally smooth brow, and the tawny eyes were intent.

Dominic smiled to himself and stepped back. Lighting a cigar, he stood behind her, feet solidly planted on the shifting deck, his body moving infinitesimally with the motion of the ship beneath him as he smoked, and smiled, and looked over the small ash-blond head to the horizon beyond. After about ten minutes he said, "We seem to have discovered another of your talents, Mademoiselle Genevieve."

"Oh?" She looked up at him, startled out of her concentrated trance by the lightly teasing statement.

"You can sail a ship," he said and strolled away, leaving her in charge of *La Danseuse*.

It was the most wonderful feeling, she discovered, once she had relaxed into the sense of competence. She was quite unaware of the attention the new helmsman was drawing from the crew who were staring and whispering in little knots of disapproval. It was bad enough having a woman aboard at all without having her sail the ship. But when nothing dreadful happened, and the small figure stood her trick, the wind blowing her skirts against her legs and ruffling her hair, as calmly as if she had been born and bred to it, a different feeling ran round the ship. This was no ordinary member of the female gender—no ordinary woman could have defied monsieur and withstood his fury, not once but twice. The memory of the rigging-climbing incident was still a lively one. No ordinary woman would have endured three days of below decks life either, up to her knees in cold, scummy water, scrubbing the decks without complaint. Whatever her reasons were for doing such an unheard of thing, she had certainly gone about it with a degree of grim determination.

Then suddenly, both the time and the opportunity for speculation on this fascinating subject vanished. "Land ahead," came the call from the masthead, and a cheer went up from the main deck. Genevieve strained her eyes into the distance. She could see just a faint darkening on the horizon.

"Cuba," Dominic said, appearing suddenly beside her. "We should make Yucatan Channel by nightfall. Once we're through there, we can creep down the coast to Honduras."

"Sail ahead, to port!" came the excited yell from the masthead, and the crew sprang to life, crowding the deck rail. The helmsman pushed himself away from the taffrail and took the wheel from Genevieve who relinquished it readily enough. Dominic raised his telescope.

"Masthead, what do you see now?" he bellowed.

"Battleship, monsieur," the voice sang out. "Two decker."

"Damnation!" Dominic swore softly. "They're going to try and cut us off. And they never sail alone," he added. "Signalman, send to all ships: Spread out and we'll go round her, three vessels to port, four to starboard." He stroked his chin as the semaphor flags flashed. "She'll not be able to take us all on, and we'll have the advantage of surprise. The last thing they'll be expecting is that we continue on our course, sail directly for her."

"Is it the British?" Genevieve asked, excitement and nervousness making her voice quaver.

"Yes. You'd better get below," he responded shortly.

"Please, let me stay," she begged. "I will keep out of the way, I promise, and there is no danger for the moment, is there?"

"Not for the moment," he said. "Very well, you may stay on deck until—"

"Sail ahead, to starboard," the voice from the masthead called again. "And another."

Three battleships carrying guns, eighteen ports a side, probably, would decimate the privateers, none of which had more than nine twenty-pound guns apiece. They relied on speed rather than fighting power, and they could lie several points closer to the wind than the cumbersome British ships of the line. But that would not benefit them if they could not get past the battleships. The alternative was to turn tail and run for the Straits of Florida. They could sail down the northeast coast of Cuba and through the Windward Passage into the Caribbean and across to Honduras. But it would add days to the journey. They could split the fleet, though.

Genevieve, fascinated, watched the privateer's face. Only his eyes gave any indication of the work going on behind that apparently unruffled brow, and the blue-tinged smoke from his cigar drifted carelessly around him. But there was a tautness to his body, an alert, unmistakable excitement as he faced the challenge, pitting his wits against those of the blockaders.

"Signalman," he called again, but softly as if he were still thinking. "Send: All vessels sail to within three knots of the leading blockader. *Alouette* and *Pique* take the Straits. *Colombe, Hirondelle,* and *Cygne* run for the Bay of Campeche. *Mouette* and *Danseuse* will go straight through them. We meet at Punta Gorda."

"Why will *Mouette* and *Danseuse* sail into the shark's mouth?" Genevieve inquired. There was nothing about the privateer's stance or expression to prohibit the asking of such a question and, in confirmation, he smiled, a contented little smile.

"Unless the wind changes, we can run before it, and there is no ship on earth, particularly one of His Majesty's clumsy battleships, that can outrun either *Mouette* or *Danseuse* running before the wind." He looked down at her and saw curiosity and excitement on her face; not a trace of apprehension. "Changing course for vessels of that size and tonnage is a cumbersome procedure. They do not answer rapidly to the helm, and they carry a great deal of sail which takes time to adjust. When they see us sailing directly toward them, they will not know what to think." He chuckled sardonically. "That we are madmen or blind, probably. But they will continue sailing toward *us*. When we go three different ways, they will have to decide which of them will follow which group; and having decided, make the necessary maneuvers to alter course. By which time, we shall be well away."

"But suppose they fire on *Danseuse* and *Mouette?*" Genevieve frowned. "If you sail in the middle of them, will you not be within range?"

"Yes, sprite, I fear that we shall." He pinched her cheek and laughed, a laugh of pure exhilaration. "A couple of broadsides would sink us, but, again, I am trusting to the element of surprise. They need time to run out their guns, and they will never imagine that two little frigates would dare to brave their firepower, so they won't be prepared."

"But if they are?"

He drew on his cigar and exhaled slowly. "That, sprite, is the risk in the venture."

She nodded, sobered by the thought, yet understanding exactly why the privateer had made the decision he had. It, perhaps, carried the greatest risk for two vessels of his fleet; the others would be home free without doubt. But it also carried the greatest rewards. She had spent the morning, while waiting for her clothes, pouring over the charts in the cabin, and was now perfectly familiar with the geography of these waters. This familiarity led her to the conclusion that only two out of the seven would be obliged to delay significantly their arrival in Punta Gorda; the two who were to take the Windward Passage. Those who fled to the Bay of Campeche would be able to make another try for the Yucatan Channel, and the two who sailed directly to the channel would be into the Caribbean by midnight.

"Send the men to quarters," Dominic instructed the bosun, "and have the guns loaded and run out, if you please." He seemed to have forgotten Genevieve, who fervently hoped that this absentmindedness would continue. She crept from his side to a corner of the quarterdeck from where she could look down at the activity on the main deck and was well away from the activity around the helm. Maybe, if she was very quiet and still, she would be able to stay on deck and witness the outcome of Dominic's plan.

The dark squares of the battleships' sails came inexorably close, urgent with menace, and the privateers continued steadily on their course until, with no warning, they seemed to scatter on the seas. They were still too far away to be threatened by the blockaders' guns when two peeled off to port, three to starboard, leaving just two gamely heading for the enemy. "Set the t'gallants," Dominic called to the sailors swarming up the rigging. They had clearly been waiting for the order, Genevieve decided, riveted with fascination at this orderly scene where many hands worked as if under the direction of one mind. "Helm a-starboard," came the quiet order to the helmsman. Then, when the leading blockader appeared set to run them down, Dominic roared, "Jibe her over," and the frigate came round neatly onto the port bow, taking the battleship quite by surprise.

The surprise was short-lived, however. The ship was close enough for Genevieve to read her name, *Endeavour,* on the hull, when a terrifying noise rent the air above the girl's head as a cannonball tore past her ear to throw up a fountain of water close on their starboard quarter.

"Hands to the braces!" Dominic called, his voice as calm and even as if he were giving the course in the Mississippi River. "Hard a-starboard." Again, *Danseuse* came round, hull up, the white water frothing under her bow. There was another appalling noise, and a shot buried itself in the quarterdeck a few feet from the cowering Genevieve. No one seemed to take any notice, and she watched in horror as smoke rose from the hole, then little rivulets of flame crept along the deck. She opened her mouth to call a warning, then recollected the fire bucket beside the ladder to the main deck. Crouching low, she ran for it. It was heavy, cast iron and filled with seawater, but with a supreme effort she managed to hurl its contents on the licking flames. There was a hiss and then only smoke remained.

Dominic, hearing the unexpected sound, spun round, just as Genevieve was running for the main deck and the pump, to refill the bucket. He opened his mouth on the order to go below, then closed it again. She seemed to have her wits about her, judging by that piece of quick thinking, and he could use every useful pair of hands at the present. *Danseuse* seemed to be drawing all the fire, and *Mouette,* under full canvas like her sister ships, was now clear and running well for the Yucatan Channel. If they could maneuver to avoid being hit, *Danseuse* would be joining her in no time. He gave the order to wear ship again and she came round, carrying too much canvas for strict safety, but he could not afford to shorten sail and lose speed. Genevieve grabbed hold of the deck rail and hung on, staring with a mesmerized terror at the great green wall of water into which *Danseuse* seemed about to plunge. It seemed inevitable that she would plow her way at this great speed right down to the ocean bottom. But the nimble vessel responded sweetly to the helm as her master had known she would and came up to dance over the water, leaving the *Endeavour* still wondering what had happened, clumsily trying to change course in pursuit.

Genevieve relaxed and stood staring over the stern at the British ship being left fast behind. Soon her top gallants were out of sight and only her royals visible.

"Two hours and we shall have run her mastheads under." Dominic, sounding infinitely satisfied, spoke at her shoulder.

"What happened with the others?" she asked. "Everything

252

happened so quickly, I did not have time to notice."

He shrugged. "Only one of the three blockaders tried to stop us, so it is to be assumed that the others split up and went after the two groups. They'll not catch them, though." He turned to acknowledge the bosun. "Any casualties, bosun?"

"Nothing serious, monsieur. A few splinters from a ball that hit the stern gallery."

Dominic nodded. "Damage?"

"Just the two hits, monsieur. The one there . . ." He indicated the hole in the quarterdeck. "And the one at the stern. Nothing that a bit o' patching can't put right."

"Nearly had a fire, though," Dominic said thoughtfully, looking at the smoke-blackened planking of the deck. "If someone hadn't thought quickly." He smiled at Genevieve, and she went pink with pleasure. Perhaps she wasn't entirely useless, after all. "Not that you should have been on deck in the first place," he added, but without heat, as if it were simply a form reproof.

"You did not tell me to go below," she reminded him.

"You took shameless advantage of my preoccupation," he retorted unarguably, pulling a handkerchief from his pocket and licking a corner. "You look like a chimney sweep." Holding her face, he wiped away the smears of soot and smoke. "That dress is filthy, too. You'll have to ask Silas to launder it for you."

"But then I'll have to stay in bed until it's dry," she protested. "That does not seem a just reward for my firefighting."

"No?" His eyesbrows lifted in that quizzical, teasing fashion. "That rather depends on what you do there, I would have said. Or were you not thinking of having company?"

"I thought you had a ship to sail." Her eyes sparkled with the light banter, and his own responded.

"It can manage without me for a few hours. Why don't you run along, give Silas your gown and put yourself to bed? I will join you in a very few minutes."

"Yes, monsieur," she said, knuckling her forehead in a fair imitation of the erstwhile cabin boy. "Whatever monsieur says."

"Get off this deck before I do something that you will not want witnessed!"

Chuckling, Genevieve beat a prudently hasty retreat, to be scolded by Silas on the state of her dress as if she were still in the schoolroom and had ruined her Sunday gown by climbing trees. Clearly, her exploits with the fire bucket were not considered sufficient excuse for spoiling the old sailor's craftsmanship.

They reached Punta Gorda on the morning of the fourth day, and Dominic went ashore almost immediately. Genevieve pleaded to accompany him, but in vain. He was impervious to her cajoling, to her sulks and to her bullying, repeating his denial, patiently and without raising his voice, as often as it was necessary. This lack of reaction she found even more infuriating than his refusal, but continuing to plague him was clearly as pointless as hitting her head against a brick wall, so she had to make do with sitting on the deck looking longingly at the little fishing village. It seemed a perfectly innocuous place, sleeping in the sun, its only inhabitants scrawny children rolling in the dust, bareheaded women carrying baskets of fish, and lean, bronzed fishermen. There was a distinct air of poverty about the village with its tumbledown shacks and single dusty cart track, and no sign of the Spanish authorities, who were presumably not bothered with such an insignificant spot. Genevieve assumed that that was why it had been chosen as the delivery place. For all its apparent lack of excitement, she longed to go ashore and feel solid ground beneath her feet, but as an indication of the lessons she had learned in recent weeks, she made no attempt to defy the privateer's edict. It also occurred to her that, although Silas had accompanied Dominic, there were plenty of the crew remaining on board, none of whom would scruple to prevent her if she did decide to leave.

Dominic and Silas reappeared after a long morning, and they were not alone. The three men who accompanied them struck Genevieve as distinctly villainous. They were bristling with pistols and cutlasses and looked much more like pirates than did the pirates themselves. Dominic, indeed, was almost elegant in his beautifully cut and laundered shirt and breeches, his boots of the finest leather, his silken kerchief knotted carelessly around his neck.

Leaning inquisitively over the quarterdeck rail, she looked down on the main deck as the five came aboard. They were speaking Spanish, a tongue that was almost as natural to Genevieve as French, her education in the necessities of Creole living having been thorough. They went over to the battened-down hatch, and then Dominic looked up at the quarterdeck. He saw her and pointed imperatively toward the companionway. Then he placed a finger on his lips. There was no mistaking the message. She was to go below without being seen or heard. She waited until the three visitors had disappeared into the hold, then dashed for the companionway and the seclusion of the cabin.

"Why must I hide?" she demanded of Dominic when he came into the cabin an hour later.

"I have no desire for those unsavory characters to know of your presence," he told her, pulling off his sweat-darkened shirt. "It's as hot as Hades out there."

"Why not?" Genevieve persisted.

"Pass me a clean shirt. Because there is no knowing what use they might make of it." He held out his hand for the shirt she handed him. "They wouldn't think twice about kidnapping you and holding you for ransom. The weapons are a present, as you know. But they could always do with funds."

"Oh." Genevieve contemplated this interesting piece of information with a frown.

"They would cut your throat in the end, anyway," he continued with brutal candor, "so there'd be little point in negotiating with them."

"You would not attempt to save me?" she demanded with clear indignation.

"If you were stupid enough to disobey my orders, issued purely for your protection, Mademoiselle Genevieve, you would get only what you deserved."

"How long do we remain here?" She changed the subject, since that one seemed to lead to no useful avenues.

"I will wait a couple of days for *Hirondelle, Colombe,* and *Cygne,*" he told her. "*Alouette* and *Pique* will be at least another week, even with a fair wind, so we will not wait for them."

"It is going to be very tedious, this waiting, if I cannot go ashore, or even on deck." Her mouth formed a small but unmistakable pout. Disconcertingly, Dominic laughed.

"It is not convincing, *mon coeur.* Elise's mannerisms look merely ridiculous on you, like a little girl dressing up in her mother's clothes."

"What did you call me?" Genevieve stared, openmouthed, having heard nothing but those two extraordinary words.

Dominic frowned, as if trying to remember. Then a startled, rueful look crossed his face. With a visible effort, he shrugged, trying to seem nonchalant. "*Une façon de parler,* sprite," he said lightly. "I think perhaps this is another occasion when you should adopt the britches and a cap again. That way, you may go on deck without drawing unwelcome attention from our friends ashore. But you will not leave the ship. Understand?"

Genevieve nodded and went to the door, avoiding his eye. "I will go and ask Silas for my britches."

Dominic stood for a minute looking at the closed door, then he sighed and shook his head. How had he let such an

256

endearment slip out, as if it were the most natural thing in the world to call her? He had never used those two words to anyone since Rosemarie's death. And he had never thought to do so again. But it had been quite involuntary, and Genevieve, of course, had noticed and had not the delicacy to let it pass unremarked. But then tact was not her long suit. He was just going to have to be very careful not to let it happen again. It wasn't as if it was the truth. That was one damnable complication he could not afford.

*Une façon de parler,* Genevieve thought. Yes, of course that was all it was. He had been laughing at her when he'd called her that. It might have been different, might have meant something, if it had happened during the passion of their lovemaking. She had best put it out of mind before her imagination got the better of her. It wasn't as if she wanted him to mean it. It would cause the most damnable complications.

The three privateers that had run to the Bay of Campeche appeared promptly, and the reunion was boisterous, to say the least. Their mission completed, the crews of all four vessels were relieved of all but vital duties for twenty-four hours, and the rum flowed freely. There was dancing and singing, but forays ashore in search of women had been forbidden, so they were obliged to make do with their own entertainment. Genevieve needed no instructions to keep to herself below. The words to the sailors' songs would have brought a blush to the cheeks of a harlot, and the conversation of the captains of the privateers seemed little better, as she discovered when Dominic entertained them to a celebratory dinner on *Danseuse.*

He had suggested strongly that she spend the evening alone, in the small cabin allotted to Silas, who was serving the gentlemen in the master's cabin and would not be needing it. Genevieve, with a stubbornness that she was to regret bitterly, said she would help Silas and grace the proceedings as hostess. Dominic had simply shrugged. It was a lesson she was going to have to learn for herself, he decided. She would suffer no more than embarrassment as long as he was there.

The captains of his fleet had had no idea of the presence of a woman on board *La Danseuse,* but they had no difficulty drawing the obvious conclusions. No lady would be in such a position, so it did not occur to them to moderate their tone or language in front of her when they teased Dominic for being a sly dog, stealing a march on the rest of them by bringing his own comfort with him. One or two hands groped at her as she moved around the table, trying to be as gracious a hostess as she would have been at home on Royal Street, or at Trianon. But there was no room for such niceties at this table. Their manners were atrocious, except for Dominic, who was as suave and seemingly as sober as ever, although he consumed as much wine and brandy as the others. When his azure gaze came to rest on Genevieve's set face and flushed cheeks as it did frequently, it held mocking amusement, the satisfaction of having been proven right, and he made no attempt to tone down the conversation, or to say anything that might alter the impression they had of "his woman."

Pride kept her in the room long beyond the point of near unbearable humiliation, although if Dominic had suggested that she leave, she would have jumped at the opportunity. But he did not; merely passed her his plate when it required refilling, and gestured toward the wine bottles on the side table when one needed replacing. When, at last, the table had been cleared and there seemed no further need of her services, and she could leave without it looking as if she were fleeing her mistake, she made for the door. Only to be arrested by a jovial demand from *Mouette*'s captain that she stay and entertain them. They were sorely in need of a little female company, and Monsieur Delacroix could not be so selfish as to keep her all to himself. Significant looks went to the big bed, and a rumble of eager agreement ran round

258

the table.

"Go," said Dominic evenly, without turning his head, and she went, trembling with shame, furious with herself for inviting that treatment, and quite unable to transfer that fury to Dominic, which made it even harder to bear. When they went on deck to smoke and clear their heads in the night air, Silas, radiating disapproval, came and told her that she could return to the master cabin in safety. She crept into bed, wondering how she was to face Dominic, only to discover that the privateer was more than generous in victory. Not once did he refer to the dreadful evening; not then or at any point in the future, but it was a long time before she could forgive herself and before the memory became sufficiently blunted to be tolerable.

The voyage home was enlivened by the capture of an Indiaman loaded with silks, tea, spices, and other luxuries that would find a hungry market in New Orleans. When the prize was sighted, the atmosphere on board *Danseuse* became charged, every man suddenly stiffening to attention, seeming to sniff the wind like a hound scenting the fox. Dominic stood at the helm, a smile on his lips as he looked at the clumsy vessel clawing awkwardly up to windward as if she could escape the little, fast flock of hawks that had appeared on the horizon with such obvious menace.

"Have the guns loaded and run out," he ordered calmly. "I doubt that we will need them, but it will show we mean business." He chuckled. "Should they be in any doubt of that fact."

Genevieve glanced up at him. He was about to commit an act of piracy that outside wartime would be judged a piece of blatant thievery, yet he was behaving as if it were a game. For Dominic Delacroix, it was just that, she realized, seeing the glint in the azure eyes, feeling the surge of energetic anticipation in the body standing beside her. A challenging game—one that he would win.

He caught her look, and the blue eyes offered her a

conspiratorial gleam. "If you wish to watch, sprite, you will be safest on the stern gallery."

"May I not stay here? I cannot understand what is happening if I do not hear you give the orders."

Genevieve Latour would, of course, need to understand what was happening while she watched. And she would not get in the way; that much he knew. "Very well, but keep your head below the level of the deck rail."

She took up a position sitting in the corner, beside the taffrail, where she had an uninterrupted view and could hear everything of what was said behind her. The merchantman was running out boarding nettings, and the snub noses of cannon appeared in her ports.

So she was prepared to defend herself. Dominic's smile broadened as he gave the order to bring *Danseuse* up into the wind. Her fellow privateers followed suit, and Genevieve could almost hear the panicky speculation on board their quarry. Why were the enemy coming to a halt in their pursuit? Only because they were about to concert their moves. Signals flashed between the hawks, then *Danseuse*'s bow swung to starboard, *Colombe*'s to port. Each ship, with the wind on her quarter, came racing down, a picture of malevolent efficiency with the water foaming beneath their bows. *Hirondelle, Mouette,* and *Pique* waited in the wings. If they were needed, they would join the fun.

The Indiaman sheered off in fright as *Colombe* bore down on her portside, but *Danseuse* was waiting to starboard. The privateer's crew went smoothly into action; the only voice was Dominic's, never raised, yet carrying. Grappling irons were thrown, and the boarding party went over the side, clawing their way along the swinging ropes to rip the boarding nettings with cutlass and hook. A few shots were fired from the merchantman and returned with a deadly accuracy that completely cowed the already overwhelmed vessel, untrained to fight. And it was all over.

Piracy on the high seas, Genevieve thought in inarticulate

bewilderment for the thousandth time. A deadly business that brought enormous rewards to those who dared—to those who possessed the skill and the daring. Dominic Delacroix possessed both to an inordinate degree, and she felt her heart lift as she shared the crew's excitement and Dominic's calmer satisfaction of a job well done. He had struck a heavy blow for his country against the enemy, struck against the fat purses of the British merchants who financed the war. His purse, of course, would be enriched by the shrinking of theirs, but this was war and privateering was quite legal. A little voice from the Ursuline convent murmured that from the point of view of a strict conscience, there were no excuses for thievery, but the moral aspect would not trouble the consumers of the goods any more than it appeared to trouble the privateers. And Genevieve realized with a little thrill of shock that while the question interested her, it didn't seem to worry her in the slightest.

# Chapter 16

"Genevieve, are you feeling quite well, *chère?*" Hélène looked anxiously at her stepdaughter whose expression bore all the signs of impatience, and the tawny eyes were distinctly stormy.

"Quite well," the girl replied shortly, looking across the crowded ballroom where New Orleans's finest were enjoying the first *bal de royauté* of the new *saison des visites*. "It is just so boring!"

"You must not speak like that," Hélène said in an agonized whisper. "Supposing someone should hear you."

Genevieve shrugged, the gesture clearly expressing her indifference to such a happenstance. Hélène sighed. Genevieve had become almost impossible since her return from the convent. No longer overshadowed by her elder sister's beauty, she was rapidly becoming one of the most sought-after young maidens of this season, but her habitual expression of bored disapproval would inevitably be offputting, once the novelty of her rather unusual beauty had worn off. The weeks at the convent, Hélène was obliged to admit, had wrought an amazing change in that respect. The girl had blossomed quite extraordinarily and, notwithstanding her diminutive stature, she was unmistakably a mature, most out of the ordinary young woman for whom her father was already considering a respectably long list of potential suitors.

"Mademoiselle Latour? My dance, I think." A young man, curled and pomaded, immaculate in silken knee britches and striped waistcoat, bowed before her.

Genevieve looked up at him over her fan. Antoine Dufour was becoming annoyingly persistent, and she did not like that silly little clipped moustache he wore above that overly full mouth. "I do not care to dance, I am afraid, Antoine."

The young man's face fell ludicrously. "But this is my dance," he said, indicating the dance card dangling from her wrist on a silken ribband.

"I did not know when I agreed that I would not feel like it." She rose fluidly, smiled with her lips, and left the ballroom. Her discomfitted suitor bowed to Hélène and went off in search of more willing damsels, and Hélène looked at Nicolas in horror.

"What are we to do?" she bemoaned. "She cannot behave with such rudeness without being ostracized eventually. I do not understand what she finds so distasteful. Everything is as it has always been, and everyone else is enjoying themselves."

"Genevieve is not everyone else," Nicolas said with absolute truth. "Oh, Dominic, I did not see you standing there. Hélène, you are acquainted with Monsieur Delacroix."

The privateer moved out of the shadow of the wall, where he had most conveniently blended against the gray silk hangings, and bowed before Madame Latour, raising her fingers to his lips. *"Enchanté,* madame."

Hélène fluttered a smile. For reasons that she did not fully understand, Monsieur Delacroix had quite suddenly become persona grata in society. It was something to do with the nearness of the British forces and the fighting that was taking place along the Gulf Coast. But Victor had been too impatient to explain the details to her when she had asked, and he did not care to mention the privateer's name or have it mentioned to him, for all that he was now to be met everywhere, bestowing that cynical, enigmatic little smile on all and sundry.

"I was hoping to solicit a dance from your cousin, Nicolas," he now said casually. "But I expect she is already engaged."

Nicolas shot him a sharp look. He still did not know what had passed between his cousin and the privateer during that April night, and to his knowledge, there had been no further dealings between them. Indeed, whenever they were in the same room together, Genevieve seemed to go out of her way to avoid Delacroix.

"No, she is not engaged," Hélène was saying, plucking nervously at the drawstring of her reticule. "I am certain she will return shortly."

Dominic bowed. "Then I shall hope to have the pleasure at a later time. Servant, madame. Nicolas." A slight inclination of his head and he went off in search of Genevieve. He had overheard the exchange with Antoine Dufour, as well as the conversation between Nicolas and Hélène, and it seemed incumbent upon him to take a hand in the matter before it became quite irreversible. Genevieve had made no secret to him, in the privacy of Rampart Street, of how insupportably irksome she found the life she was expected to lead since their return from freedom and adventure, but tonight was the first time he had seen how her public behavior was affected. And he was in complete agreement with Hélène. Many more displays of such blatant rudeness and Genevieve Latour would find herself a social outcast. If he was in any way responsible for her present disaffection from the life that she must lead, then it was also his responsibility to ensure that she come to terms with it. She would eventually, he was convinced. It was only that the memories of *Danseuse* were still very fresh, and she was having difficulty adjusting.

He saw the unmistakable figure in a delicate gown of rose-pink spider gauze over white satin disappearing up the wide circular staircase in the main hall. The retiring rooms were to be found upstairs and he followed her, his step apparently leisurely, except that he reached the head of the stairs only seconds after Genevieve. His lips tightened when he saw that, instead of going into the room set aside for ladies in need of rest and recuperation after the exertions of the dance floor, she made straight for the door to the rear, upstairs gallery.

"Genevieve!" His voice, though low, was sharp and arrested her just as she was stealthily opening the door. "You cannot leave the ball in this manner."

"I cannot bear another minute," she said in a stifled voice, still holding the door, poised for flight, the way she was holding herself and the delicate, transparent gauze of her gown reminding him of a butterfly settled momentarily on a leaf.

"You are behaving like a spoiled baby again," he said severely. "You were abominably rude to young Dufour and have upset your stepmother. It is all very well to storm and rage in private, but it is quite different to behave like that in public."

"Why can you be as contemptuous as you please, and I may not?" she demanded in a fierce undertone. "You make no secret of how you despise them all, and of the sort of amusement you derive from this . . . this circus! Why must I play the hypocrite?"

"Do not be naive, sprite. You know perfectly well why you must, and why I need not. It may be unjust, but it is the way of the world. Now, come downstairs and dance with me."

Slowly, she turned from the door, her gown swirling around her. A slight, rueful smile touched the tiger's eyes. "I will do so, but only because it will annoy Papa." That made him laugh, and she said with sudden intensity, "We are so alike, you and I, why can you not understand the way I feel?"

"I do understand," he said. "I understand because it is how I would feel myself. But there are realities, Genevieve, that you must accept. And first and foremost of those realities is that you are a woman."

"First and last," she said bitterly. "It says it all, doesn't it?"

"I am afraid so," replied Dominic. "Take that mutinous look off your face, my child, and start acting. We are going to dance and you are going to smile and talk vivaciously, first to me, and then to anyone else who solicits your attention. I do not find spoiled babies in the least appealing, and am certainly not prepared to share my bed with one."

"Is that a threat or a bribe?" Genevieve inquired archly, laying her hand on his gray-satin arm.

"Well, if it is a threat, it is one I sincerely hope not to be obliged to carry out," he said with a chuckle that was readily answered by her own. "That is much better," he approved. "Now, keep it up."

To Hélène's relief, Genevieve appeared to have forgotten her fit of the sullens and for the rest of the evening behaved impeccably, although the other woman could not help but feel that the lively, flirtatious belle might at any moment revert to her true colors. Fortunately, no one else seemed aware of the deception, or of the slightly brittle quality to Genevieve's laugh.

"Delacroix?"

Dominic turned from his covert examination of Genevieve to acknowledge the rotund figure of one of New Orleans's most prominent citizens. "Senor Garcia?"

"Would you join us in the card room?" the Spaniard said in ponderous accents. "There is a matter of some moment we would like to discuss." He nodded self-importantly and, taking Dominic's agreement for granted, waddled off in the direction of the card room. Dominic raised one eyebrow, took a fresh glass of negus from the hovering servent, and followed. Matters of some moment tended to have financial implications.

The six men gathered in the card room greeted him, if not effusively, at least with more politeness than he was accustomed to receiving from these denizens of Creole society. "How may I serve you, gentlemen?" he inquired, perching on the corner of the table. "I assume there is something I can do for you?" An ironic gleam shimmered in the turquoise eyes. "Monsieur Mayor?"

The gentleman addressed coughed and looked around the table as if for confirmation of his right to be spokesman. The silence granted it, and he began in solemn and weighty fashion as befitted the serious nature of his subject. Monsieur Delacroix was, of course, aware of the growing threat to the city with the British forces drawing ever closer. After the devastation they had wrought in Washington it was only to be expected that no quarter would be shown here. And they could not expect to beat off the British as General Stricker had done in Baltimore. The city was inadequately defended, and fifty British ships had been sighted in the Mississippi Delta. General Jackson was intending to intercept them at Baton Rouge, but New Orleans needed a defense of its own. Monsieur Delacroix had a fleet of ships, did he not? And highly trained crews?

He did, the privateer agreed, concealing his ironic amusement.

And presumably, the fleet was armed, given the nature of its usual activity.

It was, agreed the privateer, lighting a cigar and smiling benignly at them through the smoke.

Would Monsieur Delacroix consider placing his ships, men, and arms at the disposal of the committee for the defense of the city? There, it had been said at last. The mayor sat back with a sigh of relief.

Monsieur Delacroix seemed to consider the question for an inordinate length of time before he spoke. "I think I must ask for a seat on the committee in such an event," he said calmly. "You could not expect me to hand over such riches without having some say in their disposition." He watched their faces with huge enjoyment. Their horror was transparent. A notorious rogue to be granted the ultimate civic honor! Yet his point was absolutely valid, and they knew it. If they wanted what the privateer could offer, then they must accept the privateer.

"When the devil drives," Victor Latour stated with unconcealed bitterness into the heavy silence.

"Quite so, Latour." Dominic bowed his head at his old enemy and allowed his mind to dwell for one delicious instant on Genevieve. "Needs must," he agreed gently and stood up. "If that is all, gentlemen, I will bid you good night. You may contact me at Maspero's. Meanwhile, I will see that all is in order with my end of the bargain."

Genevieve saw him leave, recognized the glitter in his eye, expressive of some wicked satisfaction, the set of his shoulders, expressive of determination, the curve of his mouth, expressive of secret delight. And she ached with longing and with envy. She half started toward the door, driven by the desire to discover what had amused and delighted him, what plan he had formed, to laugh with him and plan with him. Then she remembered that she was a woman—condemned to prattle and convention behind the bars of ritual.

"Well, *ma soeur,* how does it feel to be Mademoiselle Latour?"

Genevieve looked up at Elise. There was a slight thickening of her waist beneath the sea-green gown, but her sister's pregnancy was still far from obvious. "To tell the truth, Elise, it feels no different from being Mademoiselle Genevieve. I am still the same person, after all."

"But you are now the daughter of the house," Elise reminded her, sitting on the little gilt chair and clearly settling down for a cozy chat. "It is amazing how you have blossomed since the summer."

Genevieve choked. It was so unfair to be denied the glory

268

of revelation! Elise was so complacent and matronly and even more condescending than ever, now that she had joined the ranks of the initiated and bore the evidence of that initiation. But at least she was careful to moderate her smug pride with Hélène who looked with such sadness at Elise's inhabited eyes, the translucent skin of pregnancy, the little pats she gave her belly every now and again.

After Hélène's third miscarriage three weeks ago, Victor had been told unequivocally that a further pregnancy would probably kill his wife. Hélène had begged him to ignore the advice of the doctor; she was as strong as a horse. Only grant her a few months' respite, and they would try again. But Victor had looked at the wan, bloodless face, the frail body, and had finally relinquished his last hope for a son. He had lost two wives on the accouchement bed, and the third had only just survived miscarriage. She was twenty years younger than he, and healthy in all other respects, so, barring sudden disease, she would probably outlive him. The revelation had done little for his temper and, for some reason, the prospect of a forthcoming grandchild was not proving helpful.

"Blossoming seems an infectious condition between sisters, then," Genevieve said. She knew Elise so well that the right remark came to her lips automatically, and now that they were not living under the same roof, irritation had ceased to set a brake on the complimentary softnesses that greased the wheels of their relationship.

Elise smiled with placid contentment, accepting the compliment as her due. "Lorenzo, of course, is overjoyed," she imparted, as if the information were news to Genevieve. "He is hoping that Papa will make some settlement on his grandson, now that . . . well, you know what I mean."

"Yes," her sister agreed in a dry tone. "But I must congratulate you on your prescience. To have foreknowledge of the sex of one's unborn child is a gift, indeed."

"It will be a son," Elise said fiercely.

"I am sure you are right. It is unthinkable to imagine Lorenzo's fathering anything else," Genevieve responded tartly. Oh, why did Elise bring out the bitch in her? she thought with genuine regret. It was just that the idea of her sister and the Castilian blithely assuming that they would benefit from Hélène's ill fortune made her want to spit!

*"Chère,* I think perhaps we should make our farewells," Hélène said gently, appearing out of the blue in her usual soft-footed fashion. "Unless you would prefer to stay a little longer. Nicolas could escort you home."

"You are tired," Genevieve said, rising instantly to her feet. "And I have had more than enough of this dissipation for one evening." She looked across the ballroom. "Besides, I do not think Nicolas would be at all happy to devote attention to his cousin at this point." The other two women followed her gaze. Nicolas was dancing with Madeleine Benoit, and it was clear that as far as the two of them were concerned, they were alone on some celestial planet.

"Do you think Papa will permit the match, Hélène?" Elise asked, forgetting Genevieve's acerbity in this much more interesting family issue.

Hélène looked unhappy. "Nicolas asked me to mention it vaguely to him, to see what his reaction might be, you understand, and I did try, but Victor did not seem to hear me. He often doesn't," she added with a self-deprecating little smile.

"No, he hears you," Genevieve said. "But if he does not wish to respond, he will pretend he did not."

They all knew the truth of this observation. "Does Nicolas have nothing of his own?" Elise asked. "I thought his mother left him her estate."

"Two thousand piasters," Genevieve said with authority. "When Nicolas came of age, Papa took him to dinner at his club and handed over his inheritance with great ceremony." Her lips tightened. "You can imagine it, I am sure. Poor Nicolas had had no idea how much there was, but he had never been led to believe that it would be barely enough to buy a small plot of land."

"How do you know?" asked Elise. Genevieve always seemed to know everything that went on.

She shrugged. "Nicolas told me that evening. He was so mortified by the way Papa had treated him, and I happened to be awake and sitting in the courtyard when he returned . . . so, he poured it all out." She shrugged again. "Nicolas is totally dependent on Papa. For as long as he stays in his good graces, he will have the means to live the life of a Creole blood, but let him once overstep the mark . . ." It was that fear, of course, that had led to Nicolas's involvement with the privateer, to his willingness to sacrifice Elise. She could blame him, but she could also understand.

"Madeleine Benoit is hardly a brilliant match." Elise stated the fact without adornment. They all knew what it meant.

Unfortunately, they did not quite understand what that *would* mean, since Victor Latour had decided to draw the threads of his various disappointments together and had concocted a scheme that would solve all problematical issues at one fell swoop.


Genevieve stretched luxuriously, curling her toes into the mattress, reaching her arms high above her head as the clever hands moved down her back, bringing her spine to life with the firm pressure of his thumbs against the vertebra. She groaned in delicious delight, the sound muffled by the feather pillow, as flat palms rotated her buttocks and the tips of his fingers pressed into the indentation of her pelvis. How did one learn how to give this pleasure? she thought distractedly. It seemed to require an uncanny knowledge of the pleasure centers of another's body. "Who is Rosemarie?" Vague memory of a curiosity she had hitherto forgotten to satisfy brought the question drifting between her lips, following the previous thought naturally, innocent of artifice or intent.

The hands on her back were abruptly stilled, and in the ensuing silence Genevieve realized with a stab of apprehension that it was a question better not to have been asked—a curiosity better left dormant. "Would you repeat that, please?" Dominic said, his voice quite expressionless.

"It was nothing," she mumbled into the pillow. "I did not mean anything."

His fingertips flicked smartly against her behind and hastily she tried to roll over, but he planted a knee in the small of her back and held her still. "I cannot believe, my dear Genevieve, that your question was meaningless. You are not in the habit of talking nonsense." His voice was silky smooth, but it rasped on Genevieve's stretched nerves like teeth on velvet. "Oblige me by repeating your question. I would like to be certain I heard it correctly."

Genevieve did not need to see his face to know that the azure gaze was ice tipped, the sculpted lips set in a thin line, and she felt a creeping desperation. Why had she asked? He would consider that she was invading his privacy again, but she had not thought of it like that. Indeed, she had forgotten all about the flowery signature in the book of Latin verse until this moment when it had just popped into her head.

"My patience is wearing a little thin," he warned, and her skin jumped in alarm as she felt his hand, flat and warm, come to rest on her buttocks.

"Let me up," she said. "I will tell you what I said. There is no need to hold me down and threaten me."

Dominic gave a short and not very pleasant laugh. "You had better have a reasonable explanation, my meddlesome, prying, little spy, or I shall do a great deal more than threaten." But he removed his knee, allowing her to turn over and sit up. While the danger was far from receding, at least she did not feel quite so vulnerable.

"I was not spying," she protested. "And I am sorry I asked.

272

I did not realize it would upset you."

"What was the question?" he repeated inexorably.

Damn the man! Why did he have to have such an appalling and unpredictable temper? She never knew when a casual remark would arouse it, and she'd be knee-deep in quicksand. "I asked who Rosemarie is," she said, meeting his eyes. "And I do not understand why that should be so upsetting."

"And just where did you hear that name?" he inquired, planting his hands on his hips, sublimely indifferent to his nakedness which did nothing to lessen the menace in the coiled tension of his stance.

Genevieve licked suddenly dry lips. "I was looking at the books in your cabin on *Danseuse,*" she explained hesitantly. "I did not think you would not like it. You did not tell me not to touch them." She shrugged helplessly, and when he offered no signs of reassurance, she continued stoically. "There was a volume of Latin verse—Catullus. He's one of my favorite poets." Was there just the faintest hint of a melt in those iceberg eyes? "There was an inscription in the front. I couldn't help but read it. I am sorry if it was wrong, but I was not spying, really I was not."

"Why did you not ask me about it before?" To her inexpressible relief, she saw that the frown accompanying the question was curious rather than threatening, and the tension had left his body.

"I did not remember to," she said frankly. "I forgot all about it until just now."

A slight smile touched his lips. "Perhaps you are not irredeemably inquisitive after all." He brushed the tip of her nose with a manicured forefinger. "I was a little harsh. I am sorry. I made an overhasty judgment based on previous experience of your capacity for delving into matters that do not concern you."

Genevieve was not at all sure how to respond to an apology that really did not qualify as such. He had turned

273

away and was pouring wine into two glasses. One he handed to Genevieve. Then, still without bothering to clothe himself, he found a cigar from the pocket of his coat and lit it, smoking in a thoughtful silence for a few minutes.

"Rosemarie was my wife," he said eventually, his tone even, as if he were imparting a piece of information that had nothing to do with him at all. Genevieve's jaw dropped, but she kept silent, praying that he would continue of his own accord, for if he did not, she knew she would not dare to question him.

"It was not a match that met with approval from either family," he went on, his eyes strangely blank as if he were looking into some other existence. "I was twenty and a Delacroix. She was seventeen and an American—the daughter of a merchant." Genevieve needed no expansion. A Creole aristocrat and the daughter of an American shopkeeper would be considered impossible marriage partners. "We eloped." His lips quirked in a sardonic, self-mocking smile. "It did not occur to either of us that one could not live on love alone. My family disinherited me, and Rosemarie's father said that he would accept her back into the fold on condition that the marriage was annulled."

Genevieve sat on the edge of the bed, breathless with the need to hear the rest, desperate at the thought that the story would end there and she would never find out because she would never be able to ask.

But he continued, his words clipped, no emotion in his voice. "So, with a pregnant wife to support and a living to earn, I took to the high seas. An apprentice privateer under Claude Tourcelle." A blue-tinged smoke ring wreathed in the air above his head. "I found it as entertaining a business as it proved to be lucrative, and came home full of self-importance with a pocket full of ducats and a trunk of the finest silks for Rosemarie, and a tongue bursting to regale her with the tales of my adventures." A bleak look shivered

274

in his eyes, bleak with a disdain that was clearly self-directed. "Rosemarie had died some two weeks earlier giving birth to a stillborn daughter. Out of loyalty to me, she had not sought the help of her own family, and had known better than to seek aid from mine. So she died without medical attention, except what was offered by an incompetent, self-styled midwife."

Genevieve wanted to reach out, to take his hand, to hold his head against her breast as the pain of relived memory now throbbed in his voice, hung in his eyes. But she did not know whether the comfort would be accepted. Perhaps it would be seen as yet further unwarranted interference. Dominic was so hard to understand, and the one thing she knew with absolute clarity was that she must not make the wrong move at this moment.

"The Delacroix were more than happy to welcome the prodigal son back to the fold after his unsuccessful little adventure of love." The bitterness burned like acid, and she shivered but still kept silent. "I decided that I preferred the life of a privateer—infinitely preferred it to the oiled hypocrisy that was the alternative. And, until you made your presence felt in my life, Genevieve Latour, I had never found room for another woman in those areas of that life not directly related to the simple fulfillment of mutual physical pleasure."

She went to him, then, slipping her arms around his waist, hugging him with an undemanding warmth, wishing that she were taller and generally larger and stronger so that she could somehow encompass him physically with her loving comfort. But he seemed to understand and to draw comfort, his hand stroking the ash-blond silk resting against his chest as the tautness left his body.

"You are a very little thing, sprite," he said softly. "But you have a very generous spirit. I was not at all kind to you, was I?"

"I do find you a little intimidating, sometimes," she confessed with a little laugh. "But I suppose I have earned the reputation for going where angels fear to."

"The auction block, and voodoo ceremonies, and the lower deck of a privateer . . ." he mused, but she could hear the rich chuckle lurking in the depths of the bland voice. "I have never met a woman like you, *mon coeur,* and that is very dangerous for both of us."

He had called her *mon coeur* again. She didn't think he had noticed, and she tried to control the sudden wild pounding of her blood, to say naturally, "Why dangerous?"

"Women and piracy do not go together, Genevieve."

"But that last voyage?" She raised her head, her eyes shining with memory. "There were only one or two moments when it was inappropriate for me to be there."

Dominic sighed. "Disreputable hoydens and piracy are one thing, *ma chère*. You cannot be forever a disreputable hoyden, and I am never going to be able to settle to an earthbound life."

Genevieve frowned. "I think you are jumping to too many conclusions. I would never expect you to settle to an earthbound life. It is the last thing I want for myself. Why cannot we simply enjoy what we are for as long as it is good for both of us?"

"And when it ceases to be good for one or both of us?" he queried quietly, continuing to stroke her hair.

"Then, we part—amicably and without regret. Each taking responsibility for themselves."

"You are still a child, sprite." But he said it gently, as if unwilling to hurt her. "Such ideal prescriptions rarely come to pass. There is hurt and anger and confusion, and a legacy of bitterness that takes too long to lose its sting. I don't want that to happen to you."

"It will not," she said fiercely, burying her head against his chest, inhaling his wonderful, familiar fragrance. "I am not the child you think me, Dominic. I take responsibility for my

276

own happiness."

"Such confidence," he murmured, tossing his cigar stub into the fire and lifting her into his arms. "I envy you the convictions of naivity, my Genevieve. But disillusion will come eventually. Until it does, or until circumstances intervene, we will enjoy what we have."

*Chapter 17*

It was a cool, pleasant Sunday morning in December when Victor Latour dropped his bombshell. He came into the *salle de compagnie* where his wife, Genevieve, and Nicolas were warming their hands at the fire after their obligatory sojourn in the drafty church of St. Louis.

"I have something I wish to say to you two." He indicated Nicolas and Genevieve. "Come into the cabinet." With no further expansion, he walked out of the parlor.

Nicolas looked alarmed and Genevieve glanced at the nervous Hélène. "What have we done? Do you know?"

Her stepmother shook her head. "He has said nothing to me. I do not think he is angry, though. He did not sound it."

"He will be if we don't hurry up," Nicolas said with absolute truth. "After you, cousin." With a mock bow, he gestured toward the doorway.

"I think, in this case, such chivalry is actually unchivalrous," Genevieve said with a grin. "You should surely enter his lair first. Being so much bigger and stronger!"

"Now, Genevieve, do try not to antagonize your father," Hélène pleaded. "If he is not in the mood for levity . . ."

"He is *never* in the mood for levity," her irrepressible stepdaughter chuckled. "I should be surprised if he knows the meaning of the word."

"Come on," Nicolas urged impatiently, pushing her toward the hall. "I have a luncheon engagement which I do not wish to miss."

"Mademoiselle Benoit?" Genevieve inquired sweetly.

"None of your business."

They reached the cabinet that served as Latour's private office when he conducted his domestic affairs. It was not a room that either of them cared for, redolent as it was of painful scenes of the past. The door stood open, and Victor was seated behind his massive carved desk, riffling through a sheaf of papers.

"Shut the door," he instructed. "I do not wish the entire household to hear what I have to say."

Genevieve closed the door and adopted her customary posture in this room, hands clasped behind her, eyes on the floor. Nicolas, she noticed with an inner chuckle, had a remarkably similar stance.

"Sit down," Latour said brusquely.

Genevieve and her cousin exchanged startled looks. Neither of them could remember ever having been invited to sit down in the patriarch's cabinet. They sat hesitantly on the straight-backed, leather chairs facing the desk and waited.

"It is time I considered naming an heir," Victor announced into the expectant quiet. Nicolas's head shot up. It had always been assumed that, in the absence of a son of his own, Victor would make his heir the son of his distant cousin, the child he had brought up from babyhood, trained in the shipbuilding business and the management of the sugar-cane plantation. But nothing had ever been said.

"It does not suit me," Victor said with his customary lack of softness, "to have my property inherited by one who is not a child of mine." His eyes rested on Genevieve, but she had herself well in hand, and her features were schooled to an expression of polite interest. "However, a woman is not competent to handle such an inheritance, even if she does spend an inordinate amount of time with her head in her

279

books in the convent."

Genevieve remained unmoving, but she could sense the slight relaxation in Nicolas at these words. "So," Victor said, "I have decided upon a compromise which should prove satisfactory to all concerned. You will marry Genevieve, Nicolas, and will thus receive all the benefits of my heir, and Genevieve's children will inherit in their turn. You are capable of managing the plantation and the shipyard and will continue to do so, receiving payment in the form of my daughter and her inheritance."

"And what does your daughter receive from this?" Genevieve's voice shook at the enormity of her father's proposal. She stood up, caution flown to the four winds, her face milk white, the tawny eyes huge and blazing.

"First and foremost, a husband," Victor told her shortly. "It is every girl's ambition, after all, and it is time you stopped gadding about and settled down. In addition, you will be sole heir to all the Latour property, and your children after you."

"I cannot believe this! I have no intention of marrying anyone at the moment, and *never* Nicolas!" She swung round on her cousin who looked as bloodless as if he he seen a ghost. "Nicolas does not wish to marry me. Do you?" When there was no immediate response, she took him by the shoulders. "Say something, for godssake! Madeleine Benoit, remember?"

"Enough!" roared Victor, rising in his turn, his face suffused. "There will be no talk of *that* match under my roof. If you wish to marry that insignificant little dab with not a penny to her name, then do so, but never come within my sight again!"

Still Nicolas said nothing. Genevieve shook him and his eyes focused slowly. Her heart sank as she stared incredulously. He was not going to stand up and fight. With a mutter of absolute disgust, she turned away from him and faced her father. "I am not going to marry Nicolas, Papa. I do not mind whom you name as your heir; it is a matter of indifference to me." She went to the door, but Victor bellowed at her to stay where she was and she stopped, her hand on the doorknob, feeling its porcelain coolness against her palm. There was no point walking away from this; it would only pursue her.

"You will do as I tell you, mademoiselle," Latour hissed, coming around the desk. "You are my daughter, and you will accept the authority of your father, or by God, I will compel you to do so."

"You cannot compel me into a repugnant marriage," she said, standing her ground although all her instincts told her to fly. "We do not live in the Middle Ages."

"Why would it be repugnant?" Nicolas spoke for the first time, and she spun around. He was still pale, but quite composed, as if he had reached some difficult decision. "We know each other very well, and we do not dislike each other. I can think of worse bargains."

"Can you?" The mocking inquiry was laced with contempt. "Perhaps I should be flattered. But, I am afraid, cousin, that I cannot think of a worse bargain."

Victor Latour exploded, and she stood still as the storm raged around her, making no move, no sound that might increase the fury of the torrent and lead him to augment the violence of his words with action. But at last, he ran out of steam and stopped, breathing heavily in the small room, one hand pressed against his heart. He was too exhausted to tell them to get out of the room, but his hand flicked toward the door and the cousins beat a rapid retreat.

"Coward!" Genevieve accused fiercely as they reached the hall. "You would sacrifice Madeleine for money! You are despicable!"

Nicolas laughed without humor. "And how am I supposed to live with a paltry two thousand piasters to my name? Tell me that, my brave, crusading cousin. I could not condemn Madeleine to such a life, and she has nothing. Her

281

grandmother barely has enough to maintain them with any degree of respectability."

"Perhaps you should take up piracy," Genevieve heard herself mutter, and then bit her lip. It had just slipped out under the bitter, involuntary comparison of Dominic Delacroix and Nicolas St. Denis in similar circumstances. Fortunately, Nicolas did not seem to have heard.

"If you will think about it unemotionally for a minute," he said, "you will see that it has some advantages. A marriage of mutual convenience that will grant us both independence. I am sure he can be persuaded to allow us to live under our own roof, and I will not interfere with you. If you do not wish to go into society, you need not. You may do exactly as you please. In what other marriage would that be so?" He looked at her shrewdly. "Unless there is more to this than I thought. Are your affections, perhaps, engaged elsewhere?"

Genevieve shook her head. Her affections were not respectably engaged elsewhere, not engaged with a possible husband in a potentially lasting commitment, which was what Nicolas meant.

"Then think about it," he said urgently. "I give you my word that I will not impose anything upon you. You may do what you please within the limits of discretion."

Such as continue to have an affair with a privateer, Genevieve thought, leaving him without a further word and going up to her chamber. If Nicolas refused to stand up for his own rights, she would have a much harder fight upon her hands, and Victor was never subtle in the methods he used to achieve his objectives. There was no knowing what his next step would be. All the while she was thinking, she was dressing in her quadroon's disguise, and it was only when she was ready that she realized that she had made no conscious decision to see Dominic. It was just something that she had to do, the only person she could turn to. A thick woolen shawl swathing her figure, she left her room, locking the door and pocketing the key. If they thought she had locked herself in her chamber after this morning's scene, no one would attempt to disturb her until her father decided to renew the attack. She sped down the gallery stairs and through the side gate.

Once in the street, she paused and wondered where to go first in search of Dominic. He would not be in Rampart Street since they had made no arrangements to meet today. Not unless he used the convenient house with some other mistress. For some reason, Genevieve did not think so. It had been one thing with Angelique, but she had a feeling he now kept the house just for them. She had no evidence for such delicacy of feeling on his part, but the house carried no sense of other occupants. She could try Maspero's, and if he was not there, then she would do what she had never before done and go to his house on Chartres Street. He would understand why she had taken such an unprecedented step when she explained the situation.

Maspero's was shut up, the doors barred, the windows shuttered, the peace of the day of rest lying over the establishment. So she continued down the street until she came to the house that Nicolas had casually pointed out to her soon after her first night in Rampart Street. Without allowing her misgivings to raise an obstructive head, she pulled the bellrope. Silas opened the door and surveyed her with his customary lack of expression.

"Now what?" he demanded unhelpfully.

"Is Monsieur Delacroix here, Silas? I must speak with him." The tawny eyes implored him and he sighed.

"Monsieur's busy, and he won't want them what's with him seeing you. You'd better go upstairs." He pulled the door wider, and she slipped into the hall. Silas gave her no time to examine her surroundings, but hustled her upstairs and into a large bedchamber that she knew immediately belonged to Dominic. It carried the scent of him; the furnishings had his distinctive elegance, and there was none of the vulgar opulence of Rampart Street. "Just wait in here," Silas said.

283

"Would it be wise of me to lock the door?"

"Oh, Silas!" She flushed ruefully. "I will not go where I am not supposed to."

"Not supposed to be here in the first place," he reminded her with a grim little smile before closing the door on her.

Dominic tapped his fingers on the rosewood table in the high-ceilinged, paneled dining room and looked around at the circle of expectant faces. "It is an appealing idea, gentlemen, I grant you. But an expensive and complicated plan to implement."

"There will be no shortage of funds, Delacroix," an elegant, ascetic man said. "And the implementation of complicated and daring plans is surely to what you devote your time and not inconsiderable intelligence, anyway."

Dominic smiled, his eyes narrowed as he refilled the glasses of his neighbors and pushed the decanter across the table. "And what will Napoleon do, once we have effected his escape from exile?"

"That will be for him to decide," another man said. "Of course, we should be overjoyed to welcome him here, should he wish it. But he may have other plans."

"Highly likely," Dominic murmured. "I cannot, somehow, see the emperor without an empire. It is said that he has created his own kingdom on Elba."

"If you succeed in this venture, Delacroix, we assume you would be willing to offer the emperor whatever further services he requires?"

"Should he decide to go to war again?" The fly-away eyebrows lifted on the question. "I would have to be convinced he would have some chance of success, gentlemen, before I committed my neck."

"Of course," the ascetic man said, not troubling to hide his scorn. "We are all aware that you are a mercenary, Delacroix, not motivated by principle or ideals."

"I am glad you are aware of that," the privateer said

gently. "A little more wine?"

This reminder of the host-guest relationship was sufficient to bring an end to barbed comments, and Silas, coming soft-footed into the dining room, heard only an exchange of pleasantries.

"What is it?" Dominic looked over his shoulder at the sailor/servant, standing attentively behind him. Silas knew better than to disturb a business meeting without invitation so his master presumed that a matter of some urgency had arisen. When Silas requested a private word, he rose immediately, excused himself to his guests and accompanied the other into the hall. "Well?"

"Mademoiselle is here," Silas said woodenly, staring into the distance.

"Is she all right?" For some reason, that seemed a more important question than the hows and the whys of this unlooked-for and inconvenient visitation.

"Seems a bit distressed, monsieur. I showed her into your chamber above stairs."

Dominic nodded briefly. "Make sure she stays there. I will dispatch my guests as speedily as I may." Returning to the dining room, he smiled serenely at the group around the table. "Gentlemen, I must ask you to excuse me. A matter of some urgency . . ." A graceful movement of one hand completed the sentence to the satisfaction of all concerned. They rose with the instant, courteous comprehension of the Creole gentleman, and bowed themselves from the house.

Dominic went upstairs with rather more haste than was his custom, and Genevieve, apprehension clear on her face, swung around from her contemplation of the courtyard as he came into the room.

"Please do not be cross, Dominic. I do not think I could bear to be shouted at again today."

"I am not cross," he said. "And when have I ever shouted at you?"

285

She smiled a little shakily. "Never. When you are angry, you become very still and quiet, which is actually even worse."

"What has happened, sprite?" He took her hands in a warm clasp and chafed her fingers. "You're freezing, Genevieve!"

"It is a little chilly outside and I forgot my gloves," she explained.

"Have you had luncheon?" Dominic decided that the tale could wait for awhile, at least until she looked a little less fragile and wan. "Let us go downstairs to the library, and Silas will bring you some soup." He eased her out of the room and into a cheerful, book-lined salon at the back of the house where a fire crackled cheerfully, and Genevieve began to relax. The world of Victor Latour seemed a long way away from the warmth and security of the privateer's very private domain. Silas brought her a bowl of seafood gumbo and, to her amazement, she consumed every last drop while Dominic sat on a scroll-ended couch, sipping wine and watching her, that tiny enigmatic smile lurking in the turquoise depths of his eyes.

"Better now?" he asked when she put the spoon down with a sigh of repletion.

"Much. How did you know I was so hungry?" Genevieve responded with a self-conscious little laugh. "I did not realize it, myself."

"The master of a ship makes it his business to know all sorts of things about those who sail with him," he said with a smile. "Now, you may tell me what has happened to distress you."

"Papa is going to try his damnedest to make me marry Nicolas," she said plainly.

Dominic stood up abruptly, turning his back on her as he walked to the long french door opening onto the courtyard. He stood staring outside onto the winter-bare square for long minutes, until he was sure he had himself well in hand again, and that strange, cold sensation in his chest had dissipated. Then he drawled, "Not a choice *I* would have made for you."

"What do you mean?" The silence had puzzled her, just as did the very clear tension between his shoulder blades. However, he suddenly shrugged his shoulders as if shaking free the tension and turned back to her, his expression quite calm, although the azure gaze was hooded and unreadable.

"Nicolas is not strong enough for you, my dear Genevieve," he said carelessly. "You will ride roughshod over him."

"But I am not going to marry him," she said tensely. "You sound as if it is a foregone conclusion, like Nicolas and Papa, and I am sure Hélène and Elise and Lorenzo will also."

"Nicolas wishes this?"

Genevieve explained Victor's plan and her cousin's situation, leaving nothing out while the privateer resumed his seat on the couch and listened in attentive silence. "And Nicolas says that we will leave each other alone, that I may do as I please within the limits of discretion, that we will be independent of Papa and it is all perfectly possible, maybe even desirable," she finished on a despairing wail. "I will *not* agree to it, Dominic."

"Come over here." He beckoned to her, and when she obeyed, drew her down onto his knee. "I want you to listen to me, and trust that I know what I am talking about," he said quietly, smoothing her hair as she rested her head against his chest. "Nicolas, for once, seems to have spoken a great deal of sense . . . No, be still and hear me out," he told her when she began to protest. "At some point, sooner rather than later, sprite, you are going to have to embrace your destiny— the life of a Creole lady."

"I cannot," she said.

"No, what you mean is that you *will* not," Dominic corrected her ruthlessly. "You are eighteen years old, Genevieve, with your whole life ahead of you. Marrying

Nicolas will not be the end of the world; indeed, it will ensure you a great deal more freedom than I can imagine your having in any other relationship."

"How can you talk in that manner?" cried Genevieve, pushing against his chest as she struggled to free herself from his hold.

"I am merely being sensible and farsighted," Dominic stated, tightening his buckskin-clad thighs beneath her wriggling bottom and holding her firmly against him. "You will be free of your father's jurisdiction if you do this, and you will have exchanged it for no more than the nominal authority of your husband. You will be financially independent, and if you choose to take no part in the society that you say you dislike so much, there will be no one to censure you. And if you do choose to take part in some of the games that are played . . ." A cynical note crept into his voice. "Then you may do so with discretion and a clear conscience, knowing that Nicolas will not suffer."

"No, because he will be playing them himself," she snapped. "I do not care for this pragmatic viewpoint. I cannot fit into that pattern that you have described with such eloquence. Maybe, I could have done once, but not now, not after the experiences I have had."

"Do I detect a note of recrimination?" inquired Dominic drily. "Is it, perhaps, my responsibility that you are no longer fit to live in the world to which you were born? Forgive me, but I was under the impression that you made your own choices, took responsibility for yourself."

"And so I do!" Taking advantage of his loosened hold, she sprang from his knee. "And for that reason, I do not need your advice. I would prefer never to be married than on the cold, instrumental terms that you and Nicolas describe."

"Oh, do not be such a romantic little fool," the privateer said impatiently. "You do not want to look for love in marriage; you will find that elsewhere—love and passion untrammeled by the practical business of living. You know

Nicolas, you know his faults, just as he knows yours. There is no reason why you should not deal together in perfect amity, partners in a business that brings you both profit."

"I would die rather than spend two weeks of a so-called honeymoon locked in a bedchamber with my cousin, Nicolas," she declared, articulating every unpalatable word. "I do not imagine Nicolas will be prepared to forego his conjugal rights simply because this is a marriage of convenience. And besides, Papa must be provided with the grandchild. That is part of the bargain, is it not?"

Dominic winced. For some reason, the thought of his passionate sprite in the arms of Nicolas St. Denis was utterly repellent, but he was not going to allow it to weaken his case. "Your cousin is young, virile and experienced," he said with brutal candor. "As are you. I do not think Nicolas will challenge your experience when he discovers that he has no shrinking maiden in his nuptial bed. Another man in different circumstances might well do so, and you might find it difficult to control your natural ardor and to conceal your skills until such time as it would be appropriate to reveal them."

Genevieve stared at him. "You talk as if you have been thinking about this for some time."

"So I have." He walked to the sofa table and refilled his wineglass. "Such a potential problem had not occurred to you, I imagine, my impulsive sprite."

"No," she said in a small voice. "But then I had . . . have . . . no intention of marrying in the foreseeable future, so why should I have thought of it?"

Dominic sighed. "What had you intended doing, then, Genevieve? You are not designed to be an old maid, I can tell you that. We have already agreed that the nunnery is out of the question. You may have as many loving adventures as you wish, if you can find yourself a complacent husband, but not while you remain under your father's roof."

"But I do not think I would want a complacent husband,"

she said slowly. "Would *you* be a complacent husband if Rosemarie was still alive?"

Dominic's face darkened ominously. "That is beside the point. We are not talking about me."

"But would you?" she persisted, stubbornly ignoring the warning signs.

"No, dammit, I would not!" he exploded softly. "But then I am not going to be anyone's husband, so it is an irrelevancy."

A smart knock on the door heralded the immediate entrance of Silas. The usually impassive features were alive, the brown eyes glowing with excitement. "Monsieur, I am sorry to disturb you, but the British have been sighted on Lake Borgne."

"What?" Dominic blinked. "Are you certain?"

"Yes, monsieur. A messenger from the mayor brought the news."

"But I thought General Jackson expected them to come up the Mississippi," Genevieve said, forgetting her own problems for the moment.

"So he did." Dominic gave a short laugh. "A devious piece of outsmarting, there. The city is quite unprepared to defend itself." He put his glass on the table with a decisive click. "We sail with the evening tide, Silas. Pass the word to the others at the quay. The rest of the fleet is already in the safe anchorage so we'll meet up with them when we reach the lake."

"What are you going to do?" Genevieve asked eagerly.

"Cut them off, hopefully," came the reply. "If they're planning on coming down river, we should be able to offer some resistance, while Jackson gets his defenses together ashore . . . No, you *may* not!" he thundered suddenly, anticipating the question that hovered on the parted lips, shone in the bright tiger's eyes.

"Please," she begged. "I promise I won't be in the way. I'll stay below."

"I said no! And if you're thinking of arguing with me, I should think again, fast!"

This was one occasion when Genevieve could see no alternative to accepting defeat. It was quite impractical, anyway, since she could not possibly manufacture on the spur of the moment a reason for her absence. Had Dominic agreed, of course, she would have gone nevertheless, and worried about the consequences later. But since he was quite clearly not going to change his mind, and attempting to persuade him to do so could be somewhat hazardous, she shrugged in acceptance. "I had best go home then."

Dominic hesitated, torn between the need to get himself organized without delay and the reluctance to leave her in this state of unresolved distress. "If you will only think about what I have said, sprite, you will see that I am right." He brushed a lock of silvery hair from her forehead. "You have a good head on your shoulders once you decide to use it, and I can promise you that it is an infinitely more reliable guide to happiness than one's heart."

"Yes," she said dully. "I expect you are right. You are much more experienced in the ways of the world than I, after all."

Could he detect a faint note of irony in the statement? Dominic frowned and decided to ignore it. "Yes, I am," he concurred without equivocation. "We will talk some more, when I return."

"*If* you return," Genevieve said, walking past him to the door.

"I have every intention of doing so! Now, come back here and kiss me good-bye."

She turned with a reluctant smile, lifting her face for his kiss. But he could feel her holding back restraining that natural, uninhibited passion that he found as entrancing as it was arousing. Deliberately, he set about eroding the defenses, his tongue alternately dancing and plundering in the sweet cavern of her mouth, the heel of his palm lifting a

291

nipple to press against the bodice of her gown, his other hand kneading her buttocks until she sank against him with a little, defeated whimper that changed to an urgent moan as his tongue moved to her ear, stroking delicately then plunging rapaciously, and she squirmed against him in a frenzy of delicious torment.

"I should not have done that," he murmured, raising his head slowly to look down at her kiss-reddened lips, the tawny eyes heavy with desire, knowing that the matching desire was clearly revealed in his own eyes. "It is never wise to begin something that one will not be able to complete."

She moved out of his arms, smoothing down her skirt, adjusting the folds of the shawl. "It is the time for making war, Monsieur Delacroix, not love," she said. "Like the rest of my sex, I will be here, waiting patiently when you return."

"You are not at all like the rest of your sex." Dominic sighed, seeing her face close against him.

"But isn't that what you would have me be?" she demanded. "I was under the impression that that was what you have been trying to explain all afternoon."

"I do not wish to quarrel with you, Genevieve. Go now, before one of us says something that we will both regret."

At the door, she turned back to him, biting her bottom lip. "Come back, safely."

"By hook or by crook," he promised. "We have some unfinished business, after all."

"Yes, so we do." She touched her fingertips to her lips and left.

The streets were in a ferment as Genevieve hurried back home. The bells of St. Louis peeled incessantly, and men were running to the square, muskets, pistols, and swords in their hands. Women were gathering on street corners, whispering, their eyes fearful as they looked at their hurrying menfolk rushing to answer General Jackson's call to arms.

Genevieve reached her bedchamber unseen and threw off her disguise, dressing rapidly before running downstairs.

292

She could hear Elise's voice raised in a whine of protesting fear from the *salle de compagnie,* and Lorenzo's deep tones, as pompous as ever, drowning out the lighter accents. Victor's voice chimed in with irascible decision, silencing his son-in-law as Genevieve slipped into the room.

"Oh, there you are, *chère,"* Hélène fluttered, her normally pale countenance deathly white. "It is so dreadful. The British are on Lake Borgne and will attack the city at any moment."

Genevieve was about to say that she knew, then remembered that she was supposed to have spent the afternoon behind a locked door upstairs. "Is that why the bells are ringing?"

"General Jackson is calling for all able-bodied men," Elise moaned. "It is said that he is unwell . . ."

"Man is suffering from an acute attack of dysentery," Latour exploded. "It's the devil's own timing."

"I do not imagine he could help it, Papa," Genevieve said, forgetting, in the heat of the moment, the need to avoid drawing her father's attention.

But Nicolas, with rare tact, jumped into the breach, diverting Victor the instant before the deep breath he inhaled could be exhaled on a bellow. "We should go at once." Nicolas pointedly checked the buckle of his sword belt. "We do not want to be the last to appear."

"No, indeed not." The idea that a Latour, by birth or extension, could be found backward in coming forward at such a moment was enough to send Victor to the door without a second thought. Lorenzo patted a tearful Elise on the shoulder and told her she would be quite safe with her stepmother, and when Elise wailed that it was not her own safety that concerned her, he patted her again and left hastily. Nicolas looked at Genevieve, seemed about to say something, then turned and followed the others. Elise and Hélène allowed their tears to flow unchecked, and Genevieve contemplated the irony of it all. She could not cry because she was not supposed to have anyone for whose safety she feared. Not that she felt in the least like crying for Dominic. She just wished she could be on the quarterdeck of *Danseuse*, listening to that cool, clear, decisive voice directing the operation of the dainty frigate with such absolute confidence; wished she had a part in those operations instead of sitting here with weeping women, twiddling her thumbs!

"Elise, it cannot be good for the baby for you to become so very upset," she said, accepting the only role she was going to be permitted to play in this final battle of the war. It was not an unimportant role, the soothing and calming of her hysterical female relatives, even if it was not an exciting one.

On the night of December 23rd, General Jackson launched a night attack against the British forces, checking their advance. It was a strange Christmas within the city, reprieved for the moment yet uncertain for how long. The church of St. Louis was filled for Midnight Mass on Christmas Eve, the celebration muted with the anxious prayers both for the safety of loved ones and the security of an accustomed life threatened by the prospect of occupation.

On New Year's Day, General Sir Edward Pakenham, to his eternal amazement, fought what he assumed would be the final battle against this ill-prepared, ill-manned motley army and found his troops outgunned by the enemy artillery. It appeared that expert marksmen from Kentucky and Tennessee were more than a match for the ritual bound, over-drilled British. Pakenham waited for reinforcements and, supremely confident, on January 8th launched his main force against the enemy crouching behind a hastily thrown-up earthwork defense.

Dominic and his crews, their ships securely anchored in the Mississippi, half a mile away from the battlefield at Chalmette, proffered their own expertise with small arms and cannon, and like their fellow soldiers in this hastily assembled army, watched incredulously as the red-coated ranks came on, straight at the enemy guns that cut through them like a scythe in a cornfield. But as each rank fell, there was another to take its place. It was as if they were so hidebound by the rigorous training and belief in the rules pertaining to a war between gentlemen that imagination had deserted them, and with it, the knowledge and acceptance of the facts. The outnumbered enemy were not going to come out from behind their barricades and fight eye to eye. They were not so stupid! It was such a tragic, pitiful waste of so much young life that Dominic could have wept. And so it went on for a blood-soaked half an hour of attrition, leaving over two thousand British troops dead or wounded and only thirteen casualties on the American side.

## Chapter 18

For the next few days, the city of New Orleans rejoiced, one *soirée de gala* following another as eager hostesses vied to honor the brave defenders and celebrate the end of the war that, ironically, had officially ended two weeks before the Battle of New Orleans. Had the news of the signing of the peace treaty in Europe reached General Pakenham in time, that dreadful, wasteful bloodletting would have been avoided.

Dominic Delacroix was a frequent guest at the celebrations, but he was to be found, for the most part, closeted with his male hosts and other interested parties, making plans for the voyage to Europe and the liberation of Napoleon from his exile on the island of Elba. It was a grand, if not grandiose, plan, entirely in keeping with the personalities of its designers, and the privateer was amused, although he concealed his amusement behind a mask of polite interest. The scope and daring of the plan was what held his interest, more so, indeed, than the financial rewards to be gained from lending his services, considerable though they were.

One matter that did concern him, however, was the absence of Genevieve Latour from the succession of parties. Her cousin was usually in attendance, looking more somber and paying less assiduous court to Mademoiselle Benoit

296

than was his wont. Madame Latour was frequently to be seen, usually in the company of her elder stepdaughter, but the vibrant, diminutive figure of the younger Latour was conspicuously absent. Dominic had sent two messages to the house on Royal Street, delivered, as usual, to the silently helpful Amelie. Two afternoons, he had waited on Rampart Street, but she had not come, and there had been no return message and, more surprisingly, no sudden, unexpected visitation. He wondered if she were sulking, and then dismissed the idea as having no relevance to Genevieve. She had many annoying characteristics, but she was never sullen or sulky. Perhaps, she just needed time to accustom herself to her father's plan and, wisely, had decided that illicit loving with the privateer would not help her accept the path she must tread. But Genevieve would have told him that.

Finally, he decided to approach Nicolas. He picked an occasion graced by almost every member of Creole society, including Victor Latour, and strolled casually across to St. Denis who was standing by the buffet, a morose expression disfiguring the handsome countenance.

"Good evening, Nicolas." Dominic took a lobster canapé from the table and popped it between his lips. Nicolas returned the greeting, but a wary look appeared in the pale eyes. "The world and his wife have turned out this evening," Dominic observed casually. "But I do not see Mademoiselle Latour anywhere." He allowed a question mark to drift into his voice, and the wary look in Nicolas's eyes deepened. An unaccountable flush tinged his high cheekbones. Dominic's lips tightened. Nicolas was so transparent! His fear of the privateer was palpable, and while Dominic would admit that Nicolas had been given sufficient cause in the past to be wary of further dealings with him, he could not help despising his inability to mask his alarm. Unlike his plucky little cousin who had faced the devil in Delacroix with grim resolution. "Indeed," he continued smoothly, "I have not seen her since before Christmas. She is not unwell, I trust?"

Nicolas muttered something about a severe cold and the need to remain within doors to avert possible inflammation of the lungs, and Dominic became quite convinced that something was going on in the Latour household that invited examination.

"Genevieve is at home on Royal Street?" he asked, and there was no polite veneer to the question which was sharp and decisive.

Nicolas, caught off guard, said, "Why, yes, of course. She is in her chamber."

"Then we will go and visit her," Dominic said, taking the other's arm at the elbow. Nicolas flinched, both at the hold and the tone of voice. But he tried for conventional indignation.

"I do not understand what you can mean, Delacroix. You cannot pay a visit to a young girl who is sick and confined to her chamber."

"You would be surprised," Dominic replied grimly. "My sick-bed manner is generally considered to be most beneficial for the patient."

"What is Genevieve to you?" Nicolas whispered, unable to resist the pressure urging him toward the door.

"I am surprised you should ask that," Dominic replied shortly. "You played a significant part in our becoming acquainted, as I recall."

They had reached the street, and Nicolas made one last attempt to dig his heels in. "That was many months ago and the business is closed. You have no right to interfere in the private affairs of our family."

"So, there is more to this 'private affair' than a severe cold," Dominic stated with harsh satisfaction. "What has Latour done to her?"

Nicolas stared at his interlocutor. "Why should you think he has done anything?"

"Oh, stop playing games, St. Denis. Surely it must be obvious to you, by now, that I know a great deal about

Latour affairs! And I know that Genevieve has been resisting her father's proposal that she should marry you."

"She told you that?"

Dominic sighed and increased his pace. "Let us make haste before Latour or his wife decides to return home. Believe it or not, Nicolas, I am on your side in this matter. You are not worthy of Genevieve, of course, but I expect you are aware of that," he added conversationally. "However, she will be better off with you who know her than with some lumpen clod who might attempt to mold her into conventional form."

Nicolas could find no rememdy for the contusions of this bruising bluntness, and they proceeded rapidly but in silence to Royal Street. "So, where is she?" Dominic demanded as they were admitted into the hall.

"In her chamber," Nicolas said. Never being one to fight against superior odds, he went toward Latour's cabinet at the rear of the house. "He keeps the key in here."

"How the hell long has he kept her locked up?" Dominic felt the stillness of fury enter his soul as Nicolas took a brass key off a ring hanging on the wall by the desk.

Nicolas sighed. "Since Christmas. Dominic, there is nothing anyone can do to prevent him. Hélène has tried, I have tried, but until she agrees—"

"Oh, do not give me those platitudes." Dominic snatched the key from him. "The man is a bully and if you stood up to him just once, he would crumble."

Nicolas shook his head. "You do not know him, Delacroix, if you believe that. Genevieve stands up to him all the time, but it has never done her any good." He led the way up the stairs, pausing outside the closed door to his cousin's bedchamber. Dominic inserted the key, turned it and swung the door open. The room was in semidarkness, only the glow of the *veilleuse* on the mantel offering any illumination. The small, night-gowned figure curled up on a chaise longue that faced the window onto the rear gallery turned her head listlessly toward the door.

"Tabitha? What are you doing at this time of the day?" Then she saw that her visitor was not the only person she had seen since Christmas Day: Tabitha, who looked after her most basic needs. "Am I dreaming?" Genevieve said, getting off the chaise longue. "It is becoming remarkably hard to distinguish dreams from reality these days."

"Wait outside," Dominic ordered Nicolas curtly and closed the door on him. Two long strides took him across the room to Genevieve. He drew her toward the light on the mantel, tilting her face for an intent scrutiny. "Has he hurt you?"

"No." She shook her head. "He is in no great hurry for my capitulation. I have not seen him since he locked the door." The slender shoulders, even more fragile than usual, shrugged. "But what are you doing here? It is madness. Unless you have come to take me away." For a second, a light glowed in the tawny eyes, then, as she read his face, it was extinguished. "But, of course, you have not."

"That is not the answer, sprite." Cupping her face, he spoke with soft insistence. "You must cease this resistance. It is doing you no good. Surely you must see that exchanging the tyranny of your father for marriage to Nicolas has to be a worthwhile exchange."

"Why must I be faced with two unpalatable alternatives?" she asked. "It is not the case with men."

Dominic shook his head. "What about Nicolas? His alternatives are no more palatable."

"No, there you are wrong!" she exclaimed fiercely. "If that were the case, he would resist as I am doing. If we both refused to do Papa's bidding, then he would not be able to impose his will."

Dominic could not deny this, but it did not alter his conviction that Genevieve must be brought to accept and embrace reality. "How long do you think you can continue like this?" he asked, gesturing around the room, which for all

300

its comfort, was undeniably a prison, and a small one. "I cannot go away, knowing that you remain confined in this fashion."

"Go away? Where are you going?" Genevieve had the dreadful feeling that if Dominic Delacroix were not in the same city, if she could not picture him going about his customary activities, she would lose all strength to persist in her resistance.

Dominic sighed. He had not intended to bring up the subject of his projected journey, but having once started, he could hardly withdraw. "To Europe," he told her, without hesitation. "The city elders, in their wisdom, have decided to effect Napoleon's escape from Elba. I have offered my services in the matter."

A change came over her. The listlessness evaporated and determination glimmered in her eyes, set hard on her features. "Then you must take me to Europe. It is the only answer. I cannot stay here without doing what Papa wants, and I will not do that. I hate this city. I have no place in this society—"

"Genevieve," he interrupted the flow desperately, hearing the low, but powerful intensity in her voice. "I cannot take you with me. What would you do?"

"You need not worry about that," she said coldly. "I will not be a burden on you. All I am asking for is passage on *Danseuse*. When you reach your destination, I will fend for myself."

"Doing what?" he asked, not attempting to hide his impatience with this fantasy. Her answer rocked him back on his heels.

"What I am good at," she informed him with a serene little smile. "I shall become a courtesan. I might have to borrow some money from you, initially, since I would need to set myself up with a house and clothes and things . . ." One hand waved in airy description of such necessities. "But I would repay you as soon as I was able. It is a lucrative way of

301

earning a living, I understand, and perfectly pleasant if one take one's lovers from the aristocracy. I can pass myself off as native French and can frequent the courts—"

"That will do!" Dominic at last recovered his breath sufficiently to call a halt to this blithe plan whose main drawback, as far as he could see, was that it was perfectly feasible for someone with Genevieve's talents and energies. "I have never heard such arrant nonsense in my life."

"And just how does it differ from the life you would have me lead here?" she demanded scornfully. "You recommend that I take as many lovers as I choose, so long as I am discreet. The only difference I can see is that one is hypocritical and the other is honest. If I must sell myself for my independence, I would prefer to do it without hypocrisy. At least, I might be able to choose who to sell myself to, instead of having to accept Papa's choice."

Dominic looked at her in horrified fascination. The comparison she had drawn was appallingly accurate if one chose to look at this arranged marriage of convenience in those terms. "I will have no part of such a nonsensical idea," he said, aware that he was blustering to conceal his knowledge of the truth of her words. "You are just being childish. There is nothing outlandish in your father's proposal. It is a situation faced by almost every *jeune fille bien elevée* in this town, unless she forms some *tendre* for an eligible *parti,* which is rare, in my experience."

"You will not help me?"

He shook his head and turned from the haunting plea, the desperation in the tawny eyes. "Not in that way. I would not be helping you, quite the opposite. I am not so irresponsible, my dear, for all that you may have thought otherwise."

He left her because there seemed no more to be said. Nicolas took one look at the privateer's grim, set face and shivered, wondering what could have taken place to have provoked that daunting look. Dominic marched down the stairs and out of the house without a word to Nicolas, who was left to lock Genevieve's door again and replace the key in Victor's cabinet, his heart thumping at the thought of discovery.

Genevieve found that her last hope seemed to have left her with Dominic's departure. She had not realized how much she had counted on being able to persuade him to help her in some way. She had pinned all her hopes on the thought of being able to leave New Orleans, although she had not thought so far afield as Europe. Any large American city would have served her purpose if Dominic lent her sufficient funds to start out. But he had reacted to her proposal with all the shocked horror she would have expected from some elderly dowager, a social arbiter, instead of a notorious rogue who flouted those rules himself with gay abandon. And without help, it could not be done. She had no money but the pin money her father allowed her, no friends outside the city to offer her shelter, no means of travel, except on foot, and she could not get far in that manner.

The next morning, Victor Latour drove the final nail into the coffin of her will to resist. He unlocked the door of his daughter's bedchamber and marched in, banging the door shut behind him. The sound echoed through the house on which an apprehensive silence seemed to have settled as soon as the master had left the breakfast table and stalked with such purpose up the stairs. There was no one, from the youngest slave to Hélène Latour, who was unaware of the situation, although no public mention was ever made of the prisoner upstairs. Only Tabitha was permitted to enter her room, an edict that even Hélène had not dared to defy.

Genevieve, having picked at her breakfast with the lack of appetite born of inactivity, was wondering whether to bother to get dressed when her father made his abrupt entrance. One look at his face, and her heart began to pound, but she forced herself to greet him with calm courtesy. "Good morning, Papa."

He ignored the greeting. "Have you come to your

303

senses, yet?"

"I will not marry Nicolas," she replied in the monotone of an automaton.

"Then you will marry no one," Latour stated. "If you do not choose to behave in a responsible manner, accepting your duty like any other Creole lady, then you and your dowry shall go to the Sisters of Mercy."

The statement, as he had known it would, proved to be the arrow that pierced the tight shell of determination that had fortified her will to withstand Latour's intent. She had tried to guess what his next move would be, but never, even in nightmare, had she imagined this fate. The sisters were a strict and impoverished order, unlike the Ursulines with whom Genevieve was so comfortable. They would be overjoyed to accept a potential novitiate of good family with a reasonable wedding portion to present when she became a bride of Christ. There would be no luxuries like books and the time to study in the convent set in swampland some fifteen miles outside the city, where the life was devoted to prayer and labor. It would be a living death, one to which she could not submit, as Victor Latour knew only too well.

"You will leave within the hour," he went on, watching her through narrowed eyes, gauging the reactions that she could not dissemble. "There will be no need to pack, since the sisters do not permit personal possessions of any kind, no books, no jewelry, no—"

"I know what they do not permit, Papa," she interrupted quietly. "Just as you know that you have won. I will do as you wish."

"As I bid," he corrected with a snap.

"As you bid," she agreed tonelessly.

"I will instruct Hélène to make preparations for the betrothal ceremony. No expense shall be spared on the reception." With that, Victor Latour strode from his daughter's bedchamber, leaving the door ajar.

No expense spared! Genevieve laughed mirthlessly,

wondering if that was her father's idea of an olive branch. Having got his way, he could afford to be generous. But, at least, her imprisonment was over, and she could leave the four walls that she had come to hate, could breathe the crisp January air, could walk and ride the stiffness from her unused muscles.

An hour later, she joined Hélène in the *salle de compagnie*. Her stepmother was overjoyed to see her, but clearly had difficulties with divided loyalty. With one breath she offered sympathy and with the next congratulation. One minute she was obliquely critical of her husband, the next full of praise for his wisdom that surely his daughter must accept was far greater than her own could ever be. "And, you know, *chère,* Nicolas will be a good husband," she said, patting Genevieve's hand. "You are friends, and there will be no surprises for either of you."

"Were you obliged to marry Papa, Hélène?" Genevieve, until now, had never been able to understand why her young stepmother would have agreed to be joined with an irascible bully, twice married, and twenty years older than herself.

Hélène blushed crimson. "What a question, *chère.* Of course it was not like that. My father believed it was the best for me, and his judgment was always correct. And Mama was quite in favor of the match, so, of course, I was delighted."

"Yes, of course," Genevieve sighed. Hélène, like most women of her kind, could not begin to understand why Genevieve should object to such a pleasant arrangement. Nicolas was attractive, wellborn; they had grown up together, and the marriage would be most generously blessed by Monsieur Latour. The fact that her cousin was weak, cowardly and self-serving would be seen as a mere peccadillo, when he could be brutish, a drunkard, gambler, womanizer, and she would have had to put up with it all like any other wife.

"Your papa wishes the betrothal to take place next week,"

Hélène said hesitantly. "It is very soon, but I think we will be able to invite all our friends who will be very happy to celebrate such an occasion with us."

"I would prefer that we do not have a reception," Genevieve said. "It is not an occasion to celebrate."

"You must not talk like that," Hélène scolded. "Your father insists that it is done right, and you cannot be so discourteous as to have a long face at your own betrothal. How would it look for poor Nicolas? You must consider his feelings."

"Mine, of course, are never to be considered again," she retorted bitterly. "Not only must I submit to this life sentence, but I am expected to look joyful about it. I am going out for a walk."

"Eh, Monsieur Delacroix, you become faster as the years go by, I swear it," panted the *maître d'armes* as his thrust in prime was parried and countered with a *flanconnade* to his left hand. "The years are supposed to slow one, but you are as fleet of foot and eye now as you were seven years ago."

Dominic merely smiled, flashed his foil in a swift salute and renewed the attack.

Nicolas, with the other young bloods who had come to spend an afternoon at this *salle d'escrime* on Exchange Alley, watched the match. Their own play was hopelessly amateur beside that of these two masters, and they all knew that they would learn more this afternoon by observation than by practicing against one another.

Dominic emerged the victor of the bout, not easily, certainly, but there had never been any doubt of his eventual success in his own mind or in his opponent's. Laughing, the two men went off to the *maître's* inner sanctum, under the envious eyes of the young men, who considered the invitation to take a glass in private with Pepe the summit of ambition.

Nicolas was exchanging a few desultory passes with a friend when the privateer emerged, shrugging into his coat. Shaking out the ruffles on his shirt and straightening his cravat, he regarded his juniors with an amused eye that seemed to Nicolas to burn its gentle cynicism into his back. He fluffed a parry and received his opponent's lunge full on the chest.

"Concentration, my dear Nicolas, is the be all and end all of fencing," Dominic observed. "If you are ready to leave, I will walk with you."

Nicolas was not, as it happened, ready to leave, but he could recognize an order when he heard one. Now what did the privateer want with him? Apprehensively, he fetched his coat and the two left, Delacroix humming to himself in the most unnerving fashion. "So, Nicolas," he said at last. "How are things proceeding in the Latour household?"

"You mean with Genevieve?" Nicolas asked, a sulk in his voice.

"I do not wish to be impolite," Dominic said gently, "but I cannot imagine finding any other member of that family remotely interesting."

"She has agreed to the betrothal," Nicolas told him. "Victor spoke with her this morning and when he came out of her chamber, she had agreed to obey him."

"Have you seen her since?" Dominic demanded, a sharp note of anxiety in his voice. There was no knowing to what methods Latour would stoop to achieve his object.

"At luncheon," Nicolas said. "But she did not say very much; in fact she hardly opened her mouth."

"But she is unhurt, as far as you could tell."

Nicolas looked blank for a minute, and then nodded as he understood his companion's concern. "Yes, I do not know how he persuaded her, but there was no violence, I am certain."

"By which you mean that the coercion was not physical," Dominic said acidly. "Well, pray accept my congratulations,

St. Denis." Swinging abruptly on his heel, he strode off in the opposite direction.

From then on, his usual calm, single-mindedness seemed to have deserted him. He could not concentrate on his final preparations for the voyage to Europe, was short with Silas who bore the surliness in stoic silence and responded by being extra attentive, which made Dominic feel guilty and therefore increased his irritability. Genevieve sat in the forefront of his mind, intruded on every waking moment and, quite uncharacteristically, he found himself in a ferment of indecision. He knew that in all fairness he must now bow out of her life, the life he had so vigorously urged upon her to accept. But he needed to see her, to satisfy himself that she was all right, that she had reached the right decision and understood, now, why it was the only sensible choice. And he needed to see her because he wanted her. He had never needed a woman the way he needed this sprite, and the realization chilled him. Rosemarie, perhaps, but it had not been quite the same; the hunger of lust was subsumed beneath the golden overlay of an ideal love forged on the anvil of authority's opposition. But that laughing, loving, passionate, infuriating, stubborn, willful, diminutive fairy child had no appetite for romantic ideals, only for the rough and tumble of lusting love, for the equality of need and its satisfaction. She seized life with both hands, was constantly searching the horizon for new experiences, jumped with glorious abandon. They were two of a kind.

Dominic Delacroix finally faced the fact that he had tried so hard to deny. If they were truly so alike, shared so many basic characteristics, how could he condemn her to a life that he would have escaped, or died in the attempt? He was as much a Creole as she, owed as much duty to his breeding and inheritance as she, but he had turned his back on both. They differed in one essential: gender. Was it reasonable of him to take the side of the society he despised in order to crush the spirit of one whom he admired? One to whom he was drawn in the most powerful way, whom he needed, whose presence he enjoyed in all her facets?

It was not at all reasonable. And clearly something had to be done. She could not possibly share a bed with Nicolas St. Denis; he would never appreciate her. And neither would any of the other empty-headed young men with an excess of time and money on their hands. No, Genevieve Latour's destiny did not lie in Orleanian society—something she had known for a long time. Where it did lie, the privateer had no idea. But he would give her the opportunity he had long ago taken for himself: to go out and look for that destiny rather than wait in female submission for its imposition.

With that decision came the plan for her rescue, fully formed and sufficiently outrageous to bring a gleam to the privateer's blue eyes. It was a plan that his sprite would appreciate to the full and would, perhaps, compensate her for the days of dreariness and depression consequent on her imprisonment and capitulation.

Silas received his orders in silence. He was offered no explanation, but reflected with a sour smile that only a half-wit would have needed them. At least monsieur seemed to have recovered from his bout of inattention and general lack of interest in the pressing matter of the imminent voyage. The old sailor, with a particular coloring in mind, spent a morning selecting silks, velvets, cambrics, and muslins from the storeroom at the back of the mercer's on Chartres Street. Then, with the precise memory of a particular size and shape, he gave minute instructions to the army of seam-stresses who had three days in which to fashion a complete wardrobe that would clothe an elegant young lady from the skin out on every conceivable occasion.

"Genevieve, *chère,* please try to smile." Hélène fussed around the still figure, adjusting the delicate ruff of antique lace at the neck of Genevieve's gown of heavy ivory satin.

The color would normally have been a good choice, but the girl was so pale and limp that it merely made her look even more washed out, the heaviness of the material seeming to weigh her down, increasing her appearance of diminutive fragility.

"You do not see slaves smiling in the coffles to the auction block," the girl retorted, then bit her lip, stricken with remorse at the thought of having made such an abominably inappropriate comparison. Spoiled baby! She could almost hear Dominic Delacroix's sardonic tone, the azure gaze stripping her of adult dignity, reducing her to the status of chastened pupil. She forced a smile and apologized to her stepmother for the brattish comment.

"It is quite all right, *chère*," Hélène reassured, her own relief transparent. "It is such a big occasion for a girl. I know exactly how you feel. I was so nervous at my own betrothal that I could barely walk, and my dear papa had to support me during the ceremony, I was shaking so badly."

There was a knock at the bedroom door, and Elise came in, radiantly pregnant and clearly bursting with the good advice that one, experienced in the ways of the world, had to impart to a baby sister. "The *grande salle* looks enchanting, Hélène," she said, bestowing a kindly kiss on her stepmother's cheek. "You must have worked so hard. Oh, Genevieve, you look like a week of wet Sundays!" She pinched her sister's pale cheeks vigorously, ignoring the recipient's indignant ouch. "Hélène, do you not think she should use some rouge?"

"Your papa would not like it," Hélène said definitely.

"No, I suppose it would not be proper, since she is not yet married," agreed Elise. "I cannot imagine why *you* are behaving as if this is the end of the world, Genevieve. It would not be surprising if Lorenzo and I thought it to be so, since it means that our children will receive nothing from the Latour estate, but have we once said anything?"

"Not in so many words, Elise," Genevieve agreed drily. "For all I care, you and Nicolas between you can share everything. Why could Papa not have had this wretched scheme when you were on the marriage mart? You would have been perfectly happy with Nicolas."

There was an uncomfortable silence, then Elise said with unconcealed bitterness, "You know perfectly well that you have always been Papa's favorite."

Genevieve looked at her, stunned. Dear God, but it was quite true! She began to laugh, peal after peal ringing through the room at the utter absurdity of it all. "He has the strangest way of showing it, then," she gasped, wiping the tears from her cheeks. "Marriage to Nicolas or the Sisters of Mercy! My dear sister, you do not know how lucky you are to have escaped the burdens of the favorite!"

Elise and Hélène were at a loss. Genevieve's laughter was no more reassuring than had been her previous miserable silence, but rescue appeared with the arrival of Tabitha who informed them that the guests were assembled in the *grande salle*. Monsieur St. Denis and Monsieur Latour and the lawyers were there, and it was time for Mademoiselle Genevieve to make her appearance.

The summons instantly sobered Genevieve, bringing her back from the brink of hysteria with a salutory jolt. "I am coming, Tabitha." She walked to the door, Elise and Hélène falling in behind her. She barely distinguished one face from another in the smiling sea as she walked up to the long table at the far end of the *grande salle* where stood her father, her cousin, and two solemn-faced men of law, a layer of crisp documents spread on the surface of the table behind them. She was conscious, on one level, of the scent of wood smoke from the two fires burning brightly at each end of the long room, of the mingled fragrances of perfume and scented candles, and the wax polish on the gleaming floors. Mantels and doorways were hung with the green shining richness of

311

smilax and holly. It was all very pretty, Genevieve thought with an abstracted interest. Hélène must have gone to a great deal of trouble; she must remember to thank her when this was all over.

Her father was talking, or rather, pontificating. The lawyers were nodding importantly and Nicolas was smiling nervously. Everyone else was very quiet, listening with fascination to the terms of the betrothal. So fascinating was it that for a few seconds no one registered the three men silently stepping into the salon from the hall, bringing a rush of cold air with them from the open front door.

One of the men was Dominic Delacroix, a heavy woolen cloak thrown casually over his shoulders, revealing a coat of blue superfine with silver buttons, buckskin britches, and riding boots—definitely not appropriate attire for attending a formal betrothal ceremony. His companions held drawn pistols; their clothes, the great gold hoops in their ears, the neat pigtails, advertising their profession, if their menacing stance and watchful eyes had not done so.

The words died on Victor Latour's lips, and the silence in the long room deepened until the hiss and pop of the fires seemed as loud as an orchestra in full wind.

Genevieve turned slowly. The privateer smiled at her and walked up the aisle formed by the ranks of guests, as she had done some five minutes earlier.

"You must forgive this interruption, Latour," drawled Dominic, reaching the table. He turned to Nicolas standing ashen and motionless as if in the grip of an old and familiar nightmare. "I find that I do not bear you sufficient ill will, St. Denis, to stand by and watch your systematic destruction at the hands of a woman who, with the best intentions in the world, will not be able to avoid annihilating you." He switched his attention to Genevieve. She did not move, but the tiger's eyes were alight with laughter and expectation. "You and I have some unfinished business, as I recall." So

312

saying, he lowered one shoulder and swept her over it.

"What the devil . . ." Latour found some words, at last, but they were directed at the retreating back of the privateer and his small burden of ivory and silver and gold. "Stop them!" he bellowed at the room at large, and at an army of servants in particular; but that army was no more a match for the two pistol-carrying sailors and the overpowering authority of Dominic Delacroix than his guests.

Genevieve began to laugh, raising her head from her imposed contemplation of the floor, to look at the receding tableau, to fix it forever in her memory.

"I was under the impression that abducted damsels were supposed to shriek in distress, not find their plight amusing," observed Dominic in the general vicinity of her quivering behind. His burden choked and Monsieur Delacroix grinned.

The grin did not escape Silas who allowed himself a grim nod of satisfaction as he and his companion backed out of the room in the wake of *Danseuse*'s master. A ripple of movement, a whisper of speech followed their retreat, as if the castle of the Sleeping Beauty had begun to stir. The front door closed, shutting off the stream of cold night air and setting the candles fluttering, the fire hissing.

Dominic swung Genevieve into the saddle of the waiting horse, mounting behind her in almost the same movement. Throwing off his heavy cloak, he wrapped it securely around her before pressing his heels into the mare's flanks. The animal was off on the instant, pounding down the street toward the quay.

"Where are we going?" asked Genevieve, tossing her head to catch the cold, fast air whistling past.

"To rescue the Emperor Napoleon from Elba," Dominic told her, chuckling. "A venture worthy of your talents, sprite."

And when we have done that? thought Genevieve as her

heart thrilled to the challenge and the excitement of the unknown, and her spirit, held for so long in captivity, soared into unbounded freedom. It didn't really matter what came next, did it? For the present, there was *Danseuse,* and Europe, and a partnership with the privateer—a partnership of love and lust and adventure.

## Chapter 19

"I have a monstrous spot on my nose!" Genevieve wailed, peering at the offending feature in the swing mirror on her dresser. "I cannot possibly seduce the so English Mr. Cholmondeley when I look like Falstaff after a particularly roisterous night."

Dominic could not help his appreciative chuckle. "Cholmondeley is so thoroughly in your toils, my dear girl, that I do not imagine he would notice if you had developed a carbuncle." Coming over to her, he tilted her chin up to the candlelight, observing, "It is not exactly monstrous, but a little shiny, I grant you."

"Hot water," Silas proclaimed from Dominic's dressing room. "If mademoiselle . . . madame, I mean . . . would hold her head over a bowl of hot water, it will steam the poison out."

"Really?" Genevieve turned on the dresser stool to regard the sailor with interest. "You do know the most amazing things, Silas."

Silas grunted and said, "I'll bring some from the kitchen. You'll find the flounce on the green silk mended. Just be careful when you step into it next time and leave your shoes off." On this admonition, he left the bedchamber.

"I wish this deception would permit a lady's maid," sighed

315

Genevieve. "Silas is quite wonderful, but . . . well, it *is* a little unusual to be looked after by an old sailor. And he's such a bully."

"I do not find him so," said Dominic, taking a strand of opalescent pearls from the opened cask on the dresser and fastening them around her neck.

"No, because he does not bully *you*," she retorted, lifting the strand with one finger, examining their deep creamy luster, an appreciative smile in her eyes. "He does not tell you not to tear your coats or wear your kid slippers in the rain or scold you when you get your gloves dirty."

Dominic laughed. "Poor sprite. It is a trial, I know, but we will not brush through this charade if anyone other than my own people are allowed to approach too close, and this bedchamber is about as close as anyone could come."

"Yes, I know." She stood up, slight and dainty in a delicate silk underdress that molded her form in preparation for the bronze satin that would skim her figure, caught beneath her breasts to fall to her ankles, just touching the indentation of waist, the curve of hip. She slid him a look brimming with mischief as she reached for the gown lying ready on the bed. "Can you imagine the reactions of the Grand Duchess Catherine or the Princess Sophia or Lady Kavanaugh at the idea of Madame Delacroix being waited upon by a pirate, one who doesn't even notice when madame is in nothing but her drawers and chemise?"

"It is something that does not bear thinking of," Dominic said fervently, taking the dress from her and dropping it over her head. "However, since that scandalous aspect is but the tip of the iceberg in this particular deception, I do not think it need cause us too many qualms." Turning her, he deftly fastened the hooks at the back of the gown, smoothing the material over her hips with a little pat.

"No, indeed." For an instant, she leaned back against him, and his hands, responding, curved over the firm roundness of her buttocks. "I do not think that the members of this

Congress of Vienna, so full of self-importance as they carve up Napoleon's Europe, would take kindly to the knowledge that they had clasped to their bosoms a pair of piratical adventurers, who pretended to be a respectably married couple—unimpeachable French aristocrats with a lineage to equal the Bourbons—emerging from exile now that the monster Napoleon has received his just deserts." Genevieve laughed with pure glee. "Not that their self-importance seems to be justified. Did you hear what the Prince de Ligne said? That 'this Congress does not make progress, it dances.'"

"Yes, and the man's quite right," Dominic said with a laugh. "The Emperor Franz is having much more success turning Vienna into the world's social capital with his balls and banquets and concerts than poor Metternich, for all his wiles, is having with his diplomatic shenanigans. But talking of the monster Napoleon . . ." He dropped a kiss on her spotted nose. "Did you discover anything in your assignation with the Grand Duke Sergei this afternoon?"

"That Talleyrand, Metternich, and Fouché do not believe that, for all his protestations, Bonaparte's ambitions are satisfied with the government and defense of a couple of small islands in the Mediterranean. And they should know, should they not?"

"If anyone does," Dominic agreed. "They have known him longer and better than anyone."

"Also, that there has been talk in the Congress of deporting him to the Azores, or maybe St. Helena," she continued. "There is a fear that Elba is too close, that if he attempts a return, there will be many on the continent to welcome him."

Dominic frowned. "If that information reaches Bonaparte, he will be all the more anxious to make an escape. I think we are going to have to make our move soon."

"Here you are, mademoiselle . . . madame, I mean." Silas marched in and plunked a steaming bowl on the dresser. "Hold some of that hot water against your nose."

Genevieve dipped the corner of a handkerchief into the bowl and pressed the burning cloth against the spot. "You do not have to call me 'madame,' Silas, since you and I know that it is not true."

Silas harrumphed. "Don't want to make any slips in public, so might as well get accustomed."

She shrugged. Silas had a point since he, apart from themselves, was the only one to know that Madame Delacroix was, in fact, still Mademoiselle Genevieve Latour. Even the handpicked group of his sailors running the house in Vienna, which Dominic had hired as their base while they infiltrated European society at the Congress, believed that the union between their commander and Latour's daughter had been solemnized.

"Tonight, you must wring out of Cholmondeley some information about the intelligence networks operating in the Italian ports," Dominic said casually. "I am certain Bonaparte has his own counterespionage system to combat the French at Leghorn. Once we know how it works, we should be able to use it ourselves."

"I will do what I can." Genevieve hoped that the handkerchief and hot water would provide sufficient explanation for her suddenly muffled tone. However many times she told herself that her role in their plan was perfectly straightforward, and quite the most expeditious method they had at their disposal to achieve their goal, it still hurt somehow that Dominic could treat so lightly the idea of her intimacy with those from whom they needed information. True, *she* had made the suggestion that the best way to get beneath a man's guard was with soft words between the sheets, but Dominic had agreed after only the barest hesitation.

He found out which of the delegates would have the most useful information and left it to Genevieve to coax, flatter and promise her way into their intimate confidence. He never questioned her as to how she garnered her intelligence,

318

never asked about the clandestine meetings she had with her eager suitors, never raised an eyebrow if she told him she would be returning late from an evening engagement. But Silas was always waiting, stealthy and silent in the shadows, to accompany her home from her assignations, and Dominic was always at home, wide awake, sipping brandy in the salon, when she returned. But all he ever wanted to know was what kernels of information she had managed to extract in her evening's work.

She abandoned the handkerchief and hot water and examined the blemish in the mirror. As Silas had foreseen, the spot had popped, and a little powder would effectively conceal the slight redness that remained. It was foolish to have these pangs—as if there were anything of romance or commitment about their relationship. It was as it had always been, as she had told him she wanted it—each enjoying each other in a loving partnership of adventure until it ceased to be good for one or both of them. Then they would part, amicably and without regret. Why had it been so easy to say those words that afternoon in Rampart Street, and now, an ocean away, was it so hard to accept them as truth? Dominic had told her, after that wonderfully staged abduction, that he was giving her the opportunity to find her own destiny, that he would help her in whatever ways she needed once their mission was completed, or even before if she chose to leave him. She was as much a free agent as he was, and the nagging thought that perhaps she did not wish to be a free agent was one that had to be quashed vigorously.

"If you are ready, Genevieve?" Dominic broke into her reverie, fastening the clasp of the silk evening cloak that Silas had placed over his shoulders.

"Yes . . . yes, I am quite ready." With an effort, she made her voice sound as cheerful as it had sounded a few minutes earlier. "It would never do to keep the Duke of Wellington waiting, would it?"

"I rather suspect that you would be forgiven such a

319

solecism," Dominic replied with a dry little smile. "That august gentleman is no more immune to your charms than anyone else." He held her cloak for her and ran one finger up the groove of her neck, bared by the coiffure that drew the silver-gold hair into a coronet on top of her head.

Genevieve shivered deliciously. The back of her neck was extraordinarily sensitive, as Dominic well knew. "The duke, as far as I can observe, does not appear to be immune to *any* member of my sex," she responded lightly, preceding him through the door.

"True enough," Dominic agreed, following her down the stairs, "but he is quite particular about his flirts, and you appear to be one of them."

"A married woman is always a safe flirt," she said. "He told me so himself. They do not expect too much, and they tend to be discreet." She stepped through the front door onto the quiet Domgasse where the house stood in the shadow of St. Stephen's Cathedral, and into the waiting carriage, Dominic's hand at her elbow.

"I have to confess, my dear Genevieve, that your capacity for discretion astounds me," he remarked, sitting opposite her on the blue-leather squab seat.

Genevieve shot him a sharp look, but in the darkness of the closed vehicle it was impossible to read his expression. "I was under the impression that discretion was the only rule, if not the only virtue, in this society."

"Indeed it is," he concurred, looking through the window as they turned onto the busy Wollzeile and passed the majestic Gothic structure of the Stephansdom dominating Vienna's exclusive inner city. "I just did not realize how quickly and easily you would learn to curb such an impulsive, inquisitive nature."

"Am I supposed to be complimented?" she inquired sweetly.

At that, he turned and smiled at her in the dark. "Yes, sprite, you are. You are a worthy accomplice in adventure."

The carriage drew to a halt outside the Wellesley mansion. The house blazed with light, the pavement crowded with linkboys running from carriage to the awning-covered flag way, lighting the path of the illustrious guests, jewel encrusted, satin gowned and velvet cloaked.

"Monsieur and Madame Delacroix," the liveried flunky intoned at the head of the grand staircase leading down to the thronged ballroom.

"Madame Delacroix, as ravishing as ever." Arthur Wellesley, Duke of Wellington, bowed low over Genevieve's hand, his long nose almost brushing her fingers. "So good of you to honor us with your company."

"The honor is all mine, Your Grace," Genevieve replied with impeccable formality, although she could not help responding to the roguish gleam in the duke's eyes. "Lady Margaret." She turned to acknowledge her hostess, the duke's sister, and the two women exchanged a few words of polite small talk until Margaret Wellesley made an announcement that shivered Genevieve to her toes.

"The Duke and Duchess of Angoulême have arrived in Vienna, my dear Madame Delacroix," Margaret said, smiling warmly. "You will be glad to talk over old times, I am sure."

Everyone would expect that the Duchess of Angoulême, the only surviving child of Marie Antoinette, who had been exchanged by her revolutionary captors for a handful of captive generals before being married off to her cousin, would know the Delacroix from the days of penniless wandering in exile through the courts of Europe. Now that the Bourbons were returned to the throne of France, it would be assumed that old friends in exile would have much to ask and offer each other.

"It may seem strange, Lady Margaret, but I do not think our paths have ever before crossed," Genevieve managed to say, glancing over her shoulder at Dominic. "Are you acquainted with Her Royal Highness, Dominic?"

"A brief meeting in Saxe Coburg, some years ago," the privateer lied smoothly. "I do not imagine the duchess will remember the occasion." He bowed over his hostess's hand and then easily removed himself and Genevieve from the awkward proximity.

"Should we keep out of their way?" Genevieve whispered, distractedly acknowledging the bows and smiles of greeting from all sides.

"Most certainly not," Dominic told her. "That would simply serve to draw attention to us. You know your background, do you not?"

"Yes, of course."

"Then you have nothing to worry about. Just stick to your story—no one will gainsay you if you show no hesitation . . . Ah, Monsieur Fouché, good evening."

Fouché, as crafty a schemer now as he had been at any point during Napoleon's ascendancy and his own rise to power on the tail of the emperor, bowed and smiled at Madame Delacroix who inclined her head, narrowed those tawny eyes and directed a most ravishing smile in his direction.

"May I procure you a glass of warm negus, madame?" he asked. "It is a wretchedly cold night."

"Yes, it is indeed, monsieur. I should be most grateful." Abandoning Dominic, she laid her hand on the crimson brocade arm of the diplomat and went off with him, mindful of Dominic's instructions to learn what she could of the spy networks on the Italian coast facing the island of Elba.

Fouché listened to the apparently artless prattle of his attractive companion, smiled, responded, and was not fooled. "What exactly is it you wish to find out from me, my dear madame?" he asked, breaking into her little prepared speech with undisguised amusement.

Genevieve looked up into the shrewd foxy eyes, read both the amusement and the very clear interest they contained. No one knew the extent of the double game played by

Fouché, but it was suspected that while he participated in the discussions at the Congress, he remained loyal to Napoleon. Whether the loyalty took concrete form was the question. If it did, then his help would be invaluable, but if it did not, then they would lose everything by revealing themselves. It was not a risk she could afford to take—not without Dominic's permission, at least.

"I am fascinated by the emperor," she said with a convincing assumption of candor and a guilty little laugh. "I was hoping you would tell me all about his life in exile."

"Why should you imagine, my dear, that I know of his life?" Fouché asked gently, taking a pinch of snuff and watching her through hooded eyes.

"Because I cannot imagine that you would not," she countered, settling for directness and realizing instantly that she had been right to do so.

Fouché chuckled. "You are quite correct, madame. I correspond regularly with the former emperor." He laid the slightest stress on "former," thus administering an implicit rebuke for her own unqualified use of the title.

"You keep him informed of matters of interest?" she hazarded, sipping her negus with apparent casualness.

"Matters of interest *and* relevance," he said, continuing to watch her.

Genevieve nodded. "I should imagine much of relevance to his life is discussed at the Congress."

"Your imagination cannot be faulted, madame."

"Madame Delacroix, I have been looking everywhere for you." Charles Cholmondeley broke into their tête-à-tête, a smile wreathing the amiable and deceptively vacuous coutenance. "You promised me the *boulanger,* if you recall."

"How could I forget the promise to such an accomplished partner, sir," Genevieve replied deftly. "Monsieur Fouché, I did enjoy our talk, but you will excuse me?"

"Not with pleasure, madame," he responded with a conspiratorial twinkle. "But I will endure my disappointment as best I may."

He watched her go off with the Englishman and then went in search of Delacroix. That gentleman played his cards remarkably close to his chest, but that was a quality both shared and respected by Fouché. If, as he suspected, the Delacroix couple were playing a devious game, then he would do well to discover what he could.

"You have not, I trust, forgotten our little wager," Cholmondeley breathed into his partner's ear as they proceeded down the set.

Genevieve flicked him an up-from-under smile that spoke volumes, and its recipient beamed complacently. "Where and when do you wish to play, sir?" she inquired softly.

"Tonight." His fingers squeezed hers. "Will you come to my lodgings?"

"Shame on you, sir," she chided, tapping his hand with the ivory sticks of her fan. "What a suggestion to make to a married lady."

The Englishman looked around the room and encountered the turquoise eyes of the husband in question. But they seemed to look straight through him and showed no apparent interest in Madame Delacroix. It was as Cholmondeley guessed. The Frenchman was quite happy to look the other way as long as nothing was forced upon his notice. It was a perfectly usual arrangement, and he presumably had his own little adventures that did not disturb his wife.

"What stakes do you choose, madame?" He looked down at his diminutive partner, deciding to ignore her earlier remark, which he correctly assumed to have been playfully flirtatious.

Genevieve frowned. She knew well what stakes Cholmondeley had in mind. The best of three games of piquet, and if she were the loser he would expect her to follow through on the promises that so far she had managed not to fulfill. The difficulty was that she did not know how good a player he was. With the others, she had been able to observe their play

324

beforehand. But Cholmondeley had worked with Mariotti, the French consul at Leghorn, a man everyone knew to be one of the allied spies doing their best to prevent communications between Elba and the continent. Only by knowing how that system operated could they circumvent it, communicate with Napoleon, and form a plan of campaign.

"What stakes do *you* choose, sir?" inquired Genevieve in dulcet tones.

Her partner's voice became suddenly thick. "The same you give to others, madame. Those who are lucky enough to earn your favor."

So, he knew about Legrand, Grand Duke Sergei, and Signor Sebastiani. What gossips these men were, she thought with a flash of scorn, wondering if they had told the truth or had boasted of a conquest that had not been theirs. The latter, most probably, she decided. None of them would have willingly admitted losing at piquet and thus being denied the soft, sensuous body so undeniably offered in the event of victory. In fact, she would have laid considerable odds that their individual defeats were known only to themselves and Genevieve. Dominic certainly did not know of them; did not know the perilous edge she walked as she gathered her information; would not consider it a perilous edge, presumably, since he seemed to think her body well spent in the exchange. He would probably be amazed that she had found it impossible to do what she had so lightly suggested and he had so easily agreed to; would probably laugh at her for being naively romantic instead of pragmatic, for losing sight of the fact that the end justified the means. For the privateer, that maxim informed all his decisions, as well she knew.

"And if *I* should emerge the victor, sir?" She made no attempt to challenge his statement but let it lie, accepted by default.

Cholmondeley licked his lips, an inadvertent gesture of mingled hunger and anxiety. "You will name your winnings, madame," he mumbled through a dry throat. Surely, even in the unlikely event of her victory, she would not withhold what she clearly wanted as much as he did. Genevieve Delacroix was rapidly becoming a legend in Vienna, her name whispered almost reverently in the bastions of male privacy where the envious warred with the successful; where the dividing line was drawn between those who had won the lady's favors and those who lacked the courage to enter the lists. And she played the devil's own game of piquet—on that, everyone was in agreement.

"Then, tonight. I will come to you when I have made my own arrangements." Her eyes skimmed toward Delacroix and her partner nodded hastily, in instant comprehension. Even a complacent husband must be disposed of discreetly.

But the apparently complacent husband was finding to his chagrin that complacency eluded him. Just observing Genevieve playing her fish with such natural art and skill set his teeth on edge, and in the images that niggled, ragged on the edges of his mind, lay madness if he allowed himself to dwell upon them. He dared not allow himself to think of what she would be doing with Cholmondeley later, any more than he had allowed himself to think of those times with the others. They were partners in a desperate venture, and she was simply playing her part. Just why did she have to play it with such damnable expertise and blatant pleasure? But he knew the answer to that only too well. Had he not himself unleashed that exuberant, wonderfully passionate nature, educated her in the ways of loving, taught her to give and to receive without inhibition? And now, behold, he looked upon his former pupil and wished he had been an inept tutor or she a less able student.

But he could not let her see that, so he simply smiled and nodded agreement when she whispered to him that she would be back late, that the Englishman would have told all by the time the evening was done, that Silas should wait for her outside Cholmondeley's lodgings on Grashofgasse, that everything was going very well and, so far, she had managed to avoid an introduction to the Duchess of Angoulême.

Her luck in that area, unfortunately, was short-lived. The Duke of Wellington, himself, came for her in the supper room. "Her Royal Highness wishes to meet you, m'dear," he said with a benign smile, "if these gentlemen can spare you for a few moments." Thus extricating her from the large circle of admirers, he led her into a small parlor where the royal couple held informal court.

To her relief, Genevieve saw Dominic engaged in apparently easy conversation with Marie Antoinette's daughter. Although her own manufactured background was engraved upon her memory, she found the thought of his support ineffably comforting and encouraging. As if he realized this, he turned as she came into the room and discreetly extended his hand, palm up, toward her. She placed her own in his, felt the strong, reassuring pressure of his fingers, and with renewed courage gave her attention to the Duchess of Angoulême.

She realized rapidly that she need have had no fears. The lady was not interested in details of another's history. She was high-spirited and vivacious, unlike her husband, who was as rigidly formal as the majority of the Bourbon clan; as majestically expectant of the reverential deference due to a descendent of the Sun King as had been his ill-fated cousin, Louis XVI. Genevieve found it was possible to flatter one with reverence and laugh with the other, and avoid all close reference to her own experiences during the years of exile. Her explanation that she had spent the years since her third birthday in a remote corner of Prussia, where her family had escaped the Terror with relatives of her father, was accepted without question.

Dominic moved to one side once he was sure that Genevieve was comfortable, her stage fright vanquished. He had to leave her to play her part now, and, as soon as he decently could, took his leave of his hosts, who found nothing extraordinary in the idea that Monsieur Delacroix was going on to a supper engagement with friends, leaving his wife to amuse herself as she saw fit. Wives, after all, required no chaperones and no one could accuse Madame Delacroix of indiscretion.

Silas heard his instructions in silence. He was to follow mademoiselle when she went to the lodgings of the Englishman and wait with the carriage to bring her home afterward. If he felt a moment's unease, he was not to hesitate, but should do whatever he had to to bring her home safely. They were his usual instructions. Discretion was urged, but if it had to be sacrificed to expediency, then so be it.

## Chapter 20

Silence reigned in the comfortable room where heavy velvet drapes kept out the night, and a cheerful log fire kept the chill at bay. Genevieve watched her host mixing punch with great concentration, sitting on a low ottoman before the fire, adding to and stirring the contents of the deep silver punch bowl. She had no intention of drinking herself, but was not about to tell Cholmondeley that. She had become adept at appearing to sip the refreshment offered her, while the level in her glass remained the same. When she played for stakes as high as those she wagered, she could not afford the slightest diminution in one's powers of concentration.

"Do you find Vienna a little dull after the excitements of Leghorn, Mr. Cholmondeley?" She broke the silence with the seemingly casual question, fluttering her fan, her eyes smiling at him over the frosted crepe.

"Must we be so formal, my dear ma'am?" he asked, reaching across to take the fan from her hands. "I would dearly love to hear my name upon those sweet lips."

Genevieve controlled her grimace quite admirably, she thought. She could never imagine Dominic saying anything so ridiculous! But it was just the sort of remark that Elise would have been accustomed to hearing. No! She must not allow her attention to wander in that way. "Why, Charles, of course there is no need for formality," she simpered. "I greatly desire to visit Leghorn, myself." She gave a little artistic shudder. "Just imagine being so close to the monster Bonaparte that one could almost see him across the channel. Supposing he should decide to escape?"

"Have no fear, my dear. Such a plan could never be formed without the French hearing of it." Her host smiled indulgently. Women did find the thought of Napoleon most alarming.

"But how?" she inquired, all wide-eyed, flattering attention.

Cholmondeley laughed. "Mariotti is more than a match for Bartolucci." He dipped the ladle into the punch bowl and filled two silver goblets with the steaming, aromatic concoction.

Genevieve smiled her thanks. "Bartolucci?" she inquired, burying her nose in the goblet. "I have not heard that name."

"Oh, he organizes Bonaparte's counterespionage at Leghorn," her host tossed off blithely, taking a long sip of his punch. "Fesch in Rome does the same thing, but it is of little concern to us, my dear Genevieve, and should certainly not alarm you."

"No, I am certain it should not," she said, offering him a brave smile. "And one of your countrymen remains with him on the island, does he not? Was he not one of the Allied commissioners who agreed to stay and keep watch over the exiled emperor?"

"Ah, Sir Neil Campbell," Cholmondeley agreed with a grave nod. "A good man who is more than capable of circumventing Napoleon's own spy system from Elba. He suspects that if Bonaparte did attempt an escape he would make for Murat at Naples. But the idea is ridiculous, of course. The channel is patrolled constantly by French and British ships, not even a fishing boat could slip through."

"I am sure that you are all more than equal to the challenge," she said, bestowing one of her ravishing smiles upon him. "The monster is safely captive."

Cholmondeley stood up, his eyes suddenly intense. "It is to be hoped that I am equal to the challenge you present, ma'am." Bending, he took her hands, drawing her to her feet. Genevieve steeled herself for the kiss that she knew was coming. One had to offer sufficient inducement to add credence to the pretense. If she showed her indifference to the salute, it would certainly puzzle the gentleman. The devil of it was that she now had all the information she required, but she *still* had to go through with the games of piquet if she were not to arouse his suspicion—and she had no idea how skilled the Englishman was. She allowed her lips to soften just a little beneath his, allowed her body to lean into his just enough, then drew back with a slight laugh.

"Do not anticipate your victory, monsieur." Somehow, she managed to make the direction sound like an invitation, and Cholmondeley flushed, transparently eager. He moved to the card table, pulling out a chair for her, then seated himself opposite.

"Shall we cut?"

"By all means," Genevieve said, feeling her body still, her mind clear. There were some things for which she could be grateful to Victor Latour, although she had never before imagined that those agonizing hours of forced play could ever have proved useful. Her father, despairing of finding a worthy partner, had created his own, recognizing in his younger daughter the innate skills and intelligence necessary to match him both on the chess board and with the cards. Genevieve had learned rapidly that he was quite prepared to lose a well-played game, but errors of inattention or stupidity were mercilessly revisited. As a result, she very rarely made either.

Now, having won the cut, Genevieve elected to deal. The pack of thirty-two cards lay on the table, and they each gathered up their hands. Her opponent glanced at his cards, a slight frown drawing thin, arched eyebrows together, then he seemed to make up his mind what to discard with no hesitation. It was the first indication she had of the quality of his play, and it was not reassuring. Charles Cholmondeley looked to be a fine player. Although she had decided on her discard as quickly as he, she deliberately seemed to take her time, knowing that he would see the hesitation as a sign of potential weakness and hoping that it might lead him to play with less caution.

She managed to spoil his attempt at *repique* with the retention of a knave, which she had seriously considered discarding, and the retention won her the first game. She smiled at him and cut again for deal. "I think I had the balance of the cards, Charles."

"Perhaps," he said shortly, and she pursed her lips in recognition of the intensity of his concentration. Winning this match mattered greatly to Charles Cholmondeley. Unfortunately, or rather fortunately, he was not aware how passionately it mattered to Genevieve Latour that *she* win, thus avoiding losing something much greater and more dearly valued.

A careless discard when she threw a guard that she should have kept lost her the second game, and the tension in the warm, glowing room became a force to be reckoned with. Each player knew it must be controlled if clarity of thought was to be achieved. The cards ran evenly throughout the third game, and precision of play and judgment were all important. Genevieve closed her mind to everything but the green baize of the card table and the thirty-two cards. Success depended on her ability to calculate the odds against finding a desired card in the pickup, and it seemed that her opponent did not lack that ability either. Whichever of them won, it would be a close-run game; no question of either being rubiconed.

And then the ten of spades fell onto the table. Genevieve let it lie for a few seconds. Was it an error in discard, or did he have some ulterior motive? If she picked it up, would she be playing to his hand? She forced herself to review the hands that had been played, hearing Victor Latour's voice going inexorably over every hand in every game played over a long evening, and her own voice, faint with weariness, following the reprise. But she knew, because of the experience of those wretched evenings, that her memory tonight was faultless. Charles had erred. Silently, she picked up her cards in the last hand.

"Your reputation is not exaggerated, ma'am," Cholmondeley said, his voice stiff with the disappointment that he tried gallantly to conceal as he counted his score.

"It was touch and go, sir," she replied, quietly formal, gathering the cards and tidying the pack. "It is late, and I must return home."

His mouth opened on the words of protest, of appeal, cajoling, then the gentleman remembered that he *was* a gentleman and that breed never questioned in matters of honor. He had lost a wager, and if the lady insisted on holding him to the consequences of the loss, he could do nothing but bow and accept with a good grace. "What prize do you claim, ma'am? As I recall, we agreed you should name what you pleased in the event of your victory."

Genevieve shook her head and smiled gently. "The game itself is prize enough, Mr. Cholmondeley." She held out her hand. "It was a most enjoyable evening."

"I could wish it had ended differently," he said, bowing over her hand. "You will allow me to escort you home."

"That will not be necessary. My servant will be waiting outside with my carriage."

Charles Cholmondeley remembered that Madame Delacroix made something of a habit of clandestine card games, although, from what he had gathered from others, the evenings did not always end so early, or so abruptly. But it was only to be expected that she made her own arrangements for transport on such occasions. With no further demur, he escorted her to the door, where she turned and bade him good night. Remembering the earlier kiss, he ventured to take her hands, to bring his mouth to hers, but she stepped back, not hastily or with any embarrassment so that he was spared any awkwardness himself, but the message was clear. He had played and lost and there would be no second chance.

A burly figure appeared from the shadow of the Heiligenkreuzerhof convent that dominated the narrow street. "Carriage is at the corner, madame."

With an overpowering relief, Genevieve followed the stolid, comforting presence of Silas. She sank onto the leather seat in the nestling darkness, but when she closed her eyes knaves, queens, and aces danced behind her eyelids and, in spite of her exhaustion, she knew sleep would not come easily tonight.

Dominic came out of the salon as he heard the front door open. Silas, coming into the hall behind Genevieve, shot his master a shrewd look and compressed his lips. Monsieur had been dipping deep in the brandy again—it was a habit he seemed to have developed on those nights when mademoiselle was out doing whatever it was she did. Not that his condition would be obvious to anyone who did not know how to recognize the signs; just a slight narrowing of the eyes and a set to his shoulders, as if he were concentrating on his posture.

"How did it go?" he asked Genevieve, holding open the door to the salon for her.

"I am tired," she said, walking past him to the foot of the stairs. "I will tell you what I have discovered upstairs."

"As you wish." He bowed with just the faintest hint of mockery. "Lock up, Silas."

"Yes, monsieur." Silas made his customary response and watched the two go upstairs. Mademoiselle had a tendency to become snappish when she was tired or under strain, and Silas strongly suspected that both conditions operated tonight. Monsieur, when foxed or preoccupied with some personal trouble, tended to run out of patience rather rapidly, and Silas strongly suspected that both conditions operated tonight. Well, he'd pick up the pieces in the morning. With a resigned shrug, the sailor went to check the bolts on the great front door.

"Will you unhook me, please?" Genevieve tossed her cloak over a chair and gave Dominic her back. He obliged, but instead of continuing to the next stage as he would normally have done, he turned away as soon as the back of her gown was opened.

Raging serpents of jealousy and suspicion roiled in his belly, filling his mind with a bitter, venomous bile at the thought of that idiot Englishman putting his hands on her, his lips, sliding between those long, creamy thighs. It was worse tonight than it had ever been! With an inaudible oath, he filled a glass from the brandy decanter on the table. "Well, are you intending to keep me in the dark, *ma chère?* Or was your evening wasted?"

Genevieve, in the act of pulling her shift over her head, spun round at his tone. "What is the matter?" The question was muffled by the folds of silk that had caught on a hairpin. Dominic made no move to help, but stood watching her gyrations as she struggled to release her head from its smothering captivity. Her raised arms lifted her breasts, stretched the skin taut over her ribs. Her hips, clad in silky white pantalettes, twisted with her efforts. Desire rose, powerful, to mingle with the unfocused rage. He wanted her, dammit! But he wanted to take, to possess, to brand. Had she enjoyed it with Cholmondeley? The very thought corroded like acid.

The shift at last untangled, Genevieve tossed it on the floor with her dress. She still could not get accustomed to living without Tabitha who had picked up after her ever since she could remember. Silas would grumble in the morning when he found the pile, but she was too tired tonight. And she was certainly too tired to deal with Dominic who seemed unaccountably vexed. Going over to the dresser, she sat down and began to release her hair from its pins. "As it happens, I discovered quite a lot." She told him of her conversation with the Englishman. "He says that Campbell suspects Napoleon of plotting to escape to Naples." Her hairbrush swished through the shining silver-gold mass.

"Rumors," Dominic said with a dismissive gesture, resisting the urge to bury his hands and lips in that fragrant, swirling river. "That is all that reach the ears in Vienna. They have no solid information. I have some, however. It appears that Fouché has advised him to escape to America."

"He told you?" She put down her brush and turned to look at him, surprised. "I had some speech with him, and he made it clear that he knew there was an ulterior motive behind my questions, but I did not feel confident enough for honesty."

"I did," Dominic said flatly, tossing off the contents of his glass. "He approached me . . . in a very roundabout way, of course. I replied in an equally roundabout fashion, but we now understand that we have the same goal. Whether he will trust me enough to share his plans, only time will tell."

"Yes. I see." Wearily, Genevieve stood up, slipping her last undergarment off her body. Dominic's tone had been somehow indifferent, seemed to discard her own information as having little importance. Depression settled in a clammy fog, exacerbating her fatigue. Did he not care at all what she had gone through this evening—the tension, the suspense, the dread of losing? But no, of course he did not even think about it. He assumed she played her part with her body and kept her mind and spirit untrammeled. It was simply a necessary task she performed, distasteful, perhaps, but necessary.

Picking up her nightgown from the bed where Silas had laid it earlier, she dropped it over her head, pushing her arms in the sleeves. Then she clambered up onto the high feather mattress of the poster bed.

"Just stay exactly as you are." The husky command froze

her as she knelt, her back to him, on the edge of the bed. A little quiver of anticipation ran down her back, but with it came the most curious hint of apprehension. Something was badly wrong. She knew, as did Silas, that Dominic had overindulged in the brandy. It happened so rarely, and had so little effect on his behavior that it had never before concerned her. But tonight, something was amiss.

He looked at the soft, enticing curve of her body as she kept obediently motionless, the inviting thrust of her backside against the fine lawn of her nightgown as she knelt, and that need to possess, to take, to brand became invincible. He trod softly to the bed. "Raise your nightgown."

"I am so tired," she whispered, but the protest was faint. It never mattered how tired she was, Dominic's lovemaking always renewed and relaxed her. If it had not been for that persistent sense of unease, she would never have articulated even that faint demur.

"Content you, *ma chère,* this time you will not need to work," he said. "Raise it for me."

Genevieve shivered. This time? What did that mean? And why was there that unmistakably cynical note in his voice? Sweet heaven! Was he referring to what he thought had happened with Cholmondeley? But she did as he asked because she could not think of one good reason why she should not, and drew the garment up her body.

"Stop there," he said when the gown reached her waist. His breathing was ragged, and she could hear the reassuring throb of desire in his voice. Reaching across the bed for the thick, fluffy pillows, he piled them in front of her. Then, placing a flat palm on her back, he pushed her over, gently but firmly. "Comfortable?"

She was perfectly comfortable, except for an overpowering sense of vulnerability, which puzzled her. Her position was far from unfamiliar; indeed, it was one that had on many occasions afforded exquisite delight for them both. His

337

hands began to stroke over her buttocks, and she felt the insidious relaxation begin, preparing her for the slow spiral of desire as his lips followed his roving fingers, taking full advantage of her body's exposure, of her enforced passivity, to play upon the moist, throbbing centers of her pleasure.

Dominic lost himself in the contemplation of Genevieve's softness, in the essence of her femininity, in her willing submission to the sensuous power of the pleasure-giver. In these moments, she belonged only and absolutely to him, in thrall to his touch, to his knowledge of what would bring her the greatest joy, her body responding with such sweet obedience to his orchestration. No one else could do this for her or to her, or receive from her the fearlessly candid acknowledgement of his supremacy in this matter of satisfying her desire. She would not whimper like this for Sebastiania or the Grand Duke of Legrand or Cholmondeley—or would she? Had she? The serpents twisted in his gut again, hissing venom.

Genevieve felt the change in his touch, and her skin rippled in alarm as apprehension pierced her glorious, self-absorbed trance. But his fingers probed in deep insistent possession, and she could not cling to her apprehension as the tidal wave took her, receding eventually to leave her beached upon the mound of pillows, her breath coming in little sobbing gasps.

Dominic kicked off his shoes, pushed off his pantaloons, held her hips, looking down at her for a second, the pale skin of her back glistening with a light sheen of sweat, the nape of her neck bared and vulnerable as her bright hair tumbled forward, spilling over the coverlet. Dear God, he thought with a dull recognition of the truth. *Mon coeur.* Very, very slowly, he sheathed himself within the opened, welcoming body, feeling the silken muscles tighten around him, enclosing him in her center. His hands moved up her back, pushing up the gown, his nails scribbling down her spine making her skin dance, her muscles contract. He moved himself inside her, watching her buttocks lift to meet him, heard her soft, sibilant whisper of mounting pleasure. His hands globed her bottom, slid over her thighs, drawing them further apart, before he planted his hands on his own hips and drove deeply, increasing his speed as she moved urgently against him, imparting her excitement even as she controlled the angle of her body.

The maelstrom hovered on the horizon, and they both fought to keep it at bay for a few more minutes of this inexpressible delight. But the swirling waters crept ever closer, and Genevieve yielded first to the magnetic force that sucked her into a moment of oblivion. Dominic heard his name ring through the room, the instant before the climactic release left her inert across the pillows, her face buried in the coverlet, her breathing rapid and shallow. In the certainty that he had taken her to her own limit, that by his ability to do so he had made her his own, his climax rushed upon him and he fell forward against her back, pressing her against his heart.

"D'ye care to make a four at whist, Cholmondeley?" Grand Duke Sergei ambled over to the Englishman who was leaning against a silk-hung wall in the salon of the Victomesse de Graçay, listening moodily to an indifferent performance on the harp by a sallow young lady in puce satin.

Cholmondeley seemed to shake himself back to awareness. "Beg your pardon, sir?"

"Whist," Sergei repeated gently, taking a pinch of snuff from an onyx box, his eyes following those of his companion. They came to rest on the diminutive figure of Madame Delacroix who appeared to be using her far from inconsiderable charms in the entertainment of Monsieur Fouché. "I wonder if she will suggest a game of pique to Fouché?" the Russian murmured.

Cholmondeley came awake abruptly, turning to stare at his companion. "Why would she?"

"I do not know, exactly, my friend," the other said thoughtfully, "but not for the pleasure of the game, of that I am sure."

There was a short silence, then the Englishman muttered, "And not for any pleasure in the prospect of paying her debt should she lose, either."

"Ahh," said the Russian. "So you have discovered that, also. The lady is adept at making promises, is she not?"

"And has the devil's own way with the cards."

"You lost, then?"

Cholmondeley flushed in angry discomfiture. "Aye, I lost."

"And perhaps hoped that the loss would not prevent the lady from fulfilling those promises?" probed Sergei. "They had been made, after all, with such ardor."

Cholmondeley remembered that kiss. Dammit! There had been no hesitancy then, nothing to lead him to suspect that she was not really interested.

"Take comfort, my friend, in the knowledge that you are not alone in your experience," the Russian continued with a sympathetic smile.

His companion looked at him, startled. "I had the impression . . ."

"That I and Legrand and Sebastiani had won?" Sergei laughed, but with little humor. "Wounded pride, my dear Cholmondeley, tends to permit of a little embroidering of the truth."

The Englishman began to feel a great deal better. "Why does she do it?"

The grand duke frowned pensively. "Perhaps Madame Delacroix is the type of gamester who only enjoys playing when the stakes are of the kind she cannot afford to pay. There are such people."

"Mmm." Charles nodded, pursing his lips. "But I cannot

help feeling that there is something else."

"Indubitably, my friend. It is a conclusion reached by myself, Legrand, and Sebastiani, also. We find ourselves rather curious to discover what the 'something' may be. Does it not strike you as a little peculiar that Delacroix should appear happily complaisant when his wife amuses herself? He does not seem to me to be the type—not one to share his possessions. Look at him watching her."

Monsieur Delacroix was, indeed, watching his so-called wife, oblivious of the fact that he, in turn, was being observed. A frown buckled his forehead. He had not told her to flirt with Fouché, but had simply suggested that she seek out the devious, elderly statesman and engage him in a conversation where it was clearly understood by both parties that they were working on the same side. But Genevieve was quite definitely exceeding her brief, treating Fouché to the full gamut of her wiles. She was a natural born courtesan, Dominic reflected sourly; no wonder she had suggested it so lightly as a means of supporting herself if he took her away from New Orleans. And it had been *her* suggestion that she use her body to gain the information they needed. Why the hell had he ever agreed to it? Because it had never occurred to him that he would be tormented in this way—that images of her body moving with that wonderful lasciviousness beneath some other man would clog his brain, would heat his blood, would obscure all the rationality of the pragmatist he prided himself upon being.

And to add insult to injury, he felt a complete fool, hung by his own petard. Genevieve Latour was what he had made her, was doing what she thought he wanted and expected of her, was adamant in her insistence on her independence; on the fact that she understood there was no commitment between them; they were partners in lust and love and adventure until the arrangement drew to a natural close. Then she would be off, presumably doing what she did best, as she put it so insouciantly! He ground his teeth, watching

341

her divert her attention from Fouché to the young son of the Vicomtesse de Graçay. The lad was about twenty and made no secret of his admiration for Genevieve—an admiration that that ravishing smile could not help but foster. Damnation! Did she have to play the coquette with such obvious relish? The young de Graçay had nothing to offer her in exchange for those smiles and that light, intimate touch of her hand. She was doing it because she enjoyed it, and Dominic Delacroix had only himself to blame. If it were any other woman, any other partner in adventure, he would have shared her enjoyment in the game, deriving his own from observing her play. As far as Genevieve was concerned, that was exactly what he was doing. And how the hell was he to tell her that he wasn't, without appearing like a jealous and naive, love-struck puppy? She would laugh at the transformation from pragmatic mentor to prating, soft-headed fool, and he could hardly blame her. She was most certainly not in love with him—in love with the excitement of the life he had made available to her, in love with the heady sense of a future that she could mold for herself, in love with loving, but not in love with Dominic Delacroix.

"Madame your wife is much in looks, tonight, Delacroix." The smooth voice of Jean Luc Legrand spoke at his back.

"I will accept the compliment for her, Legrand," the privateer responded with a bland smile. "Unless, of course, you would prefer to repeat it to her yourself."

Legrand inclined his head. "She is a little occupied at the moment. A most popular lady, Madame Delacroix."

The privateer became very still as his nerves stretched to hear and understand the danger that he suddenly realized lurked in the offing. A man who had seduced another man's wife would not taunt the cuckolded husband unless he had good reason. And especially not in this case, when said husband had gone to considerable lengths to let it be understood that his wife's little affairs were a matter of complete indifference to him. But he had to make some reply to a statement that could be taken as insulting the lady's honor and, by extension, that of her husband.

"How kind of you to say so, Legrand." The turquoise eyes glinted in the lamplight; the carved lips flickered in the travesty of a smile that contained more than a hint of menace.

Legrand offered a thin smile in return. "You must find it most gratifying, Delacroix."

Now why was he to be baited? questioned Dominic. Legrand could not be intending to provoke a duel, could he? Why on earth would he? He could have nothing against Dominic—the man who had looked the other way, for heaven's sake, when Legrand had taken his wife. Or was that the problem? An idea flickered in the recess of his mind, flickered and fanned that indefinable sense of danger that Legrand had brought with him.

Dominic bestowed on his interlocutor a smile of the broadest amiability and bowed. "*Most* gratifying, Legrand. Would you excuse me?" He strolled off across the room, leaving the Frenchman with a deeply puzzled frown. Perhaps they were wrong, and Delacroix was truly indifferent to his wife's peccadillos; although there had been a moment when Legrand had felt a stab of alarm, had almost taken an involuntary step backward, away from the suddenly flat, glittering surface of those azure eyes. But the moment had passed as quickly as it had come, and perhaps he had imagined it.

With a thoroughly gallic shrug, Legrand went off to the card room to impart the inconclusive results of the last few minutes to the other parties interested in this matter of Delacroix and the elusively promising Genevieve.

"Ah, Dominic, you startled me, creeping up like that!" Laughing, Genevieve turned to greet her husband who had appeared without warning at her elbow. "One should be very careful about doing that, you know. You might hear something not to your advantage. Might he not, gentlemen?" Her eyes danced roguishly; her dimples peeped in the small face as she included Fouché and the young Graçay in the mischievously suggestive remark.

Fouché merely smiled indulgently and cast an appraising look at Monsieur Delacroix. The lady had better have a care, he decided. Her husband did not look to be in a sufficiently equable temper to accept that type of risqué teasing. The young de Graçay flushed crimson at the implication that he might have been indulging in something improper that the lady's husband should not hear about, and hastily stammered a disclaimer.

Genevieve chuckled and patted his arm. "Do not be embarrassed, my dear sir. My husband is well able to take a joke, are you not?" She glanced up at him for confirmation, and the smile froze on her lips. No wonder de Graçay was looking so uncomfortable.

"No one, to my knowledge, has *yet* had cause to complain of my sense of humor, madame," Dominic drawled. "But there is always a first time."

Genevieve swallowed. What on earth was wrong? Or rather, what had *she* done wrong? The privateer was furious and, as always, his anger manifested itself in his body's stillness, in the unwavering blue eyes that held her own until her gaze dropped. She had been feeling marvelously sophisticated, exuberant with the knowledge of her demonstrable power to attract and amuse such diverse individuals as Monsieur Fouché and the son of her hosts, smugly enjoying the entertaining little game of lighthearted flirtation played by everyone at which she had discovered such an unexpected skill. Now, Dominic had made her feel crestfallen and subdued, like a little girl whose fantasy had been punctured by adult exasperation with the game of make-believe.

"It is time we went home," Dominic said with painful lack of the conventional courtesies.

Genevieve flushed, but with annoyance rather than

discomfiture this time. The curt statement had sounded exactly like the order it was, and he could not possibly have just cause for such public humiliation. "It is a little early, yet," she demurred, a hint of steel beneath the soft tone. "But do you leave, by all means, if you are fatigued. I will follow anon."

Fouché coughed and took the wide-eyed de Graçay by the elbow. The young man started, then, realizing what was expected of him, muttered some vague excuse and bowed himself away from the trouble spot.

"Come," said the privateer, offering her his arm.

"I am not ready to leave," Genevieve hissed furiously. "You had no right to embarrass me in that way."

"*You* were embarrassing me," he declared flatly. "And unless you wish for further embarrassment, you will take my arm with no more argument."

"What was I doing?" she demanded, making no move to take the still proffered arm.

"You know perfectly well." He took her hand and tucked it beneath his arm. "I have spent quite long enough this evening watching you simper and flirt in that idiotic, coquettish fashion, so we are going to make our farewells."

To her furious chagrin, Genevieve felt tears of dismayed hurt at this cruel injustice sting her eyes. "I was not simpering," she muttered, swallowing hard and blinking. "And why should I not flirt a little? Everyone else does so."

"You have obviously forgotten that your greatest appeal has hitherto lain in the fact that you are unlike everyone else," he snapped. "I have told you countless times that affecting Elise's mannerisms make you simply ridiculous. You do not have the presence for it."

Genevieve was crushed, decimated by this harshness that seemed to have come out of the blue, to have no basis in fact. She had not been affecting Elise's mannerisms; nothing had been further from thought or intention, and she had enough self-confidence to know that she had not inadvertently

behaved in any way like her stepsister. She realized that an
attempt to defend herself against the unfairness of the charge
at this point would probably reduce her to tears, since, in the
crowded salons of the de Graçay mansion, she could not
admit anger to her aid, and only in anger could she respond
as she wished. There seemed nothing for it but to leave her
hand on her "husband's" arm, a fixed smile on her lips, to
mouth platitudes as they progressed through the succession
of rooms, one opening out of the other, until they found their
hosts.

"Ah, *ma chère* madame, you cannot mean to leave us so
soon," protested the vicomte, with a flourishing bow
reminiscent of the heyday of the court of Versailles.
"Delacroix, you cannot be so unkind as to remove the
brightest illumination yet to grace us. It will be like snuffing
the candles, I swear it."

"Then I fear you are condemned to utter darkness,
vicomte," returned Dominic, gently sardonic. "Madame has
the headache." He bent a credibly concerned look on the
upturned face of the figure beside him. "Is it not so, *ma
chère?*"

"Too much excitement, vicomte," Genevieve murmured.
"I am desolated to be leaving so soon."

Then it was over, and they were outside in the cold night
air. Silas and the carriage appeared as if by telepathy and,
indeed, Genevieve frequently thought that the old sailor and
the privateer communicated independently of the usual
channels of sensible converse.

She sat huddled in the welcome darkness of the carriage,
vibrantly aware of Dominic opposite but stubbornly
retreating into her hurt. She had no idea why he should have
attacked her in that manner, but, if she stopped to think,
things had really not been right between them since they had
established themselves in Vienna. It was nothing definable;
just a word, a look, a feeling. And last night, when they had
made love after her return from Cholmondeley's lodgings,

there had been something amiss. He had loved her with his customary tenderness and skill, had drawn her out of her self and into the sensate realm of glory, but those flashes of apprehension had been real, although incomprehensible. And afterward, he had tucked her into bed, gently and lovingly; but then he had left her, and it was near dawn before she had felt him slide between the sheets beside her. He had fallen instantly asleep, and she had curled against him, her arm flung across his chest, her head pillowed in the crook of his shoulder until Silas had come in with coffee and had grumbled at her for her scattered clothing. Usually Dominic laughed at their nursery spats, but this morning he had barely noticed, had been locked in a reverie, indifferent to the goings-on around him.

Genevieve went up to bed as soon as they arrived home. She wanted to fight back, to shout her outrage at the injustice, to demand explanation, but Dominic's reserve was intimidating and she was tired, suddenly depressed by a sense of futility, and she knew that she could not bear further hurt tonight. It was easier to retreat into herself, warm in bed with a hot posset and the soft candlelight and the deep welcome of the feather mattress. Tomorrow. Tomorrow, she would grapple with whatever it was.

## Chapter 21

It was very late when Dominic finally dragged himself away from his moody contemplation of the dying fire in the salon and made his way up the darkened stairway to bed. The bedchamber was lit by a single candle on the mantel and the last glowing embers in the fireplace. He trod over to the bed where the curtains were drawn tight, enclosing the sleeping figure in a peaceful dark. Usually, if she came to bed before he did, Genevieve left the bed curtains open. But he could hardly blame her for this defensive withdrawal tonight.

Pulling back the brocaded silk, he looked down at the still figure. She lay on her back, her hands flung above her head, fingers twined in the ash-blond curtain veiling the pillow. The straight golden eyelashes formed half moons on the high cheekbones delicately flushed with sleep, and the straight, determined mouth was relaxed, lips slightly parted.

Why had he lashed out at her like that? Dominic sighed and shrugged out of his coat. His anger and dismay was really directed at himself, succumbing so ridiculously, so ineptly, to such a pathetic emotion as jealousy. It had no relevance to the game they played, no relevance to their relationship. And it had been grossly unjust to transfer the self-directed anger to Genevieve. Except that the exchange with Legrand had unsettled him.

Shaking back the fall of lace at the wrists of his shirt, he unfastened the tiny buttons and turned his attention to this other puzzle. The man had been testing him, without the shadow of a doubt, testing his reactions to Genevieve's behavior. Why would one attempt to stir up a complaisant husband? It was hardly in the lover's interest. Unless, Legrand suspected that the Delacroix affairs were not quite what they seemed. But what possible evidence could he have for doing so? Genevieve played her part well enough—*too* well for his own peace of mind, Dominic reflected dourly, tossing his shirt into a corner and sitting on the chaise longue to pull off his shoes. She was the giddy socialite, flirting indiscriminately, and her husband, when he bothered to notice at all, looked on with a vague, indulgent smile. Fortunately, he had managed just in time to step back from the brink of exposure this evening and respond to Legrand according to role, offering the bland smile, the easily accepting remark, ignoring the underlying taunt that a man bothered by his wife's behavior would have found impossible to ignore. But it still did not answer the two questions: Why had Legrand been testing him? And what had happened to arouse his suspicions?

Naked, he blew out the candle and padded, soft-footed, to the bed. Maybe Genevieve could throw some light on the question in the morning. Whether she could or not, he had the distinct impression that it was time to take what information they had and leave Vienna while the going was good. Thanks to Genevieve's spying, he knew now how to make contact with Bartolucci at Leghorn. If Fouché could be persuaded to honesty, then it would smooth their path even further. The first gray strokes of dawn were painting the sky when he slipped beneath the covers, pushing an arm beneath the sleeping figure beside him to roll her into his embrace. Without waking, she muttered his name, snuggling against him, and he stroked the silken silver mass that shimmered across his chest.

"Forgive me, sprite," he whispered, tracing the line of her jaw with a delicate fingertip. As if she heard him, she burrowed closer with a tiny sigh. She did have the most generous spirit, he thought, a rueful little smile tugging at the corners of his mouth. He did not think he had ever apologized to anyone as often as he had to this sprite. Even when she had provoked his temper with unimpeachable reason, he still ended by deeply regretting the harshness of his reactions. In the future, he must endeavor to be more gentle with her even when she deserved his anger. She certainly had not deserved it tonight.

But the road to heaven is paved with good intentions—a platitude that Dominic was destined to remember before another dawn came to Vienna.


"Do you attend the Polanski's masked ball this evening, Madame Delacroix?" Signor Sebastiani massaged his knuckles attentively, his meagre mouth dragged into the semblance of a smile. He was thin and dark and pointed, like a gnome, Genevieve had often thought, and he missed nothing of what went on around him.

"It is certainly my intention, signor," she responded politely. "May I offer you more coffee?" She picked up the silver pot, her head tilted in invitation.

"Thank you, but no." He declined with a sharp gesture of one elongated hand. "You will, I trust, stand up with me for the quadrille."

A minute frown twitched between Genevieve's brows. The Italian was incredibly arrogant, utterly presumptuous in his assumptions. It would not occur to him that she might have accepted another partner, any more than it had occurred to him that the morning of the ball was a little late in the day to be seeking her hand for the most popular dance.

"I am desolated, signor, but I am already promised to the

Duke of Wellington."

"Then what can I say?" Sebastiani's hands drifted through the air, and he shrugged. "The duke is an appalling dancer, but no lady could ever refuse him."

"Indeed not," she agreed softly. "And you, signor, are a superlative dancer. I am mortified to find that I have only country dances to offer you."

"My error." Another, careless shrug. "I always forget that it is necessary to solicit one's partners so far in advance of the event. It requires so much tedious forethought."

"But when you wish to stand up with the most sought-after partner in Vienna, Sebastiani, forethought is essential," Legrand put in, sipping his coffee. "I, I am happy to say, have secured the cotillion and the boulanger."

"Shame on you for your selfishness, Legrand," chided Charles Cholmondeley. "You would deprive the rest of us."

"Gentlemen, gentlemen," laughed Genevieve in protest. "You put me to the blush with your flattery. Vienna blooms with eligible damsels, as well you know."

"But none who are also unequalled at the card table," Grand Duke Sergei interpolated.

Genevieve kept the smile on her face but could do nothing about its disappearance from her eyes. Her four morning callers were not generally known as cronies, and it was unusual to see them together, but they had arrived in a party, and it had become very clear to their hostess that they shared something—be it knowledge, curiosity, or a goal, she did not know. But whatever it was had been causing her some considerable unease. It now rather looked as if they had exchanged the truth about their evenings of pique with the seductive Madame Delacroix. And when discomfiture found companions it could become menacing. One man would lick his wounds and keep his humiliation to himself; four of them would see no need for shame and might look for a way of evening the score. If only she could ask Dominic for his opinion. But she could not do that without revealing her silly scruples, and if those scruples were about to cause trouble, then the privateer would not be inclined to an empathetic understanding of her difficulty.

"Where is madame, Silas?" Dominic, at this point in Genevieve's uncomfortable reflections, strolled down the staircase. Having risen late after his dawn retiring, and having spent a leisurely hour at his ablutions, he was feeling relaxed and in the mood to soothe and pamper his partner-in-crime, making amends for the previous evening.

"In the salon, monsieur," Silas informed him with his customery stolidity, adding in offhand manner, "with her gentlemen."

Dominic paused on the bottom step. "What the devil does that mean, Silas?"

"Those she visits late at night," Silas said. "When I bring her home." He looked over Dominic's shoulder, his eyes a blank, as if, of course, he knew nothing of what the mademoiselle did on those nights.

Dominic's lips tightened, his good resolutions flown as he remembered his conversation with Legrand. Surely Genevieve had sufficient sense to keep her informant/lovers apart from each other? They were all clever men, skilled in the often inseparable arts of treachery and diplomacy. It would not take much for them to put two and two together if they compared notes on their conversations with madame. He walked into the salon.

"Good morning, gentlemen. What a pleasant surprise." His smile embraced the company, touched Genevieve with unmistakable warning so that she stiffened. They had not spoken since the previous evening, but she had woken, held fast in his arms, feeling warmly secure, no longer angry and hurt, as if, while she had slept, he had smoothed the rough stone of antagonism rendering it harmless. But now, the clear blue gaze sparked a message of admonitory warning and, forgetting her own unease at this sudden visitation of the club of suitors, she put up her chin, and the tawny eyes returned their own message.

"Do you care for coffee, Dominic?"

"No, thank you, *ma chère*," he replied, raising the sherry decanter. "I prefer something a little stronger. Will you join me, gentlemen?"

It seemed that they would, and the veneer of cordiality, so well known to the accomplished diplomat, settled over the salon where logs crackled in the hearth, the fire glow dimmed by the winter sun pouring through the long windows facing the Domgasse.

"We are in competition for your wife's partnership, Delacroix," the Grand Duke said, with a little bow in Genevieve's direction.

"Indeed?" The privateer's eyebrows lifted in faint question mark. "In what, may I ask?"

The silence before Sergei responded was tiny, but it held a wealth of innuendo, and a chill ran down Genevieve's spine. "Why, on the dance floor, monsieur. Where else?"

Dominic laughed easily. "Where else, indeed. You have, I trust, saved a waltz for your husband, my dear Genevieve?"

"But of course," she responded smoothly. "The unmasking waltz at midnight. What other partner should I have?"

A frown darkened the privateer's turquoise gaze. That remark, if what he suspected was true, skated dangerously close to thin ice. Was she genuinely unaware of the distinct but indefinable aura of menace in the room? Or was the defiant crackle in the tiger's eyes an indication that she was deliberately playing with fire to annoy him. The latter, he decided. Clearly, he had not been forgiven for yesterday.

Their four guests took their leave soon after with amiable smiles and soft-spoken pleasantries that deceived no one.

"Now, what the devil are they up to?" Dominic mused, pacing the salon.

"They happen to enjoy dancing with me," Genevieve said with a sweet smile and a little, dismissive shrug. "Why should you find that peculiar? Or is dancing now forbidden, as well as flirting?"

"Don't play the naive baby with me," Dominic snapped, responding to this blatant provocation as if he had never formed good resolutions in the dawn. "This business, my dear girl, is far too dangerous for you to play silly games."

"Silly games!" Her jaw dropped and she stood up abruptly, the impatient movement setting the delicate pale-green flowing muslin of her morning gown swirling. Was that how he thought of the tormenting tension, the agonizing struggles over the card table, the desperate search for words to form the seemingly casual questions that would draw out the informative replies? Silly games! Her fingers curled into fists and she glared at him, hating him at this moment for putting her into the impossible position that she could not admit to because, if he knew the truth, he really would consider that she was playing silly games.

"Yes," he said deliberately, refilling his glass with the rich amber liquid. "It was unpardonably foolish to make such a pointed remark. Has it not occurred to you that their presence here, all together, might have some covert purpose? I cannot imagine what could have aroused their suspicions, but I'll lay considerable odds that something has."

Genevieve, who was now convinced of what that something was, decided that she did not wish to pursue the conversation. "I am having luncheon with Lady Marjori-banks and I must change my dress."

Dominic sighed and attempted to moderate his tone. "Genevieve?"

She paused, her hand on the door. "Yes?"

"I am sorry if I seemed unjust yesterday. Can we not put it behind us?" He smiled, hopefully placating.

But Genevieve found that she was not to be placated. She shrugged. "I had put yesterday behind me, but it seems you are determined to continue with injustice and unkindness. I do not wish to talk about it anymore." She swished out of the room.

Dominic took a half step toward the sharply closed door and then shook his head irritably and returned to his sherry. Once he had extricated them both from the web of deception, unavoidable during their stay in Vienna, and had removed Genevieve from her duped informants, then they would be able to return to their old footing. He would no longer be tormented by jealousy, and the excitement of direct action would take away the sour taste of this conspiracy that was depressing them both.

He did not see Genevieve again until that evening when he returned from a session of the Congress, convinced that this world meeting was on the verge of breaking up. There had also been much talk of the reaction in France to the restored reign of the Bourbons. The latter were behaving in a manner deliberately calculated, it seemed, to alienate the army and to fan the flames of national republicanism that in 1789 had begun the world-wide turmoil that it had taken twenty-six years to quell. If, indeed, it *was* quelled now. It seemed likely that Napoleon would receive a favorable reception should he decide to return to France and fight for the restoration of his empire.

Dominic was anxious to impart this information and his thoughts to Genevieve, but he found her unresponsive, and her monosyllabic replies did not encourage expansion as they dressed for the Polanski's ball. Silas's presence precluded his bringing a halt to her fit of the sullens in the only way that occurred to him, and their presence at a glittering dinner party at the Hoffburg Palace as guests of the imperial family precluded conversation between them, intimate or otherwise.

Genevieve appeared, if it were possible, to sparkle even more than usual. Her eyes were brilliant, glowing like the great golden topaz that hung from her ears and from the delicate gold chain circling her slender throat, and the contrast between them and the shimmering, glinting silvergold hair falling in artless ringlets to her shoulders had never seemed more striking. She wore a ballgown of ivory crepe with golden velvet ribbons and managed to create an impression both ethereal and vibrant. Dominic, who was entirely responsible for her elaborate wardrobe and the contents of the overflowing jewel casket on her dresser, was disposed to consider the investment well worth while. The modestly dressed *jeune fille* of New Orleans who had taken little interest in prevailing fashion had been transformed into a strikingly elegant young woman with a naturally impeccable taste and faultless instinct about what suited her best.

Once they arrived at the Polanski mansion, however, he decided that he could not approve her behavior as wholeheartedly as her costume. The black silk loo mask and golden domino were no true disguise of her identity and, in fact, were not intended to be so. No one was in any doubt as to the identify of their various partners, and the unmasking at midnight was merely an excuse for a little games-playing. Genevieve was never without a partner, never without an eager circle of admirers of every age and reputation, and she bestowed her charming favors indiscriminately, meeting successively outrageous sallies with an equally daring response. It was as if she had thrown all caution to the wind, was in the grip of some madness, some fever that obscured her vision of the effect she was having on the shocked pillars of Vienna society.

Dominic could not avoid noticing the horrified looks sent in her direction, the quickly averted eyes when he intercepted the glances, the whispered buzz running around the room. Discretion was the only rule, and Madame Delacroix was violating that rule in the most shameless fashion. Only once did he manage to get close enough to her for private speech, and that proved to be totally unsatisfactory since he was by then too angry and mortified by his own position to try to understand what lay behind her extraordinary performance.

"What the hell do you think you're doing?" he demanded in a furious undertone. "Are you lost to all sense?"

"I am making quite sure that our suspicious friends lose their suspicions," she said with a brittle laugh, followed by a betraying little hiccup.

"How much champagne have you had?" They were dancing, and Dominic tried to ignore the fascinated, speculative looks sent in their direction. He squeezed her fingers painfully.

"Not enough yet," she responded, tossing her head. "You said something had aroused their suspicions. I am just proving that I am only what they have always believed, and you remain the indifferent, complaisant husband. No one intent on deception would make such a spectacle of themselves, would they?" She shot him a triumphant, if slightly askew smile as the dance came to an end. "I am going into supper with Major Vivian, *husband*. So you will excuse me, won't you?" Before he could say that the only place she was going was home and suit action to the words, she had twitched from his hold and turned that ravishing smile on the resplendent major come to claim his partner. Dominic was forced to yield her up with a bland smile and a mock bow. Then, in high dudgeon, he stalked out of the ballroom and into the cold winter air to smoke a cigar and attempt to regain his composure.

Genevieve seethed, resentment and anger fizzing like the wine in her glass. And the more it bubbled, the more sparkly she became with the men around her. By what possible right did Dominic presume to judge and criticize her behavior at every turn when she was only doing what he had so readily encouraged? When she did not even do what he had so readily encouraged, she amended through a fizzy haze, allowing her head to rest for a moment on the shoulder of her partner. She had played her part in the charade, performed her information-gathering task to perfection, and he barely acknowledged her efforts, let alone praised her for them. Instead, he criticized at every turn. He had accused her of behaving improperly with Fouché and de Graçay when all she had been indulging in was a very little, mutually enjoyable flirtation of the kind practiced by everyone. Well, she had decided to show him the difference between socially acceptable flirtation and the other kind. Since he was going to accuse her of behaving badly whatever she did, she might as well give him cause. At the same time, her flagrant behavior would assuredly allay any suspicions of her four would-be lovers that she was not the lady of easy virtue that they had believed. So thought Genevieve, buoyed up by champagne and justifiable anger that for the moment suppressed the weariness, the strain and indefinable depression that had dogged her throughout the Viennese deception.

By midnight, Dominic had had as much and more than he could tolerate. To his jaundiced eye, Genevieve seemed to be taunting him with every toss of her head, every flutter of her eyelashes, every note of laughter, every sweetly seductive whisper that he could not hear but could guess with tormenting accuracy. Only the thought of the inevitable ensuing scandal prevented him from dragging her forcibly from the ballroom. There would be plenty of talk about the way she had acted tonight, but it was a hair's breadth short of scandalous, and the talk would eventually die down. But if her husband publicly played the part of outraged spouse, then there would be no salvation.

"The unmasking waltz is mine, I believe, *ma chère*." He appeared at her side, taking her hand, offering a benign smile to the surrounding company. Only a blind man would have missed the looks of slightly contemptuous sympathy he received in return—a man who could not take charge of his wife—and his lips tightened with his fingers around hers.

"*La*, husband, but surely you will not hold me to the promise," Genevieve protested with a brittle laugh, giving an experimental tug of her captive fingers and fluttering her fan. "To be unmasked by one's husband must be quite the dullest thing."

"Indeed it is, Delacroix," boomed Major Vivian. "Don't be a dull dog, there's a good fellow."

"I am desolated to disappoint you all, but a promise is a promise, is it not, my love?" He smiled down at the diminutive figure, and the first slight shiver of misgiving pierced her champagne haze. The privateer was very, very angry. She could feel it in his stillness, read it in the frozen azure wasteland of his gaze. He had a right to be so, of course, but then so did she.

Her chin went up and the tiger's eyes met ice with fire. "If you can find no one more exciting to dance with, husband, then, of course, I will keep my promise. Pray excuse us, gentlemen."

They made their way into the middle of the floor already thronged by laughing couples busily unfastening the silken ribands of their partners' masks. Dominic, impatient with the game that fooled nobody, had discarded his own some time earlier. Now, he held Genevieve in the circle of his arm and deftly removed the strip of black silk from her eyes. "I must congratulate you on finding your true métier, my dear," he said, biting sarcasm in every syllable. "I had not realized how quickly and easily your whoring would become indispensable to you. Is it really so utterly pleasurable and satisfying that you must prostitute yourself publicly simply for the sake of it?"

Genevieve felt the bitter bile of outraged innocence rise in her gorge. Her whoring, he called it! Those abominable evenings teasing information from zealously aspiring lovers, keeping them at bay with her wits. How dared he, who had willingly connived in a scheme that her own innate delicacy had made impossible, accuse *her* of whoring! The melodious strumming of the musicians, the lively chatter around her faded into a distanced buzz, and she seemed to see only those mocking, derisive turquoise eyes, the cynical twist of his mouth. With an incoherent exclamation, she stopped dead in the middle of the floor, pulling her hands from his. Her hands flashed, first one and then the other, cracking against his face, powered by the full force of her arms.

The whirling room stilled; the bright voices fell silent; everyone stared in shocked horror at the two figures, for the moment sculpted in immobility, in their midst. Dominic had gone white beneath the sun's bronzing, and the raised scarlet handprints stood out startlingly against his cheeks. There was a moment when the blue eyes were utterly blank, then, as Genevieve watched in stunned horror at what she had done, they filled with that dreadful anger that meant she had again conjured up the devil in Delacroix. She turned and ran, pushing through the throng, leaving him standing, quite alone and humiliatingly conspicuous, in the middle of the floor.

Genevieve ran blindly, unaware as the ballroom returned to life. The musicians, who had continued to play throughout the scene as if to maintain some element of normality, now increased their volume and tempo, and the dangers began to move again as the deliciously scandalized whispers ran like brush fire around the room.

Genevieve ran, not noticing where, knowing only that she must put as much distance as possible between herself and the privateer. The knowledge that she would have to face him at some point lurked in the corner of her mind, but she thought only of making that time at some far point in the distant future. Leaving the sounds of the ball muted behind her, she turned into a wide corridor of tapestry-hung walls interspersed with carved oak doors. The corridor was deserted and her pace slowed at last, allowing her to draw breath and calm the violent thudding of her heart. She needed to get out of the Polanski mansion, and not by the front door opening onto fashionable Karntnerstrasse. The only trouble was that she had no idea of the geography of the house and in her headlong rush had lost all sense of direction. Even if she did achieve the outdoors, what was she to do then? It was a cold night and a crepe ball gown and satin domino were ill covering for a night's wandering. She would think of something.

A door at the end of the corridor stood ajar, and she paused. Through the angle of the door she could see long blue-velvet curtains, which billowed into the room as if the french window behind them were open. Tentatively, she stepped inside and felt instantly the reassuring draft of cold air.

"Why, if it is not Madame Delacroix."

Genevieve spun round and saw Legrand, the grand duke, Cholmondeley, and Sebastiani sitting around a whist table, brandy goblets at their elbows, a haze of cigar smoke wreathing above their heads. They must have opened the window to alleviate the stuffiness, she thought with wild irrelevance. "Wh . . . what a s . . . surprise, gentlemen," she stammered weakly. "I was in need of a little air . . . and . . ."

"And a hand of cards, perhaps?" suggested Sebastiani silkily. "We were just saying how very much we would all enjoy playing with you again."

"Pray sit down, madame." Legrand rose, pulling out a chair for her.

"Pray do." Sergei cupped her elbow and eased her into the chair. The touch looked innocent enough to a casual observer, but Genevieve felt the bruising pressure of his fingers and realized with dull despair that they were going to force a confrontation and she had not her wits about her. She seemed to have fled from one danger and stumbled right into the arms of another, and her head was too fuzzy with champagne for clear thinking, and what thoughts she had were all centered on Dominic Delacroix and his inevitable vengeance for an act which she knew with utter hopelessness had been unpardonable.

She played with her fan and attempted a light smile. "I am flattered, sirs, but I do not find myself in the mood for cards tonight, and I would not dream of disturbing your four. But I would be happy to bear you company and watch you play while I enjoy the fresh air from the window."

Legrand gathered up the pack and began to shuffle them with obvious deliberation, his heavily beringed fingers deft as the shiny-backed cards slipped and slid between them. "You must grant us the opportunity for recovering our losses, madame," said he gently, with a flickering smile. "You are a gamester, after all, and in honor bound to allow us a second chance."

Genevieve moistened her suddenly dry lips with the tip of her tongue. Her hands in contrast were clammy and slippery. "Gladly," she said, clearing her throat. "But I claim the right to choose the time and the venue."

Sebastiani smiled. "But the stakes remain the same."

Genevieve thought rapidly. By some miracle, her head seemed to be clearing—probably in response to the danger that beset her from all sides, she decided grimly. At this point, no harm would be done by seeming to go along with them, just as long as she could avoid playing tonight. She put her head on one side in a coyly coquettish gesture and allowed her lips to curve slowly, invitingly sensuous. "But of course," she murmured. "The pleasure is still to be mine, is it not?"

The words fell into silence, and she realized that they had probably not heard them. All their eyes were fixed on the door behind her. With sick apprehension, yet knowing exactly whom she would see, Genevieve crept around in her chair. The devil in Dominic Delacroix stood in the doorway, a whip in his hand.

"You cannot . . ." Genevieve heard herself croak as he shook out the thong of the whip with a menacing snap. Her throat seemed to close, and black spots danced before her eyes. Once again, she had ignored her own advice, and the consequences were going to be devastating.

He strode toward her, swooped down, it seemed to Genevieve in her horrified trance, like a hawk on its prey, seizing her wrists and jerking her to her feet. "I have killed men for less insult," he said with an appalling quietness. "And by God, you shall smart for it."

A deadly silence blanketed the smoke-hazed room. The four men at the table just sat and stared as if they could not believe the evidence of their eyes and ears. Not having witnessed the scene in the ballroom, they could only assume that it was his wife's presence in clandestine intimacy with four admirers that had driven Monsieur Delacroix to these extreme measures.

Genevieve shook her head in mute denial and appeal even through her wretched recognition that in a world of strict justice this version of an eye for an eye would be considered entirely appropriate. She felt herself spinning like a top to face the curtains billowing at the open window. A hand in the small of her back pushed her forward, and the whip cracked. It was only as she leaped for the french door that she realized the thong had not touched her.

Grand Duke Sergei adjusted the lace ruffles at his throat in the expectant silence following Delacroix's whip-cracking departure on the heels of his fleeing wife. "I do not think, gentlemen, that Monsieur and Madame Delacroix, if, indeed, that is who they are, have been entirely honest with the Congress of Vienna." Rising to his feet, he fetched the brandy decanter from the sideboard and refilled their goblets. "I do not care to feel that I have been used, but I fear that in this instance I am able to reach no other conclusion." He looked interrogatively around the table and received thoughtful nods of agreement.

"Why?" Cholmondeley asked, taking a deep draught of his brandy.

"Perhaps we can answer that, my friends, if we each go back over our conversations with the so elusive Genevieve, particularly those that took place in the privacy of those intimate rendezvous over the card table—when so much was promised and so little delivered."

"And if we find a common thread?" inquired Legrand,

cutting the shuffled pack on the table in front of him. The ace of spades was revealed.

"Then we shall know how and why we were used," Sebastiani said, cutting in his turn, showing the five of diamonds. He shrugged and took up his goblet, inhaling the bouquet.

"And then we may decide what we wish to do about this unpleasantness." Sergei cut and laid the ace of hearts on the table. "We appear to be partnered, Legrand."

Cholmondeley gathered up the cards and shuffled them, passing the pack to Sebastiani who cut for Legrand's dealing. "I do not care to be used, either," he announced firmly. "Any more than I care to be made a fool of."

"Not something to be done with impunity, I agree," Sergei declared, picking up his hand. "Most definitely not."

## Chapter 22

There was a hard frost, and the spiked grass crackled sharply beneath her thin satin slippers as Genevieve flew across the lawn at the rear of the Polanski mansion. A narrow strip of light from the room that held the four card players stretched ahead of her, but apart from that the garden was in darkness inhabited by the looming shadows of trees and bushes. Behind her came the inexorable crackle of the privateer's more solidly shod feet and when, experimentally, she slowed her pace, looking over her shoulder in an effort to establish some communication, the hiss and crack of the whip drove her on.

"Where are we going?" she gasped in desperation as they reached a gate set into a high stone wall at the end of the garden.

"Home," came the curt answer.

"But the carriage is on Karntnerstrasse," she wailed, sobbing for breath.

"You are not riding, you are running," she was informed with another encouraging whipcrack.

"Damn you, Dominic Delacroix!" Imprecations were the only weapons she had to combat the much fiercer one at his disposal, and yet, ludicrously, the funny side of this appalling situation threatened to overcome her fear and anger. The devil in Delacroix, whip hand raised and armed, was going to drive her through the back alleys of Vienna. And as long as she kept running, the whip would rise and fall without doing her the slightest harm. Quite what would happen if she stopped and challenged him, Genevieve was not prepared to find out. She had struck him twice in the middle of a crowded ballroom, subjected him to the most horrendous public humiliation, and in her heart of hearts she knew, even as she stumbled and stubbed her ill-protected toes on an uneven cobblestone, that she had the best of the bargain.

This extraordinary progression through the deserted, medieval, cobbled streets around the cathedral was just between the two of them—except for the four cardplayers, she realized suddenly. They would hardly keep such a succulent morsel of gossip to themselves. But she could not stop to think of the ramifications of that realization. The freezing air was combining disastrously with the champagne, setting her head whirling and her stomach to behaving as if it had lost all sense of gravity, but she kept running because the alternative did not bear contemplation.

The route Dominic directed kept them well way from the broad main thoroughfares where merchants plied their trade regardless of the time of night, the two-horse carriages bore enthusiastic revelers through the night-time city, and the private carriages bowled along with their sharp-eyed occupants. And Genevieve, in spite of the groans of her complaining body, could only be grateful for this unlooked for—and undeserved—consideration. At last they turned onto the peacefully residential Domgasse, and Genevieve leaned panting against the heavy wooden door, flush with the pavement, set into the imposing gray stone facade of their house. Dominic's arm reached across her shoulder for the brass knocker, and she straightened the instant before the door swung open under Silas's hand. Silas was supposed to be with the carriage waiting on Karntnerstrasse, wasn't he? Genevieve stumbled past him into the welcome warmth of the hall. Of course, Dominic must have sent him home before he had marched through the Polanski's house in search of her. Presumably, it was from Silas that he had got the whip, also.

"Upstairs!" Dominic nudged her between the shoulder blades with the cold silver knob of the whip, and she staggered up the wide flight, conscious of Silas's astounded expression as she went by. In the bedchamber, which looked amazingly just as it had when they had left an eternity ago, Dominic threw the whip into the corner of the room and strode into his dressing room, slamming the door behind him.

Silas picked up the discarded quirt, demanding roughly, "You all right?"

Genevieve now knew Silas well enough to detect the concern masked by the roughness. She nodded, sinking into a wing chair by the fire. "He did not touch me with it. Although, God knows he had sufficient cause." She eased off her bedraggled slippers with a sigh of relief, beginning to massage her feet through the silk stockings, before offering the confession that she owed Dominic in the face of Silas's shocked condemnation. "I slapped him, Silas, twice in the middle of the dance floor."

The old sailor's jaw dropped. "And you're still here to tell the tale!" He shook his head in disbelief. "I'll fetch you up a mustard bath for those feet." Muttering inaudibly but with some vehemence, he left the room and Genevieve glanced nervously at the closed door to the dressing room. Her feet hurt, her stomach churned, her head ached, her entire body strained toward the solid feather comfort of the bed, yet she knew that the night was far from done with. Wearily, she pulled up her skirt and untied her garters, rolling her stockings down and easing them off her bruised, frozen feet.

"Has Silas gone to fetch you something for your feet?" Dominic spoke abruptly from the dressing-room door.

Genevieve looked at him. He had changed into a long brocade dressing gown and, to her inexpressible relief, the devil she had conjured up had departed again to whatever murky depths he normally inhabited. The privateer was not in a good mood, by any means, but he was well in control of himself. "Yes," she said in a low voice, shivering suddenly and leaning forward to the fire's blaze, stretching out her chilled hands. "I am sorry I hit you. It was unforgivable, I know, but you had no right to say those things to me . . . after everything I have gone through, to be accused of whoring . . . and then of enjoying it . . ." She shuddered. "It was beyond bearing and I lost all sense." Her voice was still low, and she kept her eyes on the fire.

Silas reappeared before Dominic made any response. He glanced at the two of them and sniffed, setting a footbath before Genevieve and filling it with the steaming aromatic contents of a jug. "You'd best give her some brandy, monsieur," he advised. "It's cold to be roaming the streets dressed in those flimsy things." It was the first time Genevieve had ever heard a note of criticism, even of this faint kind, in the sailor-servant's voice when addressing Monsieur Delacroix.

"Leave us," Dominic said brusquely, but taking the advice and filling a glass with brandy.

Genevieve shook her head with a grimace as he held it out to her. "I cannot. I feel dreadful enough as it is."

"Not as bad as you will feel in the morning," he said with brutal candor. "But maybe you will be a little more moderate with the champagne in the future."

Tears sparked behind her eyelids, but she said nothing, merely immersed her feet in the hot water, which immediately seemed to engender a feeling of relaxation.

"Would you explain what you meant just now?" Dominic spoke very calmly as if the subject were of only mild interest. "What did you mean by 'everything you had gone through'?"

She may as well tell him the whole silly truth, Genevieve

thought dully. What difference could it possibly make what he thought of her now? "You can laugh at me if you please; it doesn't seem to matter anymore. But I don't seem to be able to be a proper spy, and I cannot do certain things even if they are the most practical way of achieving a goal. I am a hopeless adventurer, and I should have stayed in New Orleans and married Nicolas."

Dominic stared at her, the slender column of her bent neck, the tumbled ash-blond ringlets glinting in the firelight, the little hands gripped tightly in her lap, the ridiculous contrast of her bare legs and feet plunged in the bath with the richness of her gown and jewels. "I beg your pardon, but I fear I must be being very obtuse, Genevieve. What certain things can you not do?"

Genevieve sniffed and wished her head did not feel as if it were about to explode. "Whoring," she said, only it came out as a venomous hiss. "Whatever you might have thought, I *cannot* go to bed with those men. I can only pretend that I will."

The world seemed to spin on its axis, then slowly settled again. Dominic took a deep breath. "Then what have you been doing on those nights when you've been gathering information?"

"Playing piquet," she confessed, wriggling her toes in the soothing water. "I was the stake. If I lost, then . . ." She shrugged. "So I had to make sure I always won."

Dominic gawked in disbelief. "Those four are among the best cardplayers in Vienna!" Genevieve just shrugged again. He paced the room for a restless moment, then came to stand in front of her, reaching for her chin and tilting it to meet his eyes. "Are you telling me the truth?"

"Now you accuse me of lying!" Genevieve cried. "First I'm a whore, and now I'm a liar."

"I am not accusing you of anything, sprite," he said carefully. "I just want to be quite sure that I have it right this time. You gleaned your information while playing cards, promising that if your opponent was victorious he would have you. Is that right?"

"In a nutshell. A little crude, perhaps, but it was all I could think of. Only now I think that they have exchanged stories and they probably realize that I was not what I seemed. I was trying to allay those suspicions this evening."

Dominic frowned. "That was not all you were trying to do, my Genevieve."

She sighed. "No. But you had made me so angry with your insinuations and criticisms, and you didn't know the terrible strain it has all been, and I could not tell you because you would say I was having silly scruples—"

"What the devil could have given you that idea?" he broke in, wondering whether he would succumb to the urge to shake her before he hugged her.

"Well, you seemed to think it was such an obvious plan and not at all peculiar in me to have suggested it . . . only I didn't really know what it would mean when I did suggest it." Her fingers twined around themselves in an impossible knot in her lap. "It seemed at the time to be very blasé and . . . and well, appropriate for an adventurer. And that is what we are, after all. We are not respectable or anything, and we do not belong to each other. We are just sharing an adventure."

Dominic wondered how long it would take him to persuade her that perhaps there could be another dimension to their relationship. She was so very definite about the way she felt. He pushed that problem aside and returned to the more immediate one. "I do not understand why you could not trust me enough to tell me that this was something you did not wish to do," he said quietly. "You have been bearing the full burden of an abominable strain quite alone, deliberately allowing me to think something different, which has led me to add to your problems rather than alleviate them." He thought of all those unkind words, of his tormenting jealousy, all of which would have been avoided if only she had confided in him.

370

"But how was I to know you would understand?" Genevieve looked at him for the first time of her own volition. "You agreed to the idea so readily and behaved always when I came back as if nothing untoward had happened and—"

"I was mad to agree to it," he interrupted brusquely. "But you seemed so damnably sure of yourself and what you wanted to do that I did not think I had the right to prevent you. And then you seemed to do it so well and came back with all the right pieces of information, and dammit, Genevieve, you deliberately led me to believe that you were enjoying yourself!" She said nothing, allowing the accusation to pass by default. Dominic sighed. "I have been tormented by the most shaming, agonizing jealousy, Genevieve Latour. An utterly degrading emotion that I have never before felt and was not prepared to admit to. And you fed it."

"Jealous?" Genevieve mumbled, removing her feet from the rapidly cooling mustard bath. "You? Because of me?" It was the most extraordinary revelation, and in her wondering contemplation of it she forget her bodily ills for the moment.

"Exactly so!" he declared with a dry self-mocking little smile. "Jealous because of the games played by a diminutive scrap of femininity who had better promise this instant on her solemn oath never, ever again to keep to herself matters in which I have both an interest and a say." The turquoise eyes were stern.

"If you had told me how you felt, I would have told you the truth," Genevieve said unarguably, deciding that she was not going to be browbeaten into accepting the full blame for this tangle. "You did nothing to encourage the truth, quite the opposite." Bending, she rubbed her feet dry with the towel Silas had left. "I have such a headache, Dominic. Can we continue with this in the morning?"

"I want your promise." Catching her beneath the arms, he pulled her to her feet just as the vigorous hammering of the

371

great brass door knocker resounded through the tall, narrow house. "Who the devil . . ." Releasing her, he strode to the door and flung it wide, stepping out onto the landing overlooking the hall. Genevieve limped to stand beside him, peering over the gallery rail.

Silas trod ponderously to the door as the knocker sounded again. He pulled it wide and Monsieur Fouché walked past him without ceremony. "Where is Monsieur Delacroix, man? I must talk with him immediately."

"What is so urgent, Fouché?" Dominic called down, his voice deliberately light although Genevieve could feel the instant tautening of his body as he prepared to make decisions, to respond to whatever turn events were about to take.

"Ah, Delacroix." Their visitor raised a hand in greeting, then took the stairs two at a time. "You will forgive this unorthodox arrival. Madame Delacroix, your servant." He found the time to bow punctiliously to the barefoot Genevieve who returned a slightly sardonic curtsy.

"You are very welcome, monsieur," she said, moving back to the open door of the bedchamber. To her surprise, the Frenchman seemed to take the movement as invitation and followed her into the somewhat disheveled room where her stockings and shoes lay in a heap beside the footbath and the wet towel. She looked helplessly at Dominic, who bellowed for Silas over his shoulder.

"What's to do, Fouché?" he asked directly, handing his unexpected guest the glass of brandy he had poured earlier for Genevieve.

"I . . . uh . . . heard of the . . . uh . . . somewhat spectacular events at the Polanski ball," Fouché said with unusually hesitant delicacy. "It seemed that I had better lose no time in conferring with you about certain matters, since, obviously, your stay in Vienna must now be at an end."

"Obviously," Dominic agreed with another of his dry smiles. "I do not think either of us will be received again."

"No." Fouché sipped his brandy and waited as Silas removed the footbath and collected up Genevieve's discarded footwear.

"Time madame was in bed," the sailor permitted himself to observe as he left the room, closing the door with a punctuating click.

Fouché seemed not a whit put out by an earringed, pigtailed sailor playing lady's maid, but then, Genevieve reflected, Fouché had suspected for some time that the Delacroix were a somewhat unorthodox couple. Now he said, "There'll be no sleep tonight for any of us, not if I can persuade you to join forces with me."

Genevieve dropped into the wing chair again as a wave of dizziness brought a nauseous sinking feeling to add to her miseries. Any other time, and she would have responded as Dominic was doing, with brightening eye and alert posture. But tonight she was drained, emotionally and physically, and shamefully close to tears, she realized, resting her aching head on an elbow-propped hand. She could blame herself for the overindulgence in champagne, and supposed that that bore some responsibility for the evening's debacles, but her forced march through the streets and the intensity of the ensuing truth-telling session that she knew was not yet completed had squeezed the last drop of energy from bone and sinew. She did not think she could care less about Napoleon Bonaparte.

"Fouché, we will continue this downstairs, if you please," Dominic said briskly, opening the door again. "Silas will show you into the salon. I will join you directly."

Fouché followed his host's eyes and seemed to take in the whey-faced, drooping Genevieve properly for the first time. *"D'accord,"* he replied with equal briskness. "Desolated to have discommoded you, madame." With a smart click of his heels, he left the chamber.

"I do not know how long you may be able to rest, but a little must be better than nothing," said Dominic. "Come, I will help you undress."

"But since we are partners, should I not take part in whatever these plans are?" she offered in token protest, allowing him to pull her to her feet.

"At the moment, my child, you could not partner a soft boiled egg," Dominic told her, unhooking her gown. He had her between the sheets in a matter of minutes, and her eyes closed with a blissful sigh as the cool softness of the pillow cradled her throbbing head. Bending, he brushed her hair off her forehead and dropped a light kiss on the wide brow. "This that is between us must wait for awhile, I fear. But not for very much longer, sprite."

Her eyelashes fluttered in a response that he took to be agreement and, snuffing out the candles, he left her in merciful peace and darkness.

"So, Fouché, now we may be free of interruption." Closing the salon door behind him, he went to stand with his back to the fire, one arm resting casually along the carved mantel.

"You are interested in assisting Bonaparte to escape from Elba?" It was posed as a question, but both men knew that it was really a statement, and Dominic merely inclined his head in agreement. "The time is ripe for him to make a move," Fouché said, "but he will need to slip through the blockade of French and British ships patrolling the channel. You have some expertise in such matters, do you not?"

Dominic's fly-away eyebrows formed question marks and he whistled softly. "So you know who I am."

The elderly statesman chuckled softly. "Oh, yes, *mon ami.* I have known for three days. I have informants in America also, you should know."

Dominic nodded ruefully. "I should have known, certainly. I should communicate with Napoleon through Bartolucci at Leghorn, or Fesch in Rome?"

"You have done your homework." Fouché applauded.

"Genevieve has," Dominic corrected him, a shadow crossing the turquoise eyes.

Fouché pulled at his lower lip. "A resourceful lady, your wife. I congratulate you, Delacroix." He stared for a second into the fire, then recollected himself. "Napoleon has not sufficient ships on Elba, even if he could commandeer all of them under the sharp eyes of Neil Campbell, to transport some twelve hundred men. Another vessel, maybe two, must be acquired on the mainland. And a crew supplied."

Dominic nodded his understanding. "I have my own vessel and crew already at Leghorn, and sufficient men to put a skeleton crew aboard another sizable ship. Purchasing a merchantman should not present too many difficulties in a port of that size."

"Good." Fouché nodded and dismissed that matter as dealt with. "Bartolucci will provide you with introductions to Bonaparte who receives visitors regularly, and I see no reason why you and madame should not join the stream of the curious. When you see him, you will tell him that *I* am plotting to replace that reactionary with Louis Philippe. That will drive him to action if he requires further incentive." The wily old fox chuckled. "The people are calling for him. He will be swept on the tide of public opinion once he sets foot in France."

Dominic, having warmed his backside thoroughly, turned to face the fire. The Orleans, Louis Philippe, was a liberal, popular man. If he replaced on the throne of France the reactionary Bourbon, Louis XVIII, who was at present causing so much dissension among the populace, Napoleon would lose valuable support since the people of France would have less reason to clamor for his return. "And *are* you planning to do so?" he inquired.

Fouché chuckled. "If Napoleon does not make his move soon, I shall most certainly do my best. The situation cannot continue as it is."

"So, we have little time to lose," Dominic said with complete comprehension. Fouché was a tricky schemer. "If I am to talk with Bonaparte, discover his transport needs, acquire what is necessary, and evolve a plan for circumventing the blockade . . ." He turned to smile at Fouché, the quietly confident smile of the privateer facing action and decision.

"They are not light tasks, *mon ami,*" Fouché said, as if he needed reminding. "But I have little doubt that you will accomplish them to the greater good of France." Dominic's eyebrows lifted and Fouché chuckled. "But the greater good of France is not really your concern, is it?"

"I am a mercenary, Fouché," the privateer stated with a small shrug. "I have been well paid and will accomplish the tasks I have been paid for."

"A much more reliable motive than blind loyalty and patriotism," Fouché said without irony. "I, also, am a mercenary of a kind, but I pursue power rather than money."

"The two tend to march hand in hand," Dominic said and they both laughed, joined for a brief moment in the bond of recognition.

Fouché left soon after, and Dominic spent half an hour conferring with Silas who had remained, stolidly awake, in the kitchen, well aware that the events of the evening presaged an immediate alteration in the present arrangements. Silas received his instructions to close up the house, settle the lease and follow monsieur, together with the men who made up the household staff in Vienna, to Leghorn as soon as they could. There they would join up with *Danseuse* and her crew and await further instruction. The sailor then went off to fetch the carriage and rouse one of the hands to act as coachman during the Delacroix's journey to Leghorn.

Dominic went upstairs to face the unfriendly task of waking Genevieve from far too short a sleep. His resolution faltered when he held a candle over the bed and examined the figure far gone in the sleep of wine-aided exhaustion. She was going to feel abominable when she came to, and a long carriage ride, jolting over bumpy ill-paved roads to the coast of Italy would hardly aid recovery. Traveling day and night, they could accomplish the distance in two and a half days, barring accidents and supposing they could always find good horses in the mountainous wilderness. But did Genevieve have sufficient stamina to travel in that way, even if she were feeling her best?

He could always leave her to follow in Silas's charge. But, no, that would inhibit the men, slow them down, and he could not afford their arrival to be delayed. Then he smiled to himself, imagining what she would say if she could hear his cogitations. His sprite had committed herself to this venture without reservation, and she would not tolerate being left behind, and would certainly object most vociferously to the merest suggestion that she would not be able to keep up. She had the strength of youth and health on her side. He would do what he could to cushion the ordeal until her natural reserves reasserted themselves, but until they did, Mademoiselle Genevieve was going to have to endure—and not necessarily in silence, he thought with a rueful grimace, setting the candle down beside the bed. But he could afford to leave her sleeping for awhile longer, until he himself was changed and packed. Silas could pack for Genevieve, and he would wake her at the last possible moment.

It was in the dark hour before dawn that Dominic decided he could wait no longer. The portmanteau was stowed on the roof of the carriage that waited at the front door. He was warmly dressed in britches, boots, and jacket, a heavy topcoat tossed over a chair, ready and waiting. He had selected a velvet riding habit for Genevieve, silk lined for added warmth; with boots, cloak, and muff she should not suffer from the elements, at least.

Genevieve fought the hand on her shoulder, the inexorable, quiet repetition of her name. She tried to burrow beneath the pillows, to shut out the painful gleam from a lamp held close above, but there was no escape. With the return of consciousness came, as inextricable partners, nausea tugging at her belly, a drumbeat at her temples, sawdust in her mouth. Groaning, she rolled onto her back. "For pity's sake, go away and let me sleep."

"You have to get up now," Dominic said firmly, pulling back the bedcovers. "When you are dressed you shall have some coffee."

Her stomach heaved at the very thought. She could not, for the moment, imagine why Dominic should be doing this dreadful thing to her. With another groan, Genevieve turned onto her side, away from the light, curling her limbs, aching in every joint, into a tight ball.

Dominic's lips twitched in spite of his sympathy for a plight that he remembered only too well from his own youth. Slipping his arms beneath her, he lifted her bodily off the bed and set her on her feet where she swayed wretchedly, shaking her head in mute refusal to cooperate. "You do not wish me to leave you behind, do you, Genevieve?"

"Behind where?" The tawny eyes stretched open with clearly painful effort.

"Behind here," he said briskly, pulling her nightgown over her head. "I am going to Leghorn. Are you coming?"

"I think I am going to be sick," she moaned, shivering as the air brushed her bare skin.

"Oh, God," Dominic muttered. "You are even worse than I thought. Just how much champagne *did* you have?"

At the very word, Genevieve stumbled over to the commode where she hung retching in supreme misery, but without relief.

Dominic went to the door. "Silas, I need some of your kill or cure concoction!" Genevieve staggered back to the bed, crawling beneath the covers.

"I think I am going to die," she said. "I had better die here."

"You are not going to die. You may sleep in the carriage and by this evening you will feel yourself again. Silas has something which will stop the nausea, although it won't help your head, I am afraid." Silas appeared at that moment with a tray on which reposed a large glass of evil-smelling liquid. This he set down beside the bed, casting a comprehensive eye over the bed's occupant.

"Only thing for a hangover is to sleep it off," he commented, moving back to the door.

"That is not helpful, Silas, since it is not an option available at the moment," Dominic returned, picking up the glass. "Come on, Genevieve. Drink this." Sitting on the bed beside her, he hauled her up against his shoulder and held the noxious potion to her lips. "I promise you, it will make you feel a little better. And if you drink it down all at once, it will not taste so bad." He smiled reassuringly as he coaxed her.

Genevieve, who had never before experienced anything as horrible as her present condition and, indeed, was so rarely even mildly under the weather that her tolerance for ill health was almost nonexistent, looked at him in pathetic appeal, her nose wrinkling in disgust. Then, reasoning that it could not possibly make her worse and she could think of no reason why Dominic would want to do her further injury, she took the glass, closed her eyes and tossed the contents down her throat. She prayed for instant death, shuddering and gagging as the liquid, as bitter as any gall or wormwood, burned its way down her gullet, corroded in her already rebellious stomach. Her eyes streamed, her mouth opening and closing like that of a landed fish as she fought for air. Then the miracle occurred. The seething in her belly subsided, the acid burning faded, and she realized that she was not going to vomit.

"It's a harsh remedy, I know," Dominic comforted, rubbing her back gently. "I would not recommend it except in dire emergency, but we must be on the road before dawn."

Genevieve nodded with what she hoped was energetic concurrence, but the movement increased the drumbeat in her head and she winced, deciding to move only with the greatest care. Gingerly, she swung her legs over the bed and sat on the edge, reaching for her stockings. Bending her head caused the tom-tom again so she struggled to bring her feet to her hands, rather than the other way around.

Dominic could not help smiling as he observed this valiant attempt to circumvent her ailments. Her lips were set in a grim line of determination, her eyes kept open by invisible glue. "I think you had better let me help you," he said. "Lie down again." When she fell back with a moan of relief, he raised her legs to draw on her stockings, smoothing the thin silk over her calves and thighs, tying the garters carefully. Genevieve gave a little sigh and he looked at her sharply. Surely she was not capable of arousal in her present state. He, on the other hand, most definitely was. It seemed a long time since they had last made love with the gaiety and freedom of the past and that slight body was infinitely desirable. The soft rose-tipped mounds of her breasts, perfectly formed against the narrow rib cage where the ivory satin skin stretched taut; the delicate bloom of her navel, a tight whorl in the flat belly that would dance beneath his stroking tongue; the silken silver triangle at the apex of those long thighs that he would slowly draw aside to reveal the eagerly welcoming softness of her center—

With a slight shock, he realized that while he had been standing in rapt contemplation of the garden of pleasure laid out before him, the owner of the garden seemed to have fallen asleep again and dawn hung on the horizon. Picking up her pantalettes, he rolled the legs and slipped them over her feet, drawing them up her body. "Make a bridge, sprite," he instructed, slipping a flat palm beneath the warm buttocks and lifting her. She was not too lost to the world to hear and oblige, and her body stayed arched while he pulled the undergarment to her waist. The rest was relatively easy, and within twenty minutes he had her bundled up in her cloak and muff and installed in a corner of the carriage.

The next sixty hours Genevieve would remember with a shudder for the rest of her life. They stopped only to change horses and eat. For most of the first day, she slept fitfully, cradled against Dominic's shoulder, oblivious of the cramping discomfort this caused him. Sometime during that night, the toxic effects of the champagne finally wore off, which was not that much of a blessing since it left her wakeful and abominably conscious of the acute discomfort of the jolting vehicle. The inns where they made their brief halts were primitive roadside establishments, obviously unaccustomed to much traffic from outside the immediate rural neighborhood. Requests for water for washing were greeted with incomprehension; the food offered, Genevieve, at least, found to be a universally inedible mixture of greasy broth, gristle and unpeeled vegetables. The horses, in general, looked as if they were on their last journey before they found their way into the soup, and their progress along the steep, rough tracks that passed as roads was labored and slow.

Dominic remained completely unperturbed by these inconveniences, and when his companion snapped and complained and on more than one occasion wept with the cold, dirty misery of it all, he soothed and patted her as if she were a fretful child. Such treatment had the desired effect, leaving Genevieve guiltily anxious to make amends so that she forced a smile and sat up, trying to take an interest in the wild mountainous countryside through which they were passing.

Late in the afternoon of the third day, the carriage crested

381

a hill and the port of Leghorn lay below with the deep blue sea stretching to the coast of France. As they descended to the white-washed town, Genevieve made out the unmistakable, dainty shape of *Danseuse* swinging at anchor in the lee of the sea wall, and her heart lifted. *Danseuse* was the only home she had now, and never had she needed the comfort and security of home more than at this moment.

# Chapter 23

"So, Madame Delacroix, how do you find my little kingdom?" The exiled emperor waved an expansive hand around the garden terrace of the Mulini palace at Porto-Ferrajo, the gesture encompassing the beautifully landscaped gardens leading to the walled palace and the blue expanse of the bay below.

"Exquisite, sir." Genevieve returned the publicly correct response to a question that she, unlike the majority of her fellow guests, knew to be mere form. The exiled emperor was singularly uninterested in this little domain—little being the operative word. Bonaparte's eyes twinkled at her tactful circumspection. A large party of visitors was gathered on the terrace complimenting the ruler of Elba on the beauty and order of his realm as they examined the view from the strategically placed terrace—a view that allowed no vessel to enter the port unseen. They came from England, from France and from Italy curious to see and to talk to the amazing man who had dominated all but a tiny corner of Europe through conquest or alliance and who now, in exile, was chatty and amiable, talking freely of his career, defending his policies, extolling his virtues. But to those visitors like Dominic Delacroix bearing the correct introductions, he talked of other matters as Madame Delacroix was well aware.

Genevieve had not been a participant in the late night discussions in the small functional office that resembled a field tent, but Dominic had been a faithful reporter when he rejoined her in the opulently appointed guest chamber. One should not be fooled into thinking that this little fat man with his chubby face and expressive eyes had truly settled into the government and defense of his new kingdom, into maintaining a tiny army and navy, into the building and furnishing of his various palaces and country estates. He was as ambitious at forty-six as ever he had been as a young lieutenant, and the ambition was fed by the boredom and frustration of one suddenly deprived of absolute power and public reverence.

"I understand Sir Neil Campbell has sailed to the mainland," Genevieve now remarked casually, keeping pace with her host as he took a turn about the terrace, pausing occasionally to examine the flotilla of ships anchored in the bay through the field glasses held by an accompanying servant.

Bonaparte smiled. "He wished to consult a doctor at Florence about his eyesight, madame."

"I had hoped to meet him," Genevieve said casually.

"I do not expect him to return for ten days or so." The sovereign of Elba shrugged his plump shoulders. "But, of course, we should be delighted if you and Monsieur Delacroix would remain with us as our guests until then."

"You are most kind, sir." Genevieve smiled at the assembled company, all of whom had heard this seemingly casual conversation, most of whom believed that their host and those of his guests who chose would be here when Campbell returned.

"The pleasure is all mine. Shall we go up to the house for luncheon? It grows a little chilly. Do you not think the wind is freshening, Delacroix?"

The privateer raised his head, eyes narrowed into the

wind, which ruffled the nut-brown hair. Genevieve felt that now familiar thrill as she watched him covertly. She loved the way he stood when he was concentrating on the elements with which he was so at home, head thrown back, the bronzed skin of his face drawn taught across the firm jawline, the relaxed contours of his mouth, the planes of his face highlighted by a finger-ray of sun.

"I would expect no more than a gentle breeze from the south, sir," he replied after due consideration. "A clear night with a good moon, though."

"Was a bright night to their advantage?" Genevieve wondered. Bonaparte seemed quite unaffected by Dominic's statement and, indeed, the two of them were chatting quite inconsequentially as they returned to the palace as if they had not a trouble in the world. But surely a moonless night would be better for slipping through the blockade? It did seem ridiculous that she should be so ignorant after all the time she had spent aboard *Danseuse*. She was constantly asking questions, which both Dominic and Silas always found time to answer, but there seemed so much to learn about this sailing business.

Coming up beside Dominic where he walked with the emperor, she surreptitiously slipped her hand into his. He looked down at her and smiled, his fingers closing over hers, and she felt a little tingle of warmth enliven her skin. Since that last night in Vienna, Dominic seemed to have changed toward her. He had exacted from her the promise that she would never again act unilaterally in a business that concerned him, that she would never again doubt him when her comfort and safety were in question. He had made no promises in return, but she felt an almost indefinable aura of protection emanating in her direction, a gentleness that she had not previously associated with the privateer except when it was a part of lovemaking. She did not know quite what it meant, but she did know that it seemed to increase her happiness a hundredfold. Once or twice, thoughts of the future intruded on this dreamy warmth, but they were easily postponed. The present contained too much of activity, too many promises of excitement, and there had been no suggestion that she should be left out of either.

Dominic, throughout the innumerable courses of an overly lavish lunch, found himself observing her every few minutes. It was as if he had to reassure himself that all was well with her, that she was entertained by her company, her plate filled and her glass rarely emptied. He smiled to himself at the latter thought. He did not really need to worry about that. Genevieve, like the majority of the intelligent, learned from her mistakes and showed no inclination to subject herself again to the torments of intoxication. She was obviously particularly susceptible, he reflected, but that was hardly surprising with such a tiny frame, and he had hammered the point home fairly forcibly once she had recovered sufficiently to hear it.

As usual, she was entertaining and being entertained by a group of zealously admiring gentlemen, but now that natural flirtatiousness no longer troubled him—now that he knew she had been incapable of pursuing flirtation to its ultimate conclusion. He still shuddered when he thought of the abominable strain she had endured on those evenings when he had been sitting drowning his thoughts in brandy, too unimaginative to reflect on the personality that he ought to have known could never have followed through with that ingenuously made, unthinking scheme. She had been trying so damnably hard to be what she thought he expected her to be in order not to fail him as partner-in-adventure. And that was still how she saw their relationship.

The turquoise eyes darkened on the thought. He knew she did not love him yet, but he did not know if she could be brought to do so. Not by an abrupt declaration on his part, that was for sure. She was too young, too inexperienced in the ways of the wider world to be able to absorb such a volte-face without panic and disbelief. So, he had chosen to play a slow courting game and, to his amazement, was finding it most pleasurable. There had been no courting with Rosemarie—love had hit them with the blunt force of an avalanche—and wooing was an irrelevancy with the Angeliques of the world for whom an open purse was the only incentive. But in the gentling, the pampering, the loving indulgence of that tiger-eyed sprite, Dominic Delacroix had discovered a new realm of pleasure. Of course, she had behaved impeccably since they had left Vienna, and his good resolutions had not been strained in the least.

"We will adjourn to my office, Monsieur Delacroix." Napoleon Bonaparte spoke with the soft decisive voice that still commanded instant respect, and Dominic shook himself free of his reverie, returning to the important matters at hand. He was about to undertake the riskiest mission of his career, one where the greatest stakes were hazarded for its participants, and he could not afford to blunt the tiniest edge of clarity and expertise. No matter that he had already been paid; that once Napoleon was free of the blockade the privateer would have succeeded in his appointed task regardless of what destiny lay in store for Bonaparte; Dominic Delacroix found himself drawn to that destiny, his pride somehow inextricably at stake. And the privateer's pride was worth more to him than any purse. The Emperor Napoleon was returning to France, to a people clamoring for him to unseat the Bourbon and restore the glory of an empire headed by France, and Dominic Delacroix, in the short days of his acquaintance with Napoleon Bonaparte, had been touched by the grandeur of the man and his destiny. The essential pragmatist had been won to a cause.

He rose from the table. "I wish to send Genevieve back to my ship, sir. I will join you directly." Receiving a nod of permission, he strolled across the room, catching up with Genevieve as she was about to walk into the garden on the arm of Lord John Russell. "*Ma chère,* may I borrow you for a minute?" He smiled amiably at Lord John, who hastened to return Madame Delacroix to her husband.

"What is it?" Genevieve looked up at him curiously as he drew her back into the dining room inhabited only by servants clearing away the debris.

"You must return to *Danseuse,* sprite." He spoke in low-voiced, rapid English, which would not be understood by the Italian and French servants. "I will remain here with the emperor and will accompany him to the harbor when he embarks this evening."

"Why may I not do so, also?"

"If there is to be any awkwardness, I do not wish you to be part of it. Silas will take you down to the port now, and he will leave you on *Danseuse* since he is going to take command of the *Saint-Esprit* tonight."

"It is really to happen tonight?" The tawny eyes shone. "Even with a bright moon?"

"A dark night would be preferable, I grant you," Dominic said. "But the wind is fair, Campbell is absent, the ships are ready." He shrugged. "Tomorrow, there may be no moon, and no breeze, either. So we take what chance we have."

"Are the troops embarked?"

"I hope that is happening discreetly at the moment. The guests here are about to be taken on an expedition to Capo di Stella to view Bonaparte's sporting estate. It will keep them well out of the way of Port-Ferrajo for this afternoon and evening. None of the emperor's subjects on the island will raise a murmur if they see anything untoward."

"Then there should be no awkwardness," Genevieve pointed out with customary logic. "I would much prefer to remain here with you and take part in all the excitement."

The privateer's eyes narrowed. "You have not forgotten, I trust, that when you sail with me, Mademoiselle Latour, you are under authority."

Genevieve flushed at this soft-spoken reminder, all too reminiscent of the old days. She *had* forgotten that the master of *Danseuse* was master of all who sailed in her.

Nothing had occurred in recent days to remind her of that fact. "Please?" she implored, changing her tactic to one that might work with the new, frequently persuadable Dominic.

However, the new Dominic appeared not to be a permanent visitor. "No," he replied in flat denial. "I want you out of the way."

"So that you won't have to worry about me?"

"Exactly so."

"But I will—"

"Genevieve!"

Defeated, she shrugged in resignation. She was not going to win, so there was little point in marring their accord with pointless argument. "I will go and pack up our things, then."

"Silas has already done so. He is waiting for you in the bedchamber. As soon as the expedition to Capo di Stella has departed, you will leave for the harbor." Suddenly, he smiled and pinched her cheek. "Do not look so disconsolate, sprite. There will be plenty for you to see."

"But I do not like to be put out of the way like some troublesome responsibility," she grumbled. "I am not your responsibility."

It was a measure of the strength in his new resolutions that Dominic merely said patiently, "While you sail with me, you are. On land, I accept that we are equal partners, but on my ship no one is my equal. Now, Bonaparte is waiting for me, and I do not relish having to blame my delay on an argumentative miss who does not know when to take no for an answer."

"No, I can quite see that that would not add to your consequence in the least," said Genevieve with a sweetly mischievous smile. "Are you sure you do not care to come with me? I can think of many more exciting ways of spending the afternoon than closeted with Napoleon or watching the covert embarkation of his army."

"You are a minx," Dominic stated with a degree of satisfaction. "As it happens, so can I. But thinking of such things will ruin my powers of concentration. Now, be off with you. You may spend the remainder of the afternoon planning my entertainment when I do join you." He touched the tip of her nose in brief farewell and strode to the door. There, he stopped and turned thoughtfully. "Oh, and sprite, use your imagination to do your planning." Then he was gone, leaving Genevieve chuckling, unmistakable prickles of desirous anticipation lifting her skin.

An hour later, Silas handed her into a barouche at the front steps of the palace and swung up to take the reins of the eagerly pawing mare. The palace was protected from prying eyes on the landward side by a high wall, but once beyond this they found themselves on the broad, well-paved roads of Napoleon's kingdom, roads that he had spent the last nine months bringing up to his high specifications. Down in the town, the barracks of the Imperial Guard seemed quieter than usual, but it was the only indication that matters were not all that they seemed on the island.

*Danseuse* swung at anchor in the harbor, just one of the flotilla of five large vessels positioned in the port roads for sailing. Genevieve sprang nimbly into a waiting dinghy at the quayside, much experience of this exercise overcoming the disadvantages of her cambric gown and petticoats, and they were rowed to the dainty white frigate. There Silas left her and went on to the *Saint-Esprit,* a merchantman purchased by Dominic in Leghorn and manned by a skeleton crew of his own sailors. Genevieve went below to change the elegant gown suited to an imperial palace for a dimity print of simple cut. Plain sandals replaced the kid slippers; silk stockings were abandoned in favor of bare legs. The silver-gold hair was tied back with one of Dominic's kerchiefs. Thus dressed for action, she went up to the quarterdeck, taking up her accustomed position against the taffrail from where she could watch the activity in the harbor as well as what went on in the waist of *Danseuse.*

Her presence on board the frigate was now so accepted

that even the bosun treated her with a casual deference indicative of his recognition of her place—a place that the frigate's master had made clear was in no way to interfere with the smooth running of the vessel and the work of its crew. If Genevieve needed anything, be it food, coffee, or hot water, and Silas was not available or was too busy being a sailor to assume his other role as valet, it would not occur to her to ask someone to fetch it for her. She saw to her own needs and crept around the galley doing her best to appear invisible. This consideration had not gone unnoticed or unappreciated.

As she leaned over the rail examining the vessels in the harbor, it gradually became apparent that an unusual amount of activity was taking place. Napoleon's own brig, the *Inconstant,* had been painted with black port lids to resemble an English brig, and small craft plied the harbor bearing final supplies of biscuit, rice, vegetables, cheese, salt beef, drink rations, and fresh water. With Neil Campbell off the island, there was no one to question what the island's sovereign chose to do. He was no prisoner, had given no parole, had his own army and navy to do with as he wished. Only if he left Elba could the patrolling French and British ships prevent his escape. But they would have to catch him first. Genevieve shook her head in wonder. Dominic seemed perfectly confident that they would be able to evade the blockade. Napoleon, himself, was supremely confident of success—a confidence based on his absolute conviction that his destiny was to free France once again from Bourbon repression, to reestablish his empire. But it seemed to the watcher on *Danseuse*'s quarterdeck that the chances of evasion were slim. The only thing in their favor was that the planned escape had been surrounded by such impenetrable secrecy that no alert had gone out. Napoleon had prepared his fleet for escape while blandly discussing road-building, hospital arrangements, and a new form of budget for Elba for 1815.

He was as wily, as brilliantly devious as that old fox Fouché, Genevieve thought with a tiny smile of admiration. She knew that Dominic had fallen under the Napoleonic spell, and she understood why, even thought that if she had been permitted to sit in on the planning discussions she, too, would have been in thrall. As it was, she saw only the continuation of the adventure that had begun on the night of her aborted betrothal—the shared adventure that brought her closer to the man who was both the circumference of her life and its center. Without whom— But that was an impermissible thought, one that had no place in present reality. Her only hope was that she would somehow slip into the fabric of his life, and discussions of the future would not arise—it would simply happen.

A loud hail off *Danseuse*'s port bow took her to the landside of the frigate. A cutter, loaded to the gunwales with men in the uniform of gendarmes, rocked on the harbor swell below the stern ladder. The bosun bellowed orders and the cutter threw up a rope to be held by a grinning sailor, drawing the smaller vessel snug against the frigate's stern. Clumsily, the gendarmes swarmed up the precarious rope ladder, hampered by their dress swords. The sun glinted off the shining silver buttons, the gold braid of epaulettes, and the bright belt buckles.

"Two hours at sea and they'll be throwing up their guts," the helmsman said at Genevieve's shoulder. He was grinning broadly in wicked anticipation of the new arrivals' discomfiture. "Much good those smart uniforms 'll be to them, then."

Genevieve, who had only once experienced the hellish misery of seasickness during a violent storm in the Bay of Biscay, shot her companion a reproachful look, but he simply chuckled, quite unrepentant, and she couldn't prevent a responding grin. Watching the general ineptitude of the new arrivals as they tried to adjust to the moving decks, cramped quarters, and the general absence of creature comforts, she sympathized with the bosun who had been charged with seeing to their disposal and comfort. Dominic, once he came aboard, would have no wish to be bothered with complaints from either side, and any sufficiently hardy prospective objecter would receive short shrift. And the bosun, in such an event, would receive the sharp edge of the master's unpolished tongue.

One or two curious glances came her way as she stood watching the proceedings, but she kept herself apart on the quarterdeck until sunset brought a bevy of cutters dancing across the harbor from the quay. The leading cutter went to *Inconstant,* and the emperor embarked amid twittering pipes; the second came to *Danseuse.* Dominic, with no ceremony whatsoever, swung himself up the ladder and onto the deck. He was accompanied by two civilians who looked as unsure of their footing as had the gendarmes and somewhat put out at the lack of ceremony that had greeted their arrival.

The three of them arrived on the quarterdeck, and Genevieve felt laughter well deep in her bosom at the passengers' startled expressions as they were introduced to the bare-legged, windswept, so-called Madame Delacroix. They were the mayor of Porto-Ferrajo and his deputy, men clearly accustomed to ritual and reverence and the place of women in the scheme of things—that place was not on the quarterdeck of a frigate about to embark on a glorious enterprise.

"Where are they to sleep?" Genevieve whispered when the mayor and his deputy moved to the rail to look at the rest of the flotilla.

"In Silas's cabin," Dominic said. "There are two bunks in there. We sail within the hour so there is no time to cook dinner. See what you can find in the stores that might not offend their palates, will you?"

"Yes, monsieur," Genevieve responded in fair imitation of Silas, knuckling her forehead.

"You are asking for trouble," Dominic observed conversationally.

Genevieve shook her head. "Not trouble . . . but something else, certainly. You did promise, after all." Her eyes narrowed suggestively and the privateer chuckled.

"You're a shameless wanton, Genevieve Latour. Somehow or other within the next few hours, I have to negotiate an escape for the most carefully watched man in Europe, and all you can think of is seduction."

"It might clear your mind," she murmured, moving wickedly against him, blithely ignoring the presence of the others on the quarterdeck.

"Get below then." Dominic brought her mischievous teasing to an abrupt halt as he cupped her elbow and propelled her to the ladder descending to the maindeck. "We don't have much time."

"Be serious!" she choked, her feet skimming over the deck under the speed of her encouraged progress.

"Oh, but I am," he said with a bland smile. "Never more so. You began this, as I recall."

"But you have to sail the ship!" Laughter mingled with undeniable excitement at this outrageous proposal as she was hustled down the companionway and into the master cabin.

"So hurry up then." Dominic sat on the bed and pulled off his boots and stockings, stood to remove his britches, tossed coat and shirt over a chair, and flung himself on the bed, regarding Genevieve with frank speculation. This surprising turn of events had thrown her so off balance that her fingers fumbled clumsily with the buttons and hooks of her gown, and her eyes kept sliding to the naked figure on the bed—naked and mightily aroused.

"You are quite mad," she breathed, shaking her head free of the folds of her gown. "Supposing someone wants you?"

"I thought someone did," he returned with a lazy smile. "Isn't that why we're here? I'm always willing to oblige, as you should know."

Genevieve giggled in soft excitement. He was lying on the bed offering himself to her as if she were some female pasha with a male harem. Naked, she stepped over to the bed and stood looking down at him, her eyes drinking in the lean, bronzed, virile length of him.

"It is all yours, madame," he said with a wicked grin, linking his hands behind his head. "Help yourself."

Genevieve nodded, her tongue running slowly over her lips. Kneeling on the bed beside him, she began to touch him, exploring his body as if it were virgin territory. He lay absolutely still as her hands flattened over the ridged muscles of his belly, pressed hard along the sinewy thighs, absolutely still until she took the hard root of his manhood between her palms and began to create a gentle friction that increased in power, finally breaching the barriers of his control. Dominic moaned on a soft exhalation, and Genevieve smiled with satisfaction as she swung herself over his supine frame, guiding herself onto the impaling shaft.

The azure eyes glowed up at her, but he kept his hands behind his head and left it to Genevieve to call her own tune. She was clearly finding his total passivity as pleasurable as he did himself. Then the charmed circle was abruptly shattered by a loud knock at the door. "Monsieur?" came the bosun's voice. Genevieve stilled, her eyes widened in alarm. But Dominic merely smiled reassuringly. "Ten minutes," he called in the voice that none of his sailors would question even if the ship were going down.

"Don't stop," he said coolly. "You only have ten minutes of my time. I am much in demand it would seem."

That made her laugh and she bent her head to kiss him, plundering his mouth as he had so often done hers while her lower body moved with increasing speed to bring them both to a laughing, loving, shared finale.

Dominic gave her bottom a brisk little pat and put her from him. "I hope that will satisfy your near insatiable appetite for a few more hours because now I really do have a ship to sail." Swinging off the bed with undiminished energy, he dressed rapidly while Genevieve, as languid as she always was after lovemaking, lay and watched him. "Come along now, sprite, you have some guests to feed, remember."

"In here or on deck?" She sat up with a sigh and a leisurely stretch.

"In here, I do not wish them underfoot. You can play hostess, can you not? I will have to eat on deck."

"Oh, Dominic, no," wailed Genevieve, horrified at the prospect. "Can they not sup alone? It is pure chance that I am here, after all. On any other ship, they would not expect to be entertained."

"But you are here," he pointed out. "And you will pull your weight just like any other member of my crew, won't you, my Genevieve?"

The straight nose wrinkled in distaste. "I suppose so. You want me to keep them out of the way so that you don't have to be bothered with them, isn't that it?"

He smiled an affirmative. "Clever girl. Just turn on that devastating charm and with any luck we'll be in the open sea before they decide to come up and see what's happening." A short, hard kiss and he had gone, leaving her to dress and tidy the cabin, before examining the cabin stores and concocting a relatively appetizing supper.

She went on deck when they weighed anchor, keeping her usual discreet distance from Dominic and the helmsman. The two civilians, however, crowded around the wheel gesticulating excitedly as the other vessels got under way, and the *Inconstant,* with its imperial passenger, set a course alongside *Danseuse.* Genevieve could feel Dominic's irritation surging in waves across the deck as his passengers bobbed in front of him, obscuring his view and questioning incessantly.

"Messieurs, I must ask you to go below," he said at last with careful control. "I am trying to set a course that the entire flotilla may follow, and I cannot do it when you are babbling in my ear."

The mayor snorted and demanded an apology for this offensive statement. He received instead a brisk order to remove himself from the quarterdeck forthwith and to reappear only on invitation. Recognizing, albeit reluctantly, that it was time to play her part, Genevieve stepped forward with soothing smile and offers of wine and supper. The two, face saved by this invitation, allowed themselves to be escorted from the deck, and Dominic and the helmsman heaved sighs of relief.

Genevieve endured two hours of inexpressible tedium listening to the pompous pontifications of her guests. She longed to go up on deck, but was fairly certain that if she appeared prematurely, *Danseuse*'s master would simply send her back to her caretaking duties. After a rubber of three-handed whist, the mayor and his deputy began to show distinct signs of cabin fever, and Genevieve suggested that they might all go on deck, but that they should station themselves in the stern where they would not be in the way. Her companions bristled at such a suggestion, but the memory of the privateer's voice and eyes as he had banished them earlier sufficed to bring grudging agreement.

It was full night, but, as Dominic had predicted, the bright moon hung heavy in the jeweled sky. The sails stretched taut under the southerly breeze, and *Danseuse*'s hull skipped across the gentle swell. Her seven companions at sea were all making good headway although none were as fast or as elegant as Dominic's frigate. Genevieve looked up into the masthead, manned, as she had expected, by a sailor with glass. They knew that these waters were patrolled at the moment by one British ship and three French, and when the lookout called softly, "Sail to the north," Genevieve abandoned her companions and ran to the quarterdeck.

Dominic was sweeping the horizon with his telescope as she came to stand silently beside him. "Looks like the

*Partridge,"* he said. "With luck, she'll not recognize the *Inconstant* at this distance." A tense silence held the ship as they waited for some reaction from the British vessel, but nothing happened, and after five minutes Dominic lowered his glass. "What have you done with your charges?"

"Left them in the stern," she answered. "I could not keep them below any longer."

"Well, just as long as they do not come up here again." He raised his glass as another shout came from above.

"Sail to the northwest."

"What ship is it?" Genevieve stood on tiptoe, peering into the darkness as if she would thus be able to see with the naked eye.

*"Fleur-de-lys,"* Dominic said shortly. "Too far away, also, I trust. They're right where I expected them to be, so that's one satisfaction."

Genevieve looked at him with respect. She would like to have asked how he had known the positions of the French and British vessels, but now was not an opportune moment. "Will we avoid the others?" she asked instead.

Dominic stroked his chin. "Doubtful. See that island over there." He pointed to the northwest, and Genevieve strained to make out the dark hump of land. "That's Capraia, right in the middle of our course to France. I suspect that we shall run up against one of the other French ships somewhere in the vicinity."

"Will you fight?"

"Not if I can help it. If they recognize *Inconstant,* it is to be hoped Captain Taillade can bluff his way through."

"And if not?" Genevieve knew she was pushing a fine line with her questions, but Dominic seemed very relaxed, as he always did when facing danger. The higher the tension mounted, the more relaxed he became.

"If not, *Danseuse* and *Saint-Esprit* will engage battle, hopefully drawing off the enemy so that the rest can get through."

The island of Capraia drew ever closer, and Dominic raised his telescope again, his preoccupied stance signaling to Genevieve that she should attempt no further intrusion. She felt the sudden-alert ripple run through his body a few minutes before she could herself make out the sail approaching from the west. *"Zephyr,"* Dominic said quietly. "As I expected. Send the men to quarters, bosun, to stand by."

"Yes, monsieur." The bosun vanished on silent feet, the order given by whispered word of mouth so that the crew took up action stations and remained in silent watchfulness, ready to run out the guns or to stand down, whichever became appropriate. Genevieve knew that Silas would have given the same order on *Saint-Esprit*. She retreated into the shadows in case Dominic noticed her and decided to be tiresome about her presence on deck at a risky time.

A loud hail came across the moon-tipped water as *Zephyr* intercepted the *Inconstant*. Genevieve listened to the exchange, the voices through the megaphones carrying over the water on the breeze. A rustling and snuffling announced the arrival on the quarterdeck of the mayor and his deputy. Dominic silenced them with a sharply impatient gesture. The captain of the *Zephyr* was asking *Inconstant*'s business in these waters. But the request was friendly, seemingly a matter of form, and it became clear from the tone of the exchange that the two captains were old acquaintances. Captain Taillade assured the other that he was on a routine trip to Genoa, that Napoleon remained safe on Elba, and the assurances were accepted cheerfully by one who had no reason to doubt them.

Comradely farewells were exchanged and *Zephyr* changed tack, beating back into the lee of Capraia. The crew were told to stand down, but it was another two hours before Dominic, with a deep sigh of contentment, lit one of his little cigars. He had completed the task he had undertaken all those weeks ago at the behest of the burghers of

New Orleans.

"We are through?" whispered Genevieve, recognizing the signs and speaking for the first time since *Zephyr* had been sighted.

"You should be in bed," Dominic reproved, inhaling so that the tip of the cigar glowed in the gloom. "Yes, we are through by the usual combination of extraordinary luck and a modicum of good judgment. We should reach Juan Bay in three days."

"And then?" She came into the circle of his arm as he leaned against the taffrail.

"And then we shall see." He stroked her hair in that absently caressing manner that she found peculiarly comforting. It was as if she was simply a part of him, an accepted and inseparable presence. "It's a crazy adventure, sprite, and I've a mind to see it through."

"I also."

"But of course," he said quietly. And her heart lifted as she stood beside him, sharing the night, the moment of achievement, and the promise of the future.

## Chapter 24

"Mariotti says they were here last week." Grand Duke Sergei tossed his high-crowned beaver hat onto the settle in the parlor of Leghorn's most salubrious inn as he offered this piece of information to his three companions.

"But does he know where they are now, dear fellow?" inquired Cholmondeley, cracking and consuming a walnut with some concentration. He washed the sweet meat down with a generous gulp of madeira.

"Apparently, they went to Elba—joining the pilgrims." Sergei gave a short, bitter laugh. "Mariotti says that they infiltrated the networks like professionals. Bartolucci could not do enough for them."

"Madame Delacroix is presumably using the tidbits of information she somehow picked up at piquet," Sebastiani said with a snarl. "It seems to me, gentlemen, that we have a duty to apprehend such an experienced spy and ensure that she is brought to justice."

"But if Napoleon succeeds in his bid for France, my friend, Madame Delacroix will have been spying on the side of the victor," Legrand pointed out. "She will be considered a loyal follower deserving of reward rather than the spy's noose."

"Bonaparte has yet to succeed," said Cholmondeley. "He may have assumed the title of emperor again, but the

401

Bourbon still holds Paris."

"Mariotti believes that the Delacroix were instrumental in achieving Bonaparte's escape from Elba," Sergei went on, taking a seat at the table and reaching for the decanter of madeira. "Monsieur Delacroix apparently owns a frigate and, in addition, purchased a merchantman, which also sailed into Porto-Ferrajo. They are not there now, and *Zephyr*'s captain says that when he intercepted *Inconstant,* there was a fast frigate among the flotilla."

"Then they landed at Juan Bay with Bonaparte three days ago." Legrand walked to the window that looked out over the circular bay. "The question is: Do they remain with him, or do they consider their task completed and go on to fresh pastures?"

"That should not be difficult to discover. The governor of Antibes witnessed the landing at Juan Bay. He presumably made note of Bonaparte's companions. Such a distinctive figure as Madame Delacroix would be hard to miss."

"Then I suggest we proceed to Antibes." Sebastiani smiled his meagre smile. "If they are marching with Bonaparte, we should be able to come up with them without difficulty. Four men can travel a great deal faster than an emperor's glorious, conquering progress." A sardonic note informed these words. "I have little interest in the husband, myself, but am most anxious to play a little more piquet with madame."

"I, also," Legrand chimed in. "And if the law will not punish a spy, then we must do it ourselves."

The grand duke chuckled richly and rubbed his soft white hands together, the skin making a little rasping sound. It was a habit he had when contemplating something pleasurable. "Assuredly, Legrand. Spying is a heinous activity, and it matters not that the fortunes of war should have made right wrong and vice versa. Madame Delacroix must pay for her deceptions."

"I imagine that amongst us, we can contrive a suitably appropriate vengeance," Sebastiani murmured. "But let us be honest, gentlemen, and admit that our motives are largely personal." He shrugged. "Madame's spying does not concern me unduly. Her methods do." His pale eyes darted from face to face. "To be deceived in that way is more than a little mortifying. The lady had no intention of fulfilling her promises."

"Then she should perhaps be encouraged to do so," the Frenchman said softly. "It is never too late to right a wrong."

"Quite so." Cholmondeley rose to his feet, a gleam of excitement in his eyes. "To Antibes."


"He is magnificent," Genevieve breathed, stilling her mount rendered anxious by the tense expectant hush outside the town of Grenoble. Napoleon and his now rapidly grown following faced their first overtly hostile garrison since leaving Cannes.

The little round figure in his impressive uniform was sublimely unperturbed by the ranks of soldiers ranged beneath the Bourbon standard. With a superb flourish, he threw open his greatcoat, baring his breast to the enemy garrison as his voice rang grandiloquently. "Soldiers, if there is one among you who wishes to kill his emperor, he can do so: Here I am."

Dominic whistled softly, shaking his head in amazement. "They'll be eating out of his hand in two minutes."

"And can you blame them?" Genevieve whispered, watching, fascinated, as one by one the Grenoble soldiers laid down their arms. It was impossible to describe the magnetism of that sleek fat man, who looked more like a well-fed priest than a battle-hardened soldier, and who had pronounced himself emperor by the will of the people before he had even tested that will.

A great roar went up from the crowd as the emperor rode into Grenoble, the once hostile soldiers falling in behind him, cheering. Genevieve urged her horse forward and glanced up at Dominic as he rode beside her. He was habitually pensive these days, although, if she called him on it, he tended to laugh and change the subject. But being basically a stubborn soul, she persevered. "What are you thinking?" she asked now, as directly as usual.

"That this is madness," he answered her, this time frankly. "Ever since the Grand Alliance declared war on Napoleon again, his defeat has been inevitable."

Genevieve's jaw dropped. "It is heresy to say such a thing. You are doubting the outcome of this grand and glorious adventure!"

"That is all it is, sprite. A grand and glorious adventure. Napoleon has lost two great armies in two years. Where is he to find another large enough and experienced enough to meet the Allies whose armies have won the last two campaigns? He knows it, too."

"But the royal army at Lyons has defected," she pointed out. "And Marshal Ney has turned coat again and rejoined the emperor. The people of France are anxious to be rid of the Bourbon; they will stand behind Napoleon."

"Maybe so." Dominic did not, however, sound convinced. "For all his magnetism, Genevieve, Napoleon is a man scarred by resounding defeat. He has been defeated and dethroned once, and I fear that he will not be able to bounce back again."

Genevieve rode in silence for a few minutes before asking, "Why, then, do you continue to ride with him? Your task is completed and there can be no gain for you in this. Piracy awaits on the high seas, does it not?" She asked the question with a laugh in her voice, hoping the laugh would hide the desperate anxiety lurking beneath. When this escapade was over, what would happen to her? When the privateer took to the seas again, where would she go? The future beyond this adventure had not been mentioned between them since the night of her abduction, when he had offered her the opportunity to seek her own destiny.

Dominic smiled. "Perhaps it does, but I may still be of service to Bonaparte. In the event of his defeat, he will need a refuge, and America is more than willing. *Danseuse* is at Rochefort at Fouché's suggestion. Should the emperor find himself in need of swift transport . . ." He shrugged and wondered if this might be an opportune moment to broach the subject of Genevieve's own plans. It would certainly help in the formulation of his, if he could glean some idea of whether his courting tactics had at least given her something to think about beyond setting herself up as a courtesan in some European capital—a plan he had no intention of countenancing whether he could win her to his own point of view or not.

"Monsieur?" Silas, his generally impassive features carrying an anxious twist, rode up on a stout cob, ending Dominic's reflections. "A word, monsieur." He spoke softly with a meaningful glance at Genevieve.

Dominic frowned and pulled a little ahead. "Why the secrecy, Silas?"

"Maybe nothing," the old sailor said, "but I didn't want to alarm mademoiselle for no reason. I swear I saw that Italian from Vienna."

"Italian?" Dominic looked nonplussed. "Oh, you mean Sebastiani?"

"Some such," Silas agreed. "Mademoiselle spent one of her evenings in his house, and now he's hanging around in the square."

"I fail to see why he should not, Silas." Dominic shrugged. "Or why you think Genevieve might be alarmed by the news. He's probably observing Napoleon's progress for the Allies. He's not the only one along the route, you can be sure of that."

"I don't like it," Silas said with a stubborn nod. "Just a feeling."

Dominic, over the years, had developed a certain respect for Silas's feelings. He was fairly certain that by now

Genevieve's duped informants would know that they had been bled for information and why, but to pursue their deceiver across France, particularly in this time of upheaval, seemed a little extreme. He could not imagine what they could hope to achieve by it. "Well, let us find lodgings," he said to Silas, "and then you can scout around a little, see what you can dig up. I'll keep Genevieve under my eye."

"It would be best," Silas agreed. "No knowing what she'll get up to if she gets an idea in her head."

"What are you whispering about?" the subject of this comment demanded, drawing up alongside. "I don't like secrets. At least," she added, "not ones that aren't mine."

Dominic chuckled. "We were discussing lodgings, as it happens. Do you care to accept the emperor's hospitality as usual? All we need do is ride up with him."

"No," Genevieve said definitely. "There will be nothing but speeches and formality, and I am sore from riding, and my ears ache from speeches, and I am hungry, and if we dine with the imperial party there will be so much talking there will be no time for eating and—"

"Enough!" Dominic held up a protesting hand to stop the breathless torrent. "I am overwhelmed with your eloquence, madame, and take your point. We shall find a quiet inn and indulge ourselves in a little privacy."

"Now that," Genevieve stated, "sounds like the best idea anyone has had since we left Antibes."

"I might have some more if you play your cards correctly," he said, and was rewarded with that mischievous little giggle and the sensuous crinkling of those tiger's eyes.

"I'll see what the inns have to offer, then," Silas said in a dignified monotone, and turned off down a side street.

Grenoble had difficulty accommodating this triumphant and trumpeting invasion. The emperor was received in the governor's mansion, his entourage billeted in the town's best hostelries. For those seeking lodging as private citizens, little was to be found. However, Silas was a resourceful man and by dint of venturing beyond the city walls, found an agreeable landlady in the shape of a farmer's wife who offered a pretty bedchamber under the eaves. Silas was provided with a palliasse in the barn, but before he took his rest, he returned to Grenoble, eyes skinned for a sight of Signor Sebastiani.

Dominic was sitting by the open window of their chamber, breathing in the soft night air of late spring and the remembered fragrances of the now sleeping Genevieve when Silas returned, the cob's hooves clattering in the stable yard below. Dominic let himself out of the room, quietly latching the door and treading softly down the stairs, through the kitchen and out into the yard where Silas was waiting for him.

"Well?" The privateer lit a cigar and sat on an upturned rainwater butt.

"They're all here, monsieur. All of mademoiselle's gentlemen."

"I don't think you need call them that," Dominic said drily. "As far as I know, she lays no claim to any of the four."

"None of my business, monsieur," replied the sailor stolidly.

Dominic gave a short laugh. "You do surprise me, Silas. Are they together?"

"Seemingly. I ran them to earth in a tavern near the market square. Very close, they were."

"They are in the same business, on the same side," Dominic mused. "Although which side that is now, is probably a matter for debate. There have been so many turncoats in the last twelve months, there's no way of telling."

"They have the same interests," Silas declared. "Or interest." He scratched his nose and stared up at the stars. "If it's mademoiselle they're after . . ."

"Why would they be?" Dominic had no idea what Silas knew of the situation in Vienna, but the old sailor was as canny as they came, and as shrewd as he was intuitive.

Silas shrugged and continued to examine the sky. "Seems to me that if they were promised something that was not made good . . ."

"Damnation!" Dominic dropped his cigar to the cobbles and ground it out viciously beneath his boot. He had thought only in terms of the four men realizing that Genevieve had been spying and had succeeded in her object. It would annoy them, but it was a game they all played so they would surely shrug it off to experience. One won as many as one lost, after all. But Genevieve had been playing ducks and drakes in an area of intense personal pride with men who set great store by their pride. He tried to imagine how he would feel in their situation. It did not require much imagination. To have that entrancing, diminutive body promised, to have swallowed the bait offered by those wickedly sensuous eyes, that inviting little laugh, the deliciously intimate little touches, then to be deprived at the last moment because one's luck or skill at the cards ran out. And then to realize that she had never had the least intention of making good the promise. They had been played for fools in the one area where a man could not tolerate a sense of foolishness. And there were four of them to share and feed the outrage of the lover scorned.

"I won't ask you how you knew," he said to Silas.

The old sailor grunted scornfully. "Plain as a pikestaff, it was, if you were prepared to see it."

Dominic winced. *He* had not seen it. "I'll put Genevieve on her guard in the morning. Do keep close watch on our friends. I see no reason to take action at this point or to let them know that we're aware of them. Forewarned, we can forestall them if they show signs of making a move."

"Right." Silas pressed his hands into the small of his back, arching against them as if to ease cramped muscles. "I'm off to my bed, then. If you've no further need of me tonight."

Genevieve stirred and woke as Dominic climbed into bed

beside her. "Where've you been?" she muttered drowsily, curling into his arms.

"Talking to Silas," he replied. "Go back to sleep now, *mon coeur*. I will tell you about it in the morning."

*Mon coeur,* she thought with a ripple of warmth. Perhaps it was more than just *une façon de parler,* just a little bit more.

The next morning, over breakfast, Dominic told her of the presence in Grenoble of her four ex-informants.

"But why?" She frowned at him as she broke into the fragrantly steaming interior of a brioche. "Are they spying on the emperor for the Allies, do you think?"

"It's possible." Dominic shrugged. "But there may be more to it than that." He took a sip of coffee and picked his words carefully. "So, I would like you to stay within my sight at all times for as long as they remain with us."

"But why?" she asked again, her eyes widening. "What have they to do with me? Our dealings, such as they were, are long past." Spooning apricot preserve on her brioche, she popped a piece in her mouth and regarded him with genuine innocence.

Dominic sighed. Her sophistication in certain areas and the fearless bravado with which she faced all situations occasionally caused him to forget her youth, her strict Creole upbringing, and the fact that she had but newly emerged from the shelter of Victor Latour's capacious umbrella, all of which inevitably produced a degree of naive ingenuousness which, in this instance, could be dangerous. "You may think they are long past, *ma chère,* but ten to one the gentlemen in question do not. Men, in general, do not take kindly to being made fools of when their manhood is at issue, and particularly not to being made fools of by a slip of a girl with an unexpected talent for cards." He watched the light of comprehension dawn in her eyes. Ingenuous she may be, but she was never slow to grasp a point.

"You think they may wish to revenge themselves?" Her

409

voice was thoughtful as she remembered with sudden clarity the morning of Polanski's ball when they had appeared in force in her drawing room and she had been so conscious of a sense of unease. She had thought then that, gaining encouragement from each other, they might want to even the score, and that night, after the dreadful debacle on the ballroom floor, they had made it very clear that they wished for a confrontation. But she had assumed that by leaving Vienna, she had left the whole sordid episode behind her.

"It's hard to be certain. Their presence here may have nothing whatsoever to do with you. But until I am convinced of that, you will be a little more circumspect than is your wont, will you not?" His lips quirked but the azure gaze was steady and serious.

"I cannot imagine what they can possibly do to me in these circumstances," said Genevieve. "We are in the middle of an army, virtually."

"Nevertheless?" The fly-away eyebrows lifted.

"Nevertheless, I shall stick closer than your shadow," she laughed. "All the way to Paris."

She was as good as her word for the remainder of that triumphal march when at every stage the Bourbon defense collapsed. When Napoleon reached Fontainebleau on the outskirts of Paris, it was to hear that Louis had already left the capital which lay open, undefended, to welcome the returning emperor.

At Fontainebleau disappeared also the four followers of the Delacroix. Silas, far from being relieved at their sudden absence, was rendered greatly uneasy. "When I can see them, monsieur, I don't need to fret," he said worriedly, as they entered Paris by the south gate.

"Maybe we were worrying unnecessarily." Dominic glanced at Genevieve whose face wore a look of wondering exictement at the prospect of visiting this city that so many Creoles considered their spiritual home. "If their task was to report on Napoleon's progress and reception, the job would

410

be completed here. The Allies do not need observers for the grand entrance; it is quite public enough."

"They may have decided to wait until Paris," Silas muttered. "Much easier in a big city, when everyone's dispersed."

"What is much easier?" Genevieve demanded impatiently. "I think you are making mountains out of molehills, Silas. I have not even seen them, not once on this journey. Have you, Dominic?"

"I don't need to," Dominic said sharply. "Not if Silas says they are there."

Genevieve bit her lip and flashed a guiltily apologetic smile at the silent sailor. "I did not mean to doubt Silas's word. But don't you think we are making too much of this? What do you expect them to do?"

"If I knew that, mademoiselle, I would not be worried," Silas said with a distinct snap in his voice. "All I know is, there'll be many more opportunities in the city streets, and if you go gallivanting around in your usual careless fashion, there's no knowing what will happen."

"Well, I am not sitting in some inn twiddling my thumbs just because you have an overactive imagination," Genevieve retorted, nettled by a scolding criticism that she had not deserved for quite some time. Nudging her mount's flanks, she urged him into a trot, drawing ahead of her two companions.

Dominic's eyebrows lifted as he wondered which of them he should attempt to soothe first. But Silas spoke while he was still trying to make up his mind. "Best if I keep an eye out, monsieur," he said, his tone back to its usual stolid neutrality.

"Yes, we both shall," Dominic agreed in the same tone. "I've a mind to hire a house during our stay in Paris. We'll be less vulnerable."

Leaving the hopefully mollified Silas, he went ahead to catch up with Genevieve who offered no acknowledgement of his presence for quite a few minutes. Then she said, "I trust you are not going to expect me to beg his pardon. He was as rude as I was."

"He is concerned for you and has not had your advantages when it comes to learning how to express himself," Dominic informed her crisply. "It will cost you little to make peace."

There was another short silence, then Genevieve admitted, "I was going to, anyway. But I do think he is making a meal out a crumb, and I am not prepared to cower immured within doors to some stuffy inn—"

"You will not have to," Dominic interrupted. "I intend to hire a house, for a start. But you are not to go out unescorted. Is that too much to ask?"

"It might be," she said in all seriousness. "I cannot foresee every eventuality. Supposing I have to go out and you or Silas are not available?"

The privateer swallowed the sharp surge of irritation that would normally have found outlet in a harsh response. Genevieve was not being deliberately awkward, merely, as usual, stating a simple fact as simply as it struck her. "Let us hope that such an eventuality does not arise," he said mildly.

Genevieve gave a sudden, disconcerting chuckle. "Why are you being so genial, these days, Dominic? I expected you to go all quiet and cross when I said that."

"*Were* you trying to provoke me?" he demanded, half laughing because that chuckle was so infectious.

"No, not really. It's just that in the past, even if I didn't intend to provoke you, I did seem to, anyway, so I became accustomed to it. Now, I don't know where I stand most of the time."

"Would you prefer that I revert?" he asked, amused.

She shook her head. "No, most definitely not. It's just a little confusing when I don't get what I expect. But I daresay I shall become used to it. For as long as . . ." Her voice faded as she brought herself up short. For as long as we stay together, she had been about to say. But some deep-rooted fear of tempting providence kept her from mentioning the prospect of leaving. Perhaps if she never mentioned it, neither would Dominic, and it would just never happen. "Is that Notre Dame, do you think?" She pointed to the elegant, crenelated spire that pierced the skyline over the pitched, gray-slated rooftops.

Dominic wondered what she had been about to say—for as long as his new restraint lasted, probably. And then she had decided that that would be a little blunt if not downright rude. He turned his attention to satisfying her curiosity about the city as they rode down the wide boulevards that made Paris so essentially Napoleon's capital. Dominic had been here many times and had witnessed its transformation from a grubby sprawl of fetid faubourgs and narrow alleys into this wide open, beautifully designed show place of triumphal arches and magnificent monuments. In many ways, Paris could be considered one of Napoleon's greatest achievements. It would certainly be standing to his memory long after the battlefield exploits had become faded ink on the pages of history.

"An interesting, if somewhat fruitless, journey," Jean Luc Legrand observed, reposing his slim frame in an elegant Chippendale chair in the salon of his house on the rue de Rivoli.

"Aye, with Delacroix and that dour sailor keeping constant watch, she's as impossible to pry loose as a periwinkle on a rock," Cholmondeley agreed with a sour downturn of his mouth. "I'd thought, in all the mêlée of the march, that it would be easy enough to cut her out from the crowd."

"What a delightful residence, my dear Legrand," the grand duke said with punctilious observation of the courtesies before entering the discussion.

Legrand bowed in acknowledgement and pulled a tasseled

413

bellrope. "Allow me to offer you refreshment, gentlemen. And you will be my guests, I trust, until such time as we have succeeded in our little venture."

"With pleasure." Sebastiani was examining the furnishing of the salon with a knowing and appreciative eye. For all that it was a bachelor establishment, Legrand's house lacked nothing in the way of grace or amenity. He accepted a glass of burgundy offered by a liveried footman before observing, "I think a little patience might be in order. It should not be difficult to discover where they are staying in the city. The address will be known to any number of people at the court. If we were seen and recognized, although we were so careful to cover our tracks, it would explain the care they took to keep madame close. However . . ." He shrugged. "If we now drop out of sight, in a few days they will relax their guard. They have no certainty that we mean mischief, after all."

"And they will be obliged to participate in life at court, so closely involved as they have been with the emperor," Legrand said thoughtfully. "There would be no other reason for being in Paris at this time. Madame will be constantly in the open at balls, dinners, soirées. She will have to go to the dressmaker, the milliner . . ." He spread his hands in an expansive gesture to include all the myriad of mysterious activities essential to the correct appearance of a lady of the court. "No doubt, she will be accompanied by a maid, but that is easily disposed of."

"All very true, Legrand," Cholmondeley said. "But just how long is this socializing hiatus going to last? Bonaparte has to consolidate his position, and he's not going to do that by entertaining the polite world in Paris and issuing proclamations."

"No," agreed the grand duke, "he will attack the Allies before they attack him. He has never been one to wait to return an offensive. He will go to war soon enough."

"And the Delacroix will leave Paris," Sebastiani said with calm simplicity. "I do not wish to be balked of my due, gentlemen."

There was a murmur of agreement, and Sergei rubbed his soft white hands together. "I am most anxious to discover if the lady plays other games with the consummate skill she displays at piquet."

"Then we are agreed, I believe." Their host drew the unspoken threads together. "We move rapidly but with the utmost discretion. I suggest we employ others to watch for the right moment, and to . . . to put that moment to good use." He smiled. "I can lay hands on those who would be more than willing to employ what methods are necessary to achieve their objective. Madame Delacroix must set foot outside their lodgings at some point, and when she does . . ." His smile broadened.

"We will leave the matter entirely in your hands, Legrand, and look forward to a speedy resolution." An air of satisfied agreement settled over the salon as the four turned their appreciative attention to the very fine Nuits-St. Georges that their host made haste to dispense.

# *Chapter 25*

The house on the rue du Cirque was small but elegant and very well placed for the various events that marked Napoleon's triumphal return to Paris. Dominic ensured that he had ample time to show Genevieve the glories of the city in their first few days of residence, and they were seated with Napoleon's aristocracy to witness the spectacular Champs de Mai, the fete put on by the emperor to solemnize the restored monarchy, a celebration to rival the coronation of 1804. But Genevieve felt a strange pang of sadness—a ridiculous emotion, surely, admist the pomp and ceremonial magnificence of coaches and uniforms, liveries and satins and embroideries, gold and silver and gems. But none of this meant anything, unless—until?—the emperor went to war and won. And the emperor, himself, seemed curiously shrunken by the opulence and grandeur of his exhibition, as if he knew that the imperial uniform was a sham until he had earned it once again in the blood and terror of battle.

"Fouché wishes to talk with me, Genevieve," Dominic said as they left the flag-bedecked grandstand at the end of the spectacle. "I must go to the Elysée. Do you care to come, too? Or shall Silas take you home?"

"I think I will go home," she replied. "My head aches like the devil, and there is the banquet and ball tonight."

Dominic looked concerned. "It is not like you to be ailing, sprite. Unless it is your time, and it should not be for another two weeks."

She gave him a wan smile. "I find it a little disconcerting that you should be as aware of such intimate details as I am myself."

"I have a certain interest in them, do I not?" He smiled.

"Yes," Genevieve conceded. "But I suspect that your open acknowledgement of that interest is somewhat unusual amongst your sex. I wouldn't know, of course," she added with a slightly mischievous gleam. "Since my experience of such matters is limited to you and our rather irregular arrangement. I imagine, in regular arrangements, that the prospect of conception would be accepted so there's no need for such scrupulous attention to . . ." Sweet heaven, what was she saying? She was sounding almost wistful. A crimson wave of embarrassment rose hotly to her cheeks, and she turned away hastily, thus missing the light that sprang in the privateer's eyes.

Dominic hesitated. Had he mistaken that wistful note in her voice? "It's maybe time for us to talk a little about your future," he said carefully.

Your, not ours, thought Genevieve desolately. "Yes, I'm sure we should. But this hardly seems the right place." She waved an airy hand at the hustling throng swirling around them. By some miracle, her voice was quite normal, perhaps a little brisker than usual, but that was no bad thing. "Besides, I do have a headache, probably because of the crowds and all the trumpets. I would like to go home and rest for a little while."

"Yes, of course." Dominic beckoned to Silas, waiting discreetly a few paces behind them. "Would you take Genevieve home, Silas? I am going to the Elysée but will be back later this afternoon."

"Yes, monsieur," Silas responded in customary fashion. "Shall we walk, madame, or shall I try to find a chair?"

417

"Walk," said Genevieve promptly. "It may help to clear my head, and you would never find an empty chair, today, anyway."

The two set off to walk the short distance from the triumphal arch to the rue du Cirque. The streets were so crowded with the dispersing spectators that Silas branched off into the narrower but less populated side streets. They were still sufficiently busy, however, for him not to remark the closed carriage that was taking the same route and moving at walking pace just behind them. The speed was not unusually slow since the streets were filled with pedestrians who showed little inclination to keep to the sides and allow horse traffic free passage.

There was a moment when the traffic seemed to clear, the eddying crowd to fall back so that Genevieve could see the street ahead for a little way, could feel space around her as the press of bodies receded. In the split second that followed, she registered the great iron studded door standing open to a courtyard on her left, then the sharp whining crack of a whip, the clatter of hooves, and the clanging roll of iron wheels on the cobbles. A carriage appeared alongside, a figure rearing up on the box, arm raised. The thick cowhide caught Silas viciously across the head and he stumbled with an agonized groan onto his knees. The door of the carriage was flung wide, separating Genevieve from the fallen sailor, and a hand shot out, seizing her wrist. Genevieve, reacting without thought, fueled with pure adrenaline, jumped backward, slamming the carriage door closed on the capturing arm. There was an obscene bellow from within the carriage, and her wrist was released. She leaped for the open door and the courtyard, not daring to stop for Silas who was shaking the stars from his head and struggling to his feet.

Panting with fright and reaction, she hugged the shadow of the high stone wall, wondering if they would come after her. But there were voices raised in protest now, people crowding around Silas, and the carriage took off at breakneck speed, heedless of the danger to unwary pedestrians. Genevieve realized that she was crouching against the wall and straightened stiffly. Her hands were trembling. Shakily, she left her refuge and went out into the street where Silas, still groggy, was staring around him, acute anxiety in every line of the well-lined face.

When he saw her, naked relief wiped out the anxiety, but only for a minute. "Are you all right, mademoiselle?" The brown eyes clouded as he examined her white face.

"I am perfectly all right, Silas," she reassured swiftly. "But what of you?" She reached up to touch the livid, blood-edged slash across his cheek where the whip had cut.

He winced, but shook her off. "'Tis nothing. Nothing to what I deserve," he added with a grimace of disgust. "Blind fool, I should've seen them coming. Monsieur'll have my hide."

"It was not your fault!" exclaimed Genevieve indignantly. "How could you possibly have known?"

"I should've," he said grimly. "If you hadn't moved so quick, they'd have had you."

"Well, let us go home and look to that cut." She took charge on a brisk note that hid the little prickle of pleasure at the note of admiring approval in the sailor's voice. Silas rarely indicated approval, and if he did, it tended to be a little grudging.

They reached home without further incident, but Silas refused to heed Genevieve's appeals that he let her bathe his wound. "I must go to the Elysée and tell monsieur," he said firmly. "You stay inside with the doors locked and don't answer to anyone."

Genevieve sighed. "Monsieur will be back in an hour or so, Silas. The story can wait until then."

"If you think that, you don't know monsieur as well as you ought," the sailor replied. "He'd have me hanging from the yardarm as soon as look at me if I didn't tell him of this straightaway."

Genevieve shrugged. "At least let me put some salve on your face."

A tiny grin enlivened the sailor's self-reproachful expression. "Best for me if it looks bad, mademoiselle."

Silas found the corridors of the Elysée mobbed with officials, soldiers, participants in the day's fete, petitioners, and diplomats. The presence of an earringed, pigtailed sailor with a blooded weal on his cheek caused raised eyebrows from those he accosted for information about the whereabouts of Monsieur Fouché and Monsieur Delacroix. However, he was finally directed into a large rectangular room with long windows, the floor squared in black and white marble.

Dominic got up from an embroidered couch where he had been head to head with Fouché. "What the devil's happened, man?" He sprang across the room, anxiety rasping hoarse in the usually even voice. "Where is Genevieve?"

Silas swallowed, licked his lips nervously and told the tale with no embellishment and no attempt to defend his self-perceived negligence.

Dominic heard him out in silence, his face now impassive. "You need to get that cut attended to," was his only comment at story's end. He turned to Fouché. "We will have to continue our discussion some other time, Fouché. But you may rest assured that I will have *Danseuse* standing by at Rochefort until the emperor's affairs are resolved one way or another."

The statesman nodded, then said, "Whom do you suspect in this attack on madame? Or was it just chance?"

"Not chance," Dominic replied. "Jean Luc Legrand, I suspect, but I have no proof."

"Why would Legrand have that sort of interest in your wife?" Fouché asked, curiosity in the shrewd old eyes.

"That is a long story, one that is best left buried." Dominic dismissed the inquiry firmly, offering a brief bow in farewell. "Come, Silas."

"I beg your pardon, monsieur," Silas began as they walked fast through the corridors. "I blame myself. If mademoiselle hadn't acted so fast—"

"I'd have torn you limb from limb," Dominic interjected with a wry smile. "Get down to the quay as soon as you've cleaned that wound and find passage for yourself and Genevieve on a riverboat to La Havre. From there, you'll both take ship back to America."

Silas heard the sentence of banishment in stoic silence. Mademoiselle could not be sent off on such a voyage alone, for all her quick reactions, and if the nursemaiding fell to his lot he knew better than to object.

Genevieve, however, did not. She ran to greet Dominic as soon as he set foot in the hall, words of explanation and excuse for Silas tumbling from her lips. The subject of her well-meant peroration muttered something inaudible and disappeared instantly. Dominic could not help laughing as he caught her to him, the tightness of his hold the only indication of the extent of his relief. "I am not such an ogre, sprite. I have not touched a hair of the man's head!"

"Well, you put the fear of the devil into people," she said in laughing reproach. "I knew exactly how he felt."

The laughter died in his eyes and he released her, striding ahead of her into the salon. "I am going to make certain that the opportunity for such a thing does not arise again."

"We shall just be extra specially careful," Genevieve said, following him and perching on the arm of a chair. "But I am sure they will not try again."

Dominic recognized the shape of the upcoming battle and steeled himself. "I am not prepared to take that risk, Genevieve. I am sending you back to America."

The color drained from her face, the light from the tawny eyes. "I don't understand."

"Silas is going directly to book passage for you both to Le Havre. From there, you will take ship back home. There are always several vessels whose captains will be quite happy to take a couple of passengers."

"But what of you?" He could not possibly mean what he had said. She must have misunderstood him.

"I have work to do here—a commitment that I cannot renege on."

Genevieve fought the sense of unreality and kept her voice reasonable and even, as if this were a perfectly ordinary discussion. "If I must go anywhere, why can I not go on board *Danseuse?*"

"*Danseuse* must remain unencumbered at Rochefort, should Napoleon need her in haste. It is part of the commitment I have made," Dominic explained with a calm to match her own. His, however, was not feigned since he saw nothing extraordinary in the discussion. "If you are at risk of attack on board her, then she is also endangered and I cannot take that chance. For as long as you remain in France, you are in danger, and I cannot spare the time or the manpower to deal with that danger." It was all very straightforward, the privateer thought. A pragmatic plan. He had a job to do, a commitment that he had undertaken, and Genevieve's present situation would hinder him in the accomplishment of that task. For her own safety and his peace of mind, she needed to be well away from France. Maybe she would be out of danger across the channel in England, but he could not be sure of that, not when one of her pursuers was English. If he had to worry about her, and he would unceasingly if she were not well away or constantly under his eye, his efficiency would be impaired.

He was sending her away, just like that, with no preparation, no discussion. Hacking the adventure to a close, ripping apart their loving, lusting partnership without even the mention of a friendly future, sometime, somewhere. And all because she had suddenly become an awkward impediment to the completion of the task he had undertaken. Never in her bleakest conceptions of this moment had she imagined such a coldly abrupt ending simply because her place had slipped in the privateer's priorities.

"And what am I to do in America?" she demanded in a stifled voice. "I can hardly return home."

"No, of course not," he replied matter-of-factly. "What you do initially will depend on where your ship docks. I will, of course, ensure that you have more than enough funds to establish yourself."

"I do not wish to establish myself in America!" cried Genevieve in desolate horror at this neat, conscience-salving disposal of her future. Establish herself as what? She stood up, squaring her shoulders. If this was the end of the affair, then she would end it in her own way. "I have the right to make my own decisions, to choose my own destiny. Is not that what you offered me when you took me from my father's house? I will not be tidied away neatly, paid off like an outgrown mistress." Her voice caught on a sob. "You need not concern yourself about me. I am not your responsibility. I never have been, and I would not dream of interfering in your business affairs." She dashed away a recalcitrant teardrop and continued without pause. "Neither do I need your funds to *establish* myself, thank you."

Dominic had been so taken aback by this speech that he had allowed it to run its course, but now, as she turned to the door in a swirl of amber silk, he lunged for her. "Just what the hell do you think you're talking about, you silly child?" His tone was merely exasperated as if he were dealing with an infantile tantrum, and indeed, to the bitter regret of hindsight, that was truly how he saw it. He did not hear the meaning of the words, the mature anguish in her voice; he heard simply the exaggerated objections of a spoiled baby who did not wish to do what was necessary.

The words, the tone, the hard hand on her shoulder proved the last straw. Genevieve wrenched herself out of his grip and raced into the hall. Dominic, after a startled second, charged after her just as there came a loud bellow from Silas mingling with a crash and a cascading crescendo of breaking glass. Dominic stood, frozen for precious seconds in the doorway, taking in the sight of Silas flat on his back, surrounded by the shattered crystal of glasses and decanter, splattered by the deep ruby of spilled vintage port. Genevieve tore open the front door and was out in the street before either the twice-felled Silas or the utterly bewildered Dominic could gather their wits.

"Sweet Jesus!" Dominic registered the chill shaft of a sharp breeze and abandoned Silas. He ran for the door that still stood ajar. Genevieve was an amber flurry up the street, and he pounded after her, calling her name. He saw the closed carriage with plain panels standing at the corner, and panic flared as he realized that Genevieve had not seen it— that she was not aware of anything outside her own unhappiness at this moment. He yelled a warning, but with a sick fatalism he watched the scene that played out before his eyes almost in slow motion. A bulky figure sprang out of the carriage, and the diminutive Genevieve seemed to disappear in the dark cloth of his hold, the frantic swirl of her amber skirts and the white flash of petticoat the only indication of her violent protestations. Another pair of arms appeared from within the carriage and she was bundled inside, followed by the dark bulky figure. The carriage door slammed, and it had rounded the corner before Dominic could cover half the distance between them.

"Death and damnation!" Silas arrived on the scene, panting and wine bespattered as Dominic still stood immobile on the pavement. "What possessed her, monsieur?"

Dominic closed his eyes briefly, running an anguished hand through the nut-brown hair already disheveled by his headlong run down the windswept street. "My fault, Silas! Dear God, I cannot believe I could have been such an insensitive simpleton! An outgrown mistress! She thought I was packing her off because . . . and, of course, that was exactly how it sounded. How was she supposed to read my mind? I haven't said a damn word to her about how I feel . . . just somehow expected her to . . ." He swore viciously and spun on his heel, leaving Silas to follow him back to the house, trying to fill in the gaps in this self-immolating tumble of words.

"What do we do now?" Silas asked as he followed the privateer into his bedchamber, giving up the struggle for comprehension and deciding that action was easier.

"Find out where they've taken her, of course," Dominic snapped, taking a pair of pistols from a drawer.

"Yes, monsieur," said Silas woodenly. "But *how* was what I was asking."

Dominic pushed the pistols into his belt. "Fouché will be able to furnish me with Legrand's address. We start from there. I am going to need men, half a dozen. You know the type?"

Silas nodded. "Handy, you mean."

"Just so. Have them here by this evening. We cannot afford to waste time." A look of pain scudded across his features, and this time Silas had little difficulty understanding the reason for it. He nodded grimly and left the house.

Fighting to close out the images created by a fevered imagination, Dominic took horse back to the Elysée. But he found that his usual iron control over matters that might hinder the process of clear thinking and thus impair efficiency were somehow enfeebled. What the devil were they doing to her? Were they interested in hurting her? Would she have the sense to give them what they wanted without resistance? And Dominic Delacroix had a fairly good idea of what they wanted. Dear God! There had been that time in Morocco, when the crew of that galleon had invaded a fishing village in search of a missing prisoner and had found a little diversion on the way. The pictures ran rampant in his head—pictures of her body, naked, bruised, used! He could hear her piteous sobs of defeat and debasement—the sobs he had heard on that dreadful afternoon.

Fouché saw, instead of the suave, impassive, authoritative Creole, a man with haunted eyes in a gray face. A man who strode into the crowded room, pushing his way through without apology. A man with two pistols and a sword in his belt and the demeanor of one who intended to use them.

"I was about to send you a message," Fouché said. "Bonaparte is preparing to march on Brussels and engage with Wellington and Blucher."

"To the devil with Bonaparte!" Dominic spat. "Legrand has abducted Genevieve. He has a house in Paris, does he not?"

Fouché nodded. "On the rue de Rivoli. But would he take her there if he knows you will follow him?"

"He does not know for sure that I know he has her," Dominic said in a cold, flat voice, speaking the unpalatable truths as he now saw them. "But even if he did, his purpose is a limited one, I suspect. He wishes for revenge and when he has taken it, I imagine will ensure that she is not in a position to tell the tale—to identify her abductors—so that there will be no proof. He has only to keep her captive until he has finished with her and, with sufficient guards and good locks, will believe himself invulnerable."

Fouché shivered at the frozen azure depths of the man's eyes. If Legrand believed himself invulnerable to Dominic Delacroix, he was in for a severe shock. "Jean Luc Legrand is well known for his ruthlessness," he confirmed quietly. "He is not a man of scruple."

"I did not imagine he was, which is why matters are a trifle pressing." A ghastly smile, ice tipped with cynicism, touched the privateer's lips. "Nor are Sebastiani, Grand Duke Sergei, or the Englishman, Cholmondeley."

"They also?"

"Unless I am gravely mistaken. So, you will excuse me if the emperor's plans are of little interest at the moment."

"Yes, of course." Fouché frowned. "Why do you not take a party of militia and confront him?"

"On what grounds? And do you really think I would find her?" Dominic queried with a sardonic twitch of his eyebrows. "Legrand is no fool. He will have her well hidden from any obvious search party. No, I must *find* her by stealth, although I may have to *take* her by force. And for that I prefer my own men."

He left the Elysée and found Silas waiting for him in the rue du Cirque with six villainous-looking men, all sailors from the quays of the Seine. It took only a few minutes' talk for Dominic to be convinced that they would be loyal to the paymaster of the moment, would follow orders, but were far from stupid. They were experienced knife men, which Silas knew monsieur preferred when stealth was of the essence. There was all too much danger of an accidental shot escaping a pistol in moments of great strain and excitement.

One of them was dispatched to the house on the rue de Rivoli. Shaven and in the worsted britches and waistcoat of a manservant, he looked respectable enough to infiltrate the kitchen quarters of a gentleman's residence. These days there were always servants looking for odd jobs, and they were rarely turned away by their luckier fellows in possession of permanent positions.

As soon as darkness fell, Dominic and Silas slipped through the streets to the rue de Rivoli. The front of the house was impenetrable, except by the great entrance door, standing as it did in a long row of attached mansions that faced the high walls of the Tuileries Gardens. They exchanged a brief nod of silent agreement and melted into the side streets to scout out the rear. An hour later, they had found what they were looking for.

# Chapter 26

The experience was tauntingly familiar, yet this time inexpressibly more petrifying than when she had substituted herself for Elise and had been a willing victim of abduction. Then she had had only the alarming prospect of facing an angry privateer at journey's end. Now, at the end of this jolting carriage ride where she was trussed hand and foot like a chicken, a scarf pushed roughly into her mouth, there would be four of them. But she must meet them with dignity, if it was allowed her. If she was not to be dropped before them, helplessly bound and rendered mute. Their four faces floated in her mind's eye: thin, pointed Sebastiani; the fleshy lips and milk-white hands of the Russian; the bland smile and curiously flat eyes of Legrand; the false heartiness, the smooth amiability of the Englishman. She was not sure which of them frightened her the most, which of them repelled her the most. But she must get a grip on herself; must face them without fear. Dominic would come. How or when, she had no idea. But he *would* come and she must hold on until then. Unless Napoleon needed him urgently, and he could not spare the time for a rescue mission. It was her own fault this had happened, after all. But even as she thought these wretched thoughts, she knew that not even the emperor would keep him from finding her. Even though their affair was at an end, he would not desert her. His pride would not allow him to do so, whatever else he might feel.

The carriage swung violently, and she was thrown against the door, unable to protect herself with her bound hands. Her head knocked sharply against the window, but the gag stifled her involuntary yelp and she blinked back the tears rapidly. The two silent figures sitting opposite regarded her imperturbably for a minute. Apart from the few seconds it had taken them to render her helpless and dump her on the seat, half sitting, half lying, they had behaved as if she did not exist. Then one of them leaned over and helped her right herself against the cracked leather squabs. It was a small enough gesture, but Genevieve found to her horror that she was pathetically grateful for this sign of humanity in her black-clad captors who had reminded her overpoweringly of carrion crows.

The vehicle slowed and then came to a halt. One of the crows opened the door and sprang down. The other scooped Genevieve off the seat and handed her through the door into the waiting arms. She lay passive but her eyes were everywhere, taking in the high-walled courtyard, the tall, many-windowed house, the large poplar tree whose roots lifted the paving stones as it scratched for earth beneath the city's man-made surface.

She was carried through a tall, narrow doorway into a gloomy corridor. There was no sign of habitation although her eyes told her she was in the servants' quarters of a fairly affluent household. The paint work was fresh, the carpet underfoot unfrayed. Even the narrow staircase up which she was now borne was carpeted—an unusually luxurious touch on the backstairs. At the head of the stairs, her bearer pushed open a swing door, and they emerged in a wide corridor, where the paneled walls were hung with gilt-framed paintings. The corridor was lit by a tall window at the far end, presumably giving onto the view from the front of the house. But they did not get close enough for Genevieve to see out; instead they turned through an open door about halfway along the passage.

Here, she was put in an armchair and the scarf removed. She grimaced, rubbing her tongue against her lips in an effort to remove the bits of wool and fluff left by the gag. The silent crow bent to untie her ankles, then unfastened her wrists. With relief, she used her finger on her tongue.

"You'll find everything you need to tidy up." Her companion spoke for the first time, and Genevieve was so startled to hear the sound of a voice that she jumped. If the crow noticed, he gave no sign, but simply straightened up and left the room, closing the door behind him. She heard the sound of a key turn.

She was in a bedchamber, small but adequately furnished with poster bed, chaise longue, and armoire. A pier glass stood in one corner, basin and ewer on the washstand. The most distinctive feature of the room was that it was windowless. The door to the corridor had a glass pane for the top third, and this provided a dim light. A lamp, tinderbox, and flints, however, rested on a table beside the bed. The room was windowless, presumably, because it was situated in the middle of the corridor and, as she had seen from the courtyard, the house was one of a row. Any chambers not at the front or the back would be without outside light. Presumably they made excellent servants' quarters—and excellent prisons.

Curiously, but much to her relief, Genevieve found herself quite calm now that the initial terror of the kidnapping was past. There was little she could do toward escape when not even a skylight offered prospect on the outside world, so she busied herself at the dresser and washstand, finding the familiar activities therapeutically pacifying. At least she would confront the unknown with her face washed and her hair combed. She was wearing the amber silk that she had put on for the morning's festivities. It was a walking dress and, as such, singularly unprovocative in style and cut with a

430

high lace tucker and ruffles on the wrist-length sleeves. Genevieve found this most comforting, although why she should she could not imagine; presumably, if she was to be divested of it at some point, it mattered little what gown she wore. She shivered as little caterpillars of disgust inched slime down her spine. She must not think of such things, must concentrate only on the thought of Dominic, on finding ways to play for time. Because he *would* come.

A long time seemed to pass, though, a time long enough for fear and dreaded uncertainty to overcome the moments of serenity. She paced the small room, sat on the bed, contemplated the sparse furnishings, the single, unremarkable picture of a cottage by a millstream, paced some more and all the time kept the rising panic at bay with an effort that seemed to drain her of all emotional and mental energy. When, at long last, she heard the sound of the key turning smoothly, she nearly screamed in shock and her heart began to drum in noisy trepidation.

A liveried footman stood in the doorway. "The gentlemen await you in the salon, madame," he announced with a low bow, standing aside to allow her to pass.

Swallowing an overpowering sense of unreality, Genevieve found herself smiling formally as she walked into the corridor. The footman led her almost to the end of the passage where the curtains were drawn across the window. A wide, shallow flight of stairs curved down to a square hall lit by a glittering chandelier. They descended the stairs, crossed the hall where he flung open double doors onto an elegant apartment warmed by a fire in the grate, lit by the soft glow of many candles. The four men rose politely as she entered.

"I bid you welcome, madame," Legrand said smoothly, coming toward her, taking her hand and drawing her into the circle by the hearth. "May I offer you a glass of champagne? Or sherry, perhaps?"

Genevieve had not been able to abide the smell or the taste of champagne since that last night in Vienna. "Champagne, please," she said with equal formality, although without the smile. At least, she would not be tempted to take even the tiniest sip and would thus be sure of keeping a clear head.

"I trust your reception was not too uncomfortable," her host continued, handing her a fluted glass.

"It was abominably so," she returned. "Am I to know to what I owe this dubious pleasure?" It was amazing, but she was as icily calm and self-possessed as if she was in her father's *salle de compagnie*. She did not waste energy questioning why that should be so, but merely accepted the fact and was grateful for it.

"Later, madame," Sergei said and the soft skin of his hands rustled.

"We do not find the pleasure in your company in the least dubious," observed Sebastiani. "I do trust we shall be able to rectify the situation for you."

"I doubt it, signor." Placing her glass on a sofa table where the highly polished surface threw back her reflection as she bent over it, Genevieve looked calmly around the room. Her companions were in immaculate evening dress: black silk pantaloons, striped waistcoats, ruffled shirts, and starched cravats. "I must apologize for my dress, gentlemen. I was not expecting a dinner invitation this afternoon." She did not misread the flash of surprised admiration with which they received the cool statement, and it gave her heart.

"Dinner is served, monsieur." The flunky reappeared to make the dignified announcement, and the group moved across the hall and into a dining room easily rivaling the salon in elegance. Five people at the vast mahogany table left plenty of elbow room, and Genevieve's sense of unreality increased. At any minute, she thought, someone is going to come in and clap his hands, and I'll wake up beside Dominic and this will all fade into the realm of bad dreams.

Polite conversation continued throughout innumerable courses, and Genevieve was treated with all the attentive deference of an honored guest—the only woman at the table.

She responded in like manner, using it as an exercise in sharpening her wits. She was not encouraged to drink once it became obvious that her wineglass remained untouched, and their restraint puzzled her. Surely they would feel that, a little weak headed from wine, she would be more amenable to whatever plans they had for post-prandial entertainment. But perhaps it did not matter whether she was amenable or not. Those caterpillars trailed down her back again, and she felt drops of cold sweat run down her ribs, dampening the silk of her gown. That would never do! She brought herself under control again and felt the heat recede as her pulse slowed.

The covers were removed and the port decanter appeared on the table. Genevieve rose. "I expect, gentlemen, that you would like me to leave you to your port and cigars."

"On the contrary," Legrand said. "We will not smoke if you find it distasteful, but pray keep us company."

The first hint of steel! She resumed her seat with a small affirmative nod and tucked her hands in her lap to hide the slight tremor.

"The last time we had the pleasure of a conversation, madame, was in a card room during the masked ball of the Polanski's, as I recall." Sergei spoke.

When Dominic, cracking a whip, had driven her out into the night. Genevieve acknowledged the statement with another little nod and waited for what she no longer needed to hear. She knew what awaited her now in the dark corners of experience.

"I seem to remember that you agreed to a return game of piquet, madame," Legrand said with gentle menace. "Or should I say to four return games?"

"I seem to remember, Monsieur Legrand, that I claimed the right to choose the time and the venue, and that no one argued with that claim." It was pointless, of course, but the longer she kept talking, the longer would the inevitable be postponed.

Sebastiani smiled his thin smile. "Forgive us, madame, but you disappeared from Vienna in such haste that we felt that you had, perhaps . . ." His shoulders lifted and the smile grew thinner. "That you had perhaps decided not to honor the debt."

"You all lost in fair play." She spoke with calculated sharpness. "In those circumstances, I do not accept the debt."

"But, madame, you had no intention of honoring the wager whether you won or lost." It was Charles Cholmondeley, and the bitterness of the painfully deceived skulked behind the careful geniality. "You took from us all exactly what you wanted—information. You played us for—"

"I think Madame Delacroix knows just what she played us for, my dear fellow," broke in Sergei, softly interrupting the rising note that threatened to disturb the smooth surface of this black comedy.

"So, madame, we will play piquet," said Sebastiani with sudden bonhomie. "For the original stakes, of course."

"We will cut for the honor of who plays you first." Legrand smiled. "And who second, and so on."

"You are not too tired, I trust," murmured Sergei. "The night could prove to be a long one."

"Of course, we shall each expect the debt of honor to be paid immediately, as is customary," added the Englishman, his amiability restored.

The shape of the horror solidified. She could not possibly play all four of them sequentially and win against them all. They would be fresh as she grew increasingly fatigued. She would soon lose track of the discards as they became muddled with previous games and each time she lost, she would lose again in the violation of her body.

"Why do you wish to indulge in this farce?" Her voice was miraculously strong. "Why do you not simply take what you will take anyway? Does rape by any other name smell sweeter?" But even as she spoke the scornful words, she knew

434

that she would play because only thus would she gain precious moments. And Dominic *would* come.

"Come, madame, you would not deny us a little finesse to our revenge, would you?" Sebastiani almost whispered as he cracked a nut and placed it courteously on her dessert plate. "The simple exertion of force is so crude. And, besides, this way you will have at least the illusion of control."

"For which I am duly grateful," she said coldly. "Shall we begin? Or do you wish to increase your insuperable odds by waiting until I am overcome by the lateness of the hour?"

For some peculiar reason that accusation of unchivalry seemed to sting her audience. It gave Genevieve a certain satisfaction, even as she realized that she had probably done herself a disservice. The more time wasted in idle conversation the better. However, the damage was done, and the veneer of courtesy seemed to have been stripped from her companions who showed her for the first time the hard faces of enmity as they rose in a body from the table.

This time, they went into a library at the rear of the house, its long curtained windows presumably looking into the courtyard. A bright fire burned with a plentiful supply of logs in the basket. On the sideboard reposed decanters and a variety of pastries and sweetmeats. The candles were all fresh and newly lit. On the card table were six unbroken packs of cards.

"That will be all, thank you, Gaston." Legrand, having checked the room carefully, dismissed the servant. "We will need nothing between now and morning. You may send the household to bed."

Genevieve swallowed the little nut of nausea that seemed to be blocking her throat. All the preparations had been made for a long night that they could spend in this warm, well-supplied room undisturbed by servants. The door closed behind the departed Gaston, and she was alone with her tormentors.

"Let us cut, gentlemen," Legrand said, breaking open one

of the packs. "We will each draw a card; the highest plays madame first, the lowest last. Agreed?"

It was agreed, and Genevieve watched with a curious fascination to see her fate decided. Cholmondeley, she had decided, was the weaker of the four; Sergei, far and away the stronger. There was little to choose between Legrand and Sebastiani. But if the Englishman drew the high card, she would have a better than even chance of winning the first three games. But then she would never be able to beat Sergei if she was fatigued by playing against the others. Perhaps, if she played him first, while she was fresh and her head clear of the succession of games that would eventually fill it, she could defeat him again as she had done before. But she had known then that her victory on that occasion had been awarded by the fall of the cards. She could not match the Russian for skill if luck was not on her side. It was an impossible dilemma, but not one in which she had any choice as to its resolution. Legrand drew the high card, Sergei the next, Sebastiani, and then Cholmondeley. She must play a strong player, using every ounce of emotional and mental strength if she was to win, and then, weakened, she must play the strongest of them all. It could not have been worse.

With a numbing resignation, she took the seat Legrand held for her. For a second, her eyes met those of the four men in turn. They all held the same look: the eager anticipation of the greedy predator who, closing on his prey, knows that his hunger is about to be satisfied.

"There is a woman in the house, monsieur," the sailor said, drinking deep of the tankard of ale Silas had given him. "But no one's seen her except Gaston, the majordomo. He took her down to the salon before dinner."

"How many others, besides Gaston, are there in the house?" Dominic asked. He was priming his pistols, his posture relaxed as he concentrated, his voice quiet and even.

He was as calm as always before action, his mind clear of all but the plan, both brain and body prepared to adapt instantly to changing circumstances should the need arise. He was no longer tortured by fears for Genevieve—now that he knew what to do and how to do it. If she was suffering, it would not be for much longer.

"Six, monsieur, counting the boot boy," his informant replied. "And the master and his three guests."

"Yes, I know about them," the privateer commented, almost absently. "We will worry about them, once we have secured the household. Seven of you to their six." He looked around the circle of faces. "I want no killing, is that understood? There are to be no messy repercussions from this exercise." He received affirmative grunts and nodded briskly. "Very well, you will take your orders from Silas. I have my own business to attend to."

Silas slung a thick coil of rope, lead weighted at one end, over his shoulder. "Everyone got knives?" There was a rustle as the six men drew cutlasses from their belts. "Use them to threaten, if you must, but remember what monsieur said. No killing." Dominic waited until the seven men had slipped out of the house, melting into the moonless night in their dark clothes as they hugged the walls, their boots swathed in cloth, making no sound on the cobbles. Then he thrust his pistols into his belt and followed them. But he walked boldly in the middle of the street, his head thrown back, striding easily from the hip, his booted feet ringing on the pavement; a bareheaded man in britches, shirtsleeves, and riding boots, a short cloak flung over his shoulders, and implacable purpose in the turquoise eyes.

"Mine, I think, Monsieur Legrand," Genevieve said gently into the intense quiet as she laid her last hand of the third game on the table.

The Frenchman smiled his meagre smile. "I can only look

forward to our return match, madame. We will play again later, when you have fulfilled your obligations to my colleagues."

Genevieve felt the soft glow of triumph and relief turn to bleak chill. There was to be no reprieve, then. How ever many times she won, eventually she would lose to them all. She could not avoid it, playing twelve games to their three.

Sergei took Legrand's place and reached for a fresh pack. "Perhaps you would care to break for five minutes, madame," he suggested solicitously. "A glass of wine, a little walk about the room?"

Neither would help her, but she accepted the offer anyway. It meant another few minutes. She thought now only in terms of the passing time and how to buy that precious commodity. Even if Dominic was not coming for her, forestalling the horror could only be to her advantage. If she must lose to Sergei, she prayed, let it at least go to three games; let him not win outright with the first two.

The Russian cut, won and elected to deal. The cards seemed even, and she closed her mind to the three others in the room who were watching the play intently, sipping brandy, occasionally throwing another log on the fire, all waiting patiently for the turn that they knew would come, for the outcome already determined.

Genevieve won the first game, and as she gathered up the cards, her eyes met those of the Russian. He had given her the game, and they both knew it. And they both knew why. He was much the stronger player and had chosen to increase the pleasure of his secondary purpose by extending her dreadful anticipation, knowing full well that anticipation of pain was always worse than the reality.

She lost the second game but only by a handful of points and for a few minutes of foolishness, she hoped. Sergei had given her nothing that time. But when she saw her hand for the third game, she faced reality with that numb resignation. The cards would give her no help. She endured twenty minutes of exquisite anguish, counting desperately, trying to fix the discards in her head, going over every hand several times before she made her play. But there was nothing she could do. She could not even avoid the mortification of the rubicon.

As she laid her last card on the table, the silence seemed to extend into infinity. Sergei smiled, the fleshy lips curving over startling white teeth. "Finally," Sebastiani murmured. "First fall to you, Sergei."

"Yes, indeed," the Russian replied softly. "Madame?" He stood up.

Genevieve felt her head shaking in mute, desperate denial. But he came around the table and took her elbows, pulling her to her feet. They were all smiling. Sergei cupped her face with his soft white hands. "A little on account, I think. Let us give our friends a small taste of what they, too, may expect before we seek privacy." Those heavy lips came closer, seemed to fill her field of vision. Stand still, she told herself. Do not fight. It will only add to the degredation and this one, at least, will enjoy every minute of subduing you, and of doing it in front of an eager, envious audience. His lips covered hers, seemed to swallow her mouth in their fleshy wetness, and her body rebelled, broke free from the sensible, self-preserving constraints of her mind. Her hand came up, fingers clawed to rake down the smooth pink cheeks leaving crimson-dropped tracers.

Sergei exhaled in sharp pain and hurled an obscenity at her, wrenching her arm behind her back as his mouth pressed deeper, invading the tender barriers of her soul's integrity. A hand ripped at the collar of her gown, tearing away the lace, thrusting into the opened bodice to grasp with hurtful fingers the soft swell of her breast. She twisted and writhed, ignoring the screaming pain of her bent arm, managed to bring her knee up into his groin. He swore again but his hold did not relax. Instead, he twirled her, sent her spinning toward the couch. She fell forward across the arm, felt the ridged cord of edging velvet hard against her pelvis as her feet left the floor; felt the hooks at the back of her gown fly undone; realized with an anguished cry of desperation that in a second she would be exposed to every eye in the room, open and vulnerable to receive the obscene vengeance. There was a ringing in her ears, and her heart beat in rapid flutters, pressed against the seat of the couch by the weight of his body. The velvet smothered her, and a red mist danced ever closer, offering surcease, threatening the final, involuntary capitulation.

The door crashed open, and suddenly she could turn her head from the stifling press of velvet as Sergei turned around, relaxing his hold. Then the Russian seemed to fly through the air, and there was a moment of utter confusion, of voices raised in fury, of the sharp crack of a pistol shot, the splintering of wood as the warning ball buried itself in the paneling beside the hearth. In the ensuing silence, Genevieve struggled upright, the skin of her bared back prickling with the knowledge of exposure rather than cold.

"I knew you would come," she said.

"Of course," Dominic replied, calmly matter-of-fact. "Go and stand behind me by the door, now." He waited until she had obeyed, then said, "I am desolated to discommode you, gentlemen, but I must ask you to remove your pantaloons, your shoes, and your stockings." He smiled and perched on the arm of the couch over which Genevieve had been flung. The two silver mounted pistols rested across his knee, his index fingers poised on both triggers. "I am certain you will not object to madame's presence at this disrobing, since it would have formed part of your evening's entertainment at some point, anyway."

Legrand's eyes slid suddenly to the door behind the privateer, and Dominic swung around an instant too late. Genevieve's breath whistled through her teeth as an arm caught her around the neck, and something very sharp pricked with clear intent against her throat.

"An opportune arrival, Gaston," said Legrand. "Your

pistols, if you please, Monsieur Delacroix." He held out his hand.

Dominic hesitated and the tip of the knife pressed, drawing a bead of blood from the white skin of her throat. With a tiny shrug, the privateer turned the pistols around and was about to pass them, handles politely first, to the Frenchman, when a strange gurgle came from Gaston. The knife clattered to the floor and the manservant slid down to follow it. Genevieve stepped shakily to one side, and Silas straightened from the crouch that had brought him, silent and invisible, behind Gaston.

"Your pardon, monsieur," he said, wiping the blade of his knife on his britches. "I do not know if I have killed him."

Dominic shrugged and reversed the pistols again, handing one to the sailor. "Your clothes, please, gentlemen. You will give them to Silas." Without taking his eyes off the four men, he stretched his free hand behind him for Genevieve, and when she stepped forward, he held her close in the protective curve of his arm. "Are the others dealt with, Silas?"

"Yes, monsieur," replied the sailor, moving to take Legrand's pantaloons, snapping his fingers as Sergei, his face set in lines of murderous hatred, finally accepted the inevitable and unfastened his own. "We counted five. Just that one was missing." A groan came from the figure on the floor, and Genevieve slid out from the warm, firm security of Dominic's arms and went to kneel beside him. The knife thrust had gone deep between his lower ribs, but it did not seem to have pierced any vital organs as far as she could tell. As she bent over the prone figure, she felt hands on her back. Dominic was fastening her gown. The simple gesture brought back the whole horror of those few minutes, the dreadful knowledge of what had so nearly been. She looked at him, stricken with remembered terror, and the turquoise eyes deepened with compassion and remorse.

"It will fade, sprite," he said with gentle reassurance, slipping off his short cloak and draping it around her shoulders, fastening it over her torn bodice. "I will do all I can to ensure that it does."

Five of the six sailors appeared, like Silas, on stockinged feet. "Bound and gagged, monsieur," one said. "Paul is out back." They all stared with frank astonishment, not untinged with amusement, at the sight of the four gentlemen standing by the fire in nothing but their shirts. Silas, his arms full of pantaloons, shoes, and stockings, turned to the door.

"Take these with us, shall we, monsieur?"

"We can leave them in the street," Dominic replied with a careless shrug. "I wish only to ensure that our friends cannot follow us without delay. But perhaps you should tie them also. You may string them together with the rope we used to climb the tree to the window." He turned to the silent group of four who, white faced with humiliation, their eyes sliding around the room, clearly did not know where to look. "I must apologize for the indignity, gentlemen. But I am sure you understand its necessity—not to mention its justice."

Sebastiani muttered with overpowering venom, and Genevieve shivered at the potent hatred thus expressed. Silas reappeared, bearing the coiled rope with the leaded end. "If you'd just turn around and put your hands behind you, messieurs," he said with wooden courtesy. Genevieve went out into the hall, for some reason unable to bear witness to this debasement of her fallen enemies. Although, why she should have such delicacy after what they had been intending to do to her, what they had already done, she could not begin to imagine.

She felt weak and drained now. Unable to think of anything except that the terror was over and that Dominic would decide what next was to happen. She could no longer summon up the energy to care. Apart from the moment when he had given her the security of his arm and the moment when he had fastened her gown, he had not touched her. And she ached to be held.

"Come, Genevieve. We will leave Silas to tidy up around here." The privateer stepped into the hall. His expression was grave, almost stern, as he took her hand and led the way into the back quarters of the house. She recognized the corridor, the narrow door, and then they were in the courtyard where the unmarked carriage that had brought her to Legrand's house waited beneath the tall poplar tree, two horses between the shafts, the sailor called Paul upon the box. "We will borrow this, I think," Dominic said conversationally. "Our friends will not be needing it for awhile."

Her knees suddenly buckled as the hard lines of reality smudged. How could he talk in this way? His voice so pleasant, so matter-of-fact, as if nothing untoward had happened; as if he had not severed their relationship; as if she had not narrowly escaped the ultimate degradation; as if four, partly naked men were not standing in the library, their bound hands linked together by a coil of rope; as if a manservant was not lying bleeding on the carpet; as if five other men were not similarly immobilized, somewhere.

"Damn you, Dominic Delacroix!" she cried with her last ounce of strength. "Damn you!" She felt the same outraged, dazed incomprehension that she had felt on *Danseuse* when he had torn her out of the self-enclosed refuge into which she had retreated to escape the hurts he had inflicted.

He caught her up the instant before she hit the cobbles. "You may damn me as you please, *mon coeur,* but let us achieve a degree of privacy." There was gentle amusement in his voice, but also a deep throb of warmth and understanding.

"Do not call me that if you do not mean it!" she whispered, no longer able to hide the truth from him or from herself. She was bundled into the carriage where the merciful darkness cloaked her words and hid the hurt vulnerability in her eyes.

"Oh, but I do mean it. I have always meant it. I cannot

imagine why I tried to deny it to either of us—*mon coeur.*" The endearment was repeated with a firm emphasis as he drew her onto his lap.

Genevieve sighed and crept against him like a small, wounded animal. "Why must I go away then?"

"You aren't." His arms tightened. "But I would have followed you as soon as I could." He stroked her hair, cuddling her as if she were, indeed, a small, hurt member of the animal kingdom. "It did not occur to me to spell that out for you, I am afraid. I just assumed you would know it." He smiled slightly in the darkness. "You'll have to forgive me, sprite, but I fear I heard only the willful objections of young Mademoiselle Genevieve with her exasperating and dangerous habit of following her nose into trouble simply because it appealed to her. *'Mon coeur'* has left childhood behind her, but I forgot that for a moment." She said nothing, absorbing this and all its implications—implications that opened new horizons of dazzling beauty.

"Did they hurt you more than I saw?" He asked the question painfully and when she did not immediately answer, shifted her on his lap so that she was obliged to sit up. "I have to know, sprite."

"No." She shook her head vigorously. "I was afraid, but I knew that I had to play for time because you would come. My time had just run out."

Moving her head backward into the crook of his arm, he kissed her with a searing sweetness that healed the memory bruises of the Russian's violation. *"Mon coeur,"* he whispered as his lips trailed honeyed fire to her earlobe, and she reached against him, wondering at the extraordinary indomitable quality of loving desire. An hour ago, in physical revulsion, she could never have imagined feeling again the stirring, the hunger for her body's fulfillment. Yet she needed him now, almost more powerfully than she could ever remember. But there was an added dimension to that need. A demand for affirmation, a confirmation of this half-articulated understanding that was taking shape in the darkness of the carriage, in the unashamed honesty of his loving words, of the loving hold.

The carriage stopped outside the house on the rue du Cirque, but when he stepped out, holding her in his arms, there seemed no interruption of their contact. He carried her upstairs and laid her on the bed, sitting beside her, leaning over, his arms braced on either side of her body.

"It seems we need a priest, my Genevieve."

"You do not have to marry me," she said with a tremulous smile. "I have never expected it. We can continue as we are now, can we not?"

"No," he said definitely. "It is time we turned fantasy into fact, and you became Madame Delacroix in truth. If you wish it, that is." The softness left his eyes for a second as he raked her face. But it came back when she reached her arms around his neck, drawing his mouth down to hers in passionate answer.

"You have always said that you could never be earthbound," she said against his lips. "I do not wish to be so, either, so we will go on in the same way."

"We shall see," said the privateer, a smile lurking in his eyes, curving his lips. "Women have an almost universal tendency to wish for nests and babies. You may not be so wishful yet, *mon coeur,* but I expect it will come. I shall adapt to changed circumstances with little difficulty."

"I do not think it will happen for quite some time," Genevieve said, her fingers busy with the buttons of his shirt. "Where do we go now?"

*"Now,"* he said, pushing aside the ripped lace of her bodice and pressing his lips to her bosom, whispering in gentle, healing strokes across a purpling finger bruise. "Now, I am going to take you with me to the well of eternal pleasure, sweet love, where you may lose the fearful memories and know that you have my love for all time as shield against the world." Raising his head from her breast, he took her lips

445

with the same sweet tenderness so that she felt her entire self opening in love and trust. "Later," he continued in a soft murmur, "we will go to Rochefort where we will find a priest, and then we will wait on *Danseuse* for Napoleon to decide the fate of Europe—or for Wellington to decide the fate of Napoleon."

"I do not wish to look beyond the now," she said, touching his face, drowning in the azure gaze of love and promise.

"Then look no further, *mon coeur.*" His hands moved upon her and her eyes closed, turning inward on the realm of loving glory that they shared now and for all time.

# ROMANCE FROM JANELLE TAYLOR

ANYTHING FOR LOVE       (0-8217-4992-7, $5.99)

DESTINY MINE       (0-8217-5185-9, $5.99)

CHASE THE WIND       (0-8217-4740-1, $5.99)

MIDNIGHT SECRETS       (0-8217-5280-4, $5.99)

MOONBEAMS AND MAGIC       (0-8217-0184-4, $5.99)

SWEET SAVAGE HEART       (0-8217-5276-6, $5.99)

## SPINE TINGLING ROMANCE
## FROM STELLA CAMERON!

PURE DELIGHTS                    (0-8217-4798-3, $5.99)

SHEER PLEASURES                  (0-8217-5093-3, $5.99)

TRUE BLISS                       (0-8217-5369-X, $5.99)